SCAPEGOAT
THE PRICE OF
FREEDOM

SCAPEGOAT
THE PRICE OF FREEDOM

RAE RICHEN

Scapegoat: The Price of Freedom

A Novel by Rae Richen

Published in the United States of America by

Back Beat Publications
an imprint of
Lloyd Court Press
3034 N.E. 32nd Avenue
Portland, Oregon, 97212
www.lloydcourtpress.org
503-284-8532

Cover art by Frank Loudin
Cover design by Diana Kolsky
Book Design by Amit Dey
Chapter Silhouettes by Carol Sand
Book group reading guide by Back Beat Publications

ISBN: 978-0-9832242-3-5 (paperback)
ISBN: 978-0-9832242-4-2 (ebook)

Publisher's Cataloging-In-Publication Data
(Prepared by The Donohue Group, Inc.)

Names: Richen, Rae.
Title: Scapegoat. [Volume 1], The Price of Freedom / Rae Richen.
Other Titles: Price of Freedom
Description: Portland, Oregon : Back Beat Publications, an imprint of Lloyd
                Court Press, [2016, re-issue 2024] | Interest age level: 13 and up.
                | Summary: "Scapegoat: The Price of Freedom is the story of
                fourteen-year-old Gilbert Evans (Gib), his friends and favorite
                teachers who, in 1953, become victims of the anti-communist
                fear mongering of Senator Joseph McCarthy. When local
                leaders in Gib's hometown of Portland, Oregon, follow
                McCarthy's tactics, panic about communism grows into hatred
                and rage. Gilbert and friends learn that turning off, or even
                deflecting mass hysteria has become nearly impossible, and very
                dangerous."--Publisher website. | Includes bibliographical
                references.
Identifiers: ISBN 978-0-9832242-3-5 (print) |
                ISBN 978-0-9832242-4-2 (ebook)
Subjects: LCSH: Anti-communist movements--
                United States--History--20th century--Juvenile fiction. |
                Teenage boys--Oregon--Portland--History--
                20th century--Juvenile fiction. | Political culture--Oregon--
                Portland--History--20th century--Juvenile fiction. |
                Freedom of speech--United States--History--
                20th century--Juvenile fiction. | Civil rights--
                United States--History--20th century--Juvenile fiction. |
                Cold War--Juvenile fiction. | Historical fiction.
CYAC: Anti-communist movements--United States--History--
                20th century--Fiction. | Teenage boys--Oregon--
                Portland--History--20th century--Fiction. |
                Freedom of speech--United States--History--
                20th century--Fiction. | Civil rights--United States--
                History--20th century--Fiction. | Cold War--Fiction.
Classification: LCC PS3618.I34 S33 2016 (print) |
                LCC PS3618.I34 (ebook) | DDC 813/.6--dc23

"The price of freedom is the courage not to buy what power is selling."

Wilhalmena Stamps Williams

Citizen, 1915-1997

"Turning off, or even deflecting mass hysteria proves nearly impossible, and very dangerous."

Gilbert Evans

PROLOGUE

Assignment, Essay #1
Gilbert Evans
General Eisenhower School
Portland, Oregon
September 9, 1953

I am Gib Evans. Back in 1948, my family lived in Neustadt bei Wald, West Germany, near the border with Communist East Germany. In that village, I learned about the difference between Democracy and Communism.

On our side of the border, people ate and had plenty. On the other side, they starved.

When I was eight, I often hid in my favorite oak tree in the park near that border. One afternoon, from my tree, I saw a man crawl under the barbed wire fence to our side of the border. He looked up at me. He stood and ran toward my tree. He wanted me to help him.

On the other side of the border, a motorcycle revved up. A communist guard rode close to the wire and yanked out his rifle.

I just sat there, scared, but my mom ran into the park. Dad followed, carrying the baby. Dad pushed my baby sister behind my tree, then ran and pulled Mom to the ground. Bullets flew into my tree, into the grass, everywhere.

I could have yelled, ruined the guard's aim, done something. But I did nothing.

When the shooting stopped, the escaping man lay crumpled in the field on our side. Mom and Dad lay still in the grass.

Mom and Dad were badly injured. The tree saved my baby sister, but the man died hoping I could save him.

I'm fourteen now, and I live in the States again. It's 1953, but when I close my eyes, I can still see the border guard across the barbed-wire fence. When he leaned his jaw against his rifle butt and pulled the trigger, I learned to hate."

* *

That's how my famous essay of 1953 began. Here I am, an old newspaper man, more than fifty years later, still struggling to understand the events that followed my writing of that essay. Two things I've learned from my years as a journalist: One: Fear is the easiest commodity to sell; and Two: Someone is always selling.

In that essay, *I* was selling fear.

Now, with our country threatening to repeat the methods of 1953, it's time for me to tell you about the events that shaped my life.

When we came back from Germany to the United States, I thought I understood how things worked – how people thought. In my writings of that time, I am reminded of the way it felt to be fourteen, so sure, yet unsure, and very afraid. My fears fed into an enormous ugliness in our city, and our country.

Maybe, when I've told you my story, you and I will both begin to understand what happened to all of us because of my damned essay.

CHAPTER ONE

LATE SUMMER, 1953

O n Friday morning, I slide into my place at the breakfast table. I keep my head down and let my hair cover my face to hide my bruises. I don't want Dad or Mom to notice. They're against fighting. I'm against it too, but only when I lose. I don't plan to lose again.

I've got vacation plans for this Friday, the last before school starts. The first day of school is next Tuesday, September 8, right after Monday's Labor Day. I guess I have to go to school, but most of my classes are about an inch deep.

There's one good teacher at General Eisenhower School – teacher of seventh and eighth grade history and journalism, Mr. Reese. For Mr. Reese, I might stick around and figure out how to put up with other stupidness.

But today, after breakfast, I'm going where I can relax, catch a few fish and not get into a fight.

Dad folds up the newspaper and puts it on another chair, but I see the headline.

"Arrested?" I say. "Who's arrested? What for?"

Dad sighs and pulls up the newspaper to let me look. "Arrested on suspicion of being communists," he says.

I feel a stab of old terror. "Right here in Portland?" I take the newspaper from him and see there are three men who were members of some union — spies in our town.

"I don't want Russian spies taking over Portland the way they did in Germany," I say to Dad.

"Gib," Dad says. "These men have been accused, not convicted."

"Yeah? But what were they doing?"

"They were working to defeat a state senator and a congressman."

"Are the senator and congressman anti-communist?"

"They claim to be."

"Well, no wonder," I say. "Did Senator McCarthy find these guys?" Senator McCarthy heads a national committee to hunt down subversives, radicals and traitors.

"Read the whole story, son," Dad says, tapping it with his finger.

I read the front page. The arrested men encouraged union members to vote against Congressman Norblad. They also wanted to defeat State Senator Roland Johnson. He lives right here in our neighborhood.

Actually, it's Senator Johnson's kid who popped me in the eye.

I turn to the second page, and see another story about subversives. "The House committee on un-American activities (HUAC) renewed its recommendation that spies and saboteurs be subjected to the death penalty in peacetime, as they are in wartime."

I start to ask Dad if I can cut out that article for my collection, but my little sister, Justine, comes clattering down the stairs and into the breakfast room.

Dad takes the newspaper from me and says, "Gib, let me see that eye."

I duck my head down. "Big deal. So, I've got another black eye. Who cares?"

Dad puts his hand on my head and holds my face up to the light. "I care," he says. "It looks like an infection there."

Over his shoulder that eight-year wonder, Justine is staring at me. She says, "How come thee has only one black eye?"

"What's it to you?" I say.

"Thee didn't turn the other cheek," she says.

"Geez! When was the last time you followed that rule?"

Dad says, "Justine, cast not the first stone."

Justine is no Quaker angel. I'm not practicing to be one either. I'm up to here with kids who think they can push me around because I'm supposed to be a peaceful kind of guy.

I've seen where peace gets you. Peace makes you the target of bullies.

Justine's still going on. "That black and green color doesn't go good with thy freckles." She knows I hate my freckles, and she knows I don't like it when she talks like Mom and Dad – using old talk. Thee and thou are like a big poster announcing we are Quaker pacifists.

"Thy cowlick is up again," she says.

"Yeah, so what?" She bugs me. My stiff brown hair and my freckles bug me. I wish....

Dad's still looking at my eye, but he stops her from talking. "Justine, go get thy oatmeal from Mother. And bring a bowl for Gib."

"Daddy!" she whines.

Dad turns and gives her the raised eyebrow. She flounces around the table and pushes through the swinging door into the kitchen where Mom is making coffee and hot cereal.

"Thee needs to rinse that eye and not touch the lids," Dad says. "Think thee can avoid another fight with the Johnsons?"

"Nope. Rick Johnson always brings backup."

"How about following through on Mom's idea?"

"You mean go over there and talk to him at his house?"

Dad raises that eyebrow and says nothing.

"That's the craziest idea," I say. "First of all his brother will be there and he's part of the attack crew."

"And second? Dad asks.

"And second, there won't be a second. He'll just cream me again with Kenny's help."

Mom comes out of the kitchen at that moment. She sets a bowl of hot oatmeal in front of Dad and another by me. "Gilbert," she says, "thee ...you know how to take care of this. You've done it before. Show Rick what he has to gain by having a friend."

"Yeah? Like what?"

Mom's face goes a little red, but I'm not backing down.

I think about the times in Germany, right after the war, and then in Boston before we moved to Portland, Oregon. There's always someone wanting to make a fight with the outsider.

I say, "Rick's got nothing to gain, being my friend. His dad is rich, and a state senator. Rick's bigger than most kids in our class and he has lots of friends without me. They do what he tells them. I don't."

Mom speaks very softly. "I'm glad that you don't follow, son, but you could also lead."

"I'm tired of figuring out ways to make peace with some piece of..."

Dad raises his open palm to warn me to stop.

Mom says, "Be a friend. Lose an enemy."

"Like I have not heard that before," I say.

Dad's stare penetrates my anger.

But I'm not stopping. "I'm fed up with 'the Friendly Way'. I'm not going to love 'em till they holler, like Mom always says. I'm going to bust Rick's nose. The others will scram."

Mom smiles. "I understand the urge, son. Let me know how it works out."

"Christine!" Dad says.

Mom turns to him and whispers, "David, did you never want to pop someone?"

They look at each other, and I see that some memory has come, making both of them sad. They have secrets. I worry sometimes what those secrets might be. Maybe I don't want to know, but at least their memory saves me from their focus.

*   *

Pretty soon after breakfast, I'm outside and into the bright sun, carrying my fishing pole. In my fishing basket, I've hidden a sandwich and a Hershey bar. Mom wouldn't like it, where I'm headed. For that matter, I can't let Justine know where I'm going or that I have chocolate, so I had to sneak out of the house. I plan to test a theory about chocolate and fish in the creek down in Sullivan's Gulch.

Early this morning, I cut this fishing rod from our Big Leaf Maple. The rod I really want costs twenty-five whopping dollars. Ever since the war ended, prices just go up. Dad says that's to be expected, since people are earning more and wanting more. So, kids like me have to get in line for what Dad calls 'scarce commodities' – commodities means stuff.

While I save up for a real fishing rod, I make do with my maple switch.

I trot south on our street, Sixteenth Avenue, and pass near the theater on Broadway. They've got a big sign for *Red Planet Mars*. My friend, Mike, and I went last Saturday. The show was about these scientists contacting Mars. One of the scientists was a secret Russian spy. The whole thing was spooky.

In about a mile, I reach the edge of Sullivan's Gulch. The gulch is a deep ditch, cut by a stream called Sullivan's Creek. The creek runs about forty feet below street level and goes east to west through our part of town. It carries rain water from the hills to the Willamette River. The Union Pacific Railroad sits beside the stream on a high levée built of gravel. On both sides of the gulch, the steep banks are covered with blackberry vines, and lots of underbrush.

To get through the blackberry vines, I put my fishing-tackle basket in front of my face and take a solid hold on the butt end of my pole. Plunging into the overgrown brambles hurts, but I keep pushing through the first yards of skin-grabbing blackberries until I find the deer path leading down to the creek.

I check my old shirt and my arms for scratches. There are plenty – the cost of a good hiding place. These vines grow taller than me and I'm already almost six feet.

I'm lucky to have found this wilderness. Rick Johnson will not set foot in here. And where Rick will not go, neither will his brother or his gang. Rick is just like the boys I had to fight at the Army Base School in Germany. Those guys thought the son of a Quaker and a Conscientious Objector was fair game. And like Rick, they loved having a crowd of helpers along for the fun.

Of course, I let Mom and Dad think all those bruises were gained because I did turn the other cheek. When it came to blows, I learned to go the extra mile. I just made sure my extra mile hurt the other guy.

CHAPTER TWO

Assignment, Essay #1: Continued:

In Germany, on the other side of that barbed wire roll of fence I saw fields of stunted wheat and wilted potatoes. The communists had turned that farm into a prisoner-of-war camp. Sick prisoners worked there. The vegetables grew thin and the prisoners died.

* *

Down in this gulch, this hot jungle of blackberries and salal, I can push back my Portland Beaver Baseball cap and let sweat run into my shirt to cool me off. I can fish, watch trains, pick berries, and think. The green down here helps me forget the barren ground on the other side of that border wire.

I attach the bait—one square of a Hershey's bar. I'm betting it'll melt in this sluggish water before any trout even nibbles at it. This gulch reminds me of the creeks around Neustadt, our German town.

A finch swoops by on its way to catch bugs. I relax and look around me. My favorite place is right here.

Every day, freight trains roll through. Each train slows down as it approaches the Twelfth Avenue Bridge. That's because, in a half-mile or so, the tracks turn a sharp right to the north, and then another hard left to the west. Sometimes, guys jump off the freight train here because it's the best place to do it without being caught. After this place, the freight rolls across the Willamette River on the Steel Bridge, and rumbles into the rail yard in the northwest part of the town.

During spring, Sullivan's Creek is a heavy blast of rain pouring off the hills of East Portland, water crashing over brambles. The force of the water rolls huge boulders and threatens to pull down the levée of the railroad tracks. Last spring's flood was a powerhouse, but today, at the dry end of summer, a narrow, deep part of the stream gurgles through the middle of the wider bed of sun-cracked mud. The mud smells like green things waiting to grow, waiting for cooler weather. This is what a summer drought has left us of Sullivan's Creek.

Look at that! I've hooked a fish. Here he comes. Hang on. Hang on . ...

Yes! Trout for dinner.

Well, maybe for snack. He did take the chocolate bait. Too young to know better. I'm gonna lay him in the shade of this fiddle-head fern and try again. Hope for two fish from this fishing hole is slim. But I'm staying. This place is mine – quiet and safe.

Well, mostly quiet. Sometimes, the city sponsors outdoor concerts in the natural amphitheater over there, a half mile west of the bridge. Sometimes they have political rallies and speeches there. It's called 'The Bowl' because of the shape – a wide, roundish, sloped part of the north side of Sullivan's Gulch. Noisy place when it's busy, but people from The Bowl don't come over here. The blackberries between are too thick.

Some folks live down here in the gulch, but they stay to themselves. Right now, one of the silent citizens of this gulch sits above me on the hillside. He's the guy up there next to the south pier of the Twelfth Avenue Bridge.

One day this summer, that fellow walked down the tracks toward me, paying attention to shiny things like pennies and white cigarette butts. He wore a plaid shirt that no longer had cuffs or a collar. From his skinny shoulders, his overalls hung straight down, hardly touching his sides as if the overalls expected him to suddenly gain weight and fill their empty spaces.

When he ran into me where he thought he was alone, he nearly jumped out of his shirt.

"Gib Evans," I said, and put my hand out to shake his.

"Max," he said, and didn't offer a hand.

Later in the summer, he walked by me again and muttered, "Maximilian." Then on one hot day, he stopped in front of me as I hunkered over my fishing gear. He stood between me and the creek, and said, "The Emperor Maximilian."

I couldn't tell if he was kidding. Maybe he believed he was an emperor. So, I stood up, looked him in the eye and said, "Pleased to meet thee, Maximilian. Want to share my can of worms?"

"Got worms," he said, squinting into my coffee can. "Got lice, too."

"Are they good for fishing?"

Max stared at me. Then he snorted. "Good for fishing," he mumbled, shaking like I'd said the funniest thing he'd ever heard. He near bust his weary shirt seams. Suddenly, he stopped guffawing, and said. "Take your hat off to the Emperor Maximilian."

I touched my baseball hat and said, "Max, I'm a Quaker."

"So?"

"We believe the emperor, the butcher, and the fisherman—all are the same. Respect, yes. But we don't do the hat thing for royalty."

"Why not?"

"Because ...well, because everyman has something of God in him."

He jerked his head up and glared at me. "Something of God? It ain't enough to have worms and lice? I got to host God, too?"

That stopped me. I frowned at the idea, then shrugged. "I guess you and me – we all got to host him."

Max shook his head. "Don't like it," he said. "Too hard."

I felt weird, spouting this stuff at him. At home, I tell my folks I don't believe any of their Quaker quackery. But out it comes, and I'm thinking, either I'm lying to this guy, or to Mom and Dad.

Since that day, I sometimes see Max hunting for golf balls to sell to the duffers who play the Lloyd's Golf Course where it skirts the rim of the gulch. Or I see him on the hillside, picking berries. But more often, I see him sitting up at his camp, watching me. And when he does that, I think about being a host for God. He's right. It's not a job I want.

CHAPTER THREE

Assignment, Essay #1: Continued:

In Neustadt bei Wald, after World War Two, we were part of the Marshall Plan to rebuild Europe. My dad had been asked to help reconstruct a bombed out village. At first, building with Germans seemed odd, so I asked Dad, "Weren't they against us?"

"We came to help build homes," he said, "but mostly to build friendships. Thee cannot hate or fear, or war against people who are thy friends."

He was right, mostly. After a time, the Neustadters lost their fear of us and we all worked together. But on the other side of that fence, the communists were building only enemies.

* *

Here comes the ten a.m. freight. Its whistle blows way out at Sixtieth Avenue, warning people near the tracks like me. I glance out toward the sound of the train, but it is still too far to see. I feel the thumpa-clack of heavy freight through the soles of my tennis shoes. There's the whistle again. Must be about to the Forty-seventh Avenue Bridge.

I've met the guys who jump off as the train slows down. They've ridden from far places like Chicago or Des Moines. The first thing jumpers do is stagger along the creek staring at the green. They can't believe the ground is covered with plants that are lush in late summer. Huckleberry, kinnick-kinnick and elderberry. They don't seem to know those plants. Maybe they only grow in the Pacific Northwest, and Germany—most of them grew in Germany.

Train jumpers have no idea what to do with any of the plant life here except the blackberries. A fellow can get sick gorging on blackberries.

There it is, a long, hot lizard with metal skin, already slowing down for the turns. I wave at the engineer to let him know I'm watching. He waves, but he's still braking-down that heavy load behind him. His attention returns to the track and up to Max's box and cardboard home.

Over the crawling wheel-clacks, the brake-squall and the steam, I hear one of the metal freight doors slide open. About five cars back, a long, gaunt face peeks out. A satchel flies, followed by a fellow who leaps out the door. He lands hard, then rolls into a blackberry bramble and comes up stuck to it. He grunts with pain. As he scrambles to get away, the grunt becomes a curse word I can hear over the rattle of the departing train.

I drop my fishing stick and run toward him. "Hold still, friend. This takes time." He glances up, sees I'm a kid and loses some of the tightness that is fear's habit. I catch a brief glimpse of his face before he glances away. In that moment I can tell there's something wrong about the skin around his mouth. It's puckered instead of smooth.

My berry-stained hands are toughened up, so I start untangling him from his future food.

"You live here?" he asks, his voice like sandpaper on rough fir bark.

"Sure do," I say, licking my thorn-stabbed finger while I try to loosen the back of his jacket. "Name's Brer Rabbit, and I lives in the Briar Patch."

His jacket looks to be new. That's kind of weird — new clothes on a train jumper. He's a big man, but skinny, like he hasn't eaten much lately. He's missing the thumb and pointer finger on his left hand. The rest of that hand looks like it's gone through the clothes wringer on a washing machine.

As soon as I've freed his jacket, I start untangling his belt from the blackberry vines. The fellow drops his head to his palms. His voice comes out muffled, but wary and tight. "Brer Rabbit, how come you'd be helping a man with nothing? Can't be wanting what I own."

"No sir, I surely don't. But it's hard to fish in Sullivan's Creek when a man is hollering near my best pool."

He looks off toward where I was when he jumped. "Caught anything?"

"One pitiful little guy. The creek is low."

"I heard the fishing is good out this way."

"Thee must have heard about fish in the mighty Columbia River, or maybe the Willamette, which runs right through the middle of Portland. But Sullivan's Creek in late summer tries patience."

"You go to school around here?"

"Not if I can help it."

"That's a good way to stay ignorant," he says.

"And free, and out of fights." I say as I pull the last bit of blackberry vine off his belt loop. "School's not the only place to learn."

"True, just a more efficient place, if done right."

"Mostly, it's not done right, far as I can see."

"That the school's fault or yours?" he asks.

At first, I don't bother to answer. I'm puzzled by his good clothes. It even looks like he polished his shoes just before he jumped. I say,

"I learn enough down in the Gulch to know you didn't travel by train because you're broke. So what's your game?"

"Hmph." He tests his legs, pushing up to stand, but keeping his back to me. "I've no game to play. I'm just celebrating being alive, which is a miracle. And I'm here to make a living."

"Yes, sure. If you want me to believe you need a living, don't spit polish thy shoes before jumping from the freight car."

"Well, my friend, since you're so observant, perhaps thee knows a place called George Fox House?"

He's making fun of my lapse into Quaker talk. My 'thee' and 'thy' encouraged him to ask about the Quaker home for men.

"George Fox House," I say, and I reach into my pants pocket for the cards Mom gives me. I normally hand the card to a train hopper at the end of a conversation, like when I shake hands and go on home. I wonder how this guy knows to ask.

He turns only his left side toward me as I give him the card. I realize I haven't seen his whole face. He stares at the print on the front where it says. 'Need help? You've got a Friend in Portland, Oregon.' The guy glances at the card's other side. 'George Fox House, Beds, Showers, Food. 1350 Northeast Fifteenth Avenue, Portland, Oregon'.

He still doesn't look directly at me, but he asks, "That north of this creek, or south?"

"That's north a couple of blocks and three blocks east." I point up the steep hillside and beyond the bridge. "The bridge is at Twelfth Avenue."

"Thanks."

Somehow, I know he doesn't want to face me. Maybe he doesn't want to ever meet me again. So I say, "Well, I'll be going now. My name is Gilbert Evans. My fish is on that waxed paper back down the creek. Only been out of water ten minutes when … when your train showed up. Maybe you'd like to cook it. Wouldn't be enough to feed my family."

"Thank you, son." His voice is soft, like a tired sigh, but he still doesn't face me.

He waits until I'm halfway up the side of the gulch before he turns around to look at that square of wax paper, and then at the stick-and-string fishing rod lying next to the creek. From this distance, I can't see much detail in his damaged face. His clothes are the clothes of a man who is proud and has a job. That doesn't figure with train jumping.

I wonder what he's up to. And I wonder if I'd know him if I saw him in a crowd.

CHAPTER FOUR

After leaving the train jumper, I head toward home still thinking about that guy. I hope he knows how to find food from the plants. I think guys who wear suits grow up where they don't ever get to learn about things like that.

During the months after the murder, my friend Herr Grofmann and I hiked through the hills. He taught me to know all the plants and trees, but we never talked about his brother who'd been shot while escaping. I knew Herr Grofmann hiked with me because I had been there. We went everywhere, except never into the grassy area near the barbed-wire fence. There were still bullets in my oak, one right below my branch.

Two years after the shooting, our family moved to Boston and then here, to Portland, Oregon. I still write to Herr Grofmann. The communists still own his brother's old farm. And in every letter, he tells me how afraid Neustadters are that the Russians will invade their part of the valley. Even his handwriting is angry and afraid.

Just north of Sullivan's Gulch, I pass a telephone pole with a big sign stapled to it.

"Protect America from Communism! Report suspicious activity."

Every day, the *Portland Journal* headlines are about what they call revolutionary types. The kids at school talk about a program on television about a real-life spy who infiltrated Marxist-Communist groups and told the FBI what those subversives were doing. The kids say maybe our spy was telling the Russians about us, too.

On radio news, there's this spy-finding committee – that guy named Senator Joseph McCarthy. Senator McCarthy has even asked Oregon's Senator Wayne Morse to explain some stuff he's said. Senator McCarthy says Senator Morse is soft on communism. He might even be a subversive. Thinking about all this scary stuff, I stand there, dumb and staring at that sign on the telephone pole.

"Protect America from Communism!"

I can't seem to move my feet because I remember people so skinny they could hardly lift a hoe. While I lived there, Russia took over half of Europe, starved people, murdered people. For over a year, they tried to keep the people of Berlin from getting outside help and food. The newsmen say thousands have died in the Ukraine, in Hungary, in Romania because of Stalin, the Russian leader. And now they are here, Russian spies right in the U.S. of A., even arrested in Portland.

This poster asks me to Protect America, but I don't know how. I don't know how.

"Blasted communists," says a voice behind me.

I whip around and find Mr. Stockman standing there. He's a quiet kind of guy who lives around the corner at the southern end of our block. His is the big house surrounded by maple and horse chestnut trees.

"Hi, Mr. Stockman," I say.

"You're that kid rides his bicycle round and round our block, aren't you?"

"Yes, sir," I say. "I'm Gilbert Evans. Who put up this sign?"

"Huh!" he says, pointing a finger at the bottom line, small print. "We gotta find out who is lying in wait for a signal from Russia."

The small print he's pointing at says, "Provided Courtesy of Educators for Democracy"

"Who are Educators for Democracy?" I ask.

"Big committee," he says. "They lobby the state legislature and all that for more money to dig out subversive types."

I say, "The police arrested three guys yesterday for sub ... sub ..."

"Subversive activity," he says. "You know the Russians have the bomb now."

"I know."

"I'm building a bomb shelter in my basement. Your folks should be building one."

"We store water and stuff, but how do you build a bomb shelter?"

"Well, some recommend plastic – sheets of plastic. They say it keeps out the radiation. But I think you have to use lead."

"But where do you get sheets of lead?" I ask. "What's that cost?"

"You gotta ask, you can't afford it."

"Do you really think they can send a bomb from Russia clear to the west coast?"

"Gilbert, don't you realize they have submarines? Submarines can go anywhere. Atlantic, Pacific. They're out there."

At that moment the air-raid siren on the Bonneville Power building goes off. The shriek rips the air. That building is nearby, next to the concert Bowl down at the gulch. As it wails up and down, I glance at the sun. Maybe it's eleven in the morning, but maybe this one is for real.

"Gotta get inside," Mr. Stockman says. "See you tomorrow."

"Isn't this just the eleven o'clock drill?"

"You never know," he says, walking away from me. "It's eleven. So, they know we won't take it serious. Better hightail it to home, just in case."

I turn my back on the telephone pole sign, and run up Seventeenth Avenue.

"Hustle it up," Mr. Stockman yells as he tries to run, too.

I pass his house with its old trees and keep running. By the time I get to the house of my friend Mike Halverson, the siren has stopped. I realize it was just a drill, but still, I pound on the door until Mike opens it. He is football-player big, and solid. He looks at me from under blond bangs.

"You seen a bogey-man?" he asks.

I'm embarrassed that I was scared by something that happens every day, so I say, "Can you come out? Maybe play baseball?"

He stares, trying to figure out if I'm crazy. Then he shrugs and hollers back into his house. "Mom, I'm done with my chores. Can I go over to Gib's?"

"Sure," Mrs. Halverson says from the kitchen, "but don't forget to walk Buzzard at one o'clock."

*   *

Twenty minutes later, Mike and I come in our house. We're really sweaty after street ball and we want some food. Justine has her dolls spread all over the breakfast table, so we take the lunch Mom makes for us into the living room. We plop on the floor between the coffee table and the fireplace. The sun shines through the beveled angles of glass in the upper part of our front window. The glass angles turn the light into rainbows of color on the wall behind us. I like watching light move as the sun moves.

When we've scarfed down our tuna salad sandwiches, we act like slugs, lolling about on the braided rug. Mike's on his stomach. His straight blond hair hides his face as he reads *Superman* over by the cool dark fireplace. He's pulled some paper and a pencil from his pocket. Mike always has paper and pencil. He copies the action from his comic book.

I'm right next to the Motorola radio with one of the sofa pillows behind my head. Mike and me, we've got this one more Friday to read comics and not feel guilty about homework.

Our old mantle clock chimes the Big Ben tune. It bangs on and on, until I realize it must be twelve o'clock. I drop my *Kent Blake of the Secret Service* comic book and reach for the radio dials. I don't want to miss the *KGW Noon News*.

Mike glances at the Motorola. After some static, I get the dial tuned to the right place. I can tell because I recognize the advertisement.

Mike makes a girly voice and quotes the advert lines. "Aren't you glad you use Dial? Don't you wish everybody did?" Mike pretends to smell his armpits and mugs fainting.

The next ad is for a new mouthwash. I mimic it in my announcer voice. "Listerine gets rid of germs that can cause halitosis." We both crack up.

"Better make a pit stop. Don't kill your girlfriend with body odor and halitosis," I joke. We don't even want girlfriends, but all the guys use Dial and Listerine, just in case.

We shut up because the voice of Senator Joseph McCarthy crackles out of the brown-cloth speaker. The news report on the anti-spy hearings of the Senate has already started. Senator McCarthy sounds excited. "We've uncovered communists in the State Department. And now, we even find the red wind blows in positions of authority in the United States Army."

Splat!

I figure the splat sound is McCarthy's spit hitting the microphone. I can tell he's really disgusted with the spies and Army stupidness. Our country is in big danger.

McCarthy shouts, "Thanks to our investigations, supporters of the Red Army are on the run. Our brother investigators, the House Un-America Activities Committee, follow us into this dark discovery. We will hunt down these Pinkos wherever they hide. We will name names."

During the house-cleaner ads, Mike looks up from his Superman comic book. He says, "Your little sister is a Pinko. Pink pedal pushers, pink pony-tail ribbons, pink shoe strings."

"That's not what McCarthy means," I tell him.

"No?" He looks puzzled.

"Communists are Reds," I explain. "Pinkos are people who support them. They want to take over our country, like they took over in Eastern Europe."

Mike shrugs. "Your little sister would like to run everything."

I stare at him. The crinkles next to his eyes give him away. It's not the first time Mike's tricked me with his pretend-to-be-dumb act.

"Yeah," I chuckle, "Justine would like to run the world. Maybe she really is a Pinko."

A thunderclap nearly busts the radio speaker. McCarthy probably smacked the microphone. In the movie-house newsreels, I've seen him make big gestures and whack things. Or maybe the radio station makes noises, trying to sabotage his speech. He's talking again.

"We're moving our investigations into the colleges and universities of this once great nation," McCarthy snarls. "Colleges have become hot-beds of Marxist-communist sympathizers."

That makes me sit straight up. My dad teaches at Portland State, the new city college that moved into an old high school building downtown. Dad is no Pinko. I know that for sure. But Dad has friends who teach down at Corbett College, the really old campus in Portland. A few days ago, one of the teachers at Corbett College refused to take an oath of loyalty. And he wouldn't talk about if he were ever a member of the Party.

The Noon News topic shifts from McCarthy's hearings to Communist North Korea. A peace treaty was signed back in July this year. I know a kid at school whose dad died in Korea trying to keep the world safe from communists.

"In case the North Koreans get aggressive ideas," the announcer says, "our brave troops are at the ready on permanent bases in South Korea and Japan. And, for news of the home front," the announcer continues, "reaction to the recent execution of Julius and Ethel Rosenberg has calmed. Communist sympathizers no longer gather to protest the execution."

Mike asks, "Who are the Rosenbergs?"

"The FBI, or somebody, discovered the Rosenbergs sold atomic secrets to the Soviets – the Russian."

"Oh, yeah. Them," he says. "Did they really do it?"

"They were convicted." I think Mike doesn't ever listen to the news.

The pocket doors slide open between our living room and Dad's music-teaching room. Dad pokes his head into the living room. His dark hair sticks up in spikes because he runs his fingers through his hair while he writes music for his band. Dad nods at Mike, then raises his eyebrows and looks over his glasses at me. "Gilbert?"

Something about Senator McCarthy and the talk of communists always bothers Dad. I know what he wants, but I ignore it. "McCarthy has found lots of communist," I say.

"The radio needs to be off," Dad says.

I don't budge. "I gotta know what suspicious activity to report. I saw this sign on the telephone post."

Dad looks at me, one eyebrow way up in his 'do it now' stare. At that moment, I remember a weird discussion my folks had in the kitchen last week. Mom said, "McCarthy's a megalomaniac." And then Dad started whispering.

I don't want Mike to hear anything like that at our house, so I reach over and turn the dial off.

"Thanks, Gib," Dad says. "Good afternoon, Mike."

"Sir," Mike says.

Dad pulls his head back into the music room and slides the doors closed.

Mike waits a moment, and then he says, "How come he doesn't let you listen to the news?"

"Dad's got a student coming," I hope there really is a student. I don't want Mike to think about Dad's politics.

"Oh Geez!" Mike says. "Not a wheezing horn."

I'm glad he's moved to the new subject. He goes back to drawing. About five minutes later, the side door to the house opens. Squeaky tennis shoes climb the steps to the breakfast room. One of Dad's students has arrived in the nick of time, backing up my lie.

"Thanks, Mrs. Evans," I hear the kid say. Mom always hands the students a glass of juice. Believes in wetting their whistles before lessons.

"Justine, stop," Mom orders my little sister, "No paper airplanes at people." From the squeal of the hall door, we can tell the new student is dodging Justine's missiles.

Mike glances at me, shaking his head. "She's Pinko for sure."

Mike pulls his pencil from behind his ear and goes back to sketching. As he works, he asks, "What about that guy you met this morning down by the tracks?"

"What do you mean?"

"S'pose he's a revolutionary? Maybe come to work with the hobos or something?"

I wish I hadn't told Mike about the train hopper. Funny thing is, I am suspicious of him. He never looked me in the eye like an honest man.

"Naw," I say. "He wouldn't be a subversive or an organizer. Hobos have a hard time just getting food." But I'm thinking about how well dressed he was. Was he sent here by the Russians?

I pretend to concentrate on the *Adventures of Kent Blake of the Secret Service*, but I'm thinking maybe that fellow is up to no good. And I helped him.

Mike draws some more. Suddenly I'm bored with the comic book. I flap it in the air. "This Kent Blake is supposed to be a hero, but every problem, his solution is a blasting gun."

Mike glances up. His eyebrows rise into his bowl-cut bangs. "Well, you know, Kent Blake is not a Quaker."

I slap down my comic. "I didn't say that because of religion."

"No?"

"No! Dangit! This comic is boring because Blake's never clever."

"True," Mike says, "but when stuff gets bad, most guys only understand knuckles and guns."

"Besides, I'm not a Quaker," I say. "It's my folks."

Mike shrugs. But I want to be done with this Quaker stuff. If we belonged to some normal religion, I'd be going to catechism class, or studying for my Bar Mitzvah, but I just sit in Silent Meeting and wait for the voice of God. The truth is, The Big Guy has no messages for me.

The kid in the music room hits a doozer. Mike jumps. "Your dad must have nerves of steel."

"Don't believe it," I say. "Watch his face sometime when Justine practices her trombone."

"Trombone? That dinky kid?"

"Her choice," I say.

Mike laughs and goes back to his pencil work. I glance over, thinking he'll be drawing Justine trying to hold up a huge trombone, but this time he's drawn a tank driving across a field of bomb-blasted trees. An idea pops into my head.

"Let's write a comic book about your Dad in the Battle of the Bulge."

Mike grins. "Good idea. I don't draw the hands so great, but I did a tank close-up. You're looking right down the gun barrel at this screaming guy."

Sometimes, when we're out fishing in the gulch, Mike tells me his dad's great stories. Mr. Halverson nearly lost his feet to frost bite when his battalion pushed Germans back toward Berlin in the winter of 1944.

"Your dad's stories will make a great comic book," I say. "You do the drawings and I'll write." Mike hates to write.

"Yeah!" Mike agrees. "You do all the Oofs and Ows."

"What about a title?"

"Sergeant Halverson and the Nazi Menace," Mike says.

I shake my head, "In nineteen fifty-three, nobody cares about Nazis. It's Commies, now."

"But Dad wasn't fighting Marxists or communists."

"Your dad can discover communists on his way to Berlin," I say.

"How can he do that?"

"Let's make it that he's discovers these cells of Marxists who plot to run Germany after the war. He's the first to know they are the next big danger."

Mike nods, but I get the feeling he's not really listening. He says, "When we get done with the adventures of Sergeant Halverson, we can write about what your dad did in the war."

I glance toward the sliding door. No way do I want to do a comic book on Dad. Pacifists are not exciting. No adventures and no heroes. Besides, he never talks about during the war.

"I bet the Tales of Sergeant Halverson can take us through at least ten comic books. Maybe more," I say.

"Yeah," Mike agrees. "It's been eight years since the war ended, and Dad still comes out with new stories."

The clock chimes for one o'clock. "Geez!" Mike jumps up and starts for the front door. "I was supposed to take Old Buzzard for a walk so he won't bark during Mom's Canasta party. Yacky ladies and chocolate cake. Drives Buzzard nuts."

I get up to see Mike out the door. I've been thinking about the guy I met this morning. Maybe he's cooked my fish and moved on, but maybe he's teaching communism to Max and his friends. I should go back to Sullivan's Gulch and check. But right now, Mom is calling me.

CHAPTER FIVE

"**H**oney," Mom says, "I'm going to need thy… your help getting ready for our dinner guest."

Mom's trying to stop using the old talk, too. She says *thee* and *thine* makes other people uncomfortable. Discomfort doesn't sell peace. But change is hard. *Thee* and *thine* are really close to *you* and *your* words in German. We used them all the time in Neustadt.

"Dinner guest? Who's coming?" Justine asks.

A professor from Corbett College, Angus Wilson," Mom says, "But you, young lady, will be a guest at Magdalena's house."

"Me? Goody! At Magdalena's, I get to bake cookies." Justine jumps down from her chair. "I've got to get dressed up to visit."

She runs around, grabbing up dollies. Mom smiles and watches Justine's short legs chug up the steps to the bedrooms. I don't remember meeting a friend of Justine's named Magdalena, but I'm glad Justine won't be around for dinner. That kid cannot let a conversation happen without her butting into it.

Mom chuckles, and then gets back to me. "Gilbert, would thee take this bowl into the vegetable garden and gather Swiss chard and other vegetables?"

I reach for the bowl and ask, "Who is this Professor Wilson?"

Mom turns on the oven as she answers. "He's a friend of Daddy's. He teaches Art. Thy … your father will be teaching students while we get dinner ready, so I hope you'll clean vegetables while I take Justine to her dinner party."

Mom pulls a small cut of beef out of the refrigerator.

"Geez, we don't usually get beef. This guy must be special."

"He's your father's friend, and this cut was on sale."

"So, am I going to eat dinner somewhere else, too?" I ask.

Mom sets the dinky roast in the sink to rinse it. She turns on a dribble of water and glances out the window as if thinking how to answer me. She takes the roast out of the sink, and finally turns to me.

"Gilbert, we'll have a grown-up conversation tonight. In most countries you are a grown-up. I want you to stay for dinner, but you need to promise me that what we say in our home about certain ideas will stay in our home."

"Why would I go blabbing about a dinner conversation?"

"There are people who take a conversation between friends, and twist it into something bad. Those kinds of people have a lot of power right now. So thee must promise not to talk about our home conversations, not even to your best friends."

"Not to Mike?"

"Or James or Billy, and certainly not to Davie."

I snort. "Davie and me, we're not friends anymore."

"Davie and I," she corrects. Mom plops her beef into a bowl of flour and spices. "Well, that's a relief," she says. And then she adds, "Davie may become a very fine person, one day, but right now, he's a worry."

"No worry. He's off my list."

"So, no talk about our dinner outside this family?"

"Okay. But, Mom, how come we're not building a bomb shelter?"

She looks at me and lets out a big sigh. "Are you scared about bombs?"

"Mr. Stockman says you should use lead to line the walls. That's what he's doing."

"Gib, I know that many are talking about building bomb shelters. Once our country started dropping bombs, it was inevitable that others would learn to make them."

"But we dropped ours to stop a war."

"And it may have seemed necessary," she says, "or expedient. But we can wonder what might be if we hadn't taken that route."

"The Russians have the bomb," I say.

"Yes, they do."

"And they got some of that information from one of our guys who was a spy."

"That appears to be true, although that man, Mr. Fuchs, was from Eastern Germany originally. He lived under Hitler. There may have been reasons he acted as he did."

"Why did anybody in the government trust him?"

"I wish I knew, Gib. Here is your sister, coming back downstairs. How about those vegetables?"

I know Mom doesn't want Justine to worry about bombs and like that, so I let her change the subject, but I sure wish I didn't have to worry about them. "Back in a few..."I say.

"A garlic and an onion would be good, as well," she says.

Out in the garden, I think about that spy, Klaus Fuchs. He's in jail now, but he is part of the reason the Russians have the bomb. Their bombs are why we should be building a bomb shelter.

*   *

That evening, I pass the roasted veggies to Dad while I'm listening.

"Whatever happened to innocent until proven guilty?" Professor Wilson asks Dad.

Dad takes the bowl, but he's nodding at his friend. "Freedom of thought and speech – you can't teach without them."

Does Dad mean you can believe anything? Say anything?

Professor Wilson says "Senator William Benton had it right. That McCarthy should be expelled from the Senate."

I never heard about this Senator Benton.

Mom passes Professor Wilson the beef and she says, "Last year, Mr. Benton lost his own seat in the Senate because of that speech."

Dad points his fork at Wilson, saying, "Honesty is dangerous in today's government."

"Yes," Mom says, "Standing up to McCarthy caused the downfall of Senator Tydings in 1950."

"At least he had the courage of his convictions," Professor Wilson says, "unlike some local Senators."

I'm trying to figure out which local senator he means when Mom glances at me and winks. I nod to let her know I'll keep silent about this discussion. No way am I talking about this conversation to anybody. Dad might be a just a good host tonight, but Professor Wilson is talking about not signing the loyalty oath that the president of Corbett College requires. He's also talking about organizing the whole faculty and the student body to protest the campus visit of the investigators from the U.S. House on Un-American Activities Committee.

I thought he was just an art teacher, but he sounds like a plotter, maybe a revolutionary. And Dad and Mom just let him talk that way.

* *

The next afternoon, I'm riding my bike around the block to see Mike. When I pass Mr. Stockman's house, he's outside, working in his front garden where he's planted lettuce and tomatoes. He's wearing old work pants and tennis shoes, his usual gardening get-up.

"Hello," he says. "Gilbert Evans, isn't it?"

"Yes, sir," I say. I start to ride on by, but he continues, "You got a victory garden?" he asks.

I stop. "Sure, in our back yard."

He glances up at his maple trees and the fir tree in his side yard. "Not much sun anywhere in this yard except right here."

"Gotta have sun for tomatoes," I say.

I'm about to push off when Mr. Stockman says, "You want to see my bomb shelter?"

I figure it's my only chance. "Sure would. My folks haven't started one yet."

"Ought to get on it," he says. "Come on in."

I've known Mr. Stockman for years, because his sons used to play baseball and basketball out in front of his house. I feel like I've gotta talk about something, so I say, "Your sons off to college?"

"Nope," he says. He lets his hoe lean against the side of his porch and gestures me to follow him. "The boys are in the army now, off in Korea, in the demilitarized zone between North and South."

We climb the wood stairs while he talks. "Randy, that's my oldest, he's a lieutenant already. Jeffrey's a super marksman, but he's still a private. Kind of a happy-go-lucky kid, that Jeffrey, so I don't suppose he'll ever be an officer."

"They ever get leave to come home?"

"Nope. Just enough time to go into Seoul for a weekend. Costs a lot to fly across the Pacific, you know. Gotta stay there and make sure South Korea doesn't fall to communist domination."

I tell him, "The movies last week had a newsreel about spies and fifth columnists from Russia trying to move into other countries."

"You're right," he says. "There are parts of free Europe that even let them have a political party and vote and all. Just askin' for trouble."

"They can't vote communist here, can they?"

"Not if we can help it. But we gotta know who they are."

I follow him into the front hall, which is kind of dark because of all the trees outside. Walking into the back hall, we come to a door, right about where the basement stair door is in our house. Mr. Stockman's house is gloomy, so it's hard to see how much like our house his might be. He flips on the stair light and we head down to the basement.

"You gotta see how I've stocked the place," he says. "I'll be able to last a year or so after the bomb," he says. "Course there are four of you and only one of me, but I bet your folks can find a way to stock up."

"Mom buys canned goods on sale every fall. And she cans our garden veggies and fruit and stuff." I try to think of what else she does. Don't want Mr. Stockman to think we're not prepared.

We get to the far back in his basement. He opens a door and flips on another light.

"I've got kerosene lanterns, too," he says, "'cause in a real emergency there won't be electricity. They say bombs do something weird to electrical systems."

The inside of the door to his back room is covered in patches of metal that look like he's screwed them onto the door. I step inside after him and discover that the ceiling of this back room is also metal patches with screws that must follow the joists in the basement ceiling.

"Wow," I say. "This was a lot of work." It looks very smooth and like he laid the patches out carefully to decide what would fit in each space. The ceiling has a dark sheen to it, too.

"Cans," he says. "Cans flattened. Not quite as good as lead, but there is lead in the tin, I think. You and your sister could flatten cans for your dad to screw up in his basement."

"Sure. We've got a storage cupboard with shelves like this where the canned stuff is organized."

"Probably need to use another section of the basement next to your storage cupboard just to have room for four of you to sleep. But stay away from windows."

"That's a good idea, Mr. Stockman." I look over the whole space and see he's got a sleeping bag and an air mattress rolled up on one shelf. It looks like he started this project before Mrs. Stockman died because there is a second sleeping bag. I'm antsy to get to Mike's, but here's a chance to survive an invasion, so I try to keep the information coming.

"So, you stock up," I say, "and you create a metal room, right?"

"You got a bathroom in your basement?" he asks.

"No, just on the second floor."

"Well, I'd be glad to teach you and your dad something about plumbing below-grade."

"Thanks, that'd be pretty neat. You got a bathroom down here already?"

"Sure. Gotta figure all the necessities. Food, water, elimination."

"You've been working on this a long time."

"I'll show you the plans for the rest of my space."

Half an hour later, I know we should be working harder in our basement, just in case.

I say good-bye to Mr. Stockman and head up to Mike's house.

As soon as Mike answers, I ask, "Can I see how your dad has fixed up your bomb shelter?"

Mike shakes his head. "Dad says, 'The bomb comes, I just want to be gone.'"

"But…"

"My dad's tired of war. Says he's fed up with the things people do to each other when they're afraid."

"Like what?"

"You've heard Dad's stories. Those camps they liberated. Dad says people let that happen because they were afraid."

"Afraid of Jews?"

"Or afraid of the others, the ones who hunted Jews."

I stand there, amazed. Mr. Halverson would just let his son die from radiation because of stuff that happened during the war.

"Let's play ball," Mike says. "There are no bombs today."

Late into the afternoon, Mike and I play baseball on our corner. I pitch a fast one and Mike completely whizzes it.

"All right!" Mike says. "That's the kind of pitcher we want on our Eisenhower team."

"Sure," I say. "I've got the great arm, but what about when somebody hits the ball to me?"

"Yeah. What if there's a guy on first? Where do you throw?"

"Second base, then first base, right?"

"Sure" Mike says. "The guy already on first is gonna steal second base, and he'll get there faster than the batter can get to first."

"But what if I catch the ball on the fly?"

"In the mitt? Or in the gut?"

"Geez, Mike!"

By the time I moved here at age eleven, all the guys assumed everybody knew the rules for this game. I'm great at hitting and pitching, but I don't do the right defensive moves. I muff stuff other guys do automatically. Too bad nobody in the States plays soccer. That's the game I know best.

After our snack and comic reading, Mike jumps off our porch to walk Buzzard. After I close the front door, I notice Mike forgot his Superman comic. On the last page, a city full of grateful people watch Superman save Earth from an enormous asteroid.

Mr. Halverson, Mike's dad, once described how the people in the streets of Paris celebrated when the U.S. Army rescued them from the Nazis. A hero's welcome. But after the big war, the day our family landed in Germany, I asked Dad if I could see his army uniform. Dad gave Mom this odd look right before he explained to me about being a Quaker and a conscientious objector.

"I had a uniform," he said, "but now the war is over. I choose not to wear it."

So, no hero's welcome for my dad. I know he was a medic, but was that the whole truth? I'm not sure what all he did during the war, and now, after last night's conversation with Professor Wilson, I wonder.

And I'm afraid to ask.

And that's when I start thinking about those concerts in *Neustadt bei Wald*.

Back in those days, way before the murder of Herr Grofmann's brother, Dad started practicing his trombone in our Neustadt house. When they heard him, other Neustadters brought clarinets, trumpets, and a couple of tubas out of hiding from basements and sheds. Herr Erdmann helped Dad repair instruments with carved wood or pieces of brass plumbing out of bombed houses. Soon, the Neustadters had band practice two times a week in the old barn on Herr Grofmann's farm.

After the grown-up band members practiced for a few weeks, Dad received a letter. It was sent by a Russian officer from the other side of the wire fence, over in Lunaberg. The officer had heard the band practicing, so he invited the Neustadt Band to play concerts once a week for his staff. The Russian asked if our band could play at the fence near the Russian camp.

I listened to the discussion among band members, and that's how I learned that the warehouses I'd seen from my oak tree were prisoner barracks, part of a prison camp. The people I'd been watching were prisoners who used to be Nazi soldiers. Herr Grofmann told Dad that there were more than Nazi soldiers in that camp. Then they began whispering.

The band decided to play those concerts. A few weeks later, on a hot Wednesday afternoon, the bandsmen lined up. They played a march that Dad wrote, and they stepped smart, turning corners in good order, the way Dad taught them. They played a march on the way, and arrived at a new gate built near our end of town. The Russian soldiers brought blankets and sat on the other side of the fence to listen. We could hear the band from our house. Mother and her friends sat on our front porch. They knit while we kids listened and played tag or soccer. An hour and a half later, we all watched as the band marched home again. For some reason, Dad had them play the same march all the way up the road that they played on the way to the concert.

Now, I'm wondering why Dad's band got invited to play to Communist Germany every week. And then I think about that very last concert when Dad and the band actually went through the gate and marched into that prisoner-of-war camp. What was going on between Dad and those Russians?

I've got to shut up. Say nothing. I love my Dad.

I do know that after we got to Germany, except for that one trip into the camp, Dad worked for Friends World Service to help rebuild the town. Those people had been bombed and defeated by Americans. They didn't think Dad was any hero – not until later.

I toss *Superman* on the sofa and trudge toward the kitchen. I decide to tell Mom I'm going out to play, which is sort of true. She'd be scared if she knew I spend time down in Sullivan's Gulch where the hobos live. I gotta know if that guy who jumped from the train is still down there, and what he's up to.

Swinging open the door between the hall and the breakfast room, I accidentally step on a paper airplane. Justine pays zero attention. She has her dollhouse on the breakfast table. This week the dollhouse is a cardboard box. Next week her dollhouse might be a drawer from the kitchen cupboards.

Justine holds up the red-headed rag doll she calls Brick. She makes Brick, kick open the door on the cardboard dollhouse. "Hands in the air," Justine calls out, "and don't move a hair on your mustache." She draws Brick's hands together as if the doll aims a gun at somebody inside the dollhouse, just like the FBI guys in my comics.

Justine helps Brick wrestle an imaginary bad guy to the floor. I'm thinking, Justine, future leader of the peaceful Society of Friends – what a crack!

That's when I notice she's printed something on the side of the dollhouse box: "State Deportmet".

Mom picks up her apron skirt to wipe her hands, but she's looking over her glasses at me, and she whispers, "Thee influences thy sister, Gilbert. Have a care how thee wields that power."

"Justine never does what I tell her."

Mom gestures at the dollhouse. "State Department today."

"Not my fault," I say. "It's the radio news. It's the truth."

"Who decides what truth is?"

I frown. "If it isn't the truth," I say, "why is it on national radio?"

Mom just looks at me, and then changes the subject.

"Would you take a suit from the Bandbox Closet down to George Fox House?" she asks. "A new resident there needs to go to a job on Tuesday morning."

The Bandbox is Mom's name for the closet she's filled with clean, used clothes for hobos: "So they'll feel like they just stepped out of the bandbox."

"You commie spies are busted," Justine says.

I backtrack to the closet that should be for our coats. In this house, lots of rooms have changed their use since we moved in. Most of them are storage for the Society of Friends.

"What size suit?" I ask Mom.

"The suit in the bag from Broadway Cleaners. They did a nice rush job for me."

That means Mom went to Goodwill some days ago and got this suit special. When I pull it out, it's a tall size, but skinny. It's gotta be for my train fellow. Did she know the guy was coming?

"Mom, what does this new guy do for a living? Where'd he come from?"

"Gilbert, you know better. We care about the man we have, not the man he used to be."

"But what if he's a spy?" I ask.

"Son, thee cannot allow fear to dictate how thee treats thy fellow man."

"But communists..."

"Need food, shelter, dignity and freedom, just like the rest of us."

"Off to jail with you, Pinkos," Justine says.

Mom glances at Justine, raises her eyebrows at me.

"She's not my responsibility. She's a doofus."

Justine looks at me suddenly. "You're the doofus, Stupid head."

Mom says, "Thee teaches every minute. Now take that suit." I slam closed the closet, and head out the front door.

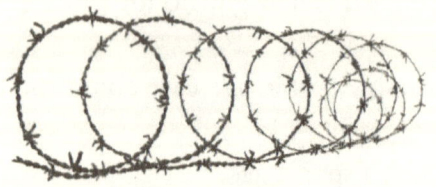

CHAPTER SIX

I'm mad because Mom wants me to be responsible in front of Justine all the time. It's not like Justine ever really listens to me. Well, except that one day in Neustadt when I was eight.

On that day, from my oak tree hideout, I heard a motorcycle roar down the road on the Russian side. The skinny man at the fence heard it, too. He dove to the ground and crawled under the fence. The spikes of wire caught his jacket. He yanked it off, leaving the jacket behind. As he crawled, I could see the teeth on the wire scrape at his head and his back, but he never stopped working toward our side. The siren in the tower wailed and wailed. That motorcycle squirreled around a bend in the road, closer to us.

Mom ran into the park. Dad chased behind her, carrying baby Justine. They raced toward the crawling man. As Dad came near the oak, he pushed Justine to the ground behind my tree trunk. He shouted at her, "Stay there." Then he charged after Mom yelling, "Christine, get down."

The man wriggled out from under the fence on our side. On the other side of the fence, the motorcycle squealed to a stop. The guard raised a fat rifle.

Dad caught up to Mom, grabbed her and pulled her to the ground. The escaping man ran toward my tree.

"Justine," I yelled, afraid she'd follow Dad, "Play rabbit in a hole. You're a rabbit hiding in a hole back there."

There was no time to jump down to her. Bullets hit everywhere, in the grass, in the dirt. I felt bullets thud into the tree trunk below me.

No! Baby sister!

The escaping man's arms flung up. Blood spread across the front of his faded blue shirt. And then he fell. Mom and Dad didn't move. The guard reached behind his back, stuffed the rifle into a backpack holster, started his motorcycle and drove off. My chest pounded. A second of silence passed when I couldn't think. Then, I jumped out of that tree.

Justine stood up, staring at me. I cried out, surprised she wasn't dead. "I a rabbit," she said.

"Good rabbit." I grabbed her hand, swung her up on my hip and ran. She was heavy, but we had to get to Mom and Dad. Mom rolled to her back, crying and shaking.

There was blood on her skirt. She reached for Dad.

I shouted, "Daddy," and fell next to them. Dad looked over his bleeding arm at Justine and me. He reached for Mom, but she already pulled off her bloody half-slip and tied it around his arm, yanking tight on the knot.

"My belt," Dad said, "Your leg."

Mom pulled his belt from its loops and tightened it around her upper leg just above where a bullet hit her.

A moment later, I glanced off at the other man, lying face down on our side of the wire. "Daddy?" I said, but I could barely make my voice come out.

Dad rolled to his feet. "Gib, keep Justine here. Hold that belt tight on Mom." I sank down again, holding the end of that belt tight against Mom's leg. Mom's face had gone gray as she watched Dad run across the field. Justine sat in silence, grabbing my shirt. While I helped with the belt, the blood slowed coming out of Mom's leg. I glanced from her to Dad.

Holding his arm close to his chest, Dad ran toward the man, collapsed to his knees, and bent over him. Then, I saw my father do something I will never forget. He made this noise, gut deep, almost silent – trying not to cry. But I knew.

"Momma," I asked. "Who is the man?"

Tears ran from her eyes and down her cheeks. "He is Herr Grofmann's brother. We would have taken him to safety." She reached her free arm and pulled me and Justine to her.

* *

On that day, I was responsible for Justine. On that one day, she listened to me and hid like a rabbit. But she doesn't mind me anymore. She's all smart mouth, when she's not pretend and dolls and girl stuff.

I walk the few blocks south to George Fox House, holding the suit hanger up and over my back. The paper bag rattles in the breeze like a big kite advertising Broadway Cleaners. South of Broadway Street, I climb stairs to the front door of the redbrick apartment house. Friend's Meeting bought this building to make temporary housing for returning service men and other displaced men. South of here is another house for women. In 1950, when we returned from Germany, Dad's first job was to organize the renovation crew for this apartment house. Four months later, by the time he had the elevator working, Dad also had landed his music-teaching job at Portland State College.

In the lobby of George Fox House, I see that Mr. Lorens is today's desk clerk. The men at Friend's Meeting take turns working here for a week at a time.

" 'lo, Gilbert. That a delivery from your mother?"

"Yes, sir. For the new man. I forget his name ..."

"Ah. That's great. Thank you very much."

"That's all right," I say. "I'll just take it on up."

Mr. Lorens puts his hand around the hanger. "Gilbert," he says, "You know the rules."

"Oh, yeah. Sorry."

Drat! I just want to know the guy's name. But maybe I can get a little information from Mr. Lorens that my too-nice folks won't give out.

"Mr. Lorens, how do you know some of the guys who come through Fox House aren't here to cause trouble?"

"What kind of trouble?"

"Oh, like here to sell bad ideas, or infiltrate the army bases, or something like that?"

"Well, kid, you oughta listen more at monthly meeting. Half the members want to take indigent people at face value and the other half think we should check out their record before we allow them to live here."

"Really? I thought all Quakers were like . . ."

"Like your mom and dad? Nope. Friends come in all kinds, just like Presbyterians and Catholics."

"But, Mom says we have to deal with the man we've got, not the man he used to be."

"That doesn't always pan out. But your mom has seen all kinds. A few times, her trust has backfired, but she hangs on to trust as the first method."

"When it backfires, then what?"

He smiles. "Ask your mom about Colonel Somervell."

"Somervell? He live here?"

"Ask her."

I let Mr. Lorens take the suit and I decide to head down to the Gulch. I want to ask Mom about Somervell, now. But I also want to see if the train jumper is in the gulch – just checking.

As I come out the front door, I see a familiar guy starting up the steps – not my train jumper guy, but Max, from under the bridge.

"Hello, Maximillian."

He gives me this grin – mostly empty spaces where teeth once lived. "I found that card you give me last summer," he says. "So, I come to get me a bath for fall."

"Gonna live here?" I ask.

"Nope, just getting rid of varmints in my overalls."

I nod my head. "Good plan. There's a laundry in the basement, and new clothes in the storage room."

"Naw," he says. "Don't want new. A man can work hard in overalls and still have pants left at the end of the day."

"How about a second shirt?"

"If I had me two shirts, I'd be inviting somebody to steal, eh?"

"I guess so." I think about asking if Max has met the scar-faced man who jumped off the train, but before I can say it, he starts talking again.

"Well, Kid, here's the card back." He hands me a grungy George Fox House card. "Don't want to get it wet," he says.

"How's that?" I say.

"Stuff in my pockets would get wet, you know."

In my mind comes this image of Max standing in the shower, plaid shirt, overalls heavy with water and still hanging off his bony shoulders. A familiar jingle rings in my head. "He uses Dial Soap. Don't you wish . . .?"

Max already is up the stairs and opening the front door. As I watch him disappear, I decide that I don't really want to know about that scarred man who jumped from the train. I'm sure the suit Mom sent is for him, because not many people are that tall and skinny. He's probably living in George Fox House, so maybe he's not talking hobos into being spies. I'll just stop thinking about him.

But maybe he and Max work together.

And then, there's that suit. The scarred man looked a lot better off than most guys who jump from the train, so why'd Mom send a second suit? And how would she know he needed it before he ever arrived?

Another thing I need to ask her about.

I head up Seventeenth Avenue. The late afternoon sun shines through the leaves and makes all the street trees on Seventeenth glow. On our streets in Portland, like the dirt lanes in Neustadt, there are maples and horse chestnuts. They must have been planted in the parking strips during the last century. By 1953, they are huge, bulging out of their six-foot-wide space. I squint ahead, hoping to get a good look at some spiny chestnuts. A half-block north, standing under one of the trees, there's a guy from my class. Davie Dashlee stares at me, hands on his belt, jingling the ring full of keys he always carries.

Davie is this curly-haired, squirrelly kind of kid – never sits still. I know for a fact he has a skeleton key that will get you into most of the garage doors on his street. Ours, too. He always has this smirk on his face, like he knows something about you that ought to be embarrassing – except he isn't going to tell.

"Hello, Davie," I say, as I come close.

He puts his hand behind his back, but I already saw the cigarette. He notices I've seen it, so he pulls it in front of him.

"It's okay," he says. "It's a Camels – the kind more doctors use." Davie gets that smirk. "You signed up for journalism class in school this year?" he asks.

"Sure, Mister Reese is great." Just to ignore his smirk, I whack a low branch of his chestnut tree. Three nuts drop and I catch one. The other two land near my shoes.

"Reese won't be teaching that class," Davie says. "They fired him." His better-than-you tone says he asked the question just so he could trot out this surprise.

"No way!" I say. "Reese is the best teacher at our school."

"Mom heard it from Missus Moriarty," Davie says. "She's the secretary for the school board."

Mrs. Moriarty lives up this street. Her house is next door to Mike's and it also backs onto our really old neighbor's yard. "Mrs. Moriarty is a gossiping old lady," I say. "I don't believe anything she says." But I still have to ask. "Reese was fired? What for?"

Davie shrugs. "He's a Commie."

I stare at Davie. "The guy made us memorize the Bill of Rights. How can he be a communist?"

He shrugs again. "Maybe the Bill of Rights is communist."

"Davie, the Bill of Rights is ours. It's from the Constitution of the United States."

"Yeah?" he says. "Get this. The Red Squad run Mr. Reese out of town."

"Without a trial?" The Red Squad is the mayor and some special police who hunt communists.

"Who needs a trial?" Davie says. "Reese admitted he went to those meetings."

I'm disgusted – but I don't know disgusted with what? "He can't be a commie," I say, and I feel my hand tighten on the spines of the nut.

Davie smirks. "You'll see."

The nut in my hand pops open along a seam line. The nut inside is still green. I want to throw it in Davie's face, but I pocket it instead. When they're brown and ripe, horse chestnuts are big enough to fit in a guy's palm, light enough to fling long distances, and hard enough to sting the enemy pretty good. I have my share of bruises, but I've given out my share, too.

The door across the street opens up.

"I gotta do my chores," Davie says, and, in a blink, he disappears toward the back of his house. I stare after his skedaddling self.

"Hey, Scaredy," Rick Johnson calls. "Whyn't you go hide out with Davie baby?" Rick stands on his porch, looking like a size D battery – powerful and weighty.

Geez! I shouldn't have hung around here so long. I'm not going to run to the Gulch this time. As calmly as I can, I bend over and pick up the other two horse chestnuts. As ammo, green nuts are better than nothing. And it looks like I might need whatever I can get. I don't look across the street, but I hear Rick's fat little brother, Kenny, clomp on their front porch to join Rick.

"Dirty Pacifist," Kenny calls.

I stride up Seventeenth Avenue, looking like 'who cares?' I barely get to the corner of Thompson Street when a smacker hits my back. Hurts like the dickens, but I pick up that nut, too.

"Dirty Commie Pacifist," Kenny yells from about thirty feet behind me.

"I'm no commie!" I swivel and pitch two green chestnuts in quick succession. Rick takes one in the face. I don't stick around to see if the other hit Kenny. I'm high-tailing it, but staying well away from my house, because if they chase me onto our porch, Dad will give all three of us his lecture on how to solve conflict at home and abroad. Plus, if he isn't teaching some trombone or clarinet student, he will even invite Rick and Kenny inside for cookies. "Won't you gentlemen come in? Let's talk this over."

Then they'll probably think Dad really is a commie pacifist.

I take a quick run up the block, across Brazee Street and start up Seventeenth Avenue toward Knott Street. The Johnson brothers never run fast, but they have more doggedness than anybody I know.

Even though I'm on Seventeenth, I'm not going to Mike's house. I don't want them mad at him, too. During last year's school board election, Senator Johnson campaigned for the guy running against Mike's dad. Mr. Johnson called Mr. Halverson 'that simple and naïve builder, just a sergeant'. Sergeant Halverson won the election to the school board anyway.

CHAPTER SEVEN

While I'm running, I look over my shoulder. Rick's not too far behind me, churning out a full head of steam. Kenny isn't in sight. I figure I have a chance if I take advantage of Kenny's absence and my uphill position, so I turn to face Rick and run toward him. Rick takes a wide stance and waits for my charge. I see him flick a look to his right, so I guess what will happen. Sure enough, at the last moment, he starts to step aside and let me fly, but I aim where he looked instead of where he was. I leap with arms out, grabbing for his shoulders. We both sprawl on the tree roots in front of Mr. Stockman's house. I get a mouthful of dirt, but I'm on top and ready to pummel him.

As I raise my left arm, a stabbing pain hits me in the back. And again. The jab near my spine is brutal. With all his wriggling to get out from under me, my left fist connects only with Rick's shoulder blade. My hand hurts a lot. And by now, I realize I underestimated Kenny. He's the pain at my back.

The next time I raise my arm, I grab Kenny's kicking boot and yank hard. Kenny goes down on his butt. I fling his untied boot in the street and go back to keeping Rick under control with my fists.

But Rick has gotten his hands loose and is turning over. I lean my forearm on his upper back and try to keep him pinned with my legs. Rick yells. "Flip him. Now."

Behind me, I hear Kenny crawling in my direction. I make the mistake of looking over my shoulder. My weight lets up on Rick, who twists enough to bring his elbow into my cheekbone.

The world darkens for a second, but I still hear Kenny scrabbling toward me. Blindly, I let fly a left jab, and catch Rick a solid one in the jaw. Kenny is nearly on me, but I move sideways. When he lunges toward me, most of his body comes down on his brother's legs.

"Aiee!" Rick shouts, just like they spell it in my comic-books. "Get off me, you fizzhead," Rick yells at Kenny.

I'm slithering out of there, but Kenny lands another blow to my kidneys, right where he kicked me before – aiming there on purpose. I try to kick at him, but I miss. Rick pops me one in the eye – the same danged eye. Kenny keeps after my back like that's the only thing he's on earth to do. Without seeing anything, I manage to give Rick another blow to the jaw. It doesn't stop him at all. As he pulls back his fist, I push his heavy little brother onto his elbow. He screams.

Rolling away from the two of them, I smack my head against the trunk of the maple tree in Mr. Stockman's parking strip. I don't know which way is up, but the brothers Johnson are fighting each other to get at me. I grab for bark, push to my feet, and step high to avoid the roots.

I think about running up the steps to Mr. Stockman's door, but he's probably down in the basement, fixing in his bomb shelter and won't hear the bell.

Once I'm on the other side of Stockman's maple trunk, my vision begins to clear, and I take off up Seventeenth Avenue in a semi-dark cloud of pain and mashed thinking capacity.

"Rick, get up." Kenny yells behind me. "Rick, he's getting away."

There is no way Kenny will come after me by himself. I just keep running full out – or as full out as pulverized kidneys will allow. Moments later, I dodge into Mrs. Moriarty's driveway.

I feel great. I stopped Rick Johnson. But, I've also made him more devoted to ripping out my innards. He knows to look in the driveways. What he doesn't know is that Mrs. Moriarty's back fence has a stile – a short set of stairs that cross over the fence to the next back yard. The stile is hidden under a huge holly tree.

If you get near this holly tree, it looks as if you'll be in a world of sticker hurt. However, if you duck behind the tree, you'll see that old Mr. Moriarty once trimmed the branches at the back. And underneath the limbed-up part, he built the stile so it was hidden from everyone's view. You sure can't see the stile from Mrs. Moriarty's back porch and yard.

My buddy, Mike Halverson, says the stile is here because Moriarty had a thing for the widow Silverberg who lives on the other side of the fence, and next door to our house. Mike claims Moriarty died of a heart attack climbing out his own window one night on his way to the widow.

Mike Halverson is full of whoohaa. Mrs. Silverberg is ugly as sin and probably as mean.

I'm already behind the holly and on the top step of the stile when I hear Rick's feet pounding up Mrs. Moriarty's driveway. If I jump down the other side, he'll hear the crackle of dried leaves. I stoop down on the top rung of the stile and try not to breathe hard.

Pretty soon I can tell Rick's got a stick and is whacking the bushes and things around the yard.

Kenny charges up the driveway. "You got him trapped?"

"There's a lump of something back under Moriarty's back porch" Rick says. "Crawl down and see if that's him."

"You crazy?" Kenny asks. "What if it's a bear?"

"That ain't no bear, dummy," Rick says, "It's gotta be that stupid Shit-and-Run Gilbert Evans."

"Come on out and take your medicine, Pacifist Commie Pig," Kenny says.

I jerk at the sound of that name again. I'm not even a pacifist. It's my dad and mom who believe all that Quaker stuff.

"Poke him again," Kenny suggests.

I hear a hiss and then a high-pitched snarl. I recognize the cat-fight scream of angry raccoons.

"Hey! Stop!" Rick yells.

There's a scuffling and drawn-out howls from the far side of the tree. Can't know who is where. I do hear Rick screeching at the same pitch as the raccoons. Then one of the raccoons races under the tree toward my stoop.

That's enough for me. Under cover of all that noise, I jump down the far side of the stile right into the crunchy dead leaves, and then I run straight into Mrs. Silverberg's dahlia patch. My raccoon plants his front paws on top of the stile, and hisses at me, teeth bared.

On this side of the fence, I turn around and discover I'm face to face with the oldest lady in the world. Garden dirt stains her apron. She's got a pair of garden loppers in one hand.

Her other hand is pointing at the purple dahlia I've smashed under my gym shoe.

"I can expl...." I start. But she raises a finger, shushing, then gestures for me to get off her purple prize. Looks like this old lady knows the business end of the loppers. She crooks her finger at me, and then turns as if expecting me to follow. The raccoon growls.

I decide to mind her. I am not going back where I'll be destroyed by the claws of huge raccoons and the boots of two Johnsons.

Behind me, on the far side of the stile, a croaking old voice shouts, "You boys take your pets out of my yard. Go on. Go on afore I hit you both upside the head with this broom." That's Mrs. Moriarty.

Mrs. Silverberg appears to smile at what she hears. On the far side of the holly tree, Mrs. Moriarty shouts. "Git. Git. Git. And take them fat creatures with you."

Mrs. Silverberg shakes her head and turns to walk into her house. On the doorstep, she says, "You look like you might haff need of some tea before you feex my dahlia." Her accent is pretty thick.

I don't know about tea, but I need a hideout, so I follow into her kitchen.

CHAPTER EIGHT

Outside a Pepto-Bismol bottle, I would never have believed so much pink could exist. But Mrs. Silverberg has found all that girlie-tint you could stomach and applied it to her kitchen. Her wallpaper is pink roses in vertical stripes. Over the sink, lace curtains show faded pink where the sun hits them every morning. She painted her oven so long ago the pink is just a blotchy memory peeling off the original white. Only her Frigidaire is still white. Maybe the failure of the oven paint made her give up the pinking process.

The room even smells pink, but I can't tell why.

Mrs. Silverberg hangs her garden apron near the back door and changes into a clean kitchen apron. She pulls back one of her breakfast table chairs and pats it for me to sit in it, so I do – pink fabric covered in plastic.

I face the stove, where she lights the gas burner and sets a painted tea kettle on the flame. The pink carnations on the kettle swirl around, oblivious of their fiery doom. Mrs. Silverberg opens a cupboard full of dishes.

`"Geebert Evans, you look shust like your fadder when he vass a young man."

"I'm only fourteen, ma'am." I think maybe, old as she is, she can't tell the difference between fourteen and thirty or forty. Besides she met Dad when she moved here, so how would she know what he was like when young?

"Und you heff his same sweet brown eyes."

Sweet eyes? Yuck.

"Und alzo, you heff his nice upright posture."

I laugh. "Posture," I say, "a short fellow like Dad has to stand straight so his band can see him. He even beats time with a big stick with a white ball on top. Even the guy marching behind the base drum can see that stick."

I'm talking too much. I feel funny, finding out that she's been paying this much attention to my family when I hardly know her.

She sets three teacups and saucers down on the little table – four pink petals in the flowers painted on the teacup – must be dogwood. Three cups. Someone else lives here, too.

"I loff to hear venn you practice de trompet." She talks as if we've known each other. I know Mom and Dad helped her move into her house, but they help everybody.

She smiles and then pours steaming water over weeds and into my cup. From a cupboard, she pulls out a fresh cake – pink frosting with red stripes. The pink smell I noticed earlier turns out to be melted Red Hot candies.

She calls into another part of the house. "Come along, Darling. Vee heff company for de afternoon snack."

I'm thinking how little I know about this lady and whoever else lives here.

Little flopping footsteps come from the room off the kitchen. In trips my little sister, Justine. She's wearing pink high-heeled sandals that are way too big. Her hair is ponytails with pink ribbons, and she's smothered in pink frothy stuff that sounds like sand paper on sandpaper – an eight-year-old dressed in a ball gown.

Magdalena. Mrs. Silverberg is Magdalena, where Justine comes to have dinner parties.

Justine stops fast. The heels on her sandals fall to the outside, and her feet slide out onto the floor. She drops a handful of paper.

"What the tookuss happened to your face?" she says.

For the first time, I realize how much my head hurts. Mrs. Silverberg looks at me. I bet she wants to know if I'll tell Justine about the fight, or the raccoons in Mrs. Moriarty's.

Justine says. "You got bark and leaves sticking out of your hair. Did you run into a tree with your bike?"

"I sort of smacked into Mister Stockman's maple," I say. Glancing down at my shirt, I realize I've dragged mud into her house.

"Geez, I'm sorry, Missus Silverberg."

"I should heff get you some ice for that cheek." Mrs. Silverberg puts her hand on my forearm. "You sit right back down."

In a moment, she has three ice cubes in a towel, gesturing for me to put them against my face. The rough towel makes me aware of the scrape on my cheek bone. Cold hits my mind. Every achy muscle throbs awake.

Justine gathers her dropped papers and puts them on the table for Mrs. Silverberg to see. She's got two brittle photographs of stiff people.

She says, "These shoes are just like the shoes in the other picture."

Mrs. Silverberg peers at them "Ah, my darling, you heff found Lottie. In dees, Lottie. She is thirteen years."

"Oh," Justine says. "This is Lottie right before."

Before what? I wonder.

Justine points at the other picture. "See, in this photo, where the little girl is next to her mother, it looks like the mother's hair is a lot of waviness. It's like Lottie's hair when she is thirteen."

"Yah," agrees Mrs. Silverberg, "Und here," she points at the mother and kid photo,

"Dee white barrette in muzzer's hair – de same barrette Lottie wears in de last picture."

In the early photo, the little girl's hair won't lie down. It reminds me of Justine's hair when she was only five – like cotton candy threads with no gravity to hold them together.

"Yah, certain," Mrs. Silverberg says. She lifts the later photo. "Diss my Lottie near to grown up."

Justine beams. "I thought so."

I lean over the table to see. Really old-time people, like from the last millennium. The little girl wears high-button boots under her dress of shiny stuff. On the woman's feet, are dress shoes, black with a strap across her foot. At the outside of each shoe, where the strap ends, is a button, big, flashy, and probably gold-colored, but you can't tell that for certain in a black and white photo.

In the other photo, Lottie at thirteen wears the same buckled shoes, but her dress is the fluff that Justine is wearing right now. My neck hairs prickle. "Who's Lottie?" I ask.

Justine glances up. "Missus Silverberg's niece. Lottie lived next door, until they took her away."

Mrs. Silverberg straightens suddenly. I see tears in the corners of her eyes, but she only says, "Gut verk, Yoosty." She pats Justine on the head. "Let us put de photos away und celebrate." The way she says my sister's name, Yoosty, with a little sound of affection mixed into the accent – it makes me realize there's stuff here. I haven't been paying attention to my sister's life.

I'm not sure what they're celebrating. And my head is aching something fierce. This place is weird. My sister dressed up is weird, and I don't understand what is going on with her and this old lady. It's like they have a life together that I never knew about.

Mrs. Silverberg cuts cake for each of us. As she pours weedy tea for Justine, she says, "I sink your muzzer vill be vonder vat happen you, Geebert. You may call her on my telephone?" She points to a black phone on its own little stand between her kitchen door and the next room.

"Yes, ma'am." I stand up. I hope Mom asks me to come home right away and help with dinner. Anything to get me out of this pinkness.

I pull the numbers around and around on the phone dial, and glance into the room Justine came from. It's a riot of green and purple curtains and wall paper. Maybe it's a dining room. I can't tell because the biggest thing in it is a bulletin board on wheels, like the movable board my teachers use to display our schoolwork. This board is covered with old photos – some black and white. Some are the brown and tan kind. Must have been taken before Columbus discovered America.

Mom comes on the other end of the phone line. "Hi, Mom. I'm at Missus Silverberg's. I accidentally stepped on her purple dahlia and I'm going to try to fix it, but first we're having tea."

"Well, give Magdalena my regards."

"Um, okay, Mom."

"And when you're done working the garden, bring Justine home with you. She needs to clean her room and set the table for dinner."

Mom didn't ask how come I stepped on the dahlia. It's like Mom believes I'm running through Magdalena's back yard since forever. I'm also remembering that Justine came to visit Magdalena for dinner the night Professor Wilson talked anti-government stuff at our house. So Mom trusts her. But then, Mom trusts Professor Wilson. And anybody else.

"Mom sends her regards," I mumble.

"Her vat, dear?"

This time I speak up. "Her regards. I guess she knows you real good, huh?"

"In English is 'very vell', yah?"

"Umm, I guess it is." I'm thinking she has learned a lot about English if she can correct me like my mother. "What is it in ... in your language?" I ask.

"In Allemande, in German ve say, 'Sie is meine Freunde.' She is my friend."

"Oh." I know German, but I thought maybe she spoke some other language, maybe Russian. And I didn't know she counted my mother as someone important in her life.

Come to that, how come she knows so much about my father's brown eyes? I don't for sure remember that they are brown.

Justine smiles at her. You'd think Justine was always a goody-goody. Actually, mud-caked jeans and arguing till your ears are bruised – that's more Justine. I don't get this thing between them.

And then I remember what Davie said about Mr. Reese. Fired for being a commie. I remember Senator McCarthy telling citizens to be alert for infiltrators, fifth columnists hiding among us. Mrs. Silverberg is sure a foreigner. Spies trick secrets out of people. They make people betray their family and friends, even betray the United States government. Russia's underground is waiting to over-throw democracy.

Could Mrs. Silverberg be spying on my family? Is she making friends with Justine to trick secrets about us out of her? What secrets have we got?

If Mr. Reese is a communist, anybody can be a communist.

I look at the big piece of cake Mrs. Silverberg has put in front of me, and I feel danged crazy for thinking about spies. She's an old lady, for Cripes sake. How could she overthrow anything?

"This is really good, Missus Silverberg," I say.

She smiles and pours more weedy water into my dogwood-flowered cup. I notice her smile is pretty nice. I wouldn't have thought that five minutes ago. Maybe I'm getting used to how wrinkly a person can be.

While Mrs. Silverberg pours into her own cup, I start thinking about how this lady knows my dad, stuff I don't know. Right before I fork into that pink frosted cake, an unwanted question slides into my mind. I've been avoiding this thought since I started listening to Senator McCarthy's speeches. But the idea won't stay away.

It's this: Where was my Dad during the war? I mean, before we worked in Nuestadt bei Wald. Where was he really? Mom said he worked for the Quakers and for peace during the war. But that Senator McCarthy talks about communist front organizations. He says they silently work for shadow governments.

One thing I've noticed about Quakers, they can be pretty silent.

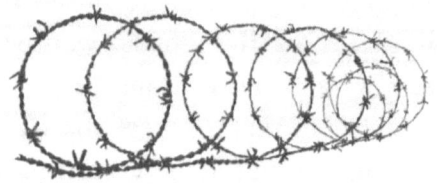

CHAPTER NINE

"Gib Evans?" The new eighth-grade science teacher calls out.

"Here," I answer. I slump sideways in a too-small desk. My long legs fill the aisle. At the same time, I watch the man try to talk. Something's wrong with him, but I haven't figured out what. His face pulls his mouth to one side whenever he says a word with an 'M' or a 'B' in it. I recognize the guy, but he's had a weekend in which to find a second suit, and I know where the suit came from. Last Friday, his hat covered the fact that the guy is bald – bald like he never had any hair.

"Ladies and gentlemen," the man says, "my name is Mr. Brendan O'Connor. I have had to come into your school abruptly, so I would like your help. We need to assess what you may have learnt prior to my advent into your lives."

This fellow talks like a hundred years ago. Maybe he's been stowed in a box while the rest of the world moved forward. I know that last Friday he stowed himself in a freight car, but I'm saying nothing about that, yet.

In the back of the room, Rick Johnson blurts out, "Where's Mr. Duncan?"

"Yeah," one of Rick's friends chimes in. "He's our real science teacher."

Real? Last year, Mr. Duncan couldn't control a herd of geese. I bet the Johnson gangsters were lying in wait for him. In fact I bet their plans for Mr. Duncan are why Rick isn't skipping school on this first day.

"Mr. Duncan has been promoted," O'Connor says. "He has become principal of Alameda School."

Uh-oh. My mother teaches English to upper grades at Alameda School. I already feel sorry for her.

Ever since Mr. O'Connor walked in this morning, I've hoped Mike doesn't get the connection with the train jumper I described. To get a job in the Portland public schools, a fellow has to have teaching credentials and a college degree. So, I'm saying nothing about train hopping, for now. We'll see if he turns out to be a fake.

Mr. O'Connor has odd pink splotches and white patches in his face and on his neck above his necktie. And there is that twitchy-ness about his mouth.

As I'm studying to figure out what caused all the problems, Mr. O'Connor raises his left fist with papers clutched tightly in his three fingers. "Miss Elizabeth Gray," he says to a new girl in the front row, "would you and Mr. Gilbert Evans from the back there take these papers and give one set to each student?"

I'm staring at those three fingers, so I'm not ready when he asks for help. I nearly upset my desk in an effort to pull my legs under me and propel myself out of a space designed for a ten year old. A couple of guys laugh.

Across the room, I can hear Rick Johnson whisper, "Retard."

But O'Connor says, "We'll have to get you a desk the right size for a future athletic star, eh, Mr. Evans?"

I straighten, desperate to keep my dignity. I glance at O'Connor, who's studying me almost as closely as I've been studying him. It's like he's testing me.

I slide sideways down the tight aisle and reached out for the quiz papers. O'Connor's three fingers have amazing strength. He doesn't let go of the papers right away, but uses the contact to look me in the eye for a second. Then he says, "I hope you will join our soccer practice this lunch time, Mr. Evans. We're putting together one great team."

Soccer, I think, who plays soccer in the United States? "Where?" I ask, thinking how I had planned to go out for football. But that was back when Reese was going to coach the team. I had all these plans that got dumped because of Reese being a fired.

Mr. O'Connor says, "We'll be at the southwest end of the playground. Bring friends. No tryouts."

Friends? Soccer? Guys here think it's a foreigner's game. I don't want any more kids thinking I'm a Red Commie. And who knows what they'll think if I start playing soccer. I answer, "I gotta check my schedule."

He smiles. "Do that."

Now he turns to the class. "Noon. You boys can come learn a new game. Everybody who shows up, plays."

One of Rick's friends says, "Soccer? That's not an American game."

Mr. O'Connor shrugs. "American? Did you know that in England soccer is called football?"

"They stole that name," Another fellow says.

"Actually," O'Connor says, "They used it first. All over Europe the game is called some variation on futbol or football."

"Even in Russia?" Rick asks.

Mr. O'Connor frowns, "You know, I'm not sure what they call it inside Russia," I wonder where Mr. O'Connor learned to play. Did he live in England?

While the new girl and I hand out the papers, Mr. O'Connor says, "Please take out your pencils. No, Mr. Dashlee, sit down again. If your tools are not already sharpened, you will have to make do with the stub end until recess."

CHAPTER TEN

"I'm telling you the guy said, 'No tryouts'," I say as Mike Halverson and I sit in the cafeteria. I've decided to give soccer a try, after all. Everybody in Europe plays it. How can Rick or anyone else accuse me of playing a subversive's game?

"No tryouts, maybe," Mike says as he chews my last oatmeal cookie. "But in the long run, fat guys will get cut. This we already know."

I watch Mike pick oatmeal crumbs from his shirtfront and I tell him, "O'Connor's different."

"I'll say. O'Connor's something of a freak."

I get up and step over the cafeteria bench to get out. "Fine. Sit on the sidelines." I drop my lunch sack in the garbage can and start out the cafeteria door.

Mike licks the last of my cookie from his fingers as he runs to catch up. "Hold up, Gib."

"Keep up, dang it. And don't be calling other people freaks." Mostly, I'm angry at myself. When O'Connor walked into our classroom, I got a shock. It just didn't seem right that a guy who looked like that got a job teaching in our school.

"All right, he's no freak," Mike says. "But you gotta admit something's wrong there."

"Doesn't affect his mind," I say. "He managed to keep Davie Dashlee in a chair for a whole class."

As we run out of the school, we can see the usual football practice down on the east side of the field. Mr. Marvin, the math teacher is now their coach. Girls are playing dodge ball and jump rope on the playground. On the southwest grassy area, Mr. O'Connor and two guys from Mrs. Hill's homeroom set up some funny cone shapes.

Mike huffs as we run, "If he's not faking the 'no tryouts' stuff, I'll give him some of my time."

"Gentlemen," O'Connor greets us, "I'm assuming you all know each other, but let's try polite introductions."

At this, Mike's face is one blank question mark. He blurts, "I'm Mike Halverson."

"Great Mister Halverson. I am Mister O'Connor. Please introduce me to your friend."

"Uh. Um. This here is Gib. I thought you knew him."

"I may know him, but we're practicing the niceties, here. Introducing each other is a way of celebrating each member of the team. It helps us play better." I think maybe O'Connor is having a private laugh on us. "Pleased to meet you, Gib,"

O'Connor says and looks over his glasses at me. "Gib, do you know these gentlemen?"

My mom taught me to do this introduction stuff in German and English.

So, I talk to the Negro guy next to me, "James Wray, I'd like to introduce you to Mister O'Connor. Mr. O'Connor, this is my friend, James Wray."

James is the only other kid in the school who is as tall as I am. Without even flinching at the missing fingers, James shakes

O'Connor's hand. He starts to introduce his friend, Billy, but Mike finally gets the point of the introduction game.

"This is Billy Mendoza," Mike says, pulling Billy forward.

Billy's the littlest guy in our class. His dad and granddad are little, too. Maybe, in the Philippines, guys are small.

"Nice to meet you," O'Connor says, shaking Billy's hand. "Let's warm up," he says, clapping his hands. The guy's got big palms. "Mike and Billy, form a team on the left." O'Connor waves at where his suit coat and hat lie far apart on the grass. "Mike," O'Connor says, "you run toward that imaginary line between my hat and coat. Billy, you follow Mike's moves as exactly as you can. Don't run over the clothes, if you please."

Mike has the look of an immovable linebacker. I hope he can move fast enough for soccer. O'Connor lifts his arm and as he drops it, he yells "Go."

Mike takes a second to get rolling, but once he moves, he does a zigzag run. Billy Mendoza has trouble matching Mike's moves. At the goal line, Mike stops, hunched over, hands on knees and breathing hard. Since he finished my oatmeal cookie, Mike has run more than I've seen during the whole last year.

O'Connor starts James across the field and I have to follow. The next minute proves that James is a dancer, but I'm as agile as a post. When James starts running, I'm aware of a tune. James crosses the finish line. The source of the tune becomes clear.

O'Connor is humming. He stops long enough to whisper "Again," and then resumes humming.

By the time James and I are on our third round, the beat is in my feet. We're joined by a third pair of players – fellows James knows, so they must be new students with him in Mrs. Hill's homeroom. James waves to them and runs, zigzagging across the field. He hums along with O'Connor.

I know that tune, but I can't remember why.

"Sweet Georgia Brown," James sings out the refrain as we reach the line. He motions for me to follow him back to the starting line. I discover that if I watch James's shoulders, I can see when he plans to zig, and follow him – almost go at the same time he does.

I watch Mike and Billy go again. On the syncopated silence, Mike suddenly stops and faces Billy who looks confused. In the next beat, Mike runs backwards, faking out his little shadow. Surprised, Billy runs straight into Mike. Mike gives Billy the hip. Billy sprawls. Mike turns and sprints toward the line.

"Nice run, Mister Halverson," O'Connor sings out. He helps Billy up and points him after Mike.

Pretty soon, all of us are singing the tune while we run. "That's good," O'Connor says. "Your lungs will get stronger the more you sing while running. Pretty soon, you'll be able to run long distances without a problem."

After a time, my mouth gets pretty dry. I stop singing because my voice cracks. So I whistle.

For the rest of that half-hour practice, O'Connor brings out what he calls "Big Hex", the only soccer ball I've seen since we left Germany. He shows the guys how to use their instep, instead of their toe to kick. We chase around, trying to keep our partner from stealing it.

O'Connor yells, "Figure the trajectories. Angle-in equals angle-out. Think about physics."

We have no idea what he's talking about, but we begin to kick and catch up with our own ball more times than not. Mike spends some time gasping on the sidelines, but he comes back. By this time, we're joined by two more guys. Twelve guys already. In Neustadt, we never found more than five to a side.

O'Connor calls a halt. "You fellows got any friends who might like this game? Don't care how good they are. Bring those gentlemen on out during our next lunch hour."

Mike is breathing hard, leaning on the fence and looking at football practice across the way. "We gonna have a team of fast guys and a team of slow stumps?"

"No, Mister Halverson," O'Connor says. "Seems like mixing it up would be fair, doesn't it?"

"More fair until we start playing other schools," James says. Maybe James is thinking those other teams won't want to play if we have a Negro on our team.

O'Connor says, "Let's mix it up and see who has the most gumption. Now, gentlemen, let's do a five-minute game. You divide yourselves."

"White shirts against blue," Mike says. So we do it.

Us guys all dress in the same colors – not like the girls, who wear all kinds of colors.

"Look at that," Mike says. "We might as well have uniforms."

Mr. O'Connor laughs and says, "Do you call each other to see what color to wear?"

Billy says, "My mama is always trying to get me to wear colors, like they used to wear in the Philippines. I got to tell her that's not what we do here."

"Why don't we?" James asks.

"You gonna wear purple tomorrow?" Mike points at me.

"You'd all laugh me off the team," I say.

"Ah," Mr. O'Connor says, "I see how it happens."

We all shrug and go on playing. White shirts win by one point – a goal by James on a pass from Billy. The bell rings. There are now twelve of us.

We troop in, sweating. As we're climbing the steps, Mike lifts his sweaty arms and says, "I've got Arrid deodorant, but you guys stink."

James says, "Yeah, and you smell like a rose."

"Si," Billy says, "I am aroz con piglet."

"Rice with ham," James translates.

Billy and the guys laugh.

I hear Rick Johnson behind us on the stairs. "Hey, Dashlee, why don't you join the foreigners playing with the cute little ball?"

I turn around to see that Davie Dashlee is struggling up the stairs, trapped between Rick and some of his followers. This could turn ugly for Davie. I yank on Billy's shirt-tail in front of me and I whisper, "Billy, stand still so they have to go around us."

"Dashlee Stashlie," chimes in one of Rick's bully friends.

Another says, "If that blob Mike Halverson can play that game, even the dwarf Dashlee might make the team."

Above me on the stairs, Billy gets James and Mike to stand with us. Rick's group doesn't see we make a big blockade.

"Did you see that ball O'Connor brought?" Rick asks, looking back at his buddies. "Bathroom floor tile, all the way. A Bathroom Ball for foreigners."

At that moment, Rick bumps into me. "Hey!"

Davie Dashlee uses that to make his escape past Rick and on up the stairs. Rick glares at me. I have a sudden thought. Instead of fighting, I'll play what Mom calls "Love 'em till they holler".

I act like I've been waiting for my old buddy Rick. "How's football?" I say. "Uh," Rick says. "It's great. Better than that silly game you guys were playing."

"I hear you're a great passer," I say.

James grins at me and starts moving our phalanx forward. Mike glances at me, his eyebrows pulled into his puzzled look. James nudges Mike to move forward, and explains, "Talk softly, but bring your big friends,"

I keep looking toward Rick, who probably wonders why I'm interested.

"I run mostly. Sometimes I pass," he says at last.

"Who's your receiver?"

His gesture includes all his friends. "None of these Bozos. You'd think every guy here greased his fingers."

I see one of his friends glance at another, his face growing red and angry.

"It takes lots of practice to know where to be on the field," I say. That angry guy glances up at me.

Rick's buddies look to him for what to do, but for a moment, he isn't sure.

Then Rick says, "Bathroom ball is a commie foreigners' game."

"Everybody in Europe plays soccer. It's not a communist game," I say.

"Europe is full of commies, my dad says."

Dang, it's hard to be nice to some people.

Mr. Marvin stares down at us from the top of the stairs. "Gentlemen, time for class."

I duck into Mr. Marvin's classroom for the first day of Journalism. I miss Mr. Reese.

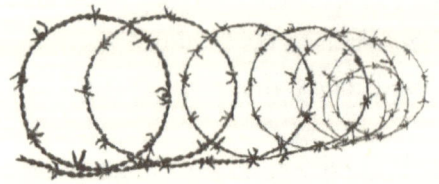

CHAPTER ELEVEN

Last year, Mr. Marvin was our math teacher. The guy is ex-Air Force, a Major, retired since the big war. In Portland, he's the head of a pretty big citizen's group I've read about in the news. I think it's called Educators for Democracy. So, his name is in the news a lot.

As soon as I enter the class, I realize it's his group that put up that poster on the telephone poles about helping find spies.

Mr. Marvin runs his classroom like a unit of the Force. Desks in straight rows, students at attention. Last year, I liked Mr. Marvin's order. This year, because they fired Mr. Reese, Mr. Marvin has become the Journalism teacher. Journalism is an elective kids can choose instead of English. Mr. Marvin has a stack of the *Portland Journal* on his desk.

James Wray, Billy Mendoza, Mike Halverson are here. So are Davie Dashlee and the new girl from Mr. O'Connor's class, Elizabeth Gray. James and Billy live across the street from each other. They've been friends for a long time, like me and Mike. Nobody seems to know this new girl.

I wonder why Davie Dashlee's in this class. He hates to write.

Mike and I lunge for back row seats. Billy, James and Davie find seats right near us. But Elizabeth takes a third row seat, near other girls by the window. The sun shines through her hair which is the light color of the beech wood at our carpenter's shop in Neustadt.

"All right, gentlemen," Mr. Marvin says. "This is journalism class. Homework to hand in every Tuesday and Thursday. Late homework is not accepted. Any questions so far?"

Mike Halverson raises his hand. "Is that anytime on Tuesday and Thursday?"

"No, Mr. Halverson. Beginning of class only. Now, gentlemen, who's been reading the newspaper?"

Lots of hands go up.

Mr. Marvin says, "That's great. And who can tell me the difference between communism and democracy?"

Billy Mendoza and James Wray raise hands. So does Elizabeth Gray, but Mr. Marvin seems not to see them. He waits for other hands to pop up.

"Mr. Jordan?"

"Communists are Russians and their spies," Jeff Jordan says.

"Communists want to kill our democracy and take us over," says another boy.

"There's this spy named Philby – he's on television."

"Karl Marx was the first communist and he didn't believe in democracy."

Mr. Marvin puts up his hand to stop everyone. "Interesting answers. However, the question I asked was 'What's the difference between Communism and Democracy?'" A few hands remain up, including the new girl, Elizabeth's. I keep my hand down, suddenly aware of how sweaty I really am from soccer. I wish I had Arrid deodorant in my locker.

James, Elizabeth and Billy still have their hands up, but Mr. Marvin calls on others first.

"Mr. Dashlee?" I'm thinking Davie reads the comics.

"Democracy is us," Davie says. "The good ol' U.S. of A. where we get to vote on stuff." So, he's been paying some attention.

After such a long time with Mr. Marvin not noticing him, Billy Mendoza quits trying and lets his hand fall to his lap.

"Miss Wilhelmi?"

"We're a democracy," one of the girls says. "That means we have real trials and not those kind of show trials they got in the newspaper where the Russians pretend to give evidence and then they shoot the guy no matter what."

"A democracy is how you vote," says another. "We get to vote on people, but the people we vote for don't have to be rich or anything. They just are Republicans or Democrats. But we don't vote for Communists."

Billy looks like he's counting the acoustic tiles. Now, only Elizabeth and James offer to answer. Last year, James liked to discuss ideas like this with Mr. Reese.

Finally, Mr. Marvin nods at James. "Your name?"

"Mr. James Wray," he says. "Same as last year."

"Glad to hear it, Jim." Mr. Marvin says. "Communism and democracy?"

"Communism is about ownership," James says. "Democracy is about who gets to vote."

Mr. Marvin shakes his head 'no' and turns to Elizabeth. "Miss?"

"Miss Gray," she tells him. "Mr. Wray is right. Communism is how they do business, like communal ownership of everything. We do business where certain people invest money to start their own business and hire others to work. It's called capitalism."

She just told Mr. Marvin that he was wrong and James Wray was right. Smart and courageous. I finally raise my hand.

"Mr. Evans," Mr. Marvin says.

"Um ...I think both are political and both are about ownership."

Some kid on the other side of the room groans out loud, but Mr. Marvin gives him the dead-eye look.

"Go on, Mr. Evans."

"Well, Sir, uh ...Communism takes over other countries like East Germany and makes those people give up their land so that communist farms can be built. That's political."

Mr. Marvin nods. "The conquest of other countries is always political."

James says, "Conquest is economics."

"Really, Jimbo?" Mr. Marvin says.

There is a moment of strange silence in the room. Something has happened between Mr. Marvin and James.

Finally James speaks. "My name is James. Economics is when the other country has better farmland, a river, or a seaport, or oil that you want. If you own it, that's money in the pocket."

"You seem to want everything to be about money, James," Mr. Marvin says.

James sticks out his chin and says, "If you look at it closely, it generally is about money. For instance, take voting in the South ..."

James knows Mr. Marvin comes from Mississippi just like James's father. They share the same soft way of slipping over their 'Rs' as they speak. Only, before they each joined the military, Mr. Marvin was not a sharecropper like James's dad.

"Jim," Mr. Marvin says, "we are not talking about the South. We are talkin' about communism."

Elizabeth says, "What about voting in the south, Mr. Wray?"

Other kids in the room shuffle their feet, or their papers. James turns to Elizabeth as if she is the only intelligent person in the room.

"Those with money get to vote." James says.

"In the south, those who can read get to vote, James," Mr. Marvin says.

"Those who get to go to school," James says to Elizabeth. "Those who have a school. Nothing very democratic about school in ol' Miss."

James Wray must have inhaled something besides oxygen on the soccer field. I try to interrupt this before Mr. Marvin blows his military cork. Elizabeth has her hand up, but at that moment, Mr. Marvin clears his throat.

"Well, James," he says in a soft voice, "aren't you glad you don't live where there is no school?"

"I am glad," James says, staring at Mr. Marvin again. "Very glad. And going to stick around to the end."

"We are pleased with your determination," Mr. Marvin says, and I'm stiff with hoping James won't keep pushing. Voting and schools in Mississippi are somebody else's problem.

Mr. Marvin turns to the rest of the class. "Now for your assignment. Have any of you read about loyalty oaths?"

Mike raises his hand and gets Mr. Marvin's nod. "That's where people who want certain jobs have to pledge they are for the U.S. of A, and have never been Marxists or believe in communism."

"Correct, Mr. Halverson. And do you have any idea why loyalty oaths are important?

Davie Dashlee shouts out. "It helps us figure out who's a Damned Roosevelt Democrat."

"Not quite, Mr. Dashlee," Mr. Marvin laughs. "And your expletive is not part of the Democratic name."

"My dad says it is."

The whole class busts up, but Mr. Marvin shushes us up pretty quickly with his stare. "Anybody have a reason for using loyalty oaths?" he asks.

For the first time today, Elizabeth Gray is sitting on her hands. Go figure.

"Mr. Gilbert Evans?" Mr. Marvin says.

"Well, sir," I say, "it's one way Senator McCarthy can figure out who believes in the over-throw of our government."

"Why would that be important, Mr. Evans?"

"We sure don't want communism in our country. In Germany, the communists took over the East German government."

"What happened then?" Mr. Marvin asks.

"The Russians owned the land and villages across the border from us. The German farmers on the other side of the barbed wire fence starved and died. Their crops belonged to the government. They were forced to grow stuff that could be sent to Russia to feed the people in Moscow."

Elizabeth Gray interrupts me. "What did the Russians think the farmers would eat?"

"Because of the war, the Russians hated the Germans. If they starved, well, more land for Russian farmers."

"And what does this have to do with loyalty oaths, Mr. Evans?" Mr. Marvin asks.

I suddenly realize that Elizabeth's narrowed eyes tell me she thinks I've gone nuts.

"They did starve," I say to her. "And one man got so desperate he climbed under the fence near our house. The guard shot him."

Elizabeth seems to have gone all white in the cheeks.

"That's enough, Mr. Evans," Mr. Marvin says. "I agree that things were bad there, but we don't need to scare the ladies."

She sinks into her seat, looks down at her feet, and I'm real sorry I went on like that.

Mike Halverson says, "Loyalty oaths just prove that people say whatever they need to say. Oaths don't prove loyalty."

The other kids in the room all start talking. "Don't you watch television?" and "We gotta have some way to find them." Most of the kids agree. We need to find out who is a communist.

"All right everybody, calm down." Mr. Marvin interrupts.

But Mike keeps talking. "A lot of people in government make oaths about being honest. Then they lie. And they get rich. And that happens on down the line, right to the filling station guy who waters his gas."

Mr. Marvin says, "Folks, I guess we have a cynic among us. For tomorrow's assignment, I'd like you all to look up this word."

He writes "c-y-n-i-c" on the black board with brand new chalk that squeals. Then he says. "And I'd like you to write an essay of two hundred fifty words on why we need loyalty oaths. Due Thursday. That's the day after tomorrow, Mister Halverson."

CHAPTER TWELVE

After class, I try to catch up with Elizabeth Gray. Her flannel skirt swishes down the hall. While I'm lengthening my stride, I watch the swing of her shiny, wide belt and the sway of her long braid. I figure out that the skirt is probably a complete circle if you lay it out on the floor.

Maybe she hears my footsteps, because she turns toward me, holding her notebook in front of her.

"Uhm . . . Elizabeth, I'm sorry I told you about that day at the border."

"You were there?"

"Yes."

"That must have been scary."

All the fear I had in that tree came back. "I thought that guy had shot my folks."

"Were they hurt?" she asked.

"Yes, but they're fine now. Dad pulled Mom to the ground before the shooting started. He knew what that guard was going to do."

"Your dad must be a very brave person."

I've been thinking my dad seems geared to avoid danger – the Quaker way.

"Well," she says. "I better get to my next class."

"Sure." I watch her walk away.

"Nice skirt," a voice says behind me. I turn around. Davie Dashlee is watching her, too. I stand between him and Elizabeth's disappearing back. Next to Davie is Mike.

"How do you guys like journalism class?" Davie asks.

"It stinks," Mike claims.

"What? Halitosis?" Davie laughs. "Gargle Listerine."

Mike ignores Davie and talks to me. "Why isn't Reese around?"

Davie says, "Reese was a Marxist back when he was a college student. The school board decided they couldn't have him teaching."

"How'd you find that out?" Mike asks.

"Some teacher accused him," Davie says. "He had to admit it, 'cause they already had called his college. Missus Moriarity told my mom the college sent lists of people who attended the Young Communists clear back to nineteen-thirty. And there he was."

Mike frowns. "1930? What's his college stuff got to do with now?"

"Don't you know?" I ask. "The communists have spies and sleeper cells of workers planted all over the country."

"Even in the State Department and the Army," Davie says. I guess he listens to the news more than I thought.

Mike glances down the hall and then back at me. "What if being a Marxist for a little while made Mr. Reese decide it wasn't good?"

"How could we ever be sure?" Davie asks. "They're even in the Unions." Mike looks at me, silent for a moment.

"Didn't you hear the news about that union organizer, that Mr. Mackie?" I ask Mike.

He doesn't say anything. So, I tell him. "They're deporting him because he's communist. That's why Marvin wants us to write about loyalty oaths."

"Right," Davie says.

There's a bunch of kids listening, now, all talking at once.

"Geez, spies were discovered in Los Angeles."

 "Right here in Portland."

"We have that siren every day because they've got the bomb."

"Some of the guys that built our bomb gave those Russkies secrets to build one, too."

Mike leans over me and says. "Didn't we memorize the Bill of Rights in Reese's class last year?"

I back up. "Practically the whole Constitution of the United States," I say.

"Well, check out the part about freedom to gather and freedom of speech," Mike says.

"Mike! Gathering in groups is okay, unless you're planning to take over the country."

Mike turns and leaves.

"Geez, doesn't he believe what's in the paper every day?" one girl asks.

I remember an article from my news collection. I once read it to Mike.

The House committee on un-American activities (HUAC) said it was shocked to find domination of some unions and locals by the Communist conspiracy."

The Oregonian, Sunday, December 28 1952

Mike gets touchy whenever I mention unions and subversives. I showed him that story and he acted just like he acted after class today. I don't say anything to the other kids. I'm not sure what makes Mike angry, but I mean to find out.

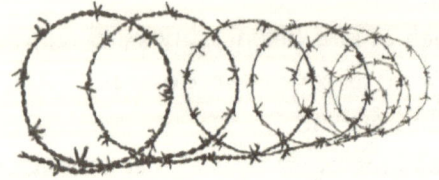

CHAPTER THIRTEEN

"**M**om," I call as I drop my books on the breakfast table. For once the table is cleared of Justine's dolls. She's probably at Mrs. Silverberg's. "Mom?" I call again.

Suddenly the door from the basement bumps open, and Mom comes into the breakfast room carrying a wicker basket full of wet clothes.

"Hi, Honey," she says, "Could you open the back door for me?"

I pull it open. She glides on out to the backyard. I follow. "Mom, how come you bought that suit before Mister O'Connor ever arrived?"

"Oh, you met him."

"He's the new science teacher. How did you know what size to get for him?"

"Honey, he's been a friend of your dad's for a long time. Here, grab this." She hands me one end of a sheet.

"A friend who arrives on a train? Without a ticket?" I hold the sheet with her, and we snap it to get the wrinkles out.

"Your father sent travel money to him, but he wanted to meet other people who travel by freight, to see why they do it." She sticks wooden clothespins in her mouth and gestures for me to help hang the sheet.

"Why?" I flip my end over the clothesline. She pulls the pins from her mouth and answers me while she forks one wooden peg over the sheet.

"He wants to understand people. So, how did school go today?"

"Reese was fired for being a communist."

"I know." She kind of droops against the clothesline. "I hoped the school board would be smarter, but ..." She stabs another pin over the middle of the sheet and hands me a third one for my end.

"If he was a communist, why shouldn't they fire him?"

She frowns. "Gib, didn't you decide that your friend Davie was not someone you wanted to be around?"

"Yeah, he was always getting me into trouble ..."

"So, for a while you thought Davie was interesting." She hands me the second sheet. "But after a time, you realized he used you to make trouble."

"Sure. I can't exactly keep him out of my life, though. He lives a block away, and he's in most of my classes."

"Didn't you like Mr. Reese?" she asks.

I snap my end of the second sheet and flip it over the line. "That was before I learned Reese might be trouble."

She stabs the wood pin over the sheet. "Gib, you learned first-hand that Davie was trouble. What do you really know about Mr. Reese?"

"That the school board fired him for ..."

"No, Gib. What do you know? Your own experience of him?"

I think a minute, trying to square what I used to believe with what I know now. "I thought he was a good teacher. I thought he believed in the United States government."

"And why did you think so?" She's working on Dad's t-shirts now, so I pick up one and pin it the way she does.

"Well, he taught us a lot about how the government works. Made us memorize the Declaration, and the Constitution and all that."

She bends over and picks up the empty basket. "We're done here. I'd like you to get your practicing out of the way before Dad comes home. He has a clarinet student at six."

But that's when I remember what Mr. Lorens said at George Fox House. "Mom, who is Colonel Somervell?"

She straightens up and stares at me. "How do you remember that name?"

Her question surprises me. I think, maybe I'll get more information if I pretend I really do remember the guy. "Well, I just kind of remember it from the past. Who was he?"

"Gib, did Mr. O'Connor mention him?"

"No. But I can't remember much." I'm lying through my teeth, but if I tell her Mr. Lorens suggested him, I bet she'll be down on Mr. Lorens and she'll tell me nothing. I don't know why I started this way, but I'm going to keep this game going until I find out something.

"I think that's something your father and I should tell you together."

So, now I really want to know.

"Gib, please just do your practicing and homework. We'll talk about this after Justine goes to bed."

"Okay," I say. Wow. That name really brought up something. The rest of the time, until I hear Dad come home, I'm in my bedroom practicing my trumpet, variations on a tune called "The Three-Cornered Hat." All the time, I'm really thinking about Mr. Reese, and why Mom asked me about once being friends with Davie. And I'm trying to remember whatever I should know about Colonel Somervell.

After Dad comes in the house, I pop downstairs. Dad sits at the breakfast table helping Justine make something for her dolls. There is a funny line on each of her arms like she recently wore something with elastic in the sleeves. I bet she's been dressing up in that old-fashioned dress over at Mrs. Silverberg's.

I peer over Dad's shoulder. He's making a cardboard cut-out of a trumpet. In Justine's hand rests tinfoil from a stick of gum. She takes the cardboard from him and wraps the trumpet so it looks shiny. While she wraps, she hums through her closed mouth, buzzing her lips to sound like a trumpet with a mute on. The tune is "The Three-Cornered Hat".

"Dad," I say, "did you know Mister O'Connor was going to apply to teach at our school?"

"Sure. He's taught in Boston ever since he finished his Masters at M.I.T."

A Master's degree . . . that is way more college than any of my other teachers. Even my Dad only has a bachelor's degree in music and composition. "How come Mr. O'Connor's not teaching at a college?" I ask. "Why eighth graders?"

"He says fourteen years old is the best time to start scientists wondering."

I'm wondering, all right, so I blurt it out. "Did he get those scars in some chemical experiment at M.I.T.?"

Dad looks at me a long time before he answers. "No, son. He got them when his airplane was hit during the war."

Now I feel cruddy. "Dad, I wasn't making fun of him. I was just asking."

Dad nods. "Okay, Gilbert. Thee . . . You have a right to ask. Now you have an answer."

He stands up. "Well, Miss Justine Evans, It's time to clear away the dolls and help thy mother set the table."

"Aw, Daddy!"

"Do you clean up at Missus Silverberg's?"

She stands taller, her chin raised toward the ceiling. "I'm her main helper."

"Thy mother is also an important person, and needs your help."

"How about Gilbert?" Justine goes into a pout.

Dad says, "I hear Gilbert helped with the laundry. He already practiced, so it's time for his homework." Dad turns to me. "Got homework, Gilbert?"

"An essay for Mr. Marvin's class," I say. "And some research for Mrs. Hill's history class."

"History," says Justine. "Like the big war and slave labor and deportations of Jews and Gypsies?"

"Maybe," I say. I glance at Dad to see if Justine's question bothers him. She's hearing about this stuff over at Mrs. Silverberg's.

Dad is studying a sheet of music and doesn't seem to notice.

"Eighth graders study the history of Oregon," I tell her.

"Oregon?" She curls up her lip. "But that's right here. What's interesting about Oregon?"

Dad glances up at her and says. "Oh, we've had our slave labor, our deportations, and our Jews and Gypsies, too."

"Wow," Justine says.

"He's kidding," I tell her. "This is Oregon, Land of the Empire Builders."

"And sometimes the Ku Klux Klan," Dad says. "Empire Building," he adds. "That's how it starts."

His clarinet student bangs open the side door, so Dad goes to meet him.

From the kitchen, Mom calls out. "Justine, you want to make the biscuits for dinner?"

Justine grins at me. "Go do your homework. I'm making dinner."

I clutch my stomach. She sticks out her tongue and flounces into the kitchen, while I go upstairs to write my essay about communism and loyalty oaths. Empire Building? Dad's got to be kidding.

* *

After dinner, it's my turn to clean the kitchen. I notice that Mom has used two cans of mushroom soup to make our dinner casserole. Mr. Stockman collected his cans for a long time, I bet. I fish those cans out of the garbage, take the paper off of them and flatten them.

I need to store them somewhere, but anywhere I store them they can't still have food. They'd attract mice, or worse. So I wash them and stuff them in a paper bag. After the dishes are washed and the pans are drying in the drainer, I take that bag to the basement and look around for a place to store them. There's a part of the basement next to the chimney that has a clothes chute on one side. On the other side of the chimney is a box that used to be our dumbwaiter. Early owners used the box and rope-pulley system to bring wood from the basement up to the wood stove they used in the kitchen. Dad closed the dumb waiter hole when he put in an electric stove. The dumbwaiter box has been sitting stuck in the basement. I stuff the sack of cans in there.

* *

After Justine is in bed, I'm still working on my essay. Mom knocks at my door. I reach over and open it. There stand both Mom and Dad.

"May we come in?"

Here it comes, I think. "Sure." I move a pile of comics off the bed and whip the covers closed. "Wanna sit?"

Dad sits. Mom starts picking things up. Can't help herself, I figure. Dad says, "Mom tells me you remember Colonel Somervell."

"Not really, much. I remember the name, but that's about it."

"You remember the band concerts, right?"

"Sure."

"Colonel Somervell ran the camp on the other side of the fence. He and I had an agreement. We'd play the concerts. He'd let the prisoners have the food we sent across the border."

"I never knew about that."

"You were seven. We didn't tell you things you didn't need to worry about."

"But Herr Grofmann and I grew vegetables."

Dad smiled. "Yes, some of the food we sent came from your garden. Everyone in town contributed."

"So, didn't Colonel Somervell live up to his part of the bargain?"

"He did. But one of the officers he most trusted reported back to Moscow about his fraternizing with the enemy."

"Us."

Dad nodded. "Moscow threatened to send him away. He told us of the threat. We played one last concert."

"The one where you went right into the camp?"

"Yes." Dad glances at Mom, and I'm certain there's something else they aren't telling me about that concert. Dad gets back to telling me. "Soon after the concert, the colonel's summons to Moscow came. The reporting officer became the commander."

"And things changed."

"Everyone in the camp was punished for the previous commander's leniency. Herr Grofmann's brother tried to escape. Soon after his death, the camp and all in it were moved to Siberia."

"What about Colonel Somervell?"

"We may never know."

CHAPTER FOURTEEN

Assignment, Essay #1: Continued:

If we allow communists in our country, we'll end up with the same problems they have in Europe. And if they take over, we'll have the same bad farming, the same bad police, the same newspapers that only print what the leaders want people to hear, and the same fear of everything that Russians cause in Europe.

* *

Today is Thursday. I have to hand in my essay on loyalty oaths. An essay so soon after school starts is kind of odd, but I guess Mr. Marvin wants to start us right out working hard. And finding out about Russian spies is a big deal in the local and national news. After learning about what they did to Colonel Somervell and the prisoners, writing this essay feels right.

And during discussion in class yesterday, I saw that most of our class has learned how dangerous communists are. We don't have a television at our house yet, but lots of kids say they can see the

McCarthy hearings on the TV. Their parents let them eat dinner while watching the six o'clock news. There is a lot of scary stuff happening because of Russia. The countries they've taken over are now this big thing called the Soviet Union, including East Germany.

Today, I have to walk Justine to school because she's taking "Share and Tell" to her third-grade class. I'm lugging her grocery sack filled with what a third grader thinks is beautiful – that pink dress with elastic in the sleeves, pink high-heeled sandals and a pink purse with what looks like little circles of shiny pink sewn all over it. And in the sack that Justine has clutched to her stomach, a photo album. Dad actually paid money to copy some of Mrs. Silverberg's old photos for that album.

I hope none of the guys meet up with us because on the way to school, Justine is practicing her speech out loud. As in fortissimo.

"So," she says, "all the thirteen-year-old girls in Lunaburg, Germany were confirmed on Sunday morning at Christ the King Lutheran Church. That afternoon, Lottie wore this dress to a party at her aunt's house." Justine gestures as if her class is in front of us. "Lottie's aunt is my neighbor and friend, Missus Silverberg."

"Justine, why tell about an old church confirmation party?" I ask.

"You listen," she says. "That night, Lottie and her best friends decided to be brave and celebrate even though the war was coming closer and closer. They could hear the American and Russian guns shooting at the Nazi camp just outside the far end of the town. The girls celebrated their confirmation and then Lottie slept that night at Magdalena's house. Everyone was very afraid. All night long there were booming guns rumbling in the fields and rifle fire on the nearby roads."

I know Justine is quoting Mrs. Silverberg exactly because Justine doesn't talk this way. I'm thinking, this stuff is too scary for a third grader to know about.

Justine keeps telling her story in Mrs. Silverberg's words.

"The next day," she says, "the shooting stopped, but they didn't know why. Lottie and the Silverbergs had breakfast of Skinny Kuchen and applesauce. Skinny Kuchen is what Missus Silverberg calls cake with no butter or sugar. Nobody had butter or sugar by the end of the war."

Now, like a drama queen, Justine points at the bag I'm carrying. "Lottie went to her house next door, but by accident, she left her party clothes at her aunt's."

A couple of guys from math class are coming behind us.

"Justine," I say, "Walk faster."

She stops. I keep walking, but I can hear what she's saying because she talks even louder. "And that early morning," she says, "Aunt Magdalena hiked around to the town walls and back, like she did to keep herself strong. She carried Lottie's things in a sack to return them at the end of her exercise.

While she walked, the German police came and took away everyone else."

The guys from math pass us, but I stop walking, stunned by what Justine said. She talks to me with tears in her eyes. "They took Lottie, and her brothers and sisters, and her parents. And next door to Lottie's house, they took Mister Silverberg who was probably sitting on the front porch smoking his pipe and looking at the sunrise.

"Why?"

"They took all the families of all the girls from the confirmation party. They threw them all on a truck and drove them away."

I stare at Justine. "Missus Silverberg was alone?"

She nods. "When she came home to the emptiness, she grabbed a blanket and ran away. She hid in the Lutheran church. All she had was that bag of Lottie's things and that blanket. When the church gardener found her, he took her to the basement and hid her behind a tomb."

"Come on ...why would the Germans bother taking them? The Germans were busy fighting the Russians and Americans."

"They took them because somebody told that Lottie's family had pretended to be Lutherans all through the war."

"Oh! But, why tell on them then, so late in the war?"

"Well, right after the war, the German who became the communist mayor of Lunaburg moved into Lottie's house. His son moved into Missus Silverberg's."

So, it's true what James says – *it's always about money.* I take a long look at my little sister. "What's in your photo album?"

"Pictures of Missus Silverberg's family. For the first days, while the Russians took over the town, the church gardener pretended to be the gardener of her house. He smuggled the photos out. One suitcase, stuffed with pictures."

"And you've been organizing those photos."

She nods. "Just this year. Before, I was too young."

Communists again, I think. They took over Lunaburg and all of East Germany. I'm glad I wrote my essay about oaths last night.

* *

In science class, Mr. O'Connor starts us on a project. We plant bean seeds in pots filled with this really dark dirt. Then we put some of the beans in a cupboard, some in the windowsills. It doesn't take a plant genius to figure out what will happen, but I guess O'Connor wants us Portland city kids to see it.

After science, we have Oregon history with Mrs. Hill. We study the Indian tribes in the Northwestern Territories before 1850. Whoa! I don't know what to do with so much fun!

But, as I leave class, I start to wonder what happened to some of those tribes. You never hear their names anymore.

Soccer at lunch now has twenty guys – guys who can't play football on Mr. Marvin's team. So, except for Mike Halverson, we're not the biggest guys in our class. Some of our fellows trip on their own shoelaces. It gets pretty messy, but O'Connor makes it fun. Even Davie Dashlee joins.

After lunch, we all troop up those stairs. The football guys make fun of soccer, of course. Rick doesn't pick on Davie. He picks on me. I think he's funny. He looks confused.

At the top of the stairs, near Mr. Marvin's classroom, Elizabeth Gray stands as if she's been listening to our jokes.

She laughs. "If guys have tongues, they must razz each other. Is that the rule?"

Rick jokes, "Is there another way?" Then he goes into the classroom.

As Rick walks to his seat, she asks, "Is that what he always wanted? Just to laugh with you?"

I glance after him. "Does a guy beat up on you to make jokes?"

She shrugs. "Gotta get your attention some way, I suppose," she says. "So, you've got your essay on oaths?"

"Sure. Plus, on the way to school this morning, I learned something new about the Marxists who took over East Germany. They really were bad, maybe as bad as the Nazis."

"You mean you learned something new about people?" she asks.

I'm puzzled, but then I see what she's getting at. "About greed," I say.

"Have you ever seen greed among Republicans and Democrats?" she asks.

"Well, yes."

"So, the Marxists in East Germany were bad when they got power. But what about people who have power right here? Is there any greed among them?"

"Sure, but communists want to control us."

"I'm guessing," she says. "Does your essay suggest we make everyone sign an oath?"

"Not everyone," I say. "Just people who work for the government."

"Aren't your parents teachers?" she asks. She raises a dark eyebrow at me, and then she shrugs one shoulder. It's a small motion, graceful. Suddenly, I can't think.

"I gotta hand in my homework," I say, but I'm talking to her back. She's already walking to her desk over by the window.

Before I drop the essay in the basket, I hesitate. I start to read it over and change some things I said, but Mr. Marvin rattles the basket and says, "Time to stop writing and get to class."

I glance at Elizabeth, who is watching me, but I drop the essay in. I tell myself it doesn't matter. It's just one assignment.

She glances out the window.

CHAPTER FIFTEEN

Each night after dinner, I collect cans and take them to the dumb waiter. Mike is collecting them for me too, so now I have three grocery bags full. Flattened, I bet they'll cover the ceiling of the canning cupboard.

I'm going to need a lot more to cover an area where we might sleep and live.

"Dad," I say when we're out in the vegetable garden. "Can we put a bathroom in the basement?"

"That would take a lot of plumbing and money, Gib. Maybe we just need to have a better bath schedule."

"But we'll need one in the basement for the bomb shelter."

Dad stops picking beans and straightens up. "Gilbert, I'm not intending to make a bomb shelter."

"But, you're a good builder and it won't cost like it would if we have to hire someone. I can help a lot."

Dad smiles. "You can help a lot, but a bomb shelter is a lot lower on the to-do list than more storage space."

"We can build storage space right into the bomb shelter, but Mr. Stockman says you have to plan for food, shelter and elimination. That's at least a toilet and a sink."

"Mr. Stockman? That's the dad of Randy and Jeffrey, right?"

"Sure. Randy and Jeff are in the Korean Demilitarized Zone."

Dad chuckles. "Doesn't it seem odd to call a place demilitarized when at least two armies are sitting there in a face off?"

Why can't he take this seriously? "Mr. Stockman says ..."

Dad looks me in the eyes, like he wants my full attention. "Gilbert, we will let other people buy into the bomb business. We're in the demilitarizing business."

"Geez! Why do you always have to put up this Quaker shit?"

"That's it, Gilbert. We can discuss, but not this way."

I stop picking tomatoes and turn away from him. "If you survive the bomb, Dad, you can set up a tent to sell peace. But you won't have a family left to sell it to." I walk off to drop the tomatoes in the kitchen.

*   *

It's class photo day at Eisenhower School. That means we hope for overcast skies but no rain so the photos can be taken out on the steps to the playground. All the girls have on their stiffest slips and their widest skirts, which leaves a narrow space for each guy. Of course I forgot photos were today, so I'm wearing an old light blue shirt which, in a black and white photo is going to look like dirty white. Good choice, Gib Evans.

Our home room is science, so we troop out to the playground with Mr. O'Connor. As we line up, James Wray pushes me in front of him. "Makes me look better by contrast," he says. "And, White Boy, you make a lot of contrast."

Billy laughs and says, "Mike, can stand in front of you, James, and then there won't be any need for contrast. You'll be gone."

"Yeah," Mike says. "In fact I can make both James and Billy disappear, easy."

The photographer has his tripod set up facing the stairs. He's kind of waving us onto the stairs, but not giving orders, so people mill around like sheep. Mr. O'Connor pulls out his stop watch. "Alphabetical order by last names. Line up now."

"We've done this before, so we're in line quickly. I know I'm in front of Elizabeth Gray, who stands in front of Mike Halverson and so forth back to James Wray.

"Minute and a half. Pretty darn good," Mr. O'Connor says. Now line up blue shirts here in Alpha order." He points to the front row. "White shirts are row two. All other colors are row three."

In the classroom and the hallway, he never lets us get too used to any style of lining up. Says he wants us to be alert at all times. So, now I'm in front with a light blue shirt next to Billy, James and Rick Johnson. Elizabeth is on the top row in her yellow blouse. As Mr. O'Connor gets into the end of the second row, just behind me, the sky darkens. Rain threatens.

The photographer glances up, hauls out a flash attachment, says the usual thing about cheese and sets off a bolt of white light. I hear a small moan and feel Mr. O'Connor crouch down.

"It's okay, sir," Mike whispers directly behind me. "Just the camera."

"Let's try that again," the photographer says. "Now everyone stand still."

His light is bright against the dark sky. This time, Mr. O'Connor stays upright, but I feel him move.

"Good enough," the photographer says, folding up his trip pod. "Better head in. It's going to rain for sure."

We break up and turn to climb the stairs. That's when I see that Mike has a grip on Mr. O'Connor's left arm. Mr. O'Connor's face has gone all clammy wet. Mike looks at me and says, "Link up."

I don't know what's going on, but I know Mike means business. I take Mr. O'Connor's other arm and start to turn him toward the door. Just then, Elizabeth steps in front of us.

"Mr. O'Connor," she says, "Could I ask you a question?"

He blinks and then focusses on Elizabeth. "Uh, yes, umm what is it?"

I can see that he's shaking off something, working really hard at coming out of it.

Elizabeth takes her time. "This is a question that's easier to answer if we all stay out here a minute. When it rains, and the sun is also out like this, where are we going to see the rainbow?"

Mr. O'Connor loosen himself from me and turns his face up to the mist that's now coming down. "Do you see where the sun is?"

"Sure," Elizabeth says. "Eight in the morning, pretty low in the sky."

"You see where the rain is coming down. The sun shines through the rain drops, right?"

"Sure. Like shining through little pieces of glass," Elizabeth says.

Mr. O'Connor blinks a little, then turns to Elizabeth, looking more like himself again. "The raindrops reflect and refract the light – a word we can explore in class on the black board. As the rays refract, we see them opposite from the sun. So, we see them west in the morning, east in the afternoon. They are organized into a rainbow of refracted light of long wavelengths like red to short wavelengths like violet and blue."

I stare at our class, where everyone is now staring at the sky with Elizabeth. Even Mr. O'Connor is staring at the sky, breathing normally and not looking so white.

Behind me, James Wray whispers to Billy, "That is one smart girl, that one." As we head inside, I see Mr. Marvin standing in the doorway, staring at Mr. O'Connor. I don't know how long he's been there. As they pass each other, Mr. Marvin says, "Well, that was interesting."

Mr. O'Connor says, "Good question about rainbows, wasn't it?"

"Lots of good questions turn up on photo day." Mr. Marvin says.

*   *

As we haul out the class science project, I look at Elizabeth who is watching Mr. O'Connor carefully. I've seen Mom look at Dad that way sometimes. Silent, concerned, and ready to help.

Last night at dinner for instance, Dad went totally still after I pushed him about building a bomb shelter. And then I saw Mom looking at him, right before she started to pray. We had a silent dinner, except for Justine yakking on and on. Dad hardly looked at me, and Mom pretended nothing was going wrong between us.

Why won't they try to save us? Why no bomb shelter for Quakers?

*   *

This morning, in Mr. O'Connor's class, I'm staring at stark-white bean plants. Anyone could have guessed this would happen. My mother serves white asparagus at Christmas dinner, for Pete's sake. Doesn't everyone know how that's done?

But, it turns out that Elizabeth, Billy Mendoza and James Wray are the only other kids in this whole classroom who grow their own vegetables

"Wow!" Mike says. "They've got no color at all. And look at that wimpy stalk."

James Wray is smiling. "Sunshine," he says, "it makes you strong, which if you are not, God help you."

Mr. O'Connor has this booming voice that comes out with a little spit. I figure that's the result of not having much control over that scarred left side of his face.

"Ladies and gentlemen, why did the cupboard not serve these beans well?"

He always calls us that: 'Ladies and gentlemen' like we are adults in a college class.

Elizabeth raises her hand, but Rick Johnson shouts out, "The girls forgot to feed 'em."

"Huh-uh," says Mike. "There's the chart. Fed once a week." He leans over Rick and adds, "Except yesterday, which was your day."

"Miss Gray?" Mr. O'Connor asks.

"James Wray is right," she says. "They have to have sun to create chlorophyll, just like people need sun to make vitamin D."

Mr. O'Connor smiles. "Miss Gray, you and Mister Wray get the blue ribbon for the day."

This, we have learned is not a fictitious blue ribbon, but a real one, like it came right off a Kentucky Derby race horse – big and ruffled with gold letters in the center of the circle-shaped upper part. The letters spell out "First Place". O'Connor says it waits for the student with the right answer, or even better, the right question.

He pulls it from a box in his desk drawer and pins it on the board. Then he gestures at Elizabeth and James to put their names next to it. Each of us has a fancy tag-board copy of our name for just this occasion. I think everybody in the class now has pinholes in their name card – even Rick Johnson, who one day got the blue ribbon for asking the question, "Why do we gotta learn about plants, anyway?"

O'Connor boomed out, "Mister Johnson earns the Big Blue for The Most Important Question of the whole term."

Rick's face flamed as he pinned his name carefully next to the ribbon.

And then that day, O'Connor asked us to imagine a world where no plants could grow. And another day, we had to imagine a whole tribe of people who had no idea what plants were safe to eat in their own forest.

When he set us to writing a story about those imagined places, I noticed that even Rick wrote. James wrote like he was racing his thoughts. And then he showed his paper to his buddy, Billy and they both laughed. Whatever he wrote must have given Billy an idea, because he started writing. Billy hardly ever writes.

Today, we've got all our plants out of the windowsills and cupboards. It's pretty obvious that bean plants like to be fed and have sun, but they hate to be fried in the western afternoon light, buried in the dark or starved.

"My friends," Mr. O'Connor says, "what kinds of food do you need to live healthy lives?"

Mike and a couple of the heftier guys are into answers like "Coca Cola", and "doughnuts", but James pops up with "collard greens". Rick starts to comment on that suggestion, but Mr. O'Connor speaks first.

"Collard greens once kept me alive," he says. "I couldn't cook them because of the smoke, but even raw, they saved my soul from death by boredom and my stomach from too much watery soup."

The whole class laughs, but I'm wondering why smoke would keep you from cooking anything.

By this week, Elizabeth knows the boys won't let her get a word in, so she blurts, "You have to eat protein and greens and trace minerals."

"Yes, Miss Gray," says O'Connor. "And where did you learn that?"

"There's an orphanage near my family's farm up in Washington. The orphans used to get nothing but corn mush. They were getting sicker than anything. Doctors studied up on them and found the corn mush they always ate didn't give them any iron and zinc and manganese – things like that."

"Boredom and watery soup," Mike says. "I could have told those doctors what was the matter."

The class laughs. I hardly hear because I'm picturing myself picking collard greens in a long row of vegetables. I'm on a farm I've never seen. In the next row, Elizabeth picks big ripe strawberries. It takes me a good minute to shake that picture and mentally return to class.

The discussion has gone on without me. Mr. O'Connor hauls out his pocket stopwatch and says, "Time to sit."

By three weeks into the year, we've learned when he says anything, he means "Do it now." So, we're in our seats in no time.

He puts away his pocket stopwatch and says, "Very good. A record so far. Thirty-four seconds. Now close your eyes and put your heads down on the table."

That means he is going to have us write about something. Writing seems weird for a science class, but I like his writing assignments better than most teachers'.

"This time," Mr. O'Connor says, "You are in a prison cell. You get no sunshine, except the little bit that comes in an upper window. It makes a narrow strip of light that moves around the opposite wall. You get corn mush for breakfast and dinner, no lunch, and you never leave this cell even to go to the bathroom.

"There is a pot in the corner for that. If you're lucky, somebody empties it once every two weeks. You see no one else. You're allowed to talk to no one else, but you know they're in other cells up and down the hall."

He pauses to let that picture sink in. Then he asks, "How will you stay healthy?"

By the time he stops describing it, I'm in that cell, starving for food, sunshine and talk. When he tells us to start writing, I have a hard time coming back to life and picking up my pen. Near me, Billy is already writing.

CHAPTER SIXTEEN

At noon, I take two steps at a time down to the school cafeteria. After imagining that prison cell during Mr. O'Connor's class, I'm starved. While I'm in the lunch line, I open my note from Mr. Marvin.

Great essay, Mr. Evans. Well thought out. You understand the Communist Threat. Because of this essay, I'd like you to take on the responsibilities of editor of the school newspaper, the 'Eisenhower Eagle'. The first edition should come out before Halloween with news, holiday poems, essays like this one, and short stories. Your main news authors should be people who get As on this first paper — people who can really write.

One essay and I have the dream job. Mr. Reese would have had two or three of us take turns. That's what happened with last year's eighth grade class. Editor. Wow! But I'll need help making the paper great.

"Gib," Mike calls from his table in the cafeteria.

"Be right over," I say. "Gotta get lunch." I head into the cafeteria line.

Mrs. Stolski plops a big spoonful of spaghetti on my plate – as in big spoonful. Mrs. Gunter smothers my spaghetti with red sauce. Mrs. Klotz gives me salad. Pretty nice. No prison rations here.

I sit down next to Mike. He says. "Look at this." He slaps a piece of paper on the table. I see the big blue F.

It slashes across the whole drawing. But behind the F, I can see a cartoon. Mike has drawn his dad in his sergeant's uniform. We can see him from the back, prying open the lock on a gate with his bayonet. On the other side of the barbed wire fence, stand emaciated people with very big eyes.

Beneath the drawing is Mike's caption. "Actions speak louder than Oaths."

"Geez, Mike, that's a great cartoon."

"So, explain the F."

I ask, "What did Mr. Marvin say?"

"He said I had to write not draw."

"Yeah," I say, relieved I don't have to tell him. "I guess it was supposed to be an essay."

"This picture says all that needs to be said," Mike says.

"Maybe, but he asked why we need oaths. This is about why we don't need them."

"You're right there, Buster," Mike says.

I don't want to argue with my friend, so I say, "You know, you can do cartoons for the Eisenhower Eagle. That'd be fun, wouldn't it?"

"So, he gave you the job?"

"Yeah. He liked my essay. We'll probably have a different editor each term, like when Mr. Reese was here."

"You think Mr. Marvin will do anything the way Mr. Reese did it?"

"Why not? Reese had a good system. The eighth grade last year put out a great newspaper."

Mike looks at me, then puts his cartoon back into the pocket of his folder and shoves the whole thing into his book bag. "I'll do cartoons for you. I can learn to do stuff for little kids. They don't care about oaths and things like that."

"Sure, that political kind of stuff is for grown up newspapers."

"Are there any?" Mike asks as he gets up.

"Any what?"

"I've got to go to gym class." Mike says.

I watch Mike go. I guess he was hoping to cartoon his way through journalism class. After a moment, I think again about his cartoon and I get this uncomfortable feeling. "Actions speak louder than oaths." Sounds like Mike has been listening to my Quaker parents. They're such dreamers. To hear them talk, you'd think nothing dangerous happens that can't be worked on through some kind of sit down over cookies. That sure won't get spies to stop digging out secrets and selling them.

There are lots of kids in journalism class besides Mike. I hunt up the kids who have As on the essay.

Billy Mendoza's essay has a B minus. "Billy, this is good," I say. "You've got a great opening sentence."

"Sure," he said, "but after I agreed that we needed an oath, I couldn't think of good reasons."

He's right. His essay reminds me of a squirrel chasing its tail. We need an oath because McCarthy wants an oath, so we need an oath.

"The truth is," Billy says. "I think oaths are so much toilet paper, but that idea isn't going to fly."

"Billy, there are subversives in lots of important places in our government."

"You've heard that?"

"Sure, on the news, all the time. If we can't find them, they'll take over."

Billy just shrugs. I guess he pretends not to be scared.

Most of the *A* essay kids seemed to have read newspapers and listened to the news. So, they have reasons for wanting an oath. For instance, a girl named Judy wrote, "We absolutely have to find the spies any way we can. I don't want to get bombed."

Her friend, Sharon, wrote, "We have a bomb shelter, but what about the people who live in apartments? Where are they going to go? If we know who is a communist, we can send them back to Russia and defend ourselves better."

I could see *A* students are more realistic than Mike and Billy. By the end of the school day, I've got a good idea how we're going to get the *Eisenhower Eagle* out by Halloween. One girl wants to write about how to make the playground safer. A fellow from Mrs. Hill's homeroom wants to ask the PTA to put up basketball courts so kids can play on the weekends. Another girl will interview local businesses that sell to students.

Everybody's got something they think is important to write about. Plus some of the teachers will contribute writing from their students.

At the end of school, I decide to ask the new girl, Elizabeth if she'd like to write a story about what it's like to come to a school where you don't know anybody. I wait for her after school where I know she usually comes out of the typing class. When she turns the corner from the classroom toward her locker, she waves goodbye to another girl. I'm glad to see that girl walk off because I don't want to have this discussion with a crowd.

"Hi, Elizabeth," I say.

She looks surprised, "Gilbert, right?"

I nod.

"Don't your friends call you Gib?"

"Yup. Nickname."

She smiles. The way her eyes light up, that kind of stops my easy-talking flow. I forget what I wanted to say and stand there like a dud light bulb.

"Can I help you with something?" she asks.

"Umm, yeah. I mean, I hope so. Would you like to write for the Eisenhower Eagle?"

She glances toward the ceiling and says. "I don't think you want me."

"Why wouldn't I? I mean you must write as good as you talk." She smiles and I think I hear her choke off a little laugh.

"I mean as well as you talk," I say.

She shakes her head and says, "First, you should see something. Then you decide if you want me to write." She stops at her locker and glances around. From the top locker shelf, she pulls out a folder that says, "Journalism". She yanks out a paper, plunks it on top of her book stack and shows it to me.

"You won't want someone like me writing for the school newspaper. I might be a bad influence."

I take her paper off the stack. An F covers her first page. With it is Mr. Marvin's comment: "Revolutionaries give up their rights. They knew that in 1776, and you should know it now."

Reading behind the blue of Marvin's handwriting, I can see that Elizabeth has memorized the Bill of Rights and the Declaration of Independence in whatever school she went to last year. But she argued against loyalty oaths.

I stare at her. "You think communism will work? Just put all the farms and companies in communal ownership and everybody will be happy?"

"Who knows? Are they afraid if we talk about it, the idea might look good?"

"It's a lousy idea."

"If it's a lousy idea, I think people could figure that out. They ought to be free to learn more about it and decide." Elizabeth draws in a deep breath. "People have a right to argue and disagree. They should have had that right in Centralia, too."

"Centralia? That up in Washington State?" I ask.

Elizabeth slaps the locker. "Centralia is in hell." She blinks and seems embarrassed.

Almost as quickly, her eyes light with defiance. "Well, it should be." That sudden change in her makes me nervous enough to laugh.

"Not funny," she says, and drops her paper back into the Peechee folder.

"We're not writing about politics and that kind of stuff in the *Eisenhower Eagle*," I say.

"Believe me," she says, "you don't want me even stapling the newspaper. I'm a revolutionary." She slams her locker and walks away. I have to close the lock for her while I watch her back. Why is she mad at me because she got an F?

I head home to ask Dad if he remembers anything about Centralia, Washington. Something makes Elizabeth Gray angry enough to cuss, and she's just not the type. My dad has a great memory for news.

CHAPTER SEVENTEEN

When I come home, I go down in the basement to look for Dad's tin snips. I want to start opening the cans in my collection before it gets too far ahead of me. I get the snips from his tool wall and head to the old dumb waiter. When I get there, all five of my sacks of tin cans are gone. I stand there staring.

I can't believe it. I run upstairs. "Mom! Dad!"

No one answers. I can't even find Justine. The back door is open. I swing through the screen door. Mom's weeding.

"I had a can collection," I call to her running down the steps to the yard. "What'd you do with my can collection?"

She stands from the lilac bed. "Gib? Cans . . . Oh, Honey, were those yours?"

"What happened?"

"I'm clearing basement space for some of my books. Why cans?"

"Where are they?"

"The garbage man . . . I didn't know."

My face goes hot. "The garbage man! Gone?"

She nods.

"Why?"

"I thought they'd been left over from when the dumb waiter was used … the previous owner."

I sit hard on the steps. "That many cans would've covered the canning cupboard. Mike helped me collect."

Mom comes to sit beside me. "Your dad said you had this thing about building a bomb shelter. Was that why the cans?"

"You and Dad never take it seriously. There's traitors just waiting and you … you weed the garden and …"

"I know how you're feeling, Gib. All the women's magazines have articles about building shelters."

"Really? With plans?"

"Gib, what I'm saying is that the danger seems huge because of all the talk, the air-raid sirens, Senator McCarthy, the news articles, accusations."

"And they've arrested those union guys right here," I say.

Mom leans her head on her gloved hand as if she's tired. "God, what power did those poor men have?"

"We don't have any power against the bomb," I say. "But we might survive. We've got to …"

"Gilbert, when people have power, they want to keep it. To keep power, they exaggerate danger. They stir people up and get their support against imagined enemies"

"But the communists are our enemies. They're not imagined, and they have bombs out there in the ocean, not just over in Russia."

"Honey, who else do you think has bombs?" she waves her arm toward the Pacific, "We have them out there, aimed at Indo-China, up there in Alaska, aimed at China, in South Korea, aimed north, and in Germany, aimed at Russia?"

"That's our only hope – protection."

Mom looks at me a long time. She kind of stretches her neck and loosens her shoulders. Then she says, "So, let's imagine for a moment. Someone with a bomb sends it at someone else. What next?"

"We bomb them right back."

"I didn't say who sent the first bomb."

All at once, I imagine being somewhere on the other side of the roll of barbed wire. All I know is that the ones on the other side, The U. S. side, are aiming their worst at me.

"We wouldn't send first," I say.

"We did. Twice. Why not a third time?"

"But ..."

"If you were on the other side, what would you do to make sure we didn't use it a third time?"

"I'd get my own."

"And then, you, on the other side, you read in your news that everyone on our side is building shelters for the Big Day. Now what do you believe those Americans will do?"

That made me stop talking. I imagined me over there. Reading their newspapers, listening to their leaders. I'd be certain sure the United States had a plan to drop the newest bomb on me. I would have heard that the U.S. has a hydrogen bomb, a thousand times more powerful than the atom bomb. I know on the other side of that border, I'd be very afraid, willing to do anything for my safety. I know it, but I don't want to admit it to Mom. Besides, what can I do about it? I'm just one kid.

"Mom," I say, "it won't help for our one family not to build a shelter. The Russians don't know about us not building."

"They don't know yet. But what if we were many families, not building shelters and many talking about not using the bomb? What if we were a growing presence, and loud about not having guns drawn and bombs aimed all the time?"

"Maybe they would hear about us," I say. "But, not until ..." Her hope seems so breakable, so unreachable.

"She says, "What if they learned that at heart, we are really scared, and just like them?"

I imagine stepping out of the woods above our little town in Germany, I look across at the emptiness that was a farm and then a prison and then nothing. I see myself, a twin kid on the other side, staring back at our side, waiting for the danger to come.

"We could send messages to them," I say. "Like 'We don't want bombs'. Maybe they will hear about us."

"Maybe they will."

I wish she were right, but I know there is a lot between what is real and what we wish. "But that's not gonna happen," I say. "Their newspapers don't tell the truth."

"Gilbert, even our newspapers tell only what the news owners decide is news."

I remember the newsreels I've seen at the movie theater on Saturday afternoons. I see enormous tanks moving in those films of the Russian May Day Parades. In my mind, their tanks are rolling toward our tanks, and every tank carries a long, powerful gun. The Russians have rockets carried on huge trucks. The rockets are ready to launch. Every rocket aims toward the west. In front of me there's this barrier of fear with no way around or over it.

"But, I don't want you to die," I whisper.

She pulls me toward her. "I don't want my son, or my family, my fellow humans to die," Mom says.

"What can we do?"

"There are choices before us. The longer we wait to speak out, the fewer choices we have. We must keep open the door to the choice of understanding."

I swallow hard. I know there's no chance we will survive what's coming.

Is this why Mike's Dad won't build? Does he want to keep open that choice? Or is it like Mike says? He just wants to be gone when the bomb comes.

*   *

Two days later, after school, I'm still tired from what I've been thinking about the world. What a mess we've made – an impossible mess.

Dad says while we try to keep the world from making the Big Mistake, we have to live. We have to enjoy life. That doesn't seem possible.

But, I try because I can't let Justine know how different the world seems now. She deserves to be a little girl and be excited about stuff like pink dresses and dolls.

I've got friends, and soccer and the fall leaves, but it's hard to act like the world is okay. Everything I look at has a dark edge around it.

I try to slog forward. I take a stack of poems from Mrs. Price's third grade to the teacher work room. As editor of the *Eisenhower Eagle*, I've gotten most of the kids in the journalism class to agree to interview somebody – the ladies in the cafeteria about how they cook for eight hundred students a day, the art teacher about her paintings in a gallery downtown. Even Davie Dashlee is going to write a story about the Beaver Baseball Team and how its season is winding up. They've been hot this year. Davie skips school for the ball park once a week, so it's a perfect assignment for him.

Here in the empty teacher work room, I'm cranking out copies of kid poems on the mimeograph machine. And I'm thinking over what Dad told me about Elizabeth's home town. In Centralia, a long time before the war, there was a riot against union workers who were suspected communists. Dad says there's still bad blood between union workers and business owners in that town, even after all these years. He says the business owners think any union guy is selling revolution. I wonder which side Elizabeth's family was on.

I'm really worried about my Dad, and maybe even Mom. Rick's dad thinks my parents are communists. Why else would Rick call me a commie pacifist? And I don't know – maybe they are. Take the other night, with Professor Wilson – what did all that mean? Was there something besides food going on in Germany with that Russian officer who asked for the band concerts?

And on top of that stuff, there is this movement Mom is part of in Friends World Service. They are working to make our country talk to the Soviets, try to get agreements to make fewer bombs, try to get Americans to visit Russia and Russians to visit here.

I hope my folks aren't radical revolutionaries, but Mom asked me not to talk about dinner with Professor Wilson. He might get fired like Mr. Reese. If someone like Rick's dad accuses you of being a Commie Pacifist, there isn't any way to prove you're not.

The world seems teetery, and dangerous.

I change mimeo masters, drop the tired one in the garbage and put on a new one. Last night after the secretaries left school, Mike and I used their new electric typewriter to copy these poems onto three master pages. Then, Mike used a sharp pen, cutting little cartoons of the kid's ideas onto the masters. Their poems are short lists of things they like about fall. One kid likes stamping around in a mud puddle until her mother hollers at her.

Mike's cartoon shows clearly that Justine is the mud puddle poet.

These pages are going to be the center of our first issue of the *Eisenhower Eagle*. Not much of a newspaper, you think? Well, because of these three pages, the third graders and their parents will read the rest of the news. And this issue will hang around in their mom's cedar chests forever. Fifty years from now, this issue will be history with cartoons by Mike Halverson. So, I'm not too corked about having to spend an hour making eight hundred copies of these poems. I just hope the mimeograph masters hold out.

And I hope the world will hold off.

This work room is right next to the teachers' room, and the teachers' door isn't quite closed, so cigarette smoke comes through the crack. As I crank the barrel of ink around and around, I'm in a haze of copy solvent and tobacco. At first, I barely notice that Mr. Marvin is in the teachers' room talking to somebody. But then I perk up.

"Where'd that O'Connor guy come from?" he says. "Nobody at the personnel office has any idea even how he got here."

I hear Mrs. Hill, our history teacher. "The personnel office isn't supposed to give you access to anyone's files."

"I got friends over there who are concerned," Marvin says. "We have to know who's teaching our students."

"Why are you asking about O'Connor in particular?" Mr. Patton, the principal, asks.

"Did you know," Marvin says, "he told his class to write about jail cells and solitary confinement? I have to ask 'Why?'"

Mrs. Hill says, "Have you seen the writing his class is doing? Some of those students, like Davie Dashlee and Rick Johnson, never wrote before unless you stood over them and dipped their pen in the ink well."

Mr. Patton chuckles.

"In his class, they're writing amazing, imaginative stuff," Mrs. Hill says.

But Mr. Marvin says, "Imaginative. How is science imaginative?"

"Mr. Einstein seems to have quite an imagination," Mrs. Hill says.

Off in this side room, I'm changing to the next mimeo master because the others wore out. I'm also thinking Mrs. Hill is right about imagination and science. Einstein's ideas create a hullaballoo, and his face is on lots of magazine covers. He's pretty wild out there.

Mr. Marvin says, "And Einstein is probably a communist, like Oppenheimer."

"You believe that these men are subversive merely because they both want us to be careful about how we use power?" Mrs. Hill asks. "Careful about the atomic and hydrogen bombs?

Mr. Patton interrupts their argument. "I don't think you need to worry about Mr. O'Connor. He has a Master's degree in Science."

"A Masters?" Marvin asks. "Why would a guy with a higher degree want to teach fourteen year olds?"

Mrs. Hill says, "If you had a Masters, who would you be teaching?"

But Marvin goes right on. "They can't account for where O'Connor was between 1945 and 1948. Isn't that a little suspicious?"

Mrs. Hill says, "Who can't account for him?"

"Personnel, of course."

"Who in personnel?" she asks.

"Can't tell you that. My informant."

"Your informant is acting illegally if he is giving you information from someone's private files."

I don't like the sound of what Mr. Marvin is doing. It doesn't seem fair. But where was Mr. O'Connor during those years?

"If O'Connor has nothing to hide, why would he need private files?" Marvin asks.

"So, I can go into your files at any time?" she asks.

"You have no reason to question my loyalty."

"Okay, my own informant in personnel will verify that for me." Mrs. Hill says. This statement is followed by a long silence. I wonder if she doesn't think it's right, would she really search his files?

Next, Mr. Marvin says, "For the sake of your students, you should want to know where Mr. O'Connor was during those missing years."

"That would be none of my business, or yours," she says. I can hear her chair creak and then the door to the hall opens and closes. I guess she left. And I guess she's right. I wouldn't want anybody searching Dad's files just because they wonder if he's a radical.

So, here I am, running the mimeo loud and clear and they are in there, just Marvin and Mr. Patton. I'm thinking, 1945 to 1948 ... where was O'Connor? According to some of these radio guys who hunt for spies, those are critical years when the Soviets began training operatives for America. They gave them American accents, American clothes and all that.

But why make a spy out of a guy who's so noticeable? His scars, his missing fingers. He's unforgettable. No way! Besides, O'Connor is really teaching us. He's a good coach, too. I'll just ask him where he was. There's gotta be an easy explanation.

From the other room, I hear Marvin talking again. "You do know that Mrs. Hill's late husband was a union organizer for the Portland longshoremen. Unionized dock workers – they could be bringing anything into the Port of Portland."

I stop cranking the machine. According to the radio news guys, communist sympathizers have tried to take over the AF of L, and the CIO. I think that's the American Federation of Labor and something – anyway, unions.

"Yes, I do know what her husband did for a living," Mr. Patton says.

"And Mrs. Hill is still active in the women's auxiliary – even on the Committee to Protect the Foreign Born Members, like Billy Mendoza's father." I stop moving.

"What are you claiming about Mr. Mendoza?" Mr. Patton asks.

"He's organizing unions at places like Jones Frozen Foods and at Cargo-Car."

"Cargo-Car? Isn't that Senator Johnson's company?"

"Mendoza wants to put them out of business – make them raise wages, put drains in the floors at Jones Frozen Foods, and other big expenses."

There is no comment from Mr. Patton, so Mr. Marvin goes on. "For a foreigner, that's pretty suspect, I say. And Mrs. Hill's group wants to protect people like that."

"And where did your family come from?" Mr. Patton asks.

"Came over on the Mayflower," Mr. Marvin says.

"I see," says Mr. Patton. "Arrived here from Holland after fleeing the law in England." The two of them are silent for a long time.

I start the machine again, slow, so I can hear over the noise.

"So, you're watching out for what she teaches, right?" Marvin asks. "U.S. History is a sensitive subject."

"I'm watching my faculty, all the time. I like to keep track of troublemakers."

"Good," says Marvin. "Real good."

I'm on my last mimeo master for the third grade poems. I've got eight hundred fifty copies, by now. The last fifty are hard to read. These mimeo masters don't last long.

I shut down the machine. I wonder what troublemakers Mr. Patton watches. And then I wonder, what if Mr. Marvin looks up Mom's records over at Alameda School? He'll see she lived in Germany during those same years. What would he think of her then?

As I step out into the hall, I see the back of Mr. Marvin heading for his classroom.

Suddenly, Justine is right beside me. "What's a communist?" she asks.

I look at the kiddy books she's got under her arm. She just came from the library. The library is on the other side of the teacher's room and that door is open sometimes, just like the one on the work room side.

"Justine," I say, "I've got a class to go to, but I'll explain communism tonight after dinner." I hope to figure out what to say by then. I'm not sure anymore.

She's all kind of breathless. "Are they scary? Can teachers be communists?"

"You and your dolls have been playing arrest the commie spies," I say. "Don't you know what you're talking about?"

I hear myself say that and I cringe. I don't know any more than she does.

"I heard your radio," she says. "They're everywhere. And they want to take over the United States, don't they?"

"Well," I say, "I think maybe we shouldn't be so worried about these ideas. Mom and Dad will take care of them."

"Can parents be spies?"

"No," I say. "Where'd you get that idea?"

"Kenny Johnson says I'm a commie Quaker," Justine says.

I stop and stare at her. She's about to cry. Of course Rick's little brother is saying this stuff.

I say, "Justine, you're a Quaker, but you're no commie. Quakers aren't anything but Quakers."

"Commie Pacifist Quaker," Justine says, and the tears are coming down for real now.

I don't want my little sister to be this scared. I get down on my haunches and look her in the eye. "Justine …"

"We are Pacifists," she sobs. "Quakers are Pacifists aren't they?"

Dang it. This is not fair for a little kid. I take my sister by the hand, and all the way toward her classroom, I try to explain that pacifist is way different from communist. I think she gets it, but she's still crying when we get to my locker.

I shove the eight hundred fifty lousy newspaper pages into the floor of my locker and take her home. Mom is not there. This is her day to do the front desk at Margaret Fox Home for Women.

So, I take Justine to Mrs. Silverberg's front door. While I'm ringing the bell, I'm kicking myself for this stupid move. What do I know about Mrs. Silverberg except that Justine feels safe with her?

Mrs. Silverberg opens her door. She looks at Justine and opens her arms. Justine runs to her and collapses. Mrs. Silverberg glances up at me and raises her eyebrows in question.

"She's afraid about foreign spies," I say, and I want to bite my tongue. Mrs. Silverberg is as foreign as they come in this neighborhood. But she's a U.S. citizen. Mom and Dad like her.

What is right? Mrs. Silverberg, Mrs. Hill, Mr. Reese, Mr. O'Connor – I like them all. Who should we be afraid of? I'm standing there like a doh-doh bird while Mrs. Silverberg hugs Justine and says.

"Vell, Geebert, I am glad you bring her home. You are a good boy. I veel take care of her until your Mama comes."

I'm kinda stuck there on the front porch. I don't know anything except that a man died in Germany, and Russian communists starved the farmers. I thought I knew everything, but I don't. I don't know anything for sure, but I do know that I shouldn't have written my essay for taking oaths. Mr. Marvin hunts for ways to ruin Mr. O'Connor and Mrs. Hill. I head home to rewrite my essay, and when I think I've got it right, I save it to send to Mr. Patton.

CHAPTER EIGHTEEN

Essay # 2
Gilbert Evans
October 05, 1953

Dear Mr. Patton,

Earlier this fall, I was asked to write an essay about loyalty oaths and about why we need them. I thought we did need them because I was afraid of communism.

Now, I realize that anyone can accuse a person they don't like of being a communist, and they can do that based on almost nothing for proof. They can drag up questions like what meetings did they visit? What religious beliefs do they have? Where did they live during and after World War II? What did their family members do for a living? And none of what these accusers do is right. If we look at the Constitution...

* *

It's morning. The sun shines into my bedroom, but I roll over to shut it out. I'm not looking forward to school on this Tuesday in October, 1953. Yesterday, I mailed my new ideas about oaths to the school principal. I'm not sure what he'll think of that essay, but I had to send it to somebody. And Mr. Patton knows what Mr. Marvin is trying to do.

This is the morning I have to tell Mr. Marvin that I asked Elizabeth, Billy and James to be the reporters and Mike the cartoonist for the Eisenhower Eagle. He said to use only A students, but those four had good ideas for stories. And besides, we're not doing politics in a school paper.

A few minutes late, I trudge down to breakfast and plop into the chair across from Justine. She seems to have gotten over her fear of spies and Kenny's accusations. Mrs. Silverberg is a good person. Justine's two braided pig-tails stick straight up from each side of her head. I study them while she leans over her book. Inside each braid, she's stashed a pencil as wood stiffening. I don't ask why because that's clearly what Justine wants me to do.

Mom comes in from the kitchen and sets down a big platter of scrambled eggs and bacon. Smells great. Dad strolls in from the piano room, a pencil behind his right ear. His hair flops over his forehead. He doesn't even notice that Justine's hair can't flop. Dad grips a tablet of music manuscript paper. His head bobs. His right hand conducts the music he probably just finished writing. "Morning, Gilbert, Justine," he says, without looking at us.

He nearly sets his music in the plate of eggs, but Justine moves the plate to the other side of her bowl. She is swift, Justine.

Mom returns with milk and coffee.

Dad smiles at her. "What are Friends up to this week?" he asks. I glance at her. I know Mom often works at lobbying government officials about peace and freedom, about more diplomacy and fewer guns. She works with the Friends World Service whenever she's not at Margaret Fox House.

"We're looking into the HUAC hearings." She stabs her pointer finger at the *Portland Journal* next to her breakfast plate. "The House un-American Activities Committee is still going to send representatives to Corbett College to question several of the professors about their . . ." She glances at Justine, "about their possible ties."

Justine is fiddling with her cereal, trying to get the flakes to stick to the backside of the spoon.

Mom smiles at Justine's antics and then opens the front section of the paper. She turns to the inside and summarizes what she's reading. "Tonight, the Portland Public School Board is having a meeting. Senator Johnson and the Educators for Democracy forced Gregory Halverson to call for a hearing about their demand for an oath of loyalty for all teachers."

I stop pouring cereal in my bowl. Gregory Halverson, that's Mike's dad. He's been on the school board since last spring. Senator Johnson, Rick and Kenny's dad, doesn't like Mr. Halverson. Mr. Johnson wanted a friend of his to win that school board position. After thinking about all this for a minute, I realize what Mom just said about the meeting tonight.

Uh-oh, I'm thinking. Loyalty oaths are a bigger topic than I thought. I ask, "They gonna debate oaths right in the board meeting where we can go and see them?"

Dad looks up, surprised. "Gib," he says, "do you remember Quaker teaching about oath taking?"

"Sure," I say. "*Yes* should mean *yes* and *no* should mean *no* without need for swearing." In Sunday school we learned this. Quakers don't swear oaths because Jesus says we should hold ourselves to a high standard of truthfulness at all times. I wish I had remembered that before yesterday.

"But, Dad," I say. "What are we going to do? McCarthy claims he's found them in the Army and in the State Department. There's all this stuff going on."

"Yes." Dad leans toward me, very tense and quiet, glancing at Justine to see if she's paying attention. Justine's still messing with her food. "Tell me specifically what McCarthy has found," he asks.

"Well, McCarthy has this list of names, people who work for the State Department and have ties to . . . uh . . . the party."

"Do you remember who is on this list he waves around?"

"I don't think he's ever read all the names, but he calls people to testify about being Reds."

Justine glances up from her plate. "Waving around? Last week, Mom and I saw this magician at library story time. He was waving a red hanky around so you couldn't tell what he was doing with his other hand."

I laugh. "Ah-ha! Are your pencil-stiff braids a red hanky? Are you trying to distract us from, say maybe, some homework that didn't get done?" She glares at me.

"Oh, my God," Mom says. And we all stop.

"Listen to this letter to the editor," she says. "It says, 'Even students in our upper grades are worried about communists, and urge that the oath be a requirement. In a recent essay, Gilbert Evans, eighth grader at Eisenhower Elementary, wrote 'I have seen the starvation and death that Russians brought to East Germans. I hope we can root out and get rid of any communists in our own country. I believe all people in positions of power should take an oath of loyalty to the United States government.'"

Mom looks up at me. "Did you write that, Gilbert?"

I'm stunned. "How did the newspaper get that?" I ask. "It was for journalism class."

She glances down at the newspaper and reads, "The letter writer says, "What greater power than to be teaching such honorable youngsters as Gilbert Evans? How easily a traitor or subversive could misuse that power! For the safety of such students, we believe our Portland Public School Board should immediately require an oath be taken by all teachers of impressionable young students."

"Signed,

Elias Marvin, Founder and President of Educators for Democracy."

When Mom finishes reading, I sit there with my head down. Mom and Dad are silent.

Nobody moves. I can't believe this has happened.

Finally, Justine says, "Is that Mister Marvin at our school?"

I nod and get ready to explain, but Mom starts talking to me. "You have a very clear writing style, Gilbert."

"Thanks," I mumble.

"Do you believe your teachers should have to take an oath of loyalty?"

I sit here, feeling befuddled. "I believed in oaths when I wrote the essay. But Mom – I wrote a different letter to the principal yesterday."

"Why did you write yesterday?"

"Because Mr. Marvin scared Justine. And he talks about other teachers behind their back, so they can't defend themselves."

Mom sees Justine launching into her story about yesterday, but Mom puts up her hand. "Magdalena told me about what you heard in the faculty room."

Dad says, "Gilbert, the faculty at Corbett College has refused to take such an oath or testify about any ties to communism they may, or may not have had. They believe forcing them to do that violates their right to free speech, and to explore ideas. They have those rights as citizens of the United States."

"I know, from the First Amendment."

Dad looks at me over his glasses frames. "Exactly. If reading about, hearing or discussing certain beliefs will destroy the United States, it must be very weak. Our acts should be our word. And we should not be forced to testify against friends, based on conversations we may have had with them about ideas – that violates your right and theirs to discuss ideas. It violates the very thing that makes people good citizens – their ability to care, to discuss and to learn."

I frown at the newspaper that Mom is holding. "But what about McCarthy and all those people he's found in the State Department?"

"So far," Mom says, "he refuses to share that list with others."

Dad glances around the room, like he's checking the windows and doors. Then he says, "Making people afraid gives him power."

I stare at my plate, afraid of what I've done. People will think I really want this oath, and I did want it. I wanted to keep us safe. But now, I don't know what is safe. If McCarthy is a liar, then his hunt is a lie. Mr. Marvin used my essay to make other people think that all kids are afraid. But he might be lying to get power, too – power over people like Mrs. Hill and Mr. O'Connor, the teachers he talks about behind their backs.

What have I done?

"And those others," I say, "the men on the House Un-American Activities Committee, and the people coming for hearings at the colleges in Portland . . . Is that just to make people afraid?"

Dad glances at Mom, then at me. "I think you should come to the board meeting tonight and see what you think."

"Me, too?" Justine pipes up.

Mom shakes her head. "Too late at night for you, Miss Justine."

"Aw, Mom!"

I think a minute. "Maybe the school board won't see Mister Marvin's letter."

Mom folds her napkin neatly at the side of her plate. "Gilbert, did Mister Marvin ask your permission to use a quote from your essay in his letter?"

I think a minute. "I don't remember if he did."

"Maybe when he made you editor of the school paper?"

I try to remember all the stuff he said that day – about how proud he was of me for writing such a good essay, for seeing the threat. I don't think he asked if he could quote me.

I say, finally, "He might have. He said a lot of things."

She nods and smooths out her napkin several times. "Well, try to remember. Right now, it's time to finish your breakfast and get off to school."

"Mom," Justine says. "I want to help you make signs for that hearing."

Mom gazes at her. "How did you know about the signs?"

"I heard you talking to Missus Silverberg about it. What's a protest?"

Mom glances at me. Then back at Justine. "Well, let's talk about it while we paint. Meanwhile, no talking about it at school. You got that?"

"You mean it's a surprise protest?" Justine asks.

Mom nods. "A big surprise."

"Are you going to a protest?" I say. "Geez! Everybody knows you're my mom."

"That's nice dear. But protesting is necessary. It's time someone in this town stood up for the Bill of Rights."

Justine raises her right fist and says, "Missus Silverberg says, 'If you are silent when things are wrong, people can't blame you. But God can.'"

CHAPTER NINETEEN

Essay # 2
Gilbert Evans
October 5, 1953

> *People frighten other people into not changing the world at all. You want a better life for workers? You must be a communist. You want to solve problems without dropping bombs? You must be a traitor.*

> *This kind of scare stuff makes people afraid to be different. But our country is full of different. Different ideas can be talked about, tested, thrown away or used because we are not afraid to try new things — at least we used to be that way.*

> *Now, though, nobody can try new things or talk about new ideas because those ideas can be labeled communist.*

* *

As soon as I set foot in school, kids are coming up to me and congratulating me about having my name in print. "My dad says you're right on," Sharon says.

John thumps me on the back, "Way to give it to the commies, Gib."

And it goes on like that until class starts in first period. I'm the celebrity every time I move from class to class. In science class, even Rick gives me the circled-fingers 'perfect' sign. Go figure. The guy is not predictable. And I am getting more and more uncomfortable with everybody thinking I'm this great patriot. I think back to what I heard Mr. Marvin doing in the teachers' room, back to my little sister so scared about possible communists that she cried all the way home. And I wonder what Mr. Patton will think of my second essay when he gets it.

During lunch hour, James Wray thumps his notebook down on the library table. I glance up and see his tight-lipped, narrow-eyed, "don't-mess-with-me" look.

"What's up, James?"

"I see you are a quoted author," he says.

"Come on. I didn't know Mr. Marvin was going to do that."

"You yanking my leg?" James says.

I glance at his leg. But today he isn't having any funny stuff. He leans down toward my face. "You really didn't know he would use your essay like that?"

I hold up my Boy Scout fingers. "But," I say. "I agreed with him when I wrote it...."

"You want our teachers to vow they've never read about Marxism, never visited any meetings where there might have been communists?"

I shrug. "I did then. Now, well, I don't think so."

"You want people to vow they've never been in a union?"

"Not the same thing, and that's not what I said even in that first essay."

"Yeah? Well, how come people say Unionism is proof of communism – the CIO and the Longshore and Warehouse men? The rail workers . . .?"

"But those are proven fronts for communist organizations," I remind him.

"You know, Gib, you are exactly the kind of guy they are looking for," he says. And he grabs his notebook and walks.

I stare after him. Some days James is so angry you can't even tell where it began. I know. I know . . . a lot of it is about being a Negro, and how hard it is to find a job and a house and all that. But why is he angry about unions?

I get up and chase after him. When I catch up, I put a hand on his shoulder and he spins around like he's thinking about hitting me.

"What's going on?" I ask.

He stands there, staring at me, then off at the walls like he's trying to decide how much to tell me. Finally, he looks me in the eye and says. "Billy Mendoza and his whole family got deported back to the Philippines."

"Aren't the Mendozas citizens?"

"Been citizens for twenty years."

"Then why?"

"Mr. Mendoza's a leader in a warehouse union, part of the Longshoremens'. He tried to organize workers at Cargo-Car. Somebody in the company claims he must be a revolutionary and treacherous because he's wants his union to ask for better wages. So Immigration deports him – and Billy, too. And all the grandparents."

"How can you deport a citizen?"

"Easy. Accuse him of something scary."

I'm thinking of Mrs. Hill. I hope she's not still working for the Longshoremen's Union Auxiliary. And then I think how scared Billy must be.

"But when was the trial?" I ask.

"No trial. Just a hearing. They also accused Mister Mendoza's lawyer of being subversive because he tried to help them. When stuff happens, bang, you're gone. And your lawyer better be real white, or he's gone, too."

"Was he?"

"Was he what?"

"White?"

"You're a doofhead," James says, and he turns on his heel leaving me to stand there in the hall.

The United States does not deport people for no reason.

Gib, you're exactly the kind of guy they are looking for.

I hope James is not so ticked at me that we can't be friends. There's things, problems I don't understand, and he can tell me about that stuff. James and I have known each other since back when we moved to Portland. And I'm going to miss Billy, a lot.

*   *

I'm bummed out about James and Billy all morning, but I have to keep going. One foot in front of the other, I guess. Foot slog, Foot slog . ....

Last week, I set up a time to interview our new principal, Mr. Patton for the *Eisenhower Eagle* newspaper. Today is the day. I've got my notebook, my questions lined up so I can take notes. I hope he doesn't ask about my letter to him and the letter in the *Portland Journal*. In my request for an interview, I asked to speak to him for ten minutes.

"He's a busy man. Ask for a short time," Dad suggested, "and then in ten minutes, you say, 'Well, our time is up.'"

"Why would I say that?"

"If you're asking him good questions, he'll invite you to stay longer. After that, time is his problem."

Mike helped me practice my questions. After we practiced, Mike drew a cartoon of me all nervous and dropping my papers down the storm drain.

This afternoon is interview time. I don't feel good about this. With James mad at me, Billy deported, my wrong letter quoted in the newspaper – the whole world feels bad.

While I wait to meet with Mr. Patton, I remember that conversation he had in the teachers' room. How does he watch for troublemakers, and who does he think makes trouble? That's what I really want to ask.

The school secretary knocks on Mr. Patton's door and tells him I'm there, so, now, there's no backing out.

"Come in, Gilbert," Mr. Patton says. "I received your second essay this morning. Thank you for thinking about your beliefs, and for sending it to me."

"I learned some stuff in between essays."

He nods. "You keep that up," he says. "Integrate new information into your thinking. I hope you do that all your life."

"Yes, sir."

He gestures me to a table near his desk. I sit in one low chair, and he folds his tall self into the other.

"So, why the short furniture?" I ask, and I'm already off my script.

He smiles. "When I was a kid, I sometimes got in trouble. In the principal's office, I didn't like sitting across a huge desk from some big, old guy. I didn't like when my legs dangled above the ground. I didn't like feeling I might get lost in the chair and never be found."

"You? What kind of trouble?" I ask. I'm a lousy interviewer. I can't help it, I'm curious.

He laughs, "Talking too much. All the usual stuff."

"All?"

He nods.

"What do kids get in trouble for the most?"

"Not thinking about what might happen. They do something. Then bad things happen because of what they did. It's hard to undo."

I nod, thinking about that one assignment that's become such a headache, then I remember another time I didn't think about what might happen. "Yeah. Last year, in Mister Reese's class, I leaned back in my chair. Broke the chair leg. He made me repair it."

Mr. Patton's smile fades. He glances up at something hanging on the wall of his office. I'm not sure what's up there behind me, but he studies it pretty closely. So, I glance around and see the edges of a sign.

Before I have a chance to twist far enough to read it, Mr. Patton says. "Ah, Mister Reese. I bet he helped you do the repair, too."

I feel myself lighten up, enjoying this memory. "He showed me how different wood has different strengths. And . . . and . . . what happened to Mister Reese?"

Now, I've really gone off course. Mr. Patton's eyelids go from soft crinkles to hard in a second. "Gilbert, that is a personnel matter and can't be discussed."

But I don't know when to stop. "Is he all right? Is he..."

He looks at the wall behind me again and says, "Gilbert, I'm sure you have questions we can talk about."

"Yes, sir." I didn't want to make Mr. Patton angry. But I liked Mr. Reese. I pull my notebook up and hunt for my questions.

"The first question on my list is, 'What changes would you like to see at Eisenhower School?'"

He loosens up again, and even leans on the low table. "I'd like to have every student in this school read for fun every day. Starting in January, we'll have a half hour every day when everything else stops. Teachers and kids, the principal and the cooks – everybody gets to sit down to read for a half an hour."

"What about kids who can't read yet?"

Our conversation goes on from there for another half an hour – good stuff which you can read about in the first issue of the *Eisenhower*

Eagle, Fall 1953. But I keep thinking about how tight his face became when I asked about Mr. Reese.

As I rise to leave, I glance at the thing behind me on his office wall – the thing he stared at sometimes. It's a sign with gold letters on a blue and white background. It says,

"Freedom Requires Your Search for Truth."

CHAPTER TWENTY

Essay #2
Gilbert Evans
October 5, 1953

I think now that we have given too much time and energy to hunt for possible insurgents and not enough time and energy to careful decision making. We've got problems like when to use the bomb, how to make sure people have enough to eat, and how to keep the United States a place where people can talk about ideas without being afraid.

I think having a loyalty oath makes these good things about our country impossible to keep safe.

* *

In the evening, Dad and I get into the car. We're headed out to the school-board hearing about oaths. In the car, I ask Dad, "How can a citizen like Mr. Mendoza be deported?"

Dad backs the car down the driveway, then stops. He takes a deep breath. When he answers, his voice sounds tired. "Back when you were in fifth grade, in 1950, Congress passed an act that allowed the FBI to spy on people they thought might be radicals."

"Sure," I say. "The Mc — Mc "

"McCarran Anti-Communist Act."

"Right."

"That act also gave the government the right to deport naturalized citizens – people born somewhere else who became citizens as adults." Dad starts driving toward the school board offices.

"Deport people without a trial?" I ask.

"It appears that they do it. It's not clear they have the right," Dad says.

"What did Mr. Mendoza do?"

"I understand he tried to form a union so Cargo-Car workers could ask for better pay."

"Mr. Johnson's company?"

"Yes, State Senator Johnson. A vice-president at his company accused Billy's father of being a communist."

"That's it?"

"And the FBI found international union organizing papers in his home – a group they claim is a Marxist-Communist front."

"Is it?"

"We may never know – the FBI doesn't have to prove those claims."

After that, Dad and I ride in silence. I'm thinking about Billy and how much I miss him. I always liked his laugh. Plus right before he was taken away, he started to believe he could write. He got up the courage to say what he thought.

A little later, I start to think maybe Quakers are on that list of suspected organizations.

We turn a corner and drive up the street near the School Administration building. As we get near, we see people on the next street corner. One guy holds a sign that says "No Commies Teach MY kids" Beyond his sign, I see a huge crowd in the open space, the plaza at the front of a big building. The crowd fills the space and spills into the street. I never expected this for just a school board meeting. We're here early, yet there are at least two hundred people under the street lamps on the sidewalks, and in the parking lot.

Others are strung out around the building. And a lot of them wave signs.

"No Communist Teachers!" "Deport foreigners!" "No Commie Spies in Schools!"

I see one sign that says, "Educators for Democracy."

"Dad, isn't that Mister Marvin's organization?"

"It is."

The men and women waggle their signs, and yell toward our car, but I can't understand what-all they're saying.

"Dear God," Dad says. "I hope Greg Halverson anticipated this mob."

I feel a chill, so I zip up my heavy jacket. Dad finally gets our car past the crowd and drives into the business area that surrounds the school offices. I look out the rear window and see that the car behind us can't get through the crowd at all. Dad slows down, glancing in his rear view mirror.

While I'm watching behind us, a big guy climbs onto the hood of that other car and starts jumping. He's rocking the other car up and down to scare someone inside.

"We might as well go on home, huh?" I say to Dad.

"I know who pumped them up to this," Dad says. He pulls our car over to the side, puts it in park, and turns to me. "I don't want you in this crowd. I'll take you home, and I'll come back."

"Why do you have to be here?"

"Because the members of the school board need to be safe. There may be a moment when I can help them."

I'm really cold, so I hunch down. "You can't keep them safe, Dad."

"I can't let Greg Halverson stand there alone."

"He's the one that ran for the school board," I say.

"He decided to run after discussing it with me," Dad says. "I told him I would stand with him when he proposed unwelcome change. I promised to be his ears in the community."

I shrug deeper into my jacket collar. "I planted his campaign signs all over the neighborhood. I have to be here, too, Dad."

Dad takes a deep breath and faces the steering wheel. I can tell he doesn't like this whole situation. I don't like it either, but I'm not letting him go into that crowd alone. He's way too nice. Somebody will pop him.

I open my door. "Let's go."

"Sit still a minute, Gilbert. We have to talk."

I close the door again. "What's to talk about? You're not going in there alone."

Dad smiles at me, but his smile is pretty bleak. "Did I ever tell you I love you?"

"I know that," I say, embarrassed. "Dad, those people are afraid of communists."

"And you're afraid of communists."

"Still am, some. But this mob, I'm more afraid of them."

"Good. If we're going in there, you and I have to agree on one thing."

"What's that?"

"You have to agree to stick with me. I can't be worried about where you are, or if you are safe. If that crowd gets dangerous, we have to be a unit."

"Sure, Dad. And we have to protect Sergeant Halverson."

"Okay. Let's do it." We roll out on our separate sides of the car.

About a block away, I see the big man jump down from the car hood. He waves the driver on. The people in the car drive past us.

I can see the woman's face in the passenger side. She's crying and shaking her head. The driver has his hand on her shoulder while he steers the car.

Dad turns to watch them go. When their car turns onto the busy street and speeds up, Dad sighs. We start walking into the wind and toward that big guy. I think about all that has happened to me in the last few days. I remember that conversation in the teachers' room.

"Dad," I say, "suppose I went into the school district office and asked to see a teacher's file; what would happen?"

Dad's eyebrows go up, startled. "Personnel files are private. Nobody can walk in and just look at them."

I nod.

"You have a teacher in mind?" he asks.

I shake my head 'No'. But, I say the opposite. "Yes. I want to know about Mister Reese."

Dad stops walking and turns toward me. "I'll tell you what it would have said in his file. For ten years, he was a great teacher, with a great curiosity which he gave to his students."

"Then why?"

"Mister Marvin accused him of being a Marxist apologist," Dad says. "Mister Reese admitted he'd visited Marxist meetings while he was a student at the university. The school board decided he couldn't be trusted. They fired him, just in case."

I feel like I can't breathe good. "Mister Halverson fired him, too?"

"No. Last spring, Mister Halverson ran for school board because Reese's hearing was going on in secrecy. Halverson believed that was wrong."

"Oh."

Dad puts his arm around my shoulder, and I start to warm up a little, but I still have this cold gripping my chest. I try to breathe into my jacket collar instead of inhaling wintery air. And I look ahead at that crowd. The same big fellow stops every car that comes down the street. Another man leans over and asks the driver something before they let them go farther. I wonder what they're asking.

Pretty soon we arrive at the edges of the crowd. There's a lot of noise – more noise than I thought from inside our car. They shout and wave their signs at passing cars, and even at us. We wait to cross the street. I see a couple of signs that say, "Communists Go Back Where You Came From."

I wonder where Billy Mendoza is tonight. In jail? On a boat?

We get into the crowd. The big man starts toward us, and I can't swallow. Dad pulls me close to him. A car comes down the street, and the man waves others toward us, but he goes back to his post in the street. We start worming our way toward the door, but the people he has sent shove us.

"Where do you think you're going?" one guy asks my dad.

"To the public meeting."

"Public is it?" The guy hovers over Dad, breathing heavy and smelling of sweat. "You believe in the oath?" he asks.

I notice that a few of his buddies have circled around us. I don't see any way for us to escape when they find out what Dad really thinks. So I start in "I believe . . ." Dad puts a hand on my arm. I glance up at him and stop.

He smiles at the hulking fellow, takes off his right glove, and raises his right hand as if he were swearing. Next he puts out that hand, offering to shake. "I'm Dave Evans," he says, "and this is my son, Gilbert."

I'm puzzled. This guy threatens us, yet Dad wants to meet him?

The guy frowns, then shakes hands with Dad. "Hi," he says. "We gotta stay out here. Marvin says we all go in together."

Dad nods, "That will make an impact, and I'm here to scout out the situation inside." "That so?" says another man in the circle, edging closer. "How come you decide that?"

Dad leans toward that man and says, as if toward a friend, "You remember, on the battlefield, when somebody could tell you how to avoid the mine fields and the barbed wire?"

The fellow straightens up and studies Dad. "You in Europe?" he says.

"Germany," Dad says, "From the Rhine to Berlin."

I stare at Dad. He never lies, but I also know he's never fought on a battlefield, so what's he saying?

Near the door, I see Mr. Marvin. He sees me, too. Marvin gets this huge grin on his face and comes over. The ring of men backs up to let him enter.

"Gilbert Evans," he says. "Glad to see you here."

"Hi, Mister Marvin. Is the door to the meeting open yet?"

"It is to you, Gilbert." Next he waves his arms and shouts to the crowd. "Folks! This is the young man I told you about – the one who wrote that essay."

I glance around and see all these people staring at me. They've stopped waving their signs. The fellow Dad was talking to puts his hand on Dad's shoulder. He looks at me and Dad as if we're his kind of folks.

Mr. Marvin says, "Go on in, Gilbert. Be sure to sign up as a speaker on the loyalty oath."

Dad and I start to go in the left hand door, but Mr. Marvin puts his arm out to stop Dad.

"Not you, sir," he says. "A lotta these people were here before you." He gestures at the sign-carrying crowd.

"Oh," Dad says very loudly to the whole crowd. "I didn't realize you all were ready to come inside. My son and I can wait for you."

I move back next to Dad. I can see that Mr. Marvin didn't expect we were together.

"Mister Marvin, this is my Dad, David Evans," I say.

"Uh . . . Well, nice to meet you Mister Evans," he says walking us toward the door.

"Actually, these folks have a job to do for a while out here before they go in and . . ."

Back in the crowd, I hear a voice. "I know him – that Pacifist guy, the Quaker fellow from around the block."

I glance over my shoulder and see Mr. Stockman. I can't believe he's saying this stuff about Dad. I thought he and I were friends.

Mr. Marvin keeps pulling us toward the door. Suddenly, I notice that Mr. Stockman has grabbed Senator Johnson and he's pointing at us. He'll get us jumped on, for sure.

I have to get us in before Mr. Marvin hears Mr. Stockman.

"My Dad's just a music teacher," I say to Mister Marvin, "you know trumpets, tubas, drums…"

Dad looks at me, a puzzled wrinkle in his forehead, but I grab Dad's hand and say, "Thanks, Sir," to Mr. Marvin. I pull Dad through the door.

The door thumps behind us. Dad pulls his hand loose from mine. "Gilbert?" he asks.

I figure it's the "Just a music teacher". That's what hurt his feelings.

"Look," I say. "I'm sorry, but Senator Johnson gets in this and we're stuck out there in a fight. Besides, how subversive can you be while playing Sousa Marches?"

"You'd be amazed," he says, taking off his gloves.

"Don't get me wrong," I say. "I like Sousa and all them, but it's not like Mister Marvin and Senator Johnson should worry about you overthrowing the government."

"I can see that you don't worry about my radical ways," he says.

"Right. Let's go to this meeting."

He stuffs his gloves in his pocket. Outside, we can hear the crowd still yelling. Dad says to me, "Gilbert, how did you feel in that crowd?"

I'm off guard, so I say straight out, "Afraid."

"Me, too," he said. I'm relieved because he was so friendly with those guys I thought he didn't realize what was going on out there.

"Dad, if they find out you're against the oath, we're in big trouble."

"Count on it. They will find out."

CHAPTER TWENTY-ONE

It's about six-thirty. The meeting will start soon and there are lots of people already inside. We first enter a lobby where there are two sets of double-wide doors, about thirty feet apart. One set of doors is closed, but the left set is open. We get in a line. I see some people from the neighborhood, like cranky Mrs. Moriarty who lives behind Mrs. Silverberg.

"'Scuse me. 'Scuse me," she keeps saying. "I am the board secretary, so you people need to let me in right now."

Dad looks at me, "Charming," he says.

I get a grip, so I don't laugh out loud. And then I think about what Mr. Stockman said. Does he know I'm David Evans' son? Has he been friendly so he can get information out of me?

Eventually, the line takes us through the left door into a huge room. Once we're inside the auditorium, I can see that there are two aisles, each about six feet wide. A lot of people are milling about in those two paths from the doors toward the front of the room. Between the aisles, there is a big center section of seats. People stand in those aisles, gesturing at each other and talking loudly.

One woman near us says to a friend, "My son's high school teacher expects him to read essays by some German fellow."

"Not Karl Marx?" a man asks.

"Mencken," the woman says, "that's the man's name. H.L. Mencken."

Dad walks up to her and says, "Hello Mrs. Shoemaker. I'm glad to see you here tonight."

The lady looks surprised, but pleased to see Dad. "Oh, Mr. Evans, my Joseph loves your band class at Portland State College."

"I'm delighted to hear it. I couldn't help overhearing your worry. I assure you that Mr. Mencken was born in Baltimore. He is safe."

"Well, if you're sure."

Dad nods. "Very sure, Mrs. Shoemaker."

"Well, that's a relief."

The man says, "You got to read everything those teachers give your kids these days."

"Oh, I do," she says. "Believe me."

A few minutes later, Dad and I walk down the aisle. Dad whispers, "Her son says their name was Schumacher until 1936. Her husband's parents arrived from Nuremburg in 1929."

I laugh, but Dad puts a hand on my arm. "Fear is in this crowd for many reasons, and we need to be aware of that fact."

*   *

There are probably a thousand wooden seats in this auditorium. And down in front, there is a high stage. I thought the school board met around a cafeteria table where they hire teachers, and custodians. Or they buy new textbooks. I never expected this big meeting room.

But, big as this place is, it's packed. All those people outside, I can't figure out where they expect to sit. Maybe there are folding chairs somewhere, ready for an overflow crowd.

The truth is, I hope the big crowd will stay out there and wave their signs, shout, and never come in. I didn't like the way they stopped cars and how they circled around us when we arrived.

On the front stage sits a long, wooden desk. Arranged on that desk, I can see embossed signs with the names of the school board members. The sign in the middle says, "Gregory Halverson, Board Chair". I knew Mike's dad was on the school board, but I didn't know he was the head of it. Sergeant Halverson comes home from war. He starts a company to build homes. But at night, he runs the school district.

A lot of people still stand in the aisle. One man says to another, "It's a good thing Marvin's group is so organized."

The other man nods, "This school board better do its job."

I want to wait and hear what job he expects the school board to do, but Dad nudges me toward seats in the center section near the left-hand aisle. We sit about halfway down the aisle where we can face the stage straight on. Dad saves the seat next to him.

"For Mike," he says. "I told his dad we'd be with him."

"Where's Mike now?"

"Helping his dad backstage."

Nearby, all up and down that same aisle stands a long line of people who aren't looking for seats. I point at that line. "What are they doing?"

"Those people want to speak about loyalty oaths. They sign up before the meeting starts."

A microphone stands at the front of the left aisle, and near it is a table with a notebook that people are writing in. That must be the list of speakers. I bet they will never get through that list in one night. Mrs. Moriarty, secretary to the school board, is getting people signed in. Mrs. Moriarty is the lady with a raccoon family under her porch.

We're facing a long meeting – longer even than Friends Meeting for Worship. The wooden chairs look hard, so I take off my coat and fold it under me before I sit. I study the people already sitting down. I don't know most of them. And most of them look angry.

Mr. Stockman comes to the speakers' line and stands there at the tail end for a minute. "Can't you hurry this line" he shouts. "Just sign your names and get on with it."

Mrs. Moriarty shouts back, "Hold your horses, Stockman."

Somebody else laughs, "Hold your horse, Stockman! That's a good one!"

Next to me, Dad groans. "What a way to make a man angry."

Mr. Stockman shouts, "Go to hell, Mrs. Crow-farty." Then he turns on his heel and stomps off to a seat on the other side of the auditorium.

As I watch him, I notice that close to the front, Elizabeth Gray sits with some adults. The lady with the blond hair must be her mom. And over there, near Elizabeth, is Rick Johnson's mom and an empty seat, probably saved for Rick's dad, Senator Johnson. I hardly ever see Mrs. Johnson come out of the house any farther than their porch flower boxes.

At the back of the auditorium, the door squeals open. I turn around to see Mr. Marvin come in by himself. He greets people in the audience as if he knows most of them, and then he stands behind the last row, near one of the doors.

Mrs. Hill, our history teacher sits in the back near the other door. In fact, I see most of the teachers from our school are back there. Mr. O'Connor gets up and walks forward to sign up to speak. Dad stands up and motions me to get in that line with him as if he wants my company while he waits to sign up. We leave our coats to save our seats.

As we stand in line, Dad asks me, "Do you want to testify about oath taking?"

"Me? I'm a kid."

"Your words were used to justify this idea. I thought perhaps you had strong feeling on this matter."

"Dad, there won't be time for a kid to talk. Look at this crowd."

"Well," he says, gazing around the room. "Do as the Spirit moves you." Dad always sounds like a Quaker. He might as well go back to using thee and thine.

It is my essay Mr. Marvin used. I ought to make a speech to stand with him. But, I didn't like the feeling outside, and I no longer trust Mr. Marvin. His big crowd was not 'organized' at all. Those people are on the edge of something, and it seemed like Mr. Marvin encouraged their mean ways.

I move forward with dad and the line of speakers. Dad greets people he knows. I watch most of the school board members come in and take their seats on the stage. Later, Mr. Halverson and a policeman come in. On the way across the stage, Mr. Halverson talks to the police officer. That policeman nods several times about whatever they're discussing, and then the officer goes back off the stage.

Mr. Halverson's blue suit looks very neat. Not a lick of plaster dust or paint on him anywhere.

Dad and I arrive at the front of the speakers' line. Mr. O'Connor turns from making his signature in the notebook and he smiles at me. I can hear people behind me gasp. I know they're seeing Mr. O'Connor's scars. His eyelid tweaks for a moment, but he keeps his gaze on me.

"Evening, Gilbert," he says. "You have a fine writing style."

"Thank you, sir," I say. Fine writing style. That's what Mom said. I don't know about Mr. O'Connor, but I do know what Mom meant: Sometimes style can get you in deep doo-doo.

After Mr. O'Connor returns to his seat, I decide to sign up to witness about oaths. I'm feeling like I have to say something because my essay was in the news. I just hope they run out of time before me.

Later, I sit in my chair next to the aisle, thinking about all the people in this room, and the mob outside. When I wrote my first essay, I never thought it would become so important.

Mike stops beside us. Dad scoots over to the third seat so Mike can sit next to me. Mike sort of hops over me and then slumps down in the second chair. Right off, he starts drawing stuff and bumping my elbow.

Me, I'm trying to figure out what to say if I have to use my turn. I squirm around because this wooden seat, even with my coat, is very hard and pokes into my bones.

Finally, I find a piece of scrap paper in my pocket. I'm scribbling on it when Mike hands me a sheet of his sketchpad.

"You need more paper," he says.

"Uh. Thanks. But I'm definitely keeping this short."

I fold his big paper in half and then concentrate on writing my ideas, until all at once, I smell something – a smell I recognize from the hills outside Neustadt. Lavender flowers. Glancing up, I nearly bump heads with Elizabeth Gray. She pulls back quickly, but holds a paper toward me.

"I saw you sign up to speak," she says. "I hope you'll read this before you do that."

It's her essay. The big F is still slashed across it. I'm puzzled, but I take it. Outside, we hear a big cheer. Elizabeth winces. She glances up the aisle toward the doors. Then she takes a deep breath and looks at me again.

"Did you know he was going to use your essay in the newspaper?" she asks.

I can tell Mike has stopped drawing. It feels like Dad and everybody else in the room is watching us. I'm not able to think about anything except all the colors there are in blond hair – and what I'll do if somebody threatens Elizabeth the way that big goon threatened the lady in the car.

"Did you know about the letter to the editor?" Mike asks, nudging my elbow.

"Uh. Nuh, nuh... no. I di... didn't."

"I'm glad," she says. Then she places her pointer finger on the paper. Her finger is long and graceful.

"Uh." I gather her paper into my chest and look her in the eyes. "I'll read it right off."

"Good," she says and straightens up. Suddenly, Dad leans over and asks, "Does Gilbert have your permission to quote from the essay?"

I'm thinking, it's her paper.

She says. "Certainly, Mister Evans." Next, she looks at me. "Do what you think is right." And then she heads off down the aisle toward her folks.

I don't dare glance at Mike or Dad because my face is hot. I guess they think Elizabeth is something to me.

Dad says, "F grade? Who is the teacher of that class?"

Mike answers. "Mr. Elias Marvin." Dad nods.

I just lay her paper on top of my notes and start reading. Pretty quickly, I can tell that Elizabeth Gray knows how to make her points, and she pulls no punches. She tells Mr. Marvin that his assignment is designed to scare students, to make them agree with his point of view.

She says the founding Fathers had a good idea when they added the Bill of Rights to the Constitution. It protects citizens during times when they disagree with each other, or with the government, or with a teacher. She tells Mr. Marvin a loyalty oath only pretends to protect us. The truth and our chance to talk about ideas – that's what really protects us.

She saw this right off.

Behind us, I hear another yell – not really a cheer, but a lot of raucous noise. The auditorium door opens again. Most of us turn around to look. Mr. Marvin lets in Senator Johnson. He walks down front to sit next to his wife, Rick's mom.

Dad leans across Mike and whispers to both of us, "I don't like the look of this. Mister Marvin will let in that whole crowd at some point, and then we'll have a mob on our hands."

Mike whispers, "Dad had a man assigned to the door. I don't know what happened to him. Maybe I'll go back and do his job."

"No," Dad says. "I promised your Dad to keep you in here, both of you boys."

"Well, then what?" I ask.

"I'm figuring," Dad says. "You be ready to work with me if something happens."

Mike and I nod. Mike goes back to drawing, but I can't think about my speech because I'm listening for that door to open again.

Mr. Halverson taps his gavel. "This meeting of the Portland Public School Board is now open."

I notice the sign-up book has been moved to a space near Mr. Halverson.

Mr. Halverson explains how the hearing will proceed. He says each person has two minutes to get to the point. No one can give their time to another. Mr. Halverson is good at this stuff. You can tell people believe he'll cut them off at two minutes sharp.

The first person up is a lady I've seen in the grocery store. She says, "We want our children to be safe in the classroom." She says other stuff, but that's her basic message.

Next is Senator Johnson. "My boys are students in our public schools. And like Mrs. Woodruff, before me, I worry about those who teach students to question the rules, teachers who sow discontent, who lay the groundwork for a Revolution in our lovely democracy."

I bet Rick wouldn't know if a teacher taught knitting or sowed discontent. Rick pays no attention in class.

Senator Johnson talks on and on about how bad things are for his two boys in the public school system. He seems to be winding up when he says, "We must insist that our children's teachers swear allegiance to all that is good in our way of living. They must give up their questioning, stop any communistic tendencies, and teach democracy."

Mr. Halverson leans toward his chairman's microphone, but Senator Johnson raises his arm and plunges on. "Students don't need to ask 'Why' about everything. They must learn to be good citizens, doing what God wills."

I glance at my dad. From his face, I can't tell if he agrees with Senator Johnson. But deep down, I think my dad wants me to ask 'Why?' Plus, he urges me to listen to an inner voice and learn what God wills for myself.

The senator seems ready to go way beyond his two minutes, when Mr. Halverson breaks in. "Thank you Senator Johnson. We appreciate your willingness to speak tonight. Next is Mrs. Pritchard."

Senator Johnson takes a deep breath. I know he is going to say more, but the next lady steps close to the microphone and smiles up at him.

Mr. Halverson says, "Mrs. Pritchard . . .."

Senator Johnson hunkers over the microphone, "Halverson, you shut off debate because you don't want these people to hear the truth."

At that moment, Mr. Marvin opens the back door. His sign-waving troops start to crowd inside. They aren't looking for seats. They churn around, buzzing like hornets. Then some of them begin to stomp down the aisle, shouting – you can't for sure tell what they're shouting, but the din in the room makes hearing impossible.

As the mob starts filling the back and the aisle, I notice several men stand up from different places all over the auditorium. The people already in the auditorium seem to rattle their seats. I think they must want to race to the exit for safety. Instead, a lot of them get up to join the crowd. One man starts to chant. "Commie! Commie!"

At that moment, Dad stands up and steps around Mike's legs. As he passes in front of me, he bends over and says, "Stay here. I'll be right back. Speak when you get the chance – if you get the chance."

He starts to climb over me too, but I see the mob coming toward him, and I grab his jacket. "You said stick together."

"This changes things", he says, and he climbs past me toward the aisle. "You have to stay. I have to be a band leader." He gets into the aisle and starts marching in place.

"Drum for me, Gilbert," he says, and I glare at him.

"Dad, you made me promise. Now you pull this."

"I need you," he says. "Be my drum."

His drum. Suddenly, I get it. We are sticking together. I turn around and pull my jacket down as I slide onto the floor. I start drumming on the wooden seat, using the cadence Dad teaches all his drumming students for the opening of a march.

Pump-pum!

Pump-pum!

Para-diddle, para-diddle,

Pump-pum!

The shouting mob is almost on Dad when Mike hands him a big piece of drawing paper. I can't see what it says on there, but Dad glances at it, smiles and holds it in the air over his head like a banner. The print is facing forward. Behind Dad, the mob crowds down the aisle toward us, waving signs and shouting.

I keep drumming and say to Mike, "Dad can turn any mob into a marching band, but he needs drummers to help."

Mike sinks to the floor next to me and imitates my drumming rhythm, two drums make a pretty good racket. Dad marches slowly toward the stage with the whole crowd behind him.

"Hey!"

I barely can hear the voice, but by sitting tall, I can see up over the back of my aisle seat. "Hey, stop that," Mr. Marvin shouts. I see he's at the back of the aisle, but he's pushing through his crowd to get to Dad.

I drum louder.

Pum, doodle

Pum, doodle

Pum, doodle

Boom.

Mike follows me into the big booms. Marvin's voice becomes part of all the noise, but he's still working toward Dad. Something holds him up for a moment, but then he seems to yank and start moving forward again, but slowly.

The crowd is now passing my chair. I have a hard time keeping the rhythm because their feet are stomping and uneven. They're far from organized, and over the seat-back I see that disorganization is a good thing. So far, Mr. Marvin can't get through as fast as he wants.

Some of the people are cheering him, slapping him on the back, but the biggest obstacle to his forward motion is one short fellow in dirty overalls who has wrapped his arms around Mr. Marvin like he wants to dance with him. I see that face. It's Maximillian, Emperor of the World, my friend from the Gulch.

I glance out into the aisle from my end-of-the-row floor space, and I hear that the people now march with our drum rhythm. As the crowd's feet beat out the march with us, Max has got his arm around Mr. Marvin's waist and has grabbed him by the belt, doing a kind of line dance with him. I don't think Mr. Marvin wants to be part of the fun.

Max sings something that sounds like, "Hava Nageela. Hava Nageela." I can't make out the rest, but it looks like Max loves the dance. Plus, he's slowing Mr. Marvin down.

Suddenly, I hear other drumming coming from somewhere else in the auditorium – a kind of jazzy syncopation based on our steady beat.

Who could that be?

Several people around us start pounding our rhythm on the backs of their seats. They're having a whale of a time. Me – I'm working up a sweat.

I glance up, and see Mrs. Hill march past me. She winks. She's got one hand banging out my rhythm on a hard book she is carrying. Crowded around her are about fifteen other older ladies, all of them clogging up the aisle between Max and Mr. Marvin and my dad. Those ladies all clap the rhythm or beat it on their purses. I don't get why, but I'm glad for their help.

Next to me, Mike says,

> "Ladies
> Auxiliary,
> Longshore-
> man's
> Union."

I glance once more at the last of Mrs. Hill's ladies, and keep drumming.

"How do you know that?" I ask.

Mike answers, while beating Pum! Pum, Pum, Pum.

> "Joint
> meets.
> Dad's
> warehouse,
> with Carpenters'
> Union
> ladies."

I glance at him. "Can you talk like that all day – in rhythm?" He laughs and does a drum rolling para-diddle.

At that moment, Mr. Marvin leans over me, screaming in my ear. "Gilbert, what the hell … heck… do you think you're doing?"

I glance up and keep drumming. "Marches make people patriotic," I say.

"What?" he shouts.

"Loyal," Mike shouts for me. "Red, white and blue."

"This is a protest," he shouts.

"Sure is," I say.

"Good crowd," Mike calls to him.

"That your Dad?" Mr. Marvin yells, pointing down toward the front.

I nod. "Loves a parade."

"Why?"

Next to me, Mike keeps drumming and says, "Ours is not to question 'Why?' Ours is but to do or die." Mr. Marvin frowns.

Mike says, "I quote Senator Johnson." And then he smiles at Mr. Marvin as if he's done the best thing.

Mr. Marvin glances down the aisle toward the stage and then leans over me again. "Do about eight more beats. Then stop."

"Yeah?" I say.

"Right," Mike says.

And Mr. Marvin starts on down the aisle, but Max is right beside him. Mr. Marvin shouts something at Max. Max looks all startled and hurt, but as Mr. Marvin walks away from him, Max glances back at me and gives me two-fists in the air.

And behind us, the sound of all the feet crescendos, thunder in a kettledrum – the mob is marching across the stage.

"Is your Dad safe?" I ask Mike.

Mike glances up and over the seat behind him.

"Board members

"Standing, and

"Clapping

"our Rhythm"

Maybe Mike really can talk like that forever. I ask, "What'd you write on that sign?"

"Big word

"says 'Freedom'

"Small words

'From Sheep'.

Uh-oh.

My hands sting. No way am I quitting. I want that crowd moving. I hope Mr. Marvin doesn't see that sign before they are out the door and long gone.

A few moments later, I see Dad again. Now he's marching up the far aisle and heading toward the door that leads out of the auditorium. I wonder if he's seen our syncopated drummer over there.

One man in the audience stands up, confronting Dad. It's our neighbor, Mr. Stockman, who called Dad a Pacifist when we were outside. Mr. Stockman steps in the aisle and grabs Dad's arms down. Dad smiles at him, and hands him the sign Mike made. I hear Dad's voice yelling so Mr. Stockman can hear. Dad's a great singer and a horn blower, with a voice that carries.

"No communist sheep here, that's for sure." Dad says.

Mr. Stockman looks at the sign. He frowns.

Dad yells again, "You're a born leader, Stockman. Go ahead and lead."

The man studies the sign, then he studies Dad's excited face. Mr. Stockman turns, he holds that sign above his head. He steps high, like the leader of a blue-ribbon band, trumpeting down Multnomah

Avenue for the Portland Rose Festival Parade. He holds Mike's sign as if it says, "Commies Go Home".

Dad steps right in behind him, keeping the march going up the aisle.

Mr. Marvin catches up with them. Dad turns his charm on, smiling at Mr. Marvin who is yelling something at him. Dad leans in a little farther, like he can't quite make out what Mr. Marvin wants.

Mr. Marvin gestures back toward me. I figure he's telling Dad to get me to stop, but there are more people than me banging on seats by now, and that won't stop on a dime.

Behind Mr. Stockman, people lift their protest signs up and down to our beat. They chant in rhythm, too. Their chant has been shortened 'Go Home, Go Home.'

Left, Right, Left, Right, with the added excitement of that syncopation – by the drummer I can't see. What started out as chaos is now organized. But I'm worried about what will happen when Mr. Stockman reaches the doors.

Even worse, what will happen to Dad if he gets them out the doors?

I hope Dad will crumple that sign Mr. Stockman now carries. Mr. Marvin for sure would understand what those words really mean.

Across the room, that syncopation drummer works with us to speed up a little and get this crowd out of here.

"Go Home, Go Home," Mike shouts with them as he drums a little faster.

My fingers grow numb. In another two minutes, I finally hear the blessed sound of the back auditorium door swinging open. We drum until the last foot shuffles out. I hear the door swing closed. I hear the sound of a lock clicking. I close my eyes and do one more set of Paradiddles. Rubbing my fingers back to life, I sit on the floor, while the other drumming all over the auditorium slows and peters out.

I'm thinking that Dad is out there with the crowd. I haven't any idea what's happening. But I know Dad. He's been planning while he marched. If he's out there, I bet Dad will shake hands with them all. He'll thank them for coming, and for participating in this impressive show of citizenship. He'll probably say something about how cold it is and how he hopes they have a safe journey home. If he's really bold, he might even offer to collect their signs 'for the next time'.

But if Mr. Marvin is out there ...

Mr. Halverson calls the meeting to order once again, and says, we can continue hearing testimony. I stand up while everyone else is re-settling themselves. I glance back at the door. Two big guys stand at each door like guards. I don't know who they are.

Where is Dad?

Just a music teacher, I said. What an idiot I've been.

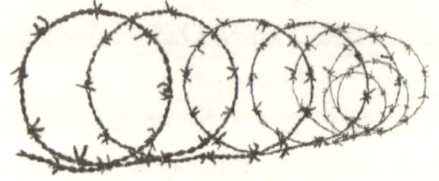

CHAPTER TWENTY-TWO

I'm stunned by my own stupidness. How could I have been so blind to my dad's courage? And blind to what other people were trying to get me to believe?

I used to soak in all I read in the newspapers. I remember shivers of fear when I cut an article out of Dad's New York Times.

Last week, the Senate Internal Security subcommittee called on states to start full-scale inquiries into communism among teachers. It said a preliminary investigation had shown that many hundreds of the nations' teachers were Communists.

New York Times, January 19, 1953

I pinned it on the wall next to my desk with the rest of my news collection. I didn't think then, how easy it is to accuse, and how impossible to prove innocence. It was in the news, so it was true.

And now my Dad is out there in a crowd that believes what I believed.

Mr. Halverson bangs his chairman's gavel once and says, "We're glad to see so many citizens out on such a cold evening. Now let us continue the hearing."

"I've got to go out, find Dad," I say.

Mike grabs my sleeve. "My dad sent one of his guys out there with your dad – a guy from the company."

"Two against that mob?"

"Better than you butting in there, Hot Head."

"I'm not . . ." But I know that I am.

Mike's eyebrows go up in a question, so I stop talking. He says, "Well, your dad said you should testify if you got the chance."

I'm worried, but I sit down, ready to jump up if I hear anything from outside.

Next to me, Mike is drawing very fast, but I can't see what he's doing.

Mr. Halverson says, "I want to remind everyone that each speaker has two minutes."

Mrs. Pritchard has her turn, talking about keeping radical new ideas away from our children.

All at once I notice that Maximillian, Emperor of the World, is at the microphone. His plaid shirt and his overalls are no cleaner than the last time I saw him at George Fox House.

I'm afraid of what he'll say – afraid these people won't understand he's really a nice guy. Those big men in the auditorium, the ones I saw before, stand up again. And next to the microphone, another big guy stands.

Mr. Halverson raises his hands, and then brings them slowly down to his table top. Somehow, that move gets everyone to calm down. All of the standing men sit down again, except the guy near the microphone.

I glance at Mike and ask, "Who are all those guys?"

"School district police."

Good planning, Mr. Halverson.

"Thank you, Harold," Mr. Halverson says to the big man who is next to Maximillian and the microphone. I've seen that guy working at Mr. Halverson's warehouse.

When the man, Harold, sits down, I realize Mr. Halverson not only has the school district police here tonight, but he also brought his own bouncers, and he just gave one of them the signal not to bounce Maximillian.

Really good planning.

Mr. Halverson looks at his list of speakers and says, "You are Mr. Million?"

"Yes, sir," Max says. "I'd like to speak about oaths and such."

Mr. Halverson smiles at him, "Go right ahead, sir."

Max leans into the mike and squints up toward Mr. Halverson. He clears his throat once. The resulting explosion makes him realize he's too close, so he backs up and then leans over.

Once he feels he's got the distance right, he says, "People who spy, can easily lie. So I say Fie! On oaths."

Someone in the audience snickers, but Mr. Halverson keeps his attention on Max.

Max says, "If a man don't act true, his oath's rotten stew. So I say P. U. on oaths."

Max stands there looking up at the school board. The board members glance toward Mr. Halverson, puzzled looks on their crinkled foreheads. I can see that one of them is starting to laugh, but Mr. Halverson glares at that board member, so the man stops himself by coughing into his handkerchief.

Mr. Halverson nods to Max.

Max says, "That's all she wrote." Mr. Halverson smiles at him.

Max laughs. And finally, the whole audience can laugh with him. Amid a wave of guffawing, he turns on his boot heel and starts back up our aisle. As he walks past me, he puts a hand on my shoulder and says, "Ya got rhythm, I'll say that."

Mr. Halverson says, "Missus Whitmore is next."

A lady near us jumps up, and heads to the front. She very carefully doesn't touch the microphone, probably thinking of Max and germs.

Mrs. Whitmore says she wants teachers to sign an oath. "And if we ever find they lied, we fire them for perjury."

And so it goes through about thirty more speakers. Most parents want this oath.

I'm listening for any sign that I should be outside. Jumpy and sweating, I should have gone out there as soon as he marched up the second aisle.

Mike looks at me and shakes his head. "Your Dad is calm. If anyone can pull this off, it's him."

So, I take a deep breath. A few speakers later, Mike leans over and shows me one of his cartoons – a crowd of people with mouths and eyes wide open, screaming in fear. They run toward Sergeant Halverson. He stands with his back to the cartoon readers. His arms are raised, to stop the stampede. But the front of the crowd is pushing Sergeant Halverson over. Off to one side of the cartoon stands a Red Cross Ambulance. Two guys run toward Halverson carrying a stretcher. The front stretcher carrier has a nametag – David Evans'. It even looks like my Dad.

Mike adds long cow horns to the heads of the front row of stampeding men.

I nod. That mad-bull mob tried to run over this meeting. Like them, I've been afraid of communists ever since I was little. But today, I was more afraid of the mass of people.

I think about all that has happened this week. I've been afraid of foreign, odd Mrs. Silverberg ever since she moved here – but Justine feels safe with her. And Justine knows that old lady's life story.

I remember what James told me this morning, "People attack the unions as radical because union people want a better life. Let me tell you Negroes want a life, too. Does that make us communists? Or just 'Uppity?'"

Mrs. Hill and her union ladies helped us keep this meeting from turning dangerous. And the men here for Mr. Halverson – union guys protecting their boss? They help make a safe meeting for all these people. Maybe some union people are communists, but these people here . . .?

I've got a lot of notes on my piece of paper. Since the mob left, I've started rewriting with new ideas. Mike hands me a second piece of drawing paper. After a few minutes, I finish scribbling new notes. But I'm so worried about Dad that I plan to get up and make it look like I might go speak. Instead, I'll go right up that aisle and outside. I can't stand this not knowing what's happening.

All over the auditorium, I hear people whisper, so I look up. Mr. O'Connor is at the microphone. I know they think he's ugly. I can tell by the tightness in the back of his neck that he knows, too. I wish they could see what I see. In his classroom, it doesn't take five minutes to stop being aware of those scars and start liking him.

He leans down to speak. "Mr. Chairman, I saw what happened in Germany when people gave up their rights in order to buy safety. The safety the Germans bought by keeping silent under Hitler, that was a trap. Discussing ideas, agreeing to disagree, yet to keep talking, that's our responsibility as citizens in a democracy. Out of fear, we could give up our freedom of speech. We might hope to save our skin, but we would instead have purchased slavery."

Mr. O'Connor touches his face with his scarred hand and continues. "And, in the long run, as you can see, such bargains cannot even save your skin."

There is sudden laughter as the crowd realizes he's made a joke about his scars. The laughers are embarrassed. Some are shushed by their neighbors, so a silence follows as Mr. O'Connor turns to go to his seat. He keeps his gaze on the wall behind the crowd, but I know he is aware. I think he wanted the laughter, to loosen everyone up about how he looks. It's the shushing, and the silence that make him stiff.

It's my turn on that list. I'll get up and go back to find Dad.

As if he reads my mind, Mike says, "Your Dad wants you to speak."

I pretend that's my plan. I shove myself up, and grab my notes. Mr. O'Connor still walks up the aisle toward me. He nods to me and keeps walking past. I glance back after him, and I see Dad standing just inside the door, right next to Mr. Marvin. Dad has a cut over one eye, but he smiles at me and nods, and waves for me to go to the microphone.

I glance down at what's left of my notes. I still have Elizabeth's essay clutched in my hand. For that, I'm glad, because now that Dad is here, I have something to say.

"Mister Gilbert Evans," Mr. Halverson calls.

CHAPTER TWENTY-THREE

I arrive at the microphone and lean toward it. Then I remember Maximillian and the microphone noise, so I stand up straight. "I am a Quaker," I say. "We have a belief that a man's honest actions show he is honest. Taking an oath is like admitting that outside the oath, at other times, he might be a liar."

Great, I think. Now, they are sure I'm a Commie Quaker Pacifist.

I take a deep breath and plunge on. "In the first week of school, I wrote an essay. I had been listening to Senator McCarthy on the radio. What he said made me afraid Russia might take over. So when Mister Marvin asked us to write about loyalty oaths, I thought we should have oaths, at that time."

There's sweat running down my sides.

"Recently, because Mister Marvin liked my essay so much, he asked me to be the editor of the school newspaper. Today at school, I told him I wanted some of the class members to interview kids and teachers, and help write the school news. He said those writers, and one really good cartoonist, come from suspect families.

"He decided they were suspect because their essays disagreed with mine, and with him, about loyalty oaths. But disagreeing doesn't make you a subversive or even suspect."

Someone in the audience hisses. Mr. Halverson hits the gavel once.

I forge ahead. "Last year, I was a student of a really good teacher. That teacher taught us to understand our country's Constitution. We memorized the Bill of Rights. We learned how our country works – how a democracy works. "Mister Reese believed in our country. But your school board fired him because back in college he visited a few meetings before he decided communism wouldn't work.

"Where is the justice in that?"

Quick! Find that spot in Elizabeth's paper. There it is.

"In an essay against oaths, one of the best writers in our class wrote:

"At the end of the Constitutional Convention, Benjamin Franklin once told a reporter 'We have given you a Democracy, if you can keep it.'

"Elizabeth Gray's last paragraph reads: 'When we demand loyalty oaths in place of freedom of speech, we give up on Democracy. Maybe we gain some feeling of safety for a short time. Maybe. But the price is too high.'"

"I agree with Elizabeth Gray. Now, I no longer want to give up my friends' right to disagree with me, or with our teacher. Let's judge our friends, and our teachers, by their actions. The question should not be 'Have they ever thought communism might work?'

"The real question is 'Have they ever done anything to destroy our government?'

"And if we accuse anyone of trying to destroy our government, we should have to have real evidence and a real trial to prove it, not some school board just firing someone for what he might think."

My two minutes must be up. I better leave the microphone.

"Please vote against oaths. Please judge us all on our actions instead."

When I turn up the aisle, Dad seems calm, but his smile is real big. Near him, Mr. Marvin stands, glowering at me. Both are inside and both safe.

And I just tossed my editors' job on the burn pile.

Across the room, Elizabeth beams at me. And up the aisle a few rows, Mr. O'Connor is trying to smile, too, but his face can't quite do it right.

Plopping down next to Mike, I know I said the truth.

Mike shoves something in my hand. It's another cartoon. He's drawn me as a dinky person, shaking my fist at a huge balloon puppet with the brushy eyebrows and the swoopy nose of Senator Joseph McCarthy. The balloon floats high overhead. Out of its mouth come the words:

"I've got you on the list . . ."

*   *

Dad slowly walks down the aisle behind Mr. Marvin. I can tell Dad's hurting by the way he holds his arms close to his chest. As he bends over to sit next to me, he takes a quick gasping breath. His skin is pale.

Mr. Marvin walks up to the microphone. Dad swipes at that cut on his forehead. I want to know where else he is hurt, but when I lean over to ask, he puts his finger to his lips.

Mr. Marvin smiles at the audience and then over at me, as if I hadn't said he accused my friends and other people with no real reason.

I stare back.

Mr. Marvin speaks with quiet calm. "The truth is," he says, "we are still at war – a cold and calculating war. And the enemy sends trained spies to our shores. He recruits and indoctrinates our students, planning to use the hidden enemy among us to get his way."

The audience rumbles.

"Russia threatens to seduce our children when they go away to places like Corbett College. We have to make certain these Russian Communist exports do not threaten the impressionable youngsters in our elementary schools, as well."

Several people behind me clap, and then others in the crowd follow their lead. Mr. Halverson raises the chairman's gavel, but it is Mr. Marvin's raised hand that brings the crowd back to order.

That moment reminds us all that Mr. Halverson may have brought the police and his own bouncers, but Mr. Marvin brought his own audience. He leans into the microphone.

"I am certain that you gentlemen will vote to make this oath a reality. Thank you for your attention."

Mr. Marvin turns from the microphone. The audience cheers.

Not waiting for complete silence, Mr. Halverson says, "Our last speaker has given testimony. We thank you all for giving your views. Sharing our concerns and ideas is the hallmark of our democratic government." A hiss sings through the crowd.

"What's going on?" I ask. "Why are they angry at Mister Halverson?"

Mike answers. "They want to have their say, but they didn't want you to have yours."

Dad's smile is tight around the eyes. He studies Mike as if becoming aware of someone he hadn't known before.

Mr. Halverson brings down his gavel. "Thank you for participating so thoughtfully. This meeting is adjourned."

The nine board members gather their papers to leave. The crowd begins to exit, too.

But Senator Johnson grabs the microphone and says. "You should vote in public."

One of the board members glances at Mr. Halverson and starts back toward his chair.

Mr. Halverson leans over and speaks into his microphone.

"It was announced that we would hold two more hearings, in other parts of the city. We will listen to everyone, deliberate, and then vote. The school district will have our recommendation after all of the hearings."

Most people get up to leave even though Senator Johnson starts a speech. His wife puts her hand on his arm in an effort to shush him. He glares at her, swings his arm back.

I'm certain he's going to hit his wife. But before anything can happen, Mr. Halverson's bouncer grabs the senator's hand, brings it down with swift force, as if about to shake it.

He says, "Sir, I'm amazed that I have a chance to see your work in real life and not just read about you in the news."

Senator Johnson blinks. Mrs. Johnson backs away from her husband. The bouncer still shakes Johnson's hand and smiles.

"I'll be keeping a watch for you at future meetings," the man says to Johnson.

Senator Johnson tries to smile, but he's angry at being stopped from speaking, or stopped from hitting. I can't tell which.

Finally, the senator says, "I'll see you at the meetings." He turns to his wife, grabbing her elbow and pushing her up the aisle.

Next to me, Mike lets out a whistle, and Dad sits back down in his seat. There are people who want to get out of our row, but Dad seems dazed. So, the people decide to go out the other way. Mike looks at me, jerking his head in a question toward my dad.

"Dad?" I say.

"That man is a born Quaker," Dad says. "I wonder where Greg Halverson found him." "Who's a Quaker?" I ask.

Mike answers again. "Our meeting bouncer, Mister Harold Burleigh. He's Dad's construction foreman. Actually, he's an Episcopalian."

Dad smiles at Mike. "Actions speak." Mike laughs.

The auditorium is nearly empty, so I ask, "Dad, where else are you hurt?"

Dad touches his forehead. "A few bruises on my chest, and a cut on my leg. As the doors shut behind us, Mr. Stockman realized he'd been locked out. He has a quick temper and a quick left jab."

"And the rest of the crowd?" I ask.

"Stockman yelled insults. A few of the fellows were set to mob me, or anybody else they could get hold of, but Mrs. Hill loudly congratulated me for leading a great show of solidarity, a democratic protest to show the fears of the people. Her friends joined in, and the fellows stopped. Mrs. Hill loaned me her handkerchief for my cut. She whispered directions for me to go in the side door entrance. Then she began collecting signs from everybody to 'keep them ready for next time', she said."

"Mr. Marvin didn't stop her?"

"No. He didn't come out with the protesters. He didn't want to miss his chance to be the last speaker."

"Dad, you gotta stop this Lone Ranger stuff. Somebody will kill you."

"That's the truth. Mrs. Hill saved my butt."

I barely have time to be amazed at his honesty when Mr. Halverson comes in from backstage. He strolls over to us. "Evans," he says to Dad, "the police are in the side hall near the superintendent's office. They're looking for you."

I jump up. "What did we do?"

Dad stands up and whispers, "Christine?"

"And Justine," Mr. Halverson says. "They were arrested for disturbing the peace outside of Corbett College tonight. They're out at the county jail near Rocky Butte. You want a ride? Some bail money?"

I feel my mouth drop open.

Dad looks Mr. Halverson in the eye, steady and long. "I've been saving bail money, but I don't know if one hundred dollars will get both of them out."

Beside me, Mike says, "They'll probably pay you to take Justine."

All three of us stare at him. He suddenly studies his shoe. "Well," he mumbles, "That's how it would be in my cartoon."

Dad bursts into a guffaw. Mr. Halverson snorts. I have to lean on a chair, I'm laughing so hard.

Clearly, Dad hurts from laughing. He lays a hand on Mike's shoulder. "Let's all go together and see if you're right." Then he says to Mr. Halverson, "But, maybe you shouldn't be seen bailing out anti-HUAC protesters."

"I'm a citizen, just like anybody else," Mr. Halverson says. "I have every right to see what price you get for taking Justine off their hands."

CHAPTER TWENTY-FOUR

Dad stops at home long enough to wash the cut on his leg, which doesn't look good. He cleans up the cut on his forehead and puts a bandage on it.

"Probably ought to get those looked at," I say.

"After we rescue the police from Mom and Justine," he says. He grabs his huge pickle jar full of change, then we head out to Rocky Butte. Mike Halverson and his dad follow us in case we need more money – or any help, as Mr. Halverson puts it.

At the jail, one of the intake officers asks if we came for Justine as well as Christine Evans. "We'll reduce the bail for Mrs. Evans if you promise your daughter will never reappear on our premises."

Mike can hardly keep the smirk off his face.

Dad says, "My daughter protests injustice. In the future, will you be arresting those who protest unfair rules and actions?"

The officer glances away, then stares at the pennies and nickels in the pickle jar. "How much you think you've got in there?"

As soon as they settle on a bail amount, Mr. Halverson and the annoyed police officer count out the pickle-jar change on the top of the in-take desk. Dad signs papers to get Mom back.

When Mom and Justine are brought into the front office, the intake officer moves out front of the desk and stands near Justine. He says, "Mister Evans, I recommend you keep better control over your women."

Justine's foot swings back. Halfway through the forward swing, Mom whips my little sister up into her arms, holds on tight and smiles her way out the door to the car. Dad follows her out. We leave the Rocky Butte jail lighter by fifty dollars of pennies, nickels and dimes. I carry what's left of the change in the jar. We better build up this bail-money collection for another go-around. Justine is jail material in any future I can see.

Mike and his dad wave from their car as we all leave the parking lot. I'm certain they'll laugh all the way home about what a screwed-up little sister I have.

Once we reach the house, Justine and Mom are in Justine's room while Justine cries and Mom croons understanding about how hard it is to be a real pacifist when everybody around you is totally provoking.

No really. Those were Justine's actual words, but she pronounced them "Totally puvokin."

I go to sleep to the sound of Mom's voice telling Dad to take Mr. Halverson's offer of help and go to the emergency ward about his cuts.

* *

This morning, I turn on my bedroom light and stumble to the window to see what the creaking sound is outside. It's just the branches in our horse-chestnut street tree. They rub against each other and the power pole. The wind in the trees makes me look up. Rain clouds pile over the hills west of town. It rains a lot in Portland, but these are thunder clouds, boiling up to high altitude.

I glance down to the street, and see a shadow veiled by the whipping rain. Someone in a slicker, stands across the street, looking up at me. I'm in my pajamas. My hair sticks straight up from my cowlick, and that person over there is hunched and focused, standing so still, I feel the concentration – the anger. I reach up and pull down the shade. As I back away, I feel foolish, but I still turn out the bedroom light. I don't want even my shadow on the shade.

I creep across the hall to Justine's room. She's asleep, but I go to her window. As I pull down her shade, I see the rain slicker turn and walk south toward Brazee Street.

Justine wakes up. "What'cha doin'?"

"Just keeping the rain out."

She laughs. "Daddy put that chalk stuff around my window. It doesn't leak."

"That's caulk."

"What I said." She jumps out of bed and beats me to the bathroom.

*   *

A while later, down at the breakfast table, Justine is already eating. Dad sits stiffly. He has stitches in his forehead.

I count black thread marks. Six stitches. "I heard you went to the hospital."

"Three hours," Dad says.

"Daddy's got tape on his ribs," Justine says, "and more stitches on his leg."

Mom says, "So, you saw Mr. Stockman at the hospital last night?"

"His nose is broken and his face is bluer than mine," Dad says.

"So much for pacifism," I say as I plunk myself down across from Justine.

Dad's smiling face is puke green with bruises. "Actually," he says, "Pacifism may not work, but physics does."

"Yeah?"

"If you let your opponent get too sure of himself, eventually you can step aside. He lands on his nose."

"Eventually is the key," Mom says, eyeing Dad's battered face, "First you have to encourage his inflated sense of self by taking a ringed fist in the face and a few solid jabs to the ribs."

"But that hurts," Justine says. "Why not just wallop him?"

We all look at Dad. He snaps out his napkin, lays it in his lap and says, "Let's all give thanks for fortitude, patience and Justine's rational ideas."

"Amen," Mom says as she reaches out to hold hands with us for prayer.

* *

This morning at school, nobody mentions my speech at the board meeting, but many of the kids must have heard. When I come near, they turn their backs on me. Three notes are on my desk when I get there. One is from Carol Bettleheim. "I thought you hated communists and wanted the oath. But Mom says you're for protecting them. How come?"

The second note is from Eli Moon. "My dad says you're a communist. Why don't you get out?"

The third note is folded up in little squares. When I open it up, I see a smudged scrawl that says, "Traitor, Real Americans will get rid of you."

What's that mean "get rid of you"? They can't send me anywhere like they did Billy. What else could it mean?

The note is written with a backward slant. I fold it up again, and stick it in my pocket.

At that moment, I remember the man outside our house this morning – that guy in the rain slicker. Was he really staring at our house? At my bedroom? Or am I just being a lame-brain because of all the stuff that happened last night. Maybe the guy was just out for a walk.

*   *

In Journalism class, Mr. Marvin hands out the assignments as if I'm not there. Then he calls Davie Dashlee up to his desk and gives him the stack of mimeographed work Mike and I have already created for the Eisenhower Eagle.

Davie goes out with all that stuff and an office pass. I figure he just became the editor of the school newspaper.

I hope that will be the last A-bomb to explode because of my speech at the meeting. I'm pretty certain Mr. Stockman will no longer be happy to see me. I wonder who else I need to be careful of – all the note writers.

But what I said last night is what I now believe.

There still is one thing I want to know about last night. I think I have a good guess about who might be good at syncopated drumming. I have seen James Wray dance with Billy Mendoza's Philippine rhythm sticks.

So, at soccer practice, while James Wray and I are doing soccer foot passes, I ask him, "Were you drumming with us at the school board meeting last night?"

"Drumming? How?

"You know, all that syncopation – the drummer that was somewhere down front and to the right facing the stage."

James traps the ball, stops and leans over me, studying my face with his nearly black eyes. "You're pulling my leg, right? Me? At the school board meeting?"

"Were you?"

"Gib that is the stupidest thing I've heard from you, yet. That is the kind of meeting that promises to turn into a lynch mob in seconds. Me and mine do not go anywhere near meetings like that."

"Oh . . . then who?"

"Syncopation?" he asks.

I nod.

Now, James closes his eyes. He shakes his head, and when he looks at me again, he says. "Brother, let me tell you something. Contrary to what you white folks imagine, not all Negroes got rhythm. I know some awkward brothers would make you look like a mix of Fred Astaire and Bo Jangles. And you, Bubba, you are one very gauche guy."

"James," I say to his back.

He glares at me over his shoulder.

I take a deep breath and blurt, "I'm sorry. Wanta punch my lights out?"

James turns around, hands on his hips. His forehead wrinkles up. He studies me. He lifts his right fist and tests the distance. Finally, he purses up his lips as if concentrating on where to plant his knuckles. "Naw," he says. "Too wide a target. Let's play ball."

As I blink, he shuffles the soccer ball in a very cool move between his feet and around his left side, then kicks the ball back to me.

I trap the ball, and then I hear a whistle. I glance up and see Mr. O'Connor's lopsided smile.

"Huddle up," Mr. O'Connor says, gesturing for all of us to gather around him.

The other guys all circle. Reluctantly, I join them, but on the far side of the circle from James.

Mike comes up behind me and says, "You eat something bad?"

I frown at him. "What you talking about?"

"That prune face you got there. That your normal look?"

Mr. O'Connor says, "Mister Halverson, we'd appreciate your humor more after the huddle."

Mike laughs, "Yeah, coach."

Mr. O'Connor reaches into a sack he's been carrying around ever since we came out to practice. Out comes a dinky little orange. I've never seen such a small orange.

"Mandarin oranges," James says.

Mr. O'Connor nods his head. "How did you know?" he asks.

James gazes out across the field, and his eyes get shiny. Then he glances at Mr. O'Connor, his face tight, like he's trying to control his muscles. He says, "Billy Mendoza's dad always brought some to our house when Mister Mendoza's sister mailed a box of them from the Philippines. She had to put them in a special box with dry ice and all that just to make sure they got here for Christmas time."

"Have you heard from the Mendozas?" Mr. O'Connor asks.

James just shakes his head slowly back and forth. A moment later, he says, "Mister Mendoza said it might not be good for us to hear from them."

Davie Dashlee pipes up. "How come? What's with the Mendozas? Didn't they just move back to where-ever?"

Mr. O'Connor glances at Davie and says, "Yes, Davie. The Mendozas went home."

Mike and James exchange a glance over Davie's head. Then James looks at me. I know not to talk about Billy.

Davie says, "So, what's a Mandarin orange?"

Mr. O'Connor reaches into his bag and brings out a second one. In fact, he starts passing them out to the guys. Then he shows us how easy it is to peel one. They are small, but very sweet.

"These are a good snack for guys who play hard," he says, "guys who sweat a lot and are going to have a game against Alameda school on Friday at three-thirty, right on the Alameda field."

"A real game?" Mike asks. "I didn't even know Alameda had a soccer team."

Mr. O'Connor nods and smiles. "Mister Berry, the gym teacher at Alameda hails from England. He wants a chance to test his new team against The Cream of Eisenhower Elementary."

Davie glances around the group. "Are we ready for them?" he asks.

Mr. O'Connor says, "Only one way to find out."

He holds the sack out for the peels. I have to pick mine up from the ground where I dropped them. Mr. O'Connor just waits while we clean up our mess. Then he says, "Let's drill stealing-the-ball for the rest of the lunch time."

* *

On our way back inside, we're all climbing up the stairs when Elizabeth Gray comes down. James stops next to her. Everyone else moves on around her and up the stairs. But I hear James ask, "That hand better?"

I whip around to see what he's talking about. She holds up her left hand. Her palm is blue, and that's all I can see because the rest of her hand is covered in a bandage.

"What did you do?" I ask, moving back down next to her.

She gets kind of red in the face. "Well, it's a long story."

James snorts and glances over at me and says, "She banged it on a wooden seat at some meeting last night."

I look into her face, but she's not looking at me – in fact she's working hard not to look at me.

"You?" I ask?

She nods. "It was stupid. I got carried away. I didn't realize until later that I banged too hard."

"Banged a syncopated rhythm?"

She steals a look at me. "Just a Beguine."

My face is hot. Beside her, I can see James, grinning at me.

"Just a Beguine," I echo. Then I take another look at that hand, and I get real concerned because the part I can see is looking pretty beat up. "Did you try ice?"

She nods. "Ice and a splint on one finger. Those chairs are not like my drum heads." James is chuckling.

I feel a shadow and look up. Mr. Marvin has come to the head of the stairs. "James Wray, what are you up to?"

Elizabeth Gray raises her head, her face suddenly still as marble. "Why are you asking, Mister Marvin?"

Mr. Marvin says, "Get in here, you three."

I turn to let Elizabeth go into the class before me, and suddenly, I have this vision of her. She is older and running toward me as if she's happy, and she's going to throw her arms around me in greeting. I blink and try hard to hold that vision in my head without letting on that anything has happened. But I know what I imagined is what I want. It's the most important thing I've ever wanted.

CHAPTER TWENTY-FIVE

On Friday, the *Portland Journal* editorial page prints an essay by Senator Johnson about some bill he's introducing in the state legislature. The bill would make it a felony to corrupt employees of any business by talk about socialist or communist ideas.

"Dad, can he do that? Isn't his bill un-constitutional?"

"His bill can't pass," Dad said, "but advertising his bill can make employees afraid to talk about unionizing."

Mom sets down her mending. "Mr. Johnson's purpose is not the bill. It is the fear."

* *

This morning, the school board voted not to require all teachers to take an oath of loyalty. I'm surprised, and inside I'm jumping for joy as I read.

Mr. Halverson is quoted in the *Portland Journal*. "This oath pries into individual beliefs and asks about vague associations. Our United States Constitution protects individual beliefs. Only actions can make a man guilty. We have precedent not to force this oath on teachers. Last year, our Oregon State legislature refused to pass a bill the bill's authors advertised as a way to 'Spot Red Teachers'. They were right not to pass it."

I remember now. That bill was supported by the guy the union men were trying to defeat. The union men were arrested on a charge of being subversive. I wonder what has happened to those men – Mr. MacKay and Mr. Mackie.

So, because of the school board vote, I think the oath problem is all over. But during the next two mornings, the newspaper and the television say they are getting a huge outcry from the public. They say people want the oath and they want it soon. Mr. Marvin's Educators for Democracy believe the oath should have a deadline.

According to the *Portland Journal*, "In many schools, the principals are asking their teachers to sign an oath despite the school board decision. They are giving the teachers until November first to declare they've never held beliefs against the United States government, never been communists or ever attended meetings of organizations that support communist ideas."

"Never even attended meetings?" I ask Dad.

Dad says, "What that means is no one is allowed to learn about Marxism, or other new ideas. That way, we'll always be afraid of the unknown."

Today, the *Portland Journal* cheers the principals' "courageous defiance of the school board". The Journal recommends that the entire school board be recalled and the subject of loyalty oaths be reconsidered for the whole district.

"Notice," Mom says. "The newspaper wrote all this on the front page – not the editorial, opinion page."

I read the pages. According to one headline, "Recall of the Left-leaning Halverson is Imperative". The front page article says, "If Mr. Halverson can't support our troops in Korea with a little bit of loyalty, he should be run out of office." Somebody is going to jump Mr. Halverson.

I think about the rain-slicker man. Does he stand outside Halverson's house sometimes?

* *

Our history teacher, Mrs. Hill, asks, "Gilbert? Are you with us?"

"No!" I say, and then I hear everyone laughing. I wake up from thinking about the news, angry and embarrassed. "I was just thinking," I say.

Pretty lame.

Mrs. Hill's stout self is leaning against her desk and smiling at me. "I'm glad to hear that. But could you think about why William Penn asked the King of England for land in the New World?"

I know this. It's Quaker history. "Penn was the King's friend," I say. "But Penn was a dissenter. So he tested their friendship and asked this one big thing."

"A bit risky, don't you think?" she asked.

"Yup. But the honey in the question was that if the King agreed, Penn would take a lot of the dissenters out of the country. No arrests. No burnings at the stake. No mess."

Mrs. Hill nods. Then she turns to the rest of the class and asks, "Did this happen anywhere besides in Pennsylvania?"

Elizabeth raises her hand, but, of course, Rick Johnson blurts without waiting.

"It shouldn't have happened even in Pennsylvania. Dissenters should be thrown in jail."

Mrs. Hill ignores him. "Miss Gray?"

Elizabeth says, "In Maryland, the king gave his friend, Lord Baltimore, land for Catholic dissenters."

"See?" Rick says.

Mrs. Hill turns to Rick and says. "Mister Johnson, I see that you have many thoughts on this subject and can't stop yourself from interrupting others. So, I'd like you to get your ideas all on paper. While the class is reading and discussing, you are to write a two-hundred word essay on how we have treated dissenters in our country."

"Two hundred words? That's not fair."

"Mister Johnson, are you dissenting?"

"Not fair," he mumbles.

Mrs. Hill says. "And while you write, think about our discussion last Friday with Mister Patton."

It's news to me, and I can tell it's news to everyone in the room that Rick has had a discussion with the principal. He starts writing. I bet Mr. Patton said something about football – the only thing Rick Johnson cares about, as far as I can see.

Mrs. Hill turns back to the class and asks, "What other religious groups were in this country before the Revolutionary War?"

James Wray raises his hand, a thing he rarely does in Marvin's class, but Mrs. Hill calls on him right away.

"There were animists." He has this tight look on his face, as if he's expecting a blow.

"Ah, yes," she says. "Can you tell the class what animists are?"

He takes a deep breath and says, "Some people believe that the spirit of an animal protects them. I guess they believe the Creator is in everything and is everywhere, and sometimes that spirit is in animals."

Mrs. Hill nods and turns to see how the class is taking this. I'm not sure I've ever heard about this before, so I want to know more.

Davie Dashlee laughs. "That's crazy."

Mrs. Hill asks, "Davie, could you define crazy for us, please?"

"Crazy? That's when you think something nobody else thinks."

"Thank you, Davie – a nice clear statement of your thought."

Rick and a few others laugh. I can tell that James is getting stiff again. I raise my hand, with, of course, no idea what I'm going to say. I just wish to drop Davie Dashlee on his head. Mrs. Hill calls on me, and that's when I remember something from way back.

"The Romans and the Greeks believed fountains and trees and animals had spirits. I guess they were animists," I say. "They did pretty well, and for a lot longer than we have, so I guess they weren't crazy."

I can see James is looking at me, waiting. So I add, "The Indians who lived here when settlers came from Europe, I think some of them were animists, too. Had been for a long time."

Davie says, "Had been. Now they know better."

Elizabeth says, "Not know better. Just got silent and hid their real selves. Most people don't say what they really think. If they are honest, someone will call them crazy, or dissenters, or communist traitors."

Davie starts to talk, but Elizabeth stands up and says directly to him, "I think each tree in the park has a spirit, and every squirrel and raccoon. I even think people have a spirit inside them. If they listen and let that spirit guide them, they will be good people. If they don't listen, they will destroy others, and themselves, too."

James Wray and Davie Dashlee both stare at her. I'm staring at her, too. She didn't raise her hand, or wait to be called on, and she just told us the most weird thing about herself. I wish I had half her courage.

Rick has stopped writing. He says to Elizabeth, "I thought you went to our church."

"What's that got to do with it?" she asks.

Mrs. Hill steps in at that moment. "Well, class, I guess we have just seen the best thing about our country. We can each think about the creator and the creation in our own way. We wrote that into our Constitution." Mrs. Hill turns to the board and picks up her chalk.

In her neat hand, she writes as she talks:

"Article Six of the Constitution of the United States says, 'No religious test shall ever be required as a qualification to any office or public trust under the United States."

Suddenly I sit up and ask myself, 'Why is she talking about this today?' Yesterday she said we were going to be studying the five tribes now living on the Warm Springs Reservation. But right off the bat this morning, she gets us going on religion, and dissent.

Next she writes, "Congress shall make no law respecting establishment of a religion, or prohibiting the free exercise thereof."

She points to the word 'free' and says, "There's more to this in the first amendment in the Bill of Rights, but this is the part we'll concentrate on this week."

And then it comes to me. She isn't going to sign that oath. She's going to refuse because of the Constitution – freedom of beliefs, and freedom of speech, freedom of peaceable assembly, the right to call the government on its bad decisions. I know even Mr. Reese would not have signed the oath.

And that's when I really start to get scared.

CHAPTER TWENTY-SIX

F riday after school, us guys on the soccer team are pretty keyed up as we walk the fourteen or so blocks over to Alameda School for our game with Mr. Berry's team.

"I hear the Alameda team has lots of big guys," Davie Dashlee says.

I've heard that, too. I glance at Mike, our only big guy.

He says, "I've got your back, Davie. When they knock you down and sit on you, I'll just come down on them like a ton of bricks."

The look of fear on Davie's face cracks up the rest of the team. "Yeah, Davie," James says. "Don't worry. We'll all help Mike protect you."

Davie stares at James, and then he says, "I'll help. I've got my shiv in my pocket."

"Shiv?" Mike asks.

Davie pulls out a Boy Scout pocket knife and waves it around.

Most of the fellows laugh, but I can't help thinking about gang action, like what you read about in the newspapers. This could be a real rumble. I hope coach knows what he's getting us into.

Mr. O'Connor reaches out and takes Davie's knife. "I'll keep this for you." Then he turns to Mike. "Soccer is a gentlemen's game – hard fought but clean."

"Clean?" James says. "I get mud on my shirt every time we practice."

So, now we're laughing as we turn into the Alameda field.

Mr. O'Connor and Mr. Berry greet each other at the grassy middle of Alameda's football field. Coach Berry has a pile of metal bars and rubber tubes on the ground next to him. He shows all of us how to set them up to be padded goals with a kind of fish net stretched across the goal space.

Then Coach O'Connor divides us and Mr. Berry's team in two groups. The guys from our group go with half of the Alameda team to set up the goal at the south end of the field. We try stuff out, watching it fall apart, looking down the field to see what the team at the other end is doing, and then trying something else that might work. After ten minutes of ringing metal poles falling down and being set up again, the coaches call us together to explain again. This time we get it. The goals go together fast, and we're ready for the game.

As we line up, Davie whispers to me, "Their big guys aren't so big, huh?"

I whisper, "You want to be goalie for the first part of the game?"

"You kidding me?" he says.

Mike becomes our goalie. Their goalie is Raymond Byers, the guy who figured out the connectors for our goal pipes – a real smart fellow about Mike's size. After fifteen minutes, we haven't had a score and neither have they. Coach O'Connor tells us we've played a fine defensive game, but we need to stop passing and take a stab at the goal.

"James and Gib, you're up front to put the ball into the net, remember?" he says.

"Sure, coach," James says, "I kick, and miss, and look like a real pro."

"Fear of mistakes loses games," Coach says. "It's been shown that eleven out of twelve kicks toward the goal go wrong, but that twelfth kick – that one is gold."

So, we start racking up kicks that go wrong. James passes to me. I pass to James or Davie, or one of the other guys, and then, whoppo! One of us sees an open spot and we smack the ball.

Over the goal, left of the goal, out of the field, but never in the net. And then James passes to Davie who passes to me and I see the opening. My foot connects. The ball flies past Ray Byers. The net stretches with the weight of the ball.

And we have a goal.

Half-time. Mandarin oranges for both teams in the middle of the field. It turns out some of these guys are in my mom's class at Alameda. They like her.

"You know," Ray Byers says, "It's okay that she makes us memorize poetry. She finds good ones – Wilfred Owens' war stuff and, you know . . . words that stick."

During the second half, I'm caught off-guard thinking Mom's class memorizes war poems? How Quaker is that?

I must have been mentally asleep because a guy named Sol Hassan gets a goal right past me, and past Mike, too. So, the score is tied one to one.

Two minutes later, I'm focused. Davie passes to me. No opening. I pass to James, and he whonks it toward the goal, but I can see that goalie Ray Byers might reach to keep it out of the net.

I run at their goalie, Ray, as if I'm going to do a football tackle. He protects himself by getting low to take the blow. James's ball hits the top of the net frame and bounces back toward us. While Ray is watching me, Davie bounces the ball off his head and puts it into the net.

Two to one. Davie grins while the team gives him the head rub for celebration.

The game ends soon after because it's getting dark. The coaches tell us we'll have another game in a month, in early November. They talk about things we can work on. It's like they are friends, and they want us to be one big team, working to get better. I've never had a coach who told the other team how to get better.

On the way home, I admit to myself that walking to Alameda I was just as scared as Davie. But their biggest guy is a new friend.

*   *

By Friday evening, I'm sure I have to worry about that loyalty oath and who will sign it or not sign it. My folks have invited people over for dinner: Mr. O'Connor, Mrs. Hill and Mr. and Mrs. Halverson. The plan is that the kids will eat in the kitchen, but the adults will eat in the dining room. I think they are getting together to decide what to do.

I hope they'll just sign it and be done with it. Anything else they might do is scary. None of them is a revolutionary, so who cares anyway?

Mom is making vegetable lasagna. I help set the table in the dining room and then I set the table in the kitchen for Mike and me and the Pest. Justine plays on the living room floor with her dolls, Lucille and Drucille – don't ask. No biffing and boffing among the dolls. Today they're all getting ready for dinner.

Before dinner, Mike comes earlier than his folks because he wants to work on our latest comic book. We've done *The Battle of the Bulge*, and *The Prisoners of Auschwitz*.

So, today we're working on whatever new idea Mike has cooked up.

As we stand in the entry way, Mike holds up his notebook. "We're gonna print this one, at least twenty copies," he says. "Dad's found this new way to make copies of things for School Board Meetings."

"Why that many copies?"

"Because it'll be our Christmas present for our families," he whispers, glancing at Justine.

I laugh and whisper back, "War stories for the pacifists? Great."

Justine still plays with her dolls. Mike sits down on the living room floor near her and the coffee table where we always draw and plan. The low afternoon sunlight comes through the beveled glass design in our front window. The light breaks into rainbow colors.

Justine says, "Look Mikey, you've got a purple-to-green face"

He glances at her, holds up his arm to see the colors. "That's pretty, isn't it, Jussy?"

She puts her Lucille doll in the light, testing different angles.

"So, what's the new printing method?" I ask.

He gets back to work. "The School District stuff is all printed on this machine called an A.B. Dick," he says. "It uses stronger master copies than that stinky mimeograph machine, and it prints a lot clearer, too. So, we can make twenty copies and then keep the master in case we want to make more. It's great."

"And this costs?"

Mike makes a zero sign. "The printer is this guy we know. Dad built his house."

"Think he'd do a newspaper, too?"

Mike glances up at me. "It's still bugging you that Marvin took away your editor's job, huh."

"Not as long as we have ourselves a comic book publisher, and maybe a newspaper publisher."

"Great!" Mike says. "Now, here's my comic book idea." He plunks down his sample – several pages of simple line drawings. He's figured out lately how simple the drawings must be so they'll work on a copying master.

"See," he says, "this is the day before Christmas, 1946."

I stare at his first page. It's just like I remember it: Barbed wire rolls cut across the land and off into the distance. On the far side of the wire you can see a dead horse lying on its back in a muddy field. Nearby are men with blunt, ugly rifles; you get the idea maybe they just shot the horse. On their uniforms are the hammer and sickle sign of Soviet Russians.

Facing the men, but on the near side of the wire is a family, Mom, Dad, big brother, little sister. Their backs are to the reader. They hold out a white flag.

"We never had a white flag."

"This is a story," Mike says. "How it might have been. Your words will describe the feelings on both sides of the fence. Everybody can see the actions."

"Okay. What's next?" I feel weird because he's taken my description of that place and made it real.

He lays it all out, page by page on the table and spilling over onto the floor. You can see that, in his story, the Russian soldiers don't trust the family, until one of the soldiers reaches his hand across and shakes the hand of the eight-year-old kid – that's me. Then the soldier makes funny faces for the little girl. She makes faces back at him, laughing. The other soldiers lower their guns as they come close to see what the little girl and her brother are laughing about.

In the upper right-hand corner of each picture, you can see a watch on a man's hairy wrist. I think that's one of the neat things about comics. You can have a disembodied clock on a person's wrist in the corner, and everybody who sees it, looks around and recognizes it's Dad's wristwatch magnified.

In Mike's comic, at midnight, Christmas Eve, Mom brings out a cherry pie and slides the glass pan and pie under the barbed wire with a note. "Merry Christmas. Treat our friends with love on your side of the fence."

The first soldier looks at the note, in the next frame, he looks at Mom. In the third frame he raises his hand in the universal Boy Scouts' three finger sign of honor.

I look at Mike's drawing, and I wish that was what happened at the barbed wire – at every barbed wire fence. And that's when I stupid-start to cry. Just like that, right in front of my friend. I'm embarrassed, but I can't stop it. These dumb tears on my face where I can't hide 'em. I feel like they've been stuck inside me since I was eight years old, since the soldier shot Herr Grofmann's brother.

Mike and Justine stare at me. All I can do is drip. Then Mike gets up and walks into the kitchen. I think he's trying to give me a chance to stop being such a nut. So, I wipe my eyes on the bottom part of my shirt, but now my nose is running, too. Justine comes over and touches me on the shoulder.

Mike comes back and hands me a stack of paper napkins. I glance up and see, Mike is sort of crying, too.

"Doesn't …" I wipe my nose and try again. "Doesn't need words." He nods.

Justine leans her mouth on my head, almost like she's kissing me, then she goes off into the kitchen.

*   *

About three minutes later, Mrs. Hill and Mrs. Silverberg arrive. They have brought dessert – cherry pie and pink ice cream. Soon, Mr. O'Connor arrives. I see by the way she looks up at him, that Mrs. Silverberg thinks Mr. O'Connor is a walking god, but I don't have a clue why. They're all off in the kitchen with Mom when Justine walks back into the living room. By now, Mike and I are laying plans for our first *Portland Community News*.

"Hey, Justine," I say. "What's with Missus Silverberg and Mister O'Connor?"

She stops and lets her head tilt to one side, her eyebrows rise as if she's amazed.

"Don't you know?" she asks, hands on her hips, eyes big. She's giving off her superior air.

"No Miss Priss ..." I start, but Mike puts out his hand to stop me.

"I don't know either, Justine," he says. "What is it?"

She talks to Mike like I didn't ask first. "Mister O'Connor saved her life in Lunaburg.

He's the reason she got across the line to live in Neustadt bei Wald with her old neighbor, Missus Goldblum."

"How did that happen?" Mike asks.

"At the very end of the war," she says, "there was chaos in Lunaburg. Mister O'Connor escaped the prisoner of war camp. He'd been there for a year and a half."

I can tell by the way Justine talks that Mrs. Silverberg has told her this story many times with exactly these words. I've been left out of all this stuff.

Justine is talking to both of us, now. "Mister O'Connor – well, he and Missus Silverberg were hidden together with lots of other people in the Lunaburg Lutheran Church. The Russians were coming into town, but the church gardener drove up with an old rattly truck. Quick like a fox, he filled that truck with the people from the church basement. Mister O'Connor and Missus Silverberg were last out of the basement. There wasn't enough room left in the bed of the truck, and it was weighted down with all the people. Mister O'Connor pushed Missus Silverberg onto the last space in that truck and then he ran back up the road to distract the Russians and let the truck get across the field, and up the road into Neustadt."

"And the Russians missed him?" I ask.

"No way. They put him back in the prisoner of war camp. He stayed there for a long time, until Daddy's band smuggled him out at the end of the last concert."

I'm bollixed. "Dad's band smuggled him?"

"Sure, Silly. You know that. You were there."

I stare at her. She was only a four-year-old back then. Mrs. Silverberg must have told her what happened. But me, I was older

– but too young to tell, because the grown-ups probably were afraid I would say something at the wrong time. Nobody ever thought to explain to me later. And, I never asked.

I remember Dad's band marching off for that one last concert. That time, the soldiers let them through the gate in the wire fence. I still feel Mom's hand squeezing mine. I feel her fear. The band had only one more concert to play because the camp would soon be moved to Siberia. I see again the bandsmen's new hats, the hats that Mom and the ladies of Neustadt spent nights making, and I realize now that the band hats were made to disguise the most conspicuous man.

"That's a great comic book story," Mike says. "Mr. Evans saves the Pilot. My dad says that's probably how O'Connor got all those burns. Plane on fire. Parachuting out. All that kind of stuff. Course, that's just my dad's guess," Mike says. "He's never asked him."

I know what Dad said about it, but I want to hear about it from Mr. O'Connor. Partly, I want to remind him how far he is now from those days. I want him to think how much he'll give up if he can't teach any more.

I walk into the kitchen. Mr. O'Connor sports this ridiculous apron that was made for Mom who's about half his weight. He's chopping vegetables while Mrs. Hill tears lettuce. Mrs. Silverberg is pouring water into the glasses at the table.

"Did you parachute out of a plane?" I ask. As soon as it's out, I hear how brassy it sounds.

But he smiles at me. "Yes. And it was on fire. And yes, that's how all this happened to me. The Germans who found me tried to take care of the burns, but they barely had enough medicine to take care of their own wounded. Things were bad for everyone in that camp."

"What were you flying?"

"It was a B17."

"When?"

"1943, July."

"So from '43 to '48 you were in a prisoner of war camp? First Germans and then Russians?"

"Yes. And to answer your question, No, they didn't try to turn me into a communist spy."

I nod. "Good. That's good."

He nods too. "It wouldn't have worked, you know."

"Oh?"

"Nope. I could see they were in a mess, and communism wasn't going to help them grow food or build bridges. Everybody could see that – even the Russians."

At that moment, a huge crash comes from the front of the house. Justine's high scream pierces the air.

"Justine!" I call. "Mike." I run with Mr. O'Connor on my heels. Dad bursts in from his music room.

Crouched on the floor, Mike holds Justine in his lap, like a papa bird hovering over his chick. He picks silvery pieces of the big front window out of her hair and the puffs of her sleeves. His own forehead bleeds like a fountain. The whole window – all the lead and the design of angled glass – the whole thing has shattered all over them.

Justine screeches. "Mike, stop. Mike, you're hurt."

"Sit very still," Dad orders. "Don't wiggle, Justine and gently close your eyes. We don't know where all the glass is."

Mr. O'Connor rips off the borrowed apron and touches Mike's forehead with it.

"There's a big piece here," he says, then he talks to my mom who has frozen beside me.

"Christine."

Mom's eyes focus on his face. "Call the ambulance," he says. "Mike has glass in his forehead."

As she runs to the kitchen phone, I can see that Mike looks dazed. I bend down next to him and Justine. "Don't keel over, Mike." I say. "You can't move until I get all this glass from the floor behind you."

I run over crunches of glass to get the broom, so, I'm the one who finds the rock with the note tied around it. I don't have time to deal with it, so I point at it, and Mrs. Silverberg picks it up. Mrs. Hill glances at it, and then takes a mop out of our broom closet. She goes after the glass on the sofas and chairs with gentle strokes.

Mom runs back from the kitchen phone. "They're on the way. Oh, my Lord." Mrs. Silverberg puts the note and the rock behind her.

Mrs. Hill picks up Mike's story stack of drawings. She glances at the top drawing and then sets it all gently on the nearest bookshelf.

The Halversons burst in, carrying their dinner hot dish. They've seen the huge jagged hole in our front window.

"The kids!" Mrs. Halverson calls.

"Ambulance is coming," Dad says.

I sweep the biggest pieces of glass out from behind Mike. I stay behind him, so he can lean on my legs and not fall on any glass that I've missed. Dad and Mr. O'Connor work with dish towels to clear glass and blood from Mike and Justine. Mike's Mom hurries in with more towels.

"Brendan," Dad says to Mr. O'Connor, "Can you lift Justine? There's glass under her, cutting both of them."

Mr. O'Connor lifts her as if she were a doll. She's covered in Mike's blood. Her eyes are unfocussed.

"Mama," I say, "she's doing that shock thing they talk about in health. But you can't wrap her in a blanket because of all the glass."

"Close your eyes, honey," Mr. O'Connor says. To my surprise, Justine does what he says. He shakes her a little and glass falls from her hair and from every part of her party dress. She seems to be asleep. Her head droops.

"The rainbow window," she whimpers. "Mikey's dying. All the rainbows are gone."

* *

Since last night when our big front window was broken, it's been three-blanket cold in our house. Last night, Mr. Halverson, Dad and I came from the hospital and covered the broken window with plywood. Dad still couldn't reach very high because of his broken ribs from Mr. Stockman. So, I helped Mr. Halverson nail across the top of each plywood sheet.

Around ten o'clock last night, our moms brought Mike and Justine home. Justine was asleep from medicine they gave her. In the dark, I hopped across Mrs. Moriarty's stile to see Mike before they took him upstairs. He was covered in bandages all across his forehead. He looked pukey, and green. He didn't feel like talking, so I scrambled back to our house before the folks missed me.

Justine has some pretty deep scratches on her arms – really all over her body, legs, neck everything. Mom told me the doctor says we were lucky the biggest shard flew at them sideways, six inches above her head, and only into the skin on Mike's forehead.

Another angle, it could have killed Mike. A little lower, it could have killed Justine.

This morning, I come downstairs to a plywood-dark living room. Dad has moved our Motorola Radio to the breakfast room so we can listen to Mom's big-band music. Maybe later I'll get to listen to my favorites, maybe "The Shadow". In the breakfast room, we can be away from the October winds.

As I walk into the kitchen to get breakfast, I hear Justine already in there, playing with her dolls. I stop in the doorway to see what those dolls have got up to this time.

She's putting bandages on them. "Oh dear," she says in a high nursey voice. "You have too many cuts for such a little dolly."

She goes on like that for a while, not noticing me. Then she takes one doll and says, "You are the detective of police. Find out who did this."

I didn't know a policeman talked to her last night, but I wonder where else she would get that idea. Each doll in turn is questioned. Each one accuses another doll. In the end, she moves the policeman from doll to doll as quick as she can, making them all yell and wave arms at each other, saying, "You did it. I know it was you. No. No. It wasn't me. It was them."

Justine is getting a little screwy. I'm about to step over there when Mom hurries in, wiping her hands on her apron. She swoops Justine up in her arms.

"Sweetheart, sweetheart," Mom croons. "It isn't our job to find out who. It is our job to get well. And look at how beautifully you are getting well."

Mom sees me. "Ah, there's your big brother," she says, turning Justine around to see me. "He can get our bacon off the stove and bring it to the table while you and I go out front and wait for Daddy."

"Out front!" Justine wails. "Not out front!"

"The sun is shining," Mom says. "We have good neighbors watching out for us. We'll wait for Daddy on the porch."

"Where's Daddy?" Justine asks.

"Can you guess?" Mom says.

"In the music room?" she says with hope. I don't blame her. Out front is where somebody stood to throw that big rock. I wonder if the rain-slicker man came back.

"No," Mom says. "Daddy and Mister Halverson are up at Engelmann's Glass, ordering new rainbows for our living room."

* *

Later in the morning, I take my newest script. I hop the back fence onto Mike's driveway. I hope Mike wants to start a new comic book or something to take his mind off the stitches in his forehead.

Mrs. Halverson answers the door. "Hello, Gilbert. Mike's at the dining table, drawing."

"That's great."

"Yo, Mike," I say as I plunk down in the chair across the table from him. "Here's my script for the next one."

He turns his pad around and shows me his picture. In it, Sergeant Halverson stirs a big pot of soup. A Red Cross officer helps a long line of people toward the chow. The Red Cross guy is my dad. I know where this story takes place – a death camp that the allied armies liberated at the end of the war.

Mr. Halverson never talks about battles. In fact, we had to do the Battle of the Bulge comic book from the library's news archives. Then we had to stick the Sergeant Halverson character into it and hope we were close.

Mr. Halverson always talks about the people he found, and he talks about the Red Cross. I didn't know our dads worked together during the war, but it turns out they became good friends. That's why the Halverson's moved to our town.

I hand Mike my script and he gives me the page from his drawing pad.

I study Mike's drawing. I can see it will fit right into the script I've got – *Aftermath of War*. This is the one where I hint that Sergeant Halverson meets a communist cell and learns they are the next threat to Europe.

Mike frowns while he reads my script. "Discovers communists?" he asks. "Why?"

"Because it will sell big," I say.

"Sell big? That's your goal?" He's looking at me like he can't believe what I just said.

I start to talk, but I feel this twitch in my left eye, like a warning. Somehow, I know if I explain my marketing idea I will ruin something between me and my friend.

Mike leans his head-bandage on one hand and goes back to drawing very careful lines on his sketchpad. After a time, he sits up and says, "That loyalty oath is a trap, you know."

"How do you figure?"

"Part of it asks you to swear you've never supported a communist or subversive organization."

"I know that. But a trap?"

"There's these cartoonists I read about in the news," he says, "like for Disney. They wanted better wages, so they got together in a union and talked about bargaining for what they want. But the Motion Picture Alliance for American Values – big studios, including Disney – they said that union was a communist front."

"So, the cartoonists just have to prove they're a regular union," I say.

"That's the point. The Motion Picture Alliance says they're communist and doesn't have to prove it. Instead, the union has to prove it is *not* communist. How do you do that?"

"You mean, if I swear I've never supported a subversive organization . . .?"

"And then," Mike says, "your organization is declared subversive because Disney doesn't like it. Now it looks like you've committed perjury. Off to jail."

That stumps me. I try to figure what I'd do. Nothing I can think of will work.

"What a nasty trap," I say.

Mike nods, and then goes back to drawing his picture. I keep staring at what I've written, trying to figure out how our country got like this.

And I know how. I bought into this stuff. And just now, I wanted to use it to get readers.

I start re-reading my script.

About fifteen minutes later, it's noon. Mrs. Halverson turns on the news.

Sure enough, the radio has Senator McCarthy is shouting accusations against an expert on China. I've heard about this guy – Owen Lattimore. I also remember Senator McCarthy shouting at Mr. Oppenheimer. He's a scientist who wants us to be careful about how we use hydrogen energy. Lattimore wants us to think about what bad things might happen if we support the wrong guy in China.

My left eyelid sits still as I listen to McCarthy. I think, probably there are Marxists in our country, and maybe some are in unions. They were in Neustadt, too. After the terrible war, people wanted to change the world. Some thought Marx had the best ideas about how to do it. Other people thought Marxists were nuts. All the same, in Neustadt, all these different kinds of our neighbors risked their lives playing a band concert to rescue one ugly prisoner of war.

I start editing my script.

Mike watches me crossing out stuff. He sits up, un-leans his bandaged forehead from his hand, stares at me, and says nothing. After a moment, he starts drawing fresh pictures.

CHAPTER TWENTY-SEVEN

After the noon news, Mike and I decide to play a little catch. I have to hunt up Mike's baseball because it hurts for him to bend over, searching under his bed and places like that. Of course, I find the ball in the bottom of his closet behind his gym shoes – smelly place.

My street is wider, so a better place to play games. We run, well Mike walks, around the block instead of over the fence because Mrs. Moriarity is sweeping her half of their shared driveway. Her half only . . . .

As we come around the corner to my side of the block, I see Rick Johnson pounding a stake in Mrs. Silverberg's front lawn. I take off toward him.

Mike yells, "Hey, Johnson."

So, Rick turns around, hammer in his hand, ready to take me on.

I yell over my shoulder, "Mike, get Dad."

I'm not thinking. I'm afraid of that big claw hammer. Rick raises it as I run toward him. I can't tell what the sign says that he's been staking in the lawn. It can't be good, but I've got my attention on whether he'll throw or pound me.

"Come to save your commie leader?" he yells at me.

His brother, Kenny, runs out from behind the next door neighbors' bushes.

I halt a hammer's throw from Rick. Kenny keeps chugging toward me.

"Don't throw," I shout, "You'll hit Kenny."

That stops Kenny's charge. Better to distract a bull than to grab his horns, as Dad says.

"Get down, doofus," Rick shouts at his brother.

Kenny backs off toward the sign. I still have my attention on that hammer and on Rick's eyes. He squints as if taking aim, raises his hammer arm and gets ready to throw.

The front door on Mrs. Silverberg's house opens up.

I let myself get distracted by the sound. She screams, "Gib! Acht!"

I duck. The hammer whistles over my left shoulder. Mrs. Silverberg charges down her porch steps. Her broom connects with Kenny's backside. My fist connects with Rick's stomach.

Behind me, something connects with my shirt collar, and then I see a long, slim hand take Rick by the collar as well.

"Gentlemen," Dad says, "That includes you, Kenny. Let us finish this at the table. Come on in and we'll hash this out calmly over cookies. Magdalena, bring your broom."

I'm pretty sure the promise of cookies is not what makes Rick and Kenny come with Dad. It helps to have the backup power of one hundred seventy-five pounds of athletic muscle in the form of Mike Halverson. Even with his bandaged head, Mike, who used to be just chubby, now looks like a serious threat to Johnson escape plans, or mine, for that matter. I'd never noticed when he got formidable.

As we turn to go back to our house, I glance at the sign. "Communast Sell Meeting House." Rick should learn to spell.

When we troop inside, Mom is taking Justine upstairs, probably to keep her fast little mouth out of the discussion. As Dad motions us to sit at the breakfast table, I ask, "Rick, what do Communists sell?"

Dad says, "Gilbert, hold onto thy cleverness."

Dad hardly ever talks in the old Quaker way anymore, so I know this is serious. I sit next to Mrs. Silverberg who has leaned her broom on the wall next to the doorway.

Rick and Kenny gaze around the kitchen and breakfast room as if at a house in a magazine. I look around, too, and I see it fresh. Dad built the table and the dish cupboard.

He taught me how to cut and fit together the room's woodwork, window frames and all. I see these things every day, but I hardly notice them. Dad does a lot more than write music and direct bands.

Dad rustles in the kitchen and comes back with cookies made by Mom. He deposits a whole bottle of milk and a tray of glasses on the table.

"Please pour for everyone," he says to me.

Mrs. Silverberg says, "Thank you, Gilbert."

Kenny glances at her and says, "Yeah, thanks." Then he jumps, and I figure Rick just kicked him.

When the glasses are full, I sit down at our big family table. Mike sits next to me.

Kenny and Rick are across the table. Mrs. Silverberg sits at the head. Dad still stands.

"Gentlemen," Dad says. "I suppose you noticed Mike's bandaged head, and the plywood in our front window."

Rick and Kenny glance at each other, then at the tabletop.

"We kept the rock and the paper," Dad says. "Finger prints. But we may not need to involve the police in these neighborhood incidents."

Rick stares at Dad, but he says nothing.

Dad continues. "Could you explain what gave you the idea for the sign?"

"We see these weird commie types going in your houses," Kenny volunteers.

Rick jerks his gaze at Kenny. Kenny shuts up. Dad strolls around the table, reaches between the two of them, and puts a chocolate chip cookie on Rick's plate, then one on Kenny's. He stands between the two of them, concentrating on Rick, his back to Kenny.

"Rick," Dad says, "Could you describe commie types to us? I'm not quite sure what they look like."

Rick tries to look around Dad at Kenny, but he can't. Kenny is leaning into the back of his chair, eating a cookie.

Rick says, "Well, you got all these people who don't believe in war."

"Uh-huh," Dad says. "And are there any other visible features they have?"

"Yeah. They're foreigners."

"I see. So, people who go into Missus Silverberg's, and I suppose you mean into our house too, are foreigners and they don't believe in war."

"Yeah."

"What kind of people would you rather see coming into our houses?"

"Real Americans," Rick says.

"Okay. And what do real Americans look like?"

"Not foreign."

"Hmm."

"And Christian, not Quakers."

I sit up, surprised by what he thinks.

Dad asks, "Did you know that Missus Silverberg saved a man from the Russians?"

Next to me, Mrs. Silverberg fidgets with her glass of milk. I'm scrambling to take in an image of this old lady in action. Who did she save?

Kenny glances at me, a question in his raised eyebrows. I shrug.

Rick says, "Her?"

"Uh-huh," Dad says. "Convinced a whole lot of people to figure out how to do it, and then worked hard to make the plan fail-safe. That man is alive because of her."

"From the Russians?" Kenny blurts.

"The Russians," Dad says.

"What about that Mister O'Connor?" Rick asks. "Mister Marvin says he was missing for three years in Communist Germany."

"Mister Marvin says," Dad repeats. "And how would Mister Marvin know that?" Dad asks.

"I don't know. He's in the Air Force."

"So, you think he may have peaked at some Air Force records, or something like that?"

Rick frowns at the implications of the word 'peaked" He says, "Marvin didn't tell me how he knew."

"You'd like to know where Mister O'Connor was," Dad says. "Would it be a good idea to ask him?"

I glance up at Dad, hoping he's not going to call Mr. O'Connor.

"Not if he's a spy," Rick says.

Kenny speaks up at that moment. "Don't you know where Mister O'Connor was?"

Dad turns finally to include Kenny in the conversation. "It's always best to get the story from the person involved. Rumor about other people is an unfair game to play."

"So, where was he?" Rick asks.

"Tell you what, gentlemen, I'll invite Mister O'Connor this evening for dessert. If he can come, I will call your family and invite all of you as well. Then, you can ask him direct."

Rick says, "My Dad won't come."

"Would you like to know the answer, Rick?"

"So! He might lie."

"Who might lie?"

"O'Connor." Rick's voice is impatient, as if it's real clear who he meant.

"Oh. I thought maybe you meant someone else," Dad says.

I get real tense because I can see the wheels turning in Rick's head. He's realizing that the person who might lie is his own dad, or maybe Mister Marvin. These possibilities have him frowning big time. I expect him to jump up and slam out of here.

But he sits there, thinking. "I can bring my dad?" he asks.

"And your mother," Dad says. "If Mister O'Connor is available."

I can see by their puzzled frowns that bringing mom is a new idea for both Rick and Kenny. I hardly ever see their mother outside the house, except at that meeting at the school board.

"Mister Evans," Rick says, "about that plywood in your window . . ."

"Yes?" Dad asks.

"You said you had a rock and paper with fingerprints."

"I do have the rock and paper," Dad says. I notice he doesn't mention the fingerprints.

"Those aren't my fingerprints," Rick says. "And for sure not Kenny's."

"Ah," Dad says.

"I don't know who did it," Rick says. "You get the police to check our prints. It's not me, I'll tell you."

Dad nods at him. "I expect to find you are right about that. I'll call your home when I have this evening arranged with Mr. O'Connor. Meanwhile, you can alert your parents to the possibility of dessert."

Kenny snorts, "Like they would come!"

But Rick glares at Kenny and says, "Mom, she says there's two sides to everything. Maybe she'll come."

"Dad would give her a . . ." Kenny blurts.

"Shut up! Just shut up!"

During the sudden silence, I look back and forth between Rick and Kenny. Kenny has this scared look. His mouth is open and he seems to be trying to figure out his brother.

Rick stares Kenny down and then turns his face from his brother. In that moment, Rick seems to have made some decision that is his alone. I feel as much on the outside and as puzzled as his little brother.

I'm really worried now. There's going to be big trouble. Dad always thinks things can be worked out with talk. But he's still wincing whenever he takes a deep breath, so we know how that worked with Mr. Stockman.

And I've seen Senator Johnson in action. He believes in fists, and a lot of people do whatever he says. He has hate plus power – a bad combination.

CHAPTER TWENTY-EIGHT

In the late afternoon of our run-in with Rick and Kenny, I'm lying on the living room floor reading the news by the firelight. *The Portland Journal* writes that in New York, "The famous rebel girl, Elizabeth Gurley Flynn, a known communist speaker", got sent to prison after a trial. *The Portland Journal* cheered that move, right in the news report. The same newspaper writer seems real happy that some Negro lady in New York named Claudia Jones, secretary of the Communist Party's Women's Commission, was arrested. They talked about how she should be deported.

Deported where, I wonder. Didn't we haul her ancestors over here without asking?

I read this section, and my skin feels tight. I sit and stare at the photos, thinking women, they're even deporting women. What will happen to Mom?

Then I turn the page and find another news article.

"Mr. Robert Harl, a city councilman, is on the hot seat for his recent lone vote to fire the Chief of Police. Councilman Harl claims

'The Chief runs a Red Squad that spies on citizens the police don't like, accusing them of radical tendencies just because they are in the way of something the chief wants.'"

The *Journal* goes on, "Portland's respected mayor says, 'Mr. Harl has always been an obstruction to our search for subversives. It makes you wonder where Councilman Harl's loyalties lie.'"

At that moment, I stop reading and think about interviewing Councilman Harl for our newspaper. I wonder if he'd talk to a kid about how the Red Squad works.

I hear Dad in the kitchen, talking on the phone. He works out with Mr. O'Connor that he will come over tonight for dessert. Then Dad dials the phone again.

Dad says, "Rick? May I speak to your Mom or Dad?"

He listens a while and then says, "That's great. When they return from the store, please tell them we look forward to an evening with them. Thanks."

On the newly vacuumed living room floor, I close my eyes, imagining the free-for-all that will happen when Justine beans Senator Johnson for calling Dad a Commie Pacifist Quaker. After a while, I go to sleep on the rug, just a nap. Last night we worked late to cover the window and get all the glass cleaned up. This night, I'll need to be alert.

By early evening, my folks have just come back from taking Justine to the home of Friends. They want only grown-up talk. So, with Justine gone, there will be no frying pan on Senator Johnson's head. Even so, I'm worried.

I step out on the porch to think. While I'm out here, Mr. O'Connor arrives.

"'lo, Gilbert," he says, and then we both see Mrs. Silverberg coming across her grass, so we wait for her.

I ask what's been on my mind since this morning. "Missus Silverberg, who did you save from the Russians?"

Her face goes all pink, and she glances at the bushes, and the sidewalk, but not at me.

Mr. O'Connor smiles. "Gilbert, let's save that story for the Johnson family, if they come."

At that moment, I look down the street and I see one lone figure running around the south corner of the block and chugging up the sidewalk. I squint to be certain he isn't carrying a rifle or a baseball bat. It's Rick, without Kenny. No parents.

Mr. O'Connor says to me. "I think you should greet Rick, Gib. But, I will be just inside the door."

I stare at him, thinking, Why me?

He says, "Make a friend, and you have a friend. At least, make an ally, and you have one less enemy."

I have to take a deep breath to stop my objections from coming out. Finally, I answer,

"Yes, sir."

He smiles that really neat, crookedy smile of his, and helps Mrs. Silverberg up the porch steps. The door closes behind them.

I face down the block again, remembering the supposed friends at Neustadt American School who used to call me names and beat up on me. They were no better than enemies, really.

As Rick runs, he glances behind him several times. By the time he gets to me, he breathes hard. I bring him up on the porch, where we are out of sight of the street. "I hope your mom makes a great dessert," he says.

I think, *That's what you care about?* And then I remember his dad pulling back a fist to hit his mother. Rick would never risk that smacking for a mere dessert.

"Mom makes pretty good apple pie," I say. "Want to come in?"

But he hesitates. "Gib, your dad ever . . . like, spank you?"

I shake my head. "Can't remember him ever doing that."

"How about that old lady, um . . . Mrs. Silverberg? And Mister O'Connor? They gonna be mad at me?"

Make an ally, I think. And then I think again. Be an ally. "Rick, I won't let anybody hurt you or yell at you."

He studies me. "You're near as big as your dad," he says. "But O'Connor . . ."

"O'Connor ever hit anybody at school?" I ask.

Rick seems to look inward, like he's seeing back over the first two months of school.

"Nobody yet," he says.

I nod. "I'm glad you came," I say.

He hesitates. Looks me up and down. Looks out once more at the darkening street. It's now dusky enough that the street lights come on and show that the sidewalk is clear of people for the whole block. Rick studies the porch, the door, the window frame with the plywood in it, and then after a moment, he nods at me to go ahead. I grab the door handle.

But before I open the door, I ask, "How come you came?"

He stares at me, screws up his face like he's figuring out why. Then he says, "Maybe I'm spying on Communists."

I nod. "Good try. You came to the wrong house."

"Pfft," he says.

At that moment Mom opens the front door for us. She greets Rick as if she's known him all his life. She re-introduces him to Mr. O'Connor and Mrs. Silverberg, then invites all of us to sit down at the table. She and Dad go out to the kitchen and return with apple pie and ice cream.

I sit next to Rick, because I promised to keep him safe. I don't want him to think I'll go back on that. My folks and Mr. O'Connor do their usual how-was-your-day kind of talk, asking Rick about football practice. After a while I think maybe they actually like football games, because they for sure are interested in how Rick practices hand-offs and kicking and all that.

After everyone has a plate full of seconds of pie and ice cream, Dad says, to Mr. O'Connor, "Rick had some questions about your war experiences, and about after the war." Dad makes it sound like Rick was purely curious.

Mr. O'Connor turns to Rick, and says, "What did you want to know about?"

"Well, I . . . well, Mr. Marvin says . . . uh, where were you?"

"Oh," Mr. O'Connor says. "My crew and I flew out of England over Germany. At first, we were bombing industries, mines, power plants, hydro-electric dams – destroying places to stop the Germans from building more planes, tanks, guns, things like that."

"At first?" Rick asks.

"Yes. During that time, I didn't think about the people who worked in the plants or at the mines. To me, I was just bombing things."

Rick says, "But there were people."

Mr. O'Connor nods. "Yes. Some worked to feed their families. Others were slaves of the German government and had no choice. Some worked there because they hoped Germany would win, and they wanted to contribute to the war effort."

"The war effort?" Rick asks. And I can tell he's thinking what I'm thinking. In news films we always hear about our war effort, never the Germans'.

Mr. O'Connor says, "Later, we bombed a city called Hamburg. By then, I knew I was bombing people. I knew it. One night, we bombed Dresden. Our plane was hit with anti-aircraft fire. We went down."

"My Uncle Rick was a bombardier," Rick says.

Mr. O'Connor studies him a moment, and then says, "That is a job that takes a lot of skill and courage. And it can make you have bad dreams for a long time."

Rick glances up at him, and then down at his fork in the pie. I think I see him nod his head, but if he does, it's a real small nod. He says, "Uncle Rick died."

Dad says, "Yes. And your Uncle Ken. How old were you when they died?"

"I was five. Grandma cried all the time, but it was Grandpa who had nightmares."

I remember when Senator Johnson ran for state senator. He talked about the sacrifice his family made during the war. I wonder if losing his brothers gave him nightmares, too.

Mr. O'Connor clears his throat. "That was a very sad time for your family, wasn't it?"

Rick seems to be seeing the past. "Uncle Rick was home for Christmas around my fifth birthday. He taught me how to ride a bike. Then he flew back to England." Around the table, everyone is silent.

Then mother gets the talk moving again by asking Mr. O'Connor, "When your plane was hit over Dresden, what happened to the crew?"

"Three men in my crew survived the anti-aircraft fire and the parachute landing. Weeks later, we were captured and taken to a German prisoner-of-war camp. Getting out of the plane, I got burned, but not as badly as one of my men. At the first camp, the German commandant had his doctor take good care of my crew. I'll never know why their commandant spent medicine and time on men who were his enemies. Before I knew him well, there was a battle near the camp. Allied air planes came in low. The commandant died."

Rick stares at Mr. O'Connor, but he asks no question, and Mr. O'Connor goes on.

"We were moved through many camps as the war went on. My navigator died of his burns and of starvation when we were in the second camp. I was separated from the other two men when they took me to the camp in eastern Germany."

"Yeah," Rick says. "Mister Marvin said you were in East Germany and got turned into a communist."

Mr. O'Connor smiles at him. "Actually, at first, it was the Germans who ran that camp, but after a time, the Allies, that's our soldiers and French, English, and Russian soldiers began to surround the town and the camp."

"Russian allies?"

"Yes, they were our allies all during the war."

"But after the war . . . ."

"After the war things went sour," Mr. O'Connor says. "The other Allies began jockeying with Russia for power over the countries of Europe."

I look at Rick and think, an ally is a friend you have to keep a watch on. But then, he'd be watching me, too. Better to be a real friend – if you can.

"So, what happened then?" Rick asks.

"The Russians took over the eastern part of Germany. The other Allies had agreed to divide Germany. We U.S. airmen didn't know about that agreement, but that's why I became a prisoner of the Russian Army. Three years later, Mrs. Silverberg and Gib's dad, Mr. Evans, here, were able to smuggle me out of that camp to freedom."

I speak up. "Mrs. Silverberg freed you?"

Mr. O'Connor nods. "She planned my escape." He glances at Mrs. Silverberg. She looks at her plate and twiddles her fork.

"Magdalena," he says to her, "Might as well 'fess up." He turns to me and says, "I was the only American pilot left in that camp by the time the band played its last concert. She made sure I got sprung like the rest of them."

"The rest of them?" Rick asks?

"Sure," he says. "Five guys, all Air Force. Like me, they had bailed when their planes were hit. To free them, Mr. Evans and his house-building friends created one very fine tunnel. Mr. Evans, here, told us about the tunnel by playing music. Their band played a concert for the Russian camp officers each week. But the songs they played were encrypted Morse code, using rhythms."

"Morse code?" Rick says. "You mean like on the decoder ring in my cereal?"

Dad nods, smiling. "Something like that," he says.

Mr. O'Connor says, "But long notes were dashes, short notes were dots. It took us a couple of concerts to realize what we were listening to."

"Ah!" I say, "That's why . . . I remember you wrote a lot of marches for the band."

Dad nods and passes the pie to Rick for thirds. He says, "Once the Americans figured out we were sending code, they began sending code back. Late at night, at fifteen minute intervals for an hour, they banged on the barrack's metal chimney – short messages to show they understood."

Rick leans toward Mr. O'Connor. "What happened in the tunnel?" he asks.

"One morning, we pretended to bury our three weakest Air Force men in the cemetery. But the grave was the tunnel. They cut through their funeral sheets and scooted through the tunnel while we said our prayers over them.

"The next morning, at roll call, we saw that the guards reinforced the barbed wire fence in places where it had the beginnings of holes – holes we had slowly been developing.

"Several of us landed in confinement for two weeks because we were suspected of escape attempts. Soon after we came out of solitary, I waited for dark and sent the other two pilots down the tunnel. I didn't think they'd last another week in that camp."

"Why didn't you go with them?" Rick asks.

"Somebody had to stay on top of the tunnel and replant the shrubbery that covered the entrance. We didn't want to expose the tunnel because there were a lot of other soldiers caught in that camp who also needed to escape."

"You told them about the tunnel?"

"I picked out the man I trusted most. He knew."

"How come the Russians didn't just give you back to the U.S.?" I ask.

Mr. O'Connor nods. "They used us as hostages. In exchange for our lives, they demanded that the U.S., France and Britain give up more German territory, and stop flying food into Berlin."

"So, the U.S. tried to get you out," Rick says.

Mr. O'Connor shakes his head. "The U.S. wouldn't admit we were there. Wouldn't talk with the men who escaped earlier, men who wanted to mount an attack to save us."

"That can't be true," I say. "The U.S. government didn't know."

But Mr. O'Connor said, "The escaped airmen couldn't get anyone at the base to listen to them. One American officer couldn't stand the betrayal, so he came to tell your Dad there would be no prisoner negotiations. That's why your Dad and Mom, and Magdalena knew they had to work on their own to get me."

"Vee hef to sneak him out in front of their nose," Mrs. Silverberg says.

"That was going to be difficult," Mr. O'Connor says.

"Because of your burns?" I blurt.

He rubs his face with his hand – the hand with the missing fingers. "My burns. My height. The fact that I have two left feet and can't march in rhythm – I was that band's nightmare rescue."

At last, Mrs. Silverberg speaks. "Vee could not leave him. Und zo, vee made hats for ze whole band, to distract from his burns. Vee hide ze uniform in ze tuba as vee go into the camp, und hope ze big bell will to cover his face on ze march out. Vee heff also gloves for everyone."

Mr. O'Connor takes her by the hand and glances at me. "Missus Silverberg thinks of the details – every detail, right down to your father having to pee when he gets to camp. One bandsman goes into the latrine with his Tuba and a clarinet inside his coat. Two come out."

Dad chuckles, "Magdalena even planned the song we played to march out of that camp the last time."

Of course I have to ask. "What song?"

"The Camptown Races," Mr. O'Connor says, smiling as big as his mouth will let him.

"Oh, Brendan," Mrs. Silverberg says, "I not chose the song."

He laughs and turns toward me. "No. Actually your dad chose that one. I think the key lines were, "Gonna run all night. Gonna run all day. Somebody bet on the bobtailed nag. I'm gonna bet on the bay."

Me, I'm starting to know my dad better, so I think Mr. O'Connor has it right. Dad chose that song as a way to thumb his nose at the camp guards when the band marched past the barbed wire and back into the free part of Germany.

"Missus Silverberg," I say, "this guy might not be able to march in rhythm, but I'm glad you rescued him."

She nods. "Vee all glad that night."

Rick sits up straight and blinks at my dad. "You went right into that camp? But you're a Commie Pacifist." He suddenly realizes what he's said and drops his fork to clap his hand over his mouth. He shrinks away from me and down in his chair, glancing at the door.

Dad sounds very calm, but I can tell from the low tone of his voice that he is working at calm. I glance at him and see a look I never saw before – sadness and anger together.

"What is a pacifist, Rick?" Dad asks.

"A guy that won't fight."

Dad shakes his head. "A pacifist is a guy, or woman, who chooses to use all the tools available to solve problems between people – all the tools except deadly weapons."

"What other tools are there?" Rick asks.

Mom says, "Can you think of one, Gilbert?"

"Um, how about talk?"

Dad nods. "Any others, Rick?"

Rick glances at Mr. O'Connor, and then says, "Uh, asking questions?"

"Good one," Dad says. "Others?" Dad glances around the table.

"Building homes," I say, understanding better than ever exactly why we were in Neustadt bei Wald all those years.

"How about playing music for your enemy," Mr. O'Connor offers with a wink.

Mrs. Silverberg laughs and says, "How about make zoup for hungry people, und maybe even pie und ice cream?"

She glances at Rick, and smiles. His eyebrows go up. He looks down at his empty plate, and I'm waiting for him to get angry because he's been eating a pacifist tool.

Instead, he laughs, a big deep laugh that gets me going, too. And then all of us are laughing. And I can see that this laughter with us, maybe that is part of why Rick came tonight.

And I wonder if for now, maybe, Rick is at least an ally.

CHAPTER TWENTY-NINE

Dad and I are sitting in the living room, reading the newspaper together. Our window has been finished and looks great, but I worry.

"Dad, did you really take the rock to the police for fingerprints?"

"Yes. I'm not sure if the policeman who came thought it was important. He says the fingerprints on it are all smudged."

"I picked it up. Mrs. Silverberg held it – maybe they really were smudged by the time the police got it."

Dad finishes the *Our City* section and hands it to me. *The Portland Journal* says the Subversive Activities Control Board used its power to list as communists and then deport several radicals. The newspaper tells about recent arrests. One is Arturo Mendoza, 'Union organizer and rabble rouser'.

That's Billy's dad. The paper quotes U.S. Immigration Officer, Roy Norene of Portland. He claims he can tell who is a communist by what they say at meetings.

In another article, *The Portland Journal* talks about deporting Hamish MacKay and William Mackie because they belonged to the radical Oregon Worker's Alliance and are "known communists". The paper's writers are glad that "the Philippino Radical, Mendoza, is already on his way back to where he came from."

"Dad, what gave Roy Norene the right to do that? Deport them?"

"That law we talked about, from 1950, allows the Subversive Activities Control Board to list people as communists and make them register as Communists. Then, if the Board decides to do it, the Subversive Activities Board can decide they should go."

"Go where?"

"They send them back to the country where they were born. Hamish MacKay is from Canada. William Mackie was born in a Scandinavian country, Finland, I believe. Others who were born here, well, the government has the right to send them to concentration camps if we have a national emergency."

"But what national emergency?"

Dad folds his newspaper closed. He shakes his head. "Seems like somebody has decided we have one, but it's not clear who has the power to make that decision."

I remember a comic book that Mr. Marvin let us guys read when we finished math homework.

"Dad, do you remember that comic about the communists taking over the U.S. – the one I borrowed from Mr. Marvin?"

"You mean Is This Tomorrow?"

"Yeah. In that book, we suddenly have a communist government in the United States. People are arrested or killed for protesting what the communist government does. Like that minister in the comic who protested. Remember, in the story, his church is blown up and he is murdered? And Congress is afraid to stand up to the head Communist."

"Pretty ironic, isn't it?"

"What's ironic?" I ask.

"People arrested for protesting against the government in the comic world. Arturo Mendoza is arrested for protesting in the real world. And our U.S. Congress is afraid of Senator McCarthy. *Is This Tomorrow* seems to be today."

*   *

Every Monday at 11:00 a.m., the bomb siren on the Bonneville Power building down near Grand Avenue at Sullivan's Gulch blares at us. Every Monday, it goes off right when we enter Mr. Marvin's class. Mr. Marvin loves to do bomb drills. 'Duck and cover", he yells and we all have to crawl under our desks and cover our heads with our hands – as if our hands could save our brains from atom bomb radiation.

After this week's school drill is over, I climb out from under my desk and back into my seat, where I start writing again. I'm not going to let bomb drills scare me. But, I'm annoyed. Mr. Marvin hovers over me every day since I testified at the school-board hearing. Not only has he made Davie Dashlee the editor of the *Eisenhower Eagle*, but he also marks everything I write with lots of red pencil and boring C or C-minus grades.

I'm keeping my marked-up essays as Exhibit Number One in the 'Mr. Marvin is Unfair Museum'. I have the whole lot of these red-penciled babies in chronological order in a file at home. James, Mike and Elizabeth have files just like mine.

Last weekend we began cleaning out my garage. On one wall, we're setting up desks and Dad's old typewriter so we can write our own neighborhood newspaper. We just have to find a company name that our printer will agree to print.

We're going to install all of our essays on the wall above our page layout table – the place where we have scissors, gummy glue, and white-out paint so we can put together the pages of our newspaper for the printer to photograph.

The printer, Mr. Kent, says, "Keep your language clean, your information truthful, and the format helpful to the neighbors, I'll do a sixteen-pager each month. Two copies for one cent."

But today, in what should be our journalism class, Mr. Marvin just fiddles with the shade on the window behind me, alternately blinding us with darkness and blinding us with the afternoon sun of early October, which is way too low in the sky for eye comfort.

I know he's just trying to make me angry. I've finished his assigned essay topic – the responsibilities of journalists to choose the right news. I must say that this paper is very good; I quote early court findings in favor of freedom of the press to go after all news, not just the news the government wants people to read.

I've thrown in a little quote from Benjamin Franklin, (I'm pretty sure it was from Ben) on the importance of news in a new democracy – this work is good enough to earn me a large F.

Mr. Marvin hates it when I'm quick, brief (like a news writer) and get my points in four short paragraphs. He never assigns a proper journalism article. I think he wouldn't recognize good journalism if it ever happened in our newspapers.

When I run a city newspaper, everyone's side will be heard. I'll be fair, and I'll print the opposition to my own point of view. And then I'll ask for the supporting evidence for both sides. If there isn't real evidence for what someone claims, then that point of view or theory is just whistling, and my newspaper will say so.

Mike says, "Easy to promise. Hard to do."

I pull out a second page and continue writing – but I'm really working on my next script.

"What's this?" Marvin asks, and I'm certain he can tell it's a script. He, however, reaches down in the storage basket under my desk and whips out my blue-covered, Special Projects notebook. He flips the pages and finds my copy of the Christmas cartoon – Mike's Christmas Cartoon.

"That's not for journalism class."

He glares at me and continues to flip the pages. I'm afraid he's going to tear them, so I reach for my notebook. He steps back.

"Mister Marvin . . . ."

"This is very interesting, Mr. Evans. I know he's staring at Mike's drawing of Mom and Dad talking through the fence to the Russians on Christmas Eve.

I speak louder. "It is my notebook, Mr. Marvin."

"You brought it to class," he says.

"To work on at lunch," I say. "It has nothing to do with journalism class."

"We'll see," he says, shuts it and drops it on my desk, letting things fall out of its back pocket onto the floor. He walks away to the front of the classroom.

I glance over at Elizabeth. She shakes her head, warning me not to react. Then James Wray stands and comes to my desk. He puts a hand on my shoulder, gets down on his haunches and says quietly, "Keep your head, Gib. Good so far."

When he rises, all my papers from the pocket are in his hand.

Mr. Marvin says, "James, you can hardly afford to be jawing over there instead of working. Your essays have not been up to snuff, lately."

"Oh?" he says. "Who's sniffing?"

The class bursts out laughing. "Sit down, Jimbo, before I put you down."

James stares at Mr. Marvin. The class is silent, watching.

After a moment, James turns to me and says in the kind of whisper that everyone can hear, "I remember that the nuts in Mississippi never fall far from the tree," he says. Then hands me my papers very slowly before he returns to his seat.

I stand up and say, "I'm going to have to leave now, Mr. Marvin."

"You don't have permission."

I wave a piece of paper off my stack as I walk to the door and open it.

I say, "I've been called out for a consultation on behavior."

"About time," Marvin says.

"Yep. I been nice way too long," I say.

Mr. Marvin starts toward me, but at that moment, Mike stands up in his way. "Permission to open the window, sir?"

"Why?"

As I close the door I hear Mike say, "Very stuffy in here, don't you think?"

I glance back inside. Marvin glares through the door at me, then at Mike, as if not sure if Mike means what he clearly means. Mike stands wide-eyed and innocent-looking – also looking very big.

Marvin checks the buttons on his suit coat, and then he says, "Sit down, Mister Halverson."

"Thank you, sir." Mike says and opens the window about four inches.

I head for home and the garage where I call and make arrangements to interview Councilman Robert Harl for "a writing project."

CHAPTER THIRTY

By four o'clock, I'm talking to Mr. Harl.

"Sure," he says, "I know Mr. Reese. He used to attend the city council meetings. We talked a lot about what was going on with the police and immigration."

"Was the police department ever your bureau on the city council?" I asked.

"No. When I joined the city council, I asked to be the commissioner in charge of police, but the mayor kept that portfolio on his own desk."

"What do you hope the citizens of Portland will do about the problems in the city?" I asked.

"I hope every citizen will watch what the city council members do with their bureaus. That's our job as citizens."

"And the Red Squad?"

"Well, as you know, the mayor says they don't exist. But on the third floor of the city building, there is a room manned by police and police staff. The files are labeled "Subversive Activities". There are rolodex files for citizens who write letters to the editor, citizens who hold signs in protest marches, citizens who were born in the countries of Eastern Europe. The files contain remarks about actions taken whenever these citizens question the status quo."

"Why?"

"Because those who want change threaten existing powers, but ninety-nine percent of the actions listed are not illegal. And they aren't damaging to our government."

That interview came to an end when Mr. Harl's chief of staff came to get him. As he opened the door to leave, he turned to me and said, "I know Reese was a great teacher, but when a teacher starts teaching the real meaning of the first amendment, power is threatened."

"How about you, sir. Aren't you a threat to power?"

"I hope so."

*   *

At four-thirty, I come to the school grounds to play soccer. I'm still thinking about what kind of threat I should be. A kid can't be much threat, but now, I'm looking for ways.

When I get to the field, Rick Johnson stands on the sidelines. He has his arm in a sling and tells Mr. O'Connor he's just curious about the rules for soccer since he can't play football at the moment. Rick even asks questions like he's really wanting to know.

Rick says he broke that arm falling down his basement stairs. I believe that until Justine meets me at home. "Kenny Johnson has a broken jaw," she says. "He came to class with it all taped shut. He's got metal holding it together, and he can only eat through a straw."

"Did Kenny fall down the stairs, too?"

"He can't talk to tell anybody." Justine says.

I've seen Kenny's dad, Rick's dad, in his angry mood. I don't know how a man with that much anger gets to be a state senator. What has happened to Rick and Kenny is not just scary. It makes me feel – I don't know – heavy in my chest, somehow.

Days later, Rick joins the soccer team. I don't quite believe it. He's still wearing that sling and a cast, but Mr. O'Connor lets him take the ball through the obstacle course and do some other easy routines.

Davie is very wary around him, but Mr. O'Connor welcomed him, so the rest of us are taking him a day at a time. On the first day, Mr. O'Connor asks Rick if he'd told Mr. Marvin he wouldn't be playing football anymore.

Rick says, "I told him Kenny would take my place on the team when he gets the bandages off."

"Kenny is younger than you are," Mr. O'Connor says.

"Yeah, but bigger. He makes a good lineman. Marvin needs linemen."

"Who needs linemen?" Mr. O'Connor asks.

Rick stares at him. Then he seems to get it. "Uh . . . Mister Marvin needs linemen."

Mr. O'Connor nods. "Yes. I noticed." Next, Mr. O'Connor says, "You know this team plays everybody. So everybody also spends time on the sidelines."

"Yeah."

"Excuse me?" Mr. O'Connor says.

Rick frowns, then brightens. "Uh . . . yes, sir. I know that."

Mr. O'Connor nods. "Then we'll do fine."

Some days later, Rick has only the sling and no cast. He says he's ready to do more, and he produces a note from a doctor about being able to do non-contact football practices.

"So, the doc thinks you're playing football?" Mr. O'Connor asks.

"I told him soccer is European football. It's fine by him," Rick says.

Mr. O'Connor stares at Rick for a moment. Rick stares back, not blinking.

"How about if you do this next exercise with Gib as your partner?" Mr. O'Connor says.

I freeze up.

Rick glances at me, a question in his rising brows.

Gotta do it sometime, I think.

"Come on," I say. So, we start the partner-fake-out routine that Mr. O'C taught us on that first day. At first, it's pretty easy to fake out Rick, but he catches on, though his sling arm slows him down. When it's my turn to follow him across the field, he fakes me pretty good – looking off to the right, but taking the ball and his feet to the left. I guess he's been watching what we were doing sometime during the last weeks.

*   *

Rick keeps coming to lunch-time practice, and he's learning pretty fast how to use his feet to move the ball. After about four days, he gets paired up with Davie for a partner practice. This time, we're supposed to face our partner, try to take the ball around the other guy, or try to steal the ball. I watch Davie and Rick from the sidelines because I know there might be things said or done between those two.

Mr. O'Connor stands next to me. He says, "Taking care of bad blood is my job, Gib. Go get James into this exercise with you."

That's a relief. He knows what might happen. I start across the field toward James when suddenly Davie sticks a foot between Rick's legs. He takes the ball and puts Rick on his rear end in one motion. I didn't know Davie could be so fast.

"Hey, Stupid!" Rick yells, pulling his arm into his chest as if it hurt him.

Everybody on the field stops, waiting. Mr. O'Connor, silent as a tree, gazes at Davie with those eyes, and that sideways smile of his. If he had an eyebrow, it would be up, waiting for Davie to do something.

Davie stares at Mr. O'Connor. Rick rolls enough to get to his knees. I can see he is about to flatten Davie. Mr. O'Connor puts one hand out and down, a signal. Davie glances from Mr. O'Connor to Rick, then all of a sudden, Davie puts his hand out and down toward Rick.

"Sorry," Davie says. "I didn't think the grass was that mucky."

This speech surprises Rick into looking up at his enemy. That hand seems to be waiting to help. I can see Rick sliding his glance side to side, checking who is watching and what we all might be thinking.

Davie says, "You don't want to stay down there, Buster. You might sink to China."

Rick pushes himself up to his feet. Instead of taking the hand, Rick tags Davie on the shoulder, as if in a friendly bump.

"Or," Rick says, "I could take you down next, Davie, 'cause now I've learned the move from you."

Davie laughs. "You can try." He grabs the ball with his left foot and passes it downfield, runs and catches up with it before stabbing it into our imaginary goal line.

Rick laughs. "Try that again, when I'm looking."

Mr. O'Connor laughs, too. So, I know it's going to be okay, this time.

On the way into class, Rick comes up next to me. "You know Stockman?" he asks.

"Sure. Round the end of the block?"

"He told my dad he was going to cream you for stealing his ideas about bomb shelters."

"What? He showed me. He wanted to show me."

Rick shrugs. "Watch for him." Then he goes into class without looking back.

* *

That afternoon, in the school hall, I step out of the library. Around the corner, I hear Mr. Marvin talking to Mr. O'Connor.

"You make a habit of stealing my players?"

"I believe Rick made that decision."

"You bribe him?"

"Sure," Mr. O'Connor says, chuckling. "Told him I'd help him with his math homework."

"This is not a laughing matter," Mr. Marvin says. "His father wants him to get a football scholarship to the U."

"He's an eighth grader, Elias. He's got plenty of time for football in high school. Besides, he's already learning a lot about footwork by playing soccer. Might be an even better quarterback because of it."

"You'll be hearing from the Senator, you can bet on it."

"That would be better than hearing from his secretary," Mr. O'Connor says.

I decide to go out of school the other way. No way Mr. Marvin will like it if he thinks I'd heard that zinger.

CHAPTER THIRTY-ONE

Two weeks after our dessert with Rick Johnson, the *Portland Journal* features the President of Oregon Educators for Democracy, Mr. Elias Marvin. Top left of the page is a photo of him in front of a huge American flag.

The story reads:

> "*Mr. Marvin, an ex-Air Force officer, served out of England during World War Two. He and Senator Johnson's brother, Richard, were mates in the same crew. It was during this time that Marvin and Johnson first became aware of the frightening future represented by communism among the labor parties of England and other European countries.*
>
> "*Today, Marvin is vigilant, serving with Portland's political leaders as eyes and ears, seeking out probable spies and Red supporters in our region. He helped Senator Johnson write the proposed state bill that would have allowed Oregon to force*

all the states' teachers and others to take an oath that they had never been members of, nor supported the Communist Party."

"We encourage Marvin and Johnson's further efforts to reintroduce the bill to incarcerate, without bail, any suspected Communists teachers up to trial and, or deportation. This needed bill was ignominiously held up by the left-leaning members of the State Education Committee of our legislature. Johnson, with Marvin's help, vows "We will continue to present this bill until we can make our state safe from these hidden, spy-infested cells and their operatives."

I glance over at my dad. He's editing some music he's written, but he looks up at me.

"Reading the trash liner?" he asks.

"Can't get it in the can fast enough," I say, but I can't help myself. I keep reading and it gets worse.

"Elias Marvin says he has discovered certain teachers at local colleges and other educational institutions whose politics are 'suspect'.

In the next paragraph, he describes, but doesn't name Mr. O'Connor, Mrs. Hill and Mr. Halverson. His descriptions are so specific he might as well have named them. Then he goes for one more.

'Just one of many examples of suspect classroom teachers is a music teacher at Portland State College. This man is a known draft dodger who spent several years after the war meeting weekly with Communists in East Germany'."

He means my dad, but he doesn't need to name him. Portland State isn't a big college. It has only one teacher who was a Conscientious Objector during the war and lived in Germany after the war. I don't know how Marvin knows about the weekly band concerts, but he makes them sound bad.

* *

After school, Rick waits for me in the hall. Davie is stuck in Mrs. Hill's detention again, because of not handing in homework. So, I get Rick outside and away from the school. He fiddles with his arm sling. As he stretches his arm out, I ask my question.

"You read about Mister Marvin in the news this morning?"

"Sure did." He's silent a moment, like he's thinking about what to say next, and then he adds, "Dad made sure I read that article. Said that ought to show me why he's telling me I can't play for Mister O'Connor. Says Mister O is a bad influence."

"But you played with us at noon today."

"And Mister Marvin will phone him up tonight to tell him I played."

"So, you choose to be in trouble?"

He stretches out his arm again. "I have to."

"When he finds out, what will happen?" I ask.

"He'll beat me up, when he gets home from Salem."

"Rick, I . . . ."

"He'll try, but he's getting old."

I stare at Rick, who is really only a little bigger than me. My stomach roils just thinking about him fighting his own father. Plus, his dad is not that old, not old enough.

"Don't worry about me," Rick says. "Worry about my mom. Worry about Kenny who has all that metal holding his jaw together, but he still thinks Dad runs the world. Kenny is bigger than Dad, but he's so afraid, he can't fight back."

He stops talking suddenly, and I look up. We're walking past a lady weeding her rose garden. I think about how it would feel to go home to fist fights and beatings. Then, when we get out of ear-shot of the gardener lady, I ask my next question.

"So how did Mister Marvin know about my Dad's concerts in East Germany?"

Rick glances over at me. "You think I told him?"

"Don't know how else he would know."

Rick studies his size large tennis shoes. I figure he's deciding whether to admit he told. He says, "My dad has access to all kinds of records because he's a senator. One thing he does real well is look for dirt. He gets Mister Marvin to look up teachers' records, and people's secrets. It turns out the Army commander at that base where you lived, he kept records. He called those concerts 'unauthorized fraternization' between Americans and Communists."

I feel my neck hairs cool. "Mr. Marvin works for your Dad?"

"Tight buddies. And both of them work with the Chief of Police. They love the hunt."

"Hunt for Communists?"

"The hunt for anyone who gets in their way. Which reminds me, he thinks you're working on a community newspaper and I'm supposed to warn you not to publish."

"What? How does he know that?"

"Somebody who didn't buy an advertising space from you because you and Mike are related to known revolutionaries."

I'm so ticked off I almost don't hear the next thing he says. "Dad says I can't have anything to do with you and your family because of your school board speech."

What he says sinks in slowly. When I realize what it means, I stop walking and face him. "But you waited for me after school."

"Dad's not home today. Down in Salem at the state capitol until the Friday before Halloween. He's busy passing laws to stop foreigners from taking over our country, or more importantly, from changing the rules at his company."

*   *

The next day, I know I have to do something about stopping everything that Senator Johnson and Mr. Marvin are trying to do. I get together with Mike, Elizabeth and James. We decide to start the *Eisenhower Neighborhood News* as soon as we can.

We plan a lot, how we'll sell more ads (Elizabeth will do that, because she's not homely like Mike or hard to talk to, like me), how we'll distribute (first three issues free, after that a nickel an issue unless advertising covers our costs), and how we'll find stories, (doesn't everyone love to see a story about themselves or their friends?).

I'm really hot to find out more about Mr. Johnson and Mr. Marvin – how they work together and why. So, I skip school and take the bus down to Longshoremens' and Warehousemen's' headquarters. I've called ahead and made an appointment to talk to the Secretary-Treasurer Lincoln Greene. I told them I was doing a news article for *Eisenhower Neighborhood News* on the rights of unions.

"You're a kid." The guy says when I come in his office.

"Yes, sir. But I'm the editor of the *Eisenhower Neighborhood News* with a circulation of five hundred in Northeast Portland, (the number of houses where we figure we can drop off our first sample edition).

"Pretty sharp. You sell ads?"

"Yes, sir. Half page is fifteen dollars and a quarter page ad is ten."

"What? You printing on eight by eleven?"

"No sir, eleven by seventeen. So your half page ad would stand out."

"You're good, kid. I'll give it some thought. But, you said you wanted to interview me about, um," he looks at his appointment notebook.

I take out my pencil and notebook. "About the rights of unions to organize. I'm a friend of the Mendoza family, sir, and that's what made me think about this."

His face goes still. "Mendoza. I bet you know Billy."

"I do. Classes. Soccer team."

"What do you know about the working conditions at Cargo Car?"

"Nothing. Can you tell me about it?"

"Twenty men injured this year by unsafe machinery, welding, cranes dropping sheet metal recklessly – or maybe on purpose. And when old cars need cleaning, no fans to push out the air made toxic by the solvents. Five men this month overcome by fumes during cleaning."

I'm writing fast. "That five on top of the twenty who were injured?"

"Yes. And then, Mendoza was trying to organize at Jones Frozen Foods. His wife worked there. Icy water up to the ankle on that floor, and exposed electrical wiring snaking around near the water – place is ripe for a lot of deaths, and short of that, a lot of illness from working in that water. Workers get sick, there's no way they can stay home. Five have had pneumonia and two of those died. The other three lost their jobs because they didn't come to work when they were in the hospital."

"So that means the workers need representation to have safer conditions, but what right do they have to demand to be represented by a union?"

"In this country? None outside the right to assemble. And the factory owners would like to keep it that way. They sell the government and everybody else on the idea that union representation is Socialist, or worse, a Communist idea."

"How would you describe the idea of union organizing?"

"In the United States, all people have the right to assemble, even if they assemble to discuss organizing and to work toward making representation a reality. They have a right to strike and picket peaceably, but picket lines are broken up by the police and picketers arrested for disturbing the peace. And then, some, like Billy's dad, get deported on the trumped up charge that they are Communists."

"Why do the police break up picket lines?"

"They are not working for John Q. Public."

"Can you prove that?"

"Not yet, kid. But I'll let you know when I can."

We talk a little more, then I shake hands with Mr. Greene and go out into his outer office. I sit down, trying to put my notes into a story. I see a big guy walk into the office. I recognize the rain slicker, and the man inside it.

He doesn't notice me, but I know Mr. Stockman despite the bandage on his nose. He pushes past the bookkeeper in the outer office and barges into Secretary –Treasurer Greene's office.

"Senator Johnson sent you again? Can't he wait until that nose heals?" the Secretary asks.

I hunch over my notes and listen. Three fellows from the next room come into the outer office. They're clearly listening to this conversation, waiting to pounce if necessary.

I don't think Mr. Stockman has any idea he's walked into a potential fight.

"You're on notice, Greene," Mr. Stockman says in the other office. "Johnson is not taking 'No' for an answer. You lay off Cargo Car or he'll see to it you meet with the interesting end of a shovel."

"Stockman, I believe that message came from Johnson. You never have anything that colorful to say."

Stockman says, "You're nothing but a Commie stooge, trying to ruin Johnson's source of income. The first sign of a strike and you're off to Australia."

"I know how this works, Stockman. I hope you are very certain the Chief is in your master's pocket."

"Why wouldn't he be? He doesn't like Commies any better than the rest of us."

"That's hardly the reason the Chief does Johnson's work. I notice the guy is driving a car he didn't buy and lives in a house he didn't pay for. What do you get for your efforts?"

"I get to clean this country out of people like you."

"We'll see who gets cleaned out. Now you can leave."

Stockman opens the office door and sees the three men. "Out of my way," he says. They step back between me and him. One of them actually bows and waves him out the door. None of them pay any attention to me.

Now, I have a story. Wonder if that bit about the chief of police is true. If I use that, I think that's liable if I can't prove it. But I can ask who paid for the chief's car and house. Would that be liable?

And another question: when did Mr. Stockman become the voice of Mr. Johnson at union headquarters?

After a while, when he's had time to start his truck and move on, I go outside to wait for the bus.

"You little shit." That's Mr. Stockman. "I thought those were your tennis shoes I saw in there. Now, I know you and your dad are in this union stuff." Stockman's moving in on me. His fist is balled up.

"I'm a reporter," I say. "I'm here to interview the union head."

"Yeah? That what you were doin' when you barged into my basement?"

"You invited me in."

He grabs my jacket front, and pulls back his arm. "But you kept from me some vital information, didn't you?"

His fist smashes into my face. I know I'm falling, but I don't know much else. As I hit the ground, I hear him say, "The whelp of that pacifist, stealing my plans to pass to the Reds."

That's when the pain starts.

* *

Hours later, I wake up in a hospital bed with Mom holding my hand and Justine hovering over her shoulder, crying. Mom says Mr. Greene brought me to the hospital. My nose hurts like something exploded in my head. I guess it did. The doctor says it's a good thing I'm nearly grown up. That blow would have done a lot more damage to a kid's head.

The phone company helped Mr. Greene find my parents by going through the phone records of calls to his office. I didn't know they kept records like that. Do they always do that? Or just keep records on calls to suspected Communist unions?

* *

Today, I've got to take this nose to school. My face is still blue, but my nose is in a cast just like Mr. Stockman's. I bet that was his revenge on dad. Stepping aside may have worked for Dad, but I didn't have a choice.

Dad looks at my face and says, "I'm sorry, son."

"It's not you, did this," I say. "Got some newspaper I can read around this plaster?"

Justine says, "That's your proboscis."

"What?"

"Justine," Mom says. "We aren't in need of new words for nose, this morning. We need some quiet."

My hand goes to my plaster. I don't know if I can face the kids at school wearing this.

Justine stares at her plate and whispers, "An elephant has a proboscis. An anteater has a probos…"

Mom puts her hand on Justine's arm. "Enough." Justine stops.

Dad hands me the paper. In today's *Journal,* Mr. Marvin has an opinion piece. He says,

"There are teachers working with very young children and with youth athletic teams who have much to answer for in their background. One teacher of my acquaintance," Marvin says, *"was in Eastern Germany for nearly three years after the war, and no one knows what Communistic influences he may have picked up during this un-accounted time."*

Later in the story he cites examples of the negative influence these types can have on their own children as well as their students. And then he describes the comic book he *"discovered in the notebook of the child of one suspect teacher."*

Me? A child? I've got a nose that will prove I'm not. And it still hurts.

"This concocted and slap-dash comic book," he says, *"is the joint creation of that child and the son of a prominent member of the school board. It graphically depicts friendly relations with Communistic types."*

Slap-dash?

The article ends, "Such clear examples of subversive influence on our students cannot be ignored."

Marvin sounds like Senator McCarthy. And just like McCarthy, he hints that he has found many, when he really only mentions three. He uses the word 'communistic' over and over. I think McCarthy made that word up himself.

Two months ago, I imitated McCarthy, too. But, Mr. Marvin is getting dangerous, and the *Portland Journal* seems to love quoting him. In my heart, I refuse to call him Mr. Marvin anymore – he is just Marvin.

We're going to lose our favorite teachers. And, my parents won't sign. Quakers refuse to take oaths. Their acts speak for them. Or so they believe.

*   *

Sure, I get a lot of questions when I come to school. The most interesting is the question I don't get. Mr. Marvin never asks about my nose.

First thing, as I enter the building, Rick meets me, like he's been waiting.

"Is your nose going to be all right?"

"Doc thinks so. Might be a little crooked, but he's put all the bones in the right place."

"Can you breathe?"

"Mostly through my mouth."

He shakes his head. "That damned guy. He's out of control."

I look at Rick. Doesn't he know who controls Mr. Stockman? I'm not going to say what I heard, and now, I'm wondering what's the right thing to do for a friend? Does a real reporter write what he knows even if it's going to hurt someone?

During lunch, I convince James and Elizabeth to wait in the hall after school. Then I ask Rick to get Davie out of there. "Tell Davie I'm doing research and can't walk home with you guys."

"Yeah. The goody-goody excuse."

"What?"

"Davie will believe it," Rick says. "He already thinks you study too much."

I laugh. "Anything more than zero is too much for Davie." Laughing makes my whole face hurt.

After school, only Mike and I enter Mr. Marvin's empty classroom.

"Hello, boys," Marvin says. "What can I do for you?" His eyes are working to ignore my face.

"You can produce proof," I say, "Or you can take back your accusations."

"Whom did I accuse?"

Mike says, "You didn't need to name the people. Everyone knows who voted against you at the school board hearing."

And then, I add, "And everybody knows you're copying Senator McCarthy. Not very creative."

He glances at me, his face tight. Mr. Marvin knows I've just quoted some of his red-pencil remarks on my papers.

"If I were you . . ." He starts, then seems to think of a new tactic and turns on Mike.

"Michael Halverson, do you have any idea how many signatures Portland Safe Democracy has on the recall campaign for your father?"

"Does it matter?"

"It should matter to you. Your father's reputation is not good. That will begin affecting his building business."

Now Marvin turns to me. "And I've had quite an interesting conversation with the president of Portland State College. That school is an indulgence in this state. We have two very good colleges in Oregon already. Any damage to Portland State's reputation will mean reduced funding by the legislature."

"You are a credit to your kind," I say.

I heard Mom say that once, when she was talking to a man who gossiped about everybody. At the time, I thought she'd given him a compliment. So did the gossiping man.

Marvin isn't fooled, though. His eyes narrow as he stares at me. "I have asked our principal, Mister Patton, to move you to a study hall instead of my class because of your disruptive attitude. We don't need people who always get into fights."

I feel like I've been hit again. He thinks he can turn this smashed nose on me?

Plus, I need this class to graduate from the eighth grade. I know it. And Marvin knows it.

Mike whips around and calls over his shoulder, "Come on, Gib. There's no talking to the two-per-centers."

Mike has this theory that only two percent of the population is really stupid enough to believe McCarthy's incendiary scare tactics. The other ninety-eight percent are more scared of McCarthy than of spies or of Russians. Mike never reminds me that I used to be a two per-center myself.

I take a last look at Marvin. He's smiling at me. It's not a nice smile.

Out in the hall, we find James and Elizabeth.

Mike says to them, "I think I got enough quotes to use in our editorial. Let's go to work."

The three of them leave me there in the school hall with my job to do. They go out the door, heading to my garage, where they are going to start writing the first edition of *The Eisenhower Neighborhood News.* Mike's first editorial will be about our conversation with Mr. Marvin – revealing his threatening tactics.

Next, Mike plans to interview his dad about how the Red Cross served during the fight to save France, and then to liberate prisoners in the extermination camps. That will be Mike's way of revealing my dad's part in the war. I've borrowed – really taken over – Dad's old Brownie Box camera, so I can have photos of Mr. Harl, Mr. Greene, Mr. Halverson and Dad in the newspaper.

My three friends have a plan to do a lot more good old neighborhood news: stories about local shop owners, neighbor gardens, anything to get people to want to see their name in print and build a big readership. We've agreed on all this beforehand.

My job is to make sure our best teachers sign the loyalty oath, so they will be here all year, and into the future, like for Justine's future. I'd hate for Justine to spend a year in the wooden chairs in the principal's office just because she's left with Marvin for a teacher.

CHAPTER THIRTY-TWO

I swing into Mrs. Hill's classroom. She has one student cleaning erasers and black boards, so I can't talk to her. I sit down in a desk and wait.

When she notices me, she tells the other kid, "Tommy, those are clean enough for today. Let's not have a similar meeting tomorrow."

The kid looks at her angrily, then at me. "What you in here for?" he asks.

"Beating around the bush," I say.

He looks puzzled. "What?"

Mrs. Hill looks at me over her glasses as if urging less smart-mouth. Hold onto thy cleverness, I remind myself.

"I'm just kidding," I say to the student. "I talk too much in history, not about history."

The kid nods. "I read too much, not about history." He grabs up his jacket and heads out the door.

Mrs. Hill still studies me. "Well, Gilbert. I hear you are taking up news-papering outside of school hours."

I'm surprised. "Where'd you hear that?"

"From Elizabeth Gray. And Mr. Greene, the Union Secretary-Treasurer. How's the nose feel?"

"It hurt all day. But we're starting on the paper tonight. Cleaned out the garage last weekend. It's our office. Did you read the article in the *Portland Journal*?"

"You mean the one quoting our local spy hunter?"

I nod. Now comes the hard part. I say, "One afternoon, you were in the teachers' room, and the door to the mimeograph room was open."

She smiles and sits down at a desk near me. "You overheard Mister Marvin talking about Mr. O'Connor." I guess my relief must show, because she smiles at me and she goes on. "I heard the mimeograph machine running over-time. Figured it was our student news editor. No teacher tries to force a mimeo stencil to last through that many copies."

I laugh. "Yeah."

"And," she says, "You've come to warn me about what Mister Marvin said after I left the room."

"How'd you know?"

"I've been warned by another informant," she says. Then she seems to hear what she just said, and she chuckles. "'Informant' sounds like conspiracy talk, doesn't it?"

"Yeah. All the comic books call it that." Of course I know her other informant has to be Principal Patton. Who else could it be?

Now I can get down to business. "Missus Hill, me and ... I mean James, Elizabeth, Mike and I are hoping you'll sign the loyalty oath."

She looks around at the empty desks in the empty room. "James Wray? Mike Halverson? Elizabeth Gray?"

"Yes. They're not here because they're working on our first news edition. Also, we figured if all of us talk to you, Marvin might figure out what's going on."

She nods. "Thinking strategically, are you?"

I shrug. She reaches over and writes the word 'strategically' on my notebook. "Look it up." She's like my mom – always teaching.

"Are you talking to other teachers?" she asks. "Mister O'Connor, for instance?"

"He's next on my list."

She puts her hand on my arm. "Do your parents know about your 'Please sign' campaign?"

I shake my head.

She frowns. "I thought not," she says. Then she straightens her suit buttons, smooths down her worn skirt front, and finally says, "That article took the starch out of me, I'll tell you. Can't lie about that."

"Mike and I, we tried to talk to Mister Marvin about how unfair it was, but, well, we weren't very good at it."

"Not very Quaker-like, eh?"

My face grows hot. "Dad's good at it. Mom, well, sometimes Mom says exactly what she means when she's angry."

"Like your little sister, I wager."

I'm surprised she knows Justine that well. "Yeah. I mean 'yes'."

She smiles at me. "We can all practice to be more like both your dad and your mom. Both ways of working are effective, like union negotiators – the tough negotiator and the compromising negotiator – one is scary to bosses who mistreat their workers, so they think about accepting the compromise offered by the other one."

I wonder about her husband, the Union Man. And I wonder about accusations against unions. Are they really hotbeds of Communism? I file my questions away as future research for our newspaper.

Right now, I have to convince her. "Will you sign the oath? We need you here at school. If you don't sign, they'll fire you. Like Mister Reese."

She gazes at me. "Look at this part of the oath," she says, holding the papers toward me.

Even before I look, I know the part she means. It's the part that Dad objects to, and Mom.

I see where her finger points: ' ... the foregoing shall not prevent any inquiry as to whether the applicant, employe [sic] or eligible has any beliefs inimicable [sic] to the government or who advocates or is a member of an organization which advocates the overthrow or resistance by force of our form of government.'

"I know," I say, "nobody should ask you about your beliefs, only your actions. My dad and mom say that, too."

"Separation of church and state," she says. "No religious test applied. And I'm not even mentioning freedom to gather peaceably in groups."

I know she's right. All that is in Article One of the Bill of Rights – stuff that Mr. Reese made us memorize in seventh grade.

"But we need you," I say. "Isn't staying here one of the actions you can do to help us?"

"I don't know, Gilbert. I have to think on it."

"Okay," I say. "We just wanted you to know we hope you will do it."

"Thank you," she said. "And thank the others. It's good to know you care."

"Please don't leave us with this."

She holds up her hand, probably to stop me from saying bad things about others. "Gilbert Evans, I can imagine how it will be if I don't sign. But I must think about it, carefully."

I nod and stand up. I guess I've said all I can, but I leave her classroom feeling real low. It sounds like her husband was a fire-eater, the tough negotiator she talked about, and she admired him. She's not going to sign.

I wonder if a person can get into high school without graduating from eighth grade. I don't think I'll make it six or seven more months here.

Out in the hall, I gather my courage and am about to shove on into Mr. O'Connor's classroom, when James Wray comes around the corner from the boy's bathroom.

"Came to warn you, Gib," he says. "Marvin's meeting with Mister Patton right now."

As we duck back to the doorway near the bathroom, I say, "Mister Patton? He wouldn't believe Mister Marvin. He even warned Missus Hill about the guy."

James looks up and down the hall before he answers me. "Maybe Mister Patton got scared," James says. "Maybe he has to listen to The Whisperer these days."

"The Whisperer?"

"Yeah," James says. "Marvin – the guy that whispers lies in everyone's ears."

I'd laugh, but then I can't think it's so funny. "Would a principal be afraid of a screwball teacher?"

James nods. "Ever since the school board meeting, Marvin's got more power than any principal."

I stand there like my feet have been glued to the floor tiles. Things are so upside down.

"You've got to convince Mister O'Connor," James says.

"Want to come in with me?" I ask. "I don't want to be the one who fails to convince him."

James shakes his head. "No. We agreed it should be just one of us. And you've known him best and longest."

That's when I realize Mike must have told James about my meeting with O'Connor at the railroad tracks. I didn't think Mike had guessed Mr. O'Connor was the same guy.

CHAPTER THIRTY-THREE

Mr. O'Connor hunches over his desk. He pinches the bridge of his nose with his good hand. In his damaged hand, he holds the loyalty oath papers. I recognize them. Dad has the same papers on his desk at home.

"Sir?" I say.

He sits up, as if waking suddenly. His eyes blink, the way mine do when I clear out the memory of a dream. Then he glances across the room, but doesn't seem to see.

"It's just me," I say. "Gilbert Evans."

He sighs down deep, and then, at last he looks at me, at here and now.

"Come on in, Gib," he says. "What can I do for you?"

I shrug. "Talk?"

"Maybe I should pop the guy who popped you?" He smiles, so I know he's just kidding.

"Don't think my dad would approve."

"Probably not, satisfying though it might be."

I grab a chair and drag it backwards up to his desk. I want to do this right.

I straddle the chair and say, "I'm here for some kids in the class – for me and others. We figured Mister Marvin better not see a crowd coming into your room."

He puts the papers down and waits. His silence makes me fidget. It's like he's telling me to get to the point.

"We hope you'll sign the loyalty oath. We want you to be our teacher, and we don't see any other way."

"No other way? Why do you believe that?" he asks.

"The school board meeting. Well, people make assumptions, and they're afraid."

"You're afraid."

"We're not afraid of radicals. We just don't want the school board to think you are one."

"You and some of the other students. Let me guess. Mike, Elizabeth, maybe one or two others?"

"James Wray."

"Ah, yes. James."

Mr. O'Connor puts both of his hands on his desk and stares at his missing thumb and pointer finger. "Gilbert, if I sign that oath, what will I be teaching you?"

I stare at his hand, too. I think about how that happened. I imagine shoving back the top of a burning fighter plane and jumping into empty space, hoping the chute isn't too damaged. I imagine bullets flying at me.

"Thee . . . You wouldn't be teaching me that you are loyal to America. I already know that."

His hand moves to hide in his jacket pocket, like he knows what I've been imagining and it embarrasses him. "So, Gilbert. What would you learn if I sign this oath?"

"That you want to stay and be our teacher."

"Don't you already know that?"

I look up at his face, his blotchy skin, his dark blue eyes, his twitchy, puckered mouth. "Yes sir, I know you spend a lot of time and your own money getting us stuff for experiments, and helping us figure out what it all means – gravity and motion, and plant food, sun, and all that science stuff."

His face loses some of its tightness. "Stuff," he repeats, chuckling.

I'm embarrassed because I want to convince him we've been drinking it all in like we're thirsty, but it sounds like I've just barely understood – like I've kind of absorbed a little of his lesson, not gulped it down.

So, I try again. "I'm not saying it the best way, but I know you want us to learn how things work."

He nods. "And if I sign this oath of loyalty, what will you know about how people work?"

When he says that, that's when I'm certain I can convince him. So, I blurt it all out, not the way I planned, but the way it feels.

"I already see how they work," I say. "I see people grow afraid of something. I see other people make them be afraid. And then people can't think. Like me – I didn't think. I read these news stories. I listened to the hearings and the news on the radio."

I rattle on. "I thought there were all these scary people, communist spies, trying to take over our world, and it took me way too long to figure out that it was the people making me afraid on purpose. McCarthy, and Marvin, and the Educators for Democracy Committee, and the House and Senate Hearings, and all of them, those are the people taking us over. And they have taken over because everybody believes them, or is afraid of them."

He puts his good hand on my arm, and I stop. He's looking at me in a way I've never seen before, kind of like he's my dad, and I've fallen and broken my leg.

But I'm not broken, and it's him I'm worried about.

"Gilbert," he says, "Do you remember the day I arrived on the train?"

I've never mentioned I know that was him.

When I don't answer, he tilts his head down a little, looks me in the eye so deeply that it's like we're locked onto the truth, and I can't look away. Then he says. "Remember?"

So, he doesn't mind that I know. "Yes, sir," I say.

"You were not afraid of me that day."

"No, sir."

"And you've never been afraid of the Emperor Maximilian."

"You've met Max? Down in Sullivan's Gulch?"

"Often," he says, and I try to imagine him sitting under the bridge overpass, talking to Max over a cold can of tuna fish.

"He's not scary," I say, "just skinny and tired."

"And scared of you."

"Why me?"

"He says you made him be a host to God, and he can't get away from it. He has to be different because of it."

"I remember that day. I just meant . . ."

Mr. O'Connor nods. "I know what you meant. Your mother and father used that phrase "something of God in every man". They used it on me when I lay in the Vets' Hospital after the camps. Back early in the war, I had to jump from that burning airplane because I was shot while dropping bombs on a city. And even after your dad's band rescued me, the memory of burning cities, and the thought of burning people is what kept me sick for a long time.

"Because of your folks, I tried to find the Something of God in myself. And when at last, I got a glimpse, it shone as a small flicker of light. It needed all my attention to keep it in the world. Working at saving that bit of light, that helped me get well."

I realize that because of Max, I did start to think differently about me, too.

Mr. O'Connor says, "Two months ago, you were afraid of communists."

"Yeah."

"Now, you're afraid of other people's fear. If I sign this oath, you will still be afraid."

I feel coldness between my shoulder blades. "But if you don't sign it, you won't be here to teach me anything."

He nodded. "So, I must decide what lesson I most want you to learn."

That's the moment I know I will lose him. "But then we'll be left with teachers like Mr. Marvin."

"I know, Gib," he says. "But, this is what I want you to remember." He pulls the papers toward him, takes up a pen in his left hand and writes across the first page. "I refuse."

He glances at me and smiles. And then he puts those papers in an envelope that already has the stamp and Mr. Patton's name and address on the front.

"Want to walk with me to the post box near my rooming house?" he asks.

I stand. "Yes, sir."

CHAPTER THIRTY-FOUR

On the Friday before Halloween, Eisenhower School always has a party. Today is party day. Justine is an embarrassing pain in the butt all the way to school. Her costume for the Halloween party can't get wet. Her hair can't get wet. Justine has no homework to carry, but both her hands are busy holding her rain slicker over the silly hoopskirt of her costume.

From our house on Sixteenth Avenue to the school at Thirteenth Avenue, I have to hold a huge umbrella over her with one hand while trying not to drop my notebook and the grocery bag carrying my own costume. I won't be caught wearing a costume on the way to school. I'm not even sure I have the nerve to wear it for the party.

Sometimes I marvel at Justine's belief in her own importance. She never seems to imagine that anyone might laugh at the Queen of the Night – black velvet dress (cut down from some old gown of mom's), black lace gloves, black and silver crown of construction paper and the silver wrappers from chewing gum.

Her crown bobs at a jaunty angle over very short brown curls made droopy by Portland's wet air. We arrive at the busy intersection of Fifteenth Avenue and Brazee Street, near Ventnor's Market. The seventh grade crossing guard, Dwight Smith, starts to hold out his guard flag to stop traffic for us.

But he never gets it out because the city bus revs up its motor and aims itself at the curb and the rain puddle. I pull Justine out of the way of a big splash.

Dwight Smith jumps back onto the curb, yelling, "Hey!" The bus screeches to a halt.

Dwight says, "It's that crabby Mr. Schmidt, again."

The front door opens, and the driver acts like he thinks we'll climb aboard. I'm sure he saw the crossing flag, because Dwight is a tall kid for seventh grade.

Justine pokes her head out from under the umbrella and shakes her scrawny fist at the driver. "That not funny," she yells. "You come out here in the rain and see if you like it."

"Sorry, lady," the driver says in a deadpan drone.

"You 'bout hit Dwike," Justine yells.

"Kids shouldn't try to stop a city bus," Mr. Schmidt says.

"I have your bus number and I'll call your boss," Justine hollers just before the door hisses shut.

I duck my head to cover a snort of laughter. But my little sister turns on me. "You moved the umbrella."

The bus pulls away while Justine glares at me. Dwight stares at her in what looks like big-eyed admiration.

"Where'd you get that bus number idea?" I ask, trying hard to be straight-faced.

Justine's hands fist. Her chin pushes out at me. "You remember when the policeman arrested Momma at that meeting about loyalty oaths at colleges?"

I nod. I sure do remember. "Yeah," I say, "Dad and I had to bail you both out."

Dwight is all ears for this conversation.

"Well," Justine continues. "Momma wrote down that policeman's badge number and his name. He tried to take the paper away from her. She knocked his hand back, and that's when he arrested us for 'saulting an officer."

I didn't know about assaulting an officer. All I knew was that Mom had been in a cell with most of the members of the quilting bee from Friends' Meeting House. For peaceful people, Quakers seem to go to jail more than most.

Justine doesn't wait for me to sort out that memory and her reasoning. She elbows Dwight's flag out for him and starts across the Fifteenth Avenue, one hand pulling her coat around her and the other pulling my sleeve so the umbrella will keep up with her.

Dwight holds his flag like a stupefied robot. "Good luck, Gib," he says.

I ignore him.

"You're weird, Jussy," I mutter. "Why does Mom's arrest make you think it's a good idea to threaten the bus driver with his name and number?"

"Momma was arrested because she scared the policeman. That Mr. Schmidt-bus-driver is probably praying I don't remember the bus number all the way to my classroom."

"A lot of good prayer will do him," I joke.

"Right. It's number Five-nine-oh-nine on the Broadway Line going north at 8:15 in the morning," Justine nods so big she has to let go of her coat and grab her crown.

I want out of the job of being her brother.

We arrive at the school side door and stand under the last of the cherry tree leaves as Justine turns her freckled face up at me. "Gib, we got to stand up to people."

"What?"

"You know what Momma says?" I shake my head.

"She says, 'Just because we are Quakers doesn't mean we have to do the quaking'."

With that, Justine takes the umbrella handle out of my hand and shoves her way through the door. I stare after her as her umbrella, still open, bobs down the hall toward Mrs. Price's third-grade classroom.

A fight a day. Two on a good day. My nutty little sister. Someday, I'll have to buy season tickets to Weekly Ladies' Wrestling where the star will be Justine Evans, Queen of the Night.

CHAPTER THIRTY-FIVE

It turns out that this Halloween Friday all the guys at Eisenhower School decide to wear costumes. I haul my Dracula cape out of the shopping bag. It's damp.

I stick the wax dog teeth in my mouth and growl across the aisle. Elizabeth laughs, but she covers her throat with one hand and leans away from me in mock fear.

These teeth kind of hurt my broken nose, but they make the costume.

At the change of classes from History to Science, Mike comes up dressed as Babe Ruth, complete with beer-gut pillow. He holds open a large shopping bag. "I've got those glass cleaner things you asked me for."

Startled, I stare down into the sack at the big suction cups. Back when we were cleaning out my folks' garage, he'd joked with James about having these things for window cleaning on tall buildings. They keep stuff like this at Mr. Halverson's construction warehouse.

"Wow! Theeth are geaaat!" I say, but the dog teeth make talking hard, so I just slip one of the suction cup's elastic handles over my hand.

"I got some for your knees, too."

There in his grocery bag, attached to even bigger bands of elastic, sit two suction cups nearly as large as the high-hat cymbal on the school drum set.

"Thankth, Mi'e."

Mike grins, then adds. "Dad says, 'Don't try to leap tall buildings in these things'."

I take out the dog teeth for a moment. "Be right back for science class." I stash teeth in my mouth again and step into the short arched hallway that leads to the Men's room.

Over the recessed doorway it still says 'Boys'.

Once inside the empty room, I pull the leg bands over my chinos, and admire the way the knee suction cups look. I could climb just about any building with these things on. I shove the hand bands over my fingers, positioning the cups on my palms.

I test the hand suction on the metal wall of a nearby toilet stall. My left sticks until I lift my palm. Then it pulls right off. But the right hand is stuck tight. I yank, but it won't come loose. I yank harder. The metal wall bulges toward me.

"Hey," a familiar voice yells from inside the next stall.

It's Rick Johnson. I can hear Rick's tennis shoe squeak and then his foot slams the flusher on the toilet. His stall door bangs open and Rick comes out. He stows a comic book in the back of his pants, but not before I notice the image of Superman.

Rick also studies me. "Oh, this is priceless," Rick says. "Dracula climbs castle walls and can't get down before sunrise. Death to the vampire."

"Fffery funny," I say through my wax teeth. I start to shake off the left suction cup so I can use that hand to pull the right one off the wall.

"Hold on there," Rick pulls a skinny wooden handle out of his pocket, holds it away from himself, pushes something and pops out a long blade. I have heard about these new switchblade knives, but I've never seen one. I glance at his face. He has me trapped by the stall. His hair hides a lot, but not the gleam in his eyes.

"Be real still," Rick says, "so's I don't hurt you much."

I hold out my left hand and its suction cup like a shield. Rick laughs softly and takes a step toward me. I crouch, ready to bat at his knife arm. I think, maybe he really is the one who threw the rock that shattered our living room window. In one swift movement, Rick slides his knife under my stuck suction cup. It falls with a plop to the floor. There is a scratch in the ugly green paint on the metal wall.

"Got to break the seal, is all," Rick says, smiling at me. "What'd you think I was going to do?"

I spit out the teeth. "I don't get it. Why are you friendly these days? Why play soccer when you're so good at football?"

"Well, let's put it this way," he says. "I got tired of saying 'yes, sir'. So, I'm going out of my way to dare him to bust my nose."

"What's that mean?"

"It means I do what I have to so's I can live my own life."

"Yeah? So, you play soccer. That's a dare. You play for O'Connor when he wants you to play for Marvin. That's a dare. But what about Kenny?"

"Kenny's going to have to figure out what he wants. If he wants out, I'm there for him. Meanwhile, he's still saying 'yes'."

"So, has anybody busted your nose?"

"Not like yours," he says, reaching his fist toward my face as if to bust me again. I stand still, working not to duck.

Rick smiles at me. "But Dad will. He'll get out his ...well ...he'll start to steam. When he blows, his neck veins bulge. Not pretty." Rick glances toward the bathroom entry door. "The bell's rung for science class."

"Uh- oh," I say.

"Me," Rick says, "I'm a hobo today. Hobos just hang out, so I'm headed for the football field to watch the high school work outs. Maybe I'll meet up with Kenny after school. For you, Dracula, if you want to slink up and down the halls, I recommend not using the suction stuff."

Rick clicks his knife back into its handle and walks out the door. I stand there, overwhelmed by the idea that Rick dares to argue with his dad. Senator Johnson is a big man with a big temper and a lot of power in this state.

Moments later, I stuff the wax teeth back in my mouth so I can pull the glass cleaners' suction pads off my knees. I pick up the smaller ones from the floor and stuff them all back in Mike's shopping bag. I go out into the alcove just outside the bathroom and lean against the doorjamb, trying to get rid of the thought of Mr. Johnson's neck veins popping as he hits Rick.

I hear the next classroom door open.

Mr. Marvin's room. I hang back in the alcove entry to the restroom, hoping Mr. Marvin won't pass by and give me trouble about missing class. Next thing, I hear Mr. Marvin talking to someone.

"You just go knock on O'Connor's door," Marvin says. "Keep the weapon out. He'll think it's a great joke. He hasn't seen one of these for years."

"But Mr. O'Connor doesn't know me, sir." That voice is Dwight Smith, the crossing guard from Fifteenth Avenue.

"It's okay," Marvin says. "He'll get a real thrill out of the outfit you've got on. Probably want to know all about how your dad got it."

"Like I told you . . . .."

"Yes. You told me. Now tell O'Connor. And keep the weapon drawn when he comes to the door."

Dwight starts shuffling down the hall, seeming unsure. I hear Marvin close his classroom door. I hope it is safe to come out of the alcove. I poke out my head. Marvin is in his room with the shade drawn over the door window. Off to my right, I see Rick's back as he heads toward the steps out to the playground. And to my left is Dwight.

From behind him, I watch Dwight walk toward the science class. As he gets closer to the door, I stare at what he's wearing. It's some kind of wool suit, black pants and gray- green jacket. It fits like Dad's band director's uniform.

Not only is Dwight really tall for thirteen years old, but he also looks more grown up than a lot of eighth graders I know. In that uniform, he looks like an adult.

As he passes Mrs. Hill's classroom, Dwight puts on a cap – gray- green upper part with a black band and visor. As soon as I notice the matching black collar on the gray- green coat, I know Dwight is wearing a World War II German SS uniform. I've seen them in the war comics.

The black pants are a little big even for Dwight, but he seems to have them hitched up with a bulging belt that pushes out the back of the field coat. As Dwight reaches Mr. O'Connor's door, he shoves up the back of the field coat and pulls an awkward, long-nosed gun out of a holster.

My hair prickles. I know something bad is about to happen. I spit out my wax teeth and start running.

"Don't," I shout. But Dwight has already knocked on the door.

"Don't do it," I yell again, running toward Dwight's back. Before I can catch up with Dwight, Mr. O'Connor opens the door. The look of horror on Mr. O'Connor's face makes me freeze.

Mr. O'Connor screams over his shoulder, back toward his class. "Drop and cover. Drop and cover."

He grabs for Dwight's gun arm, twisting it toward the side. Behind O'Connor, the classroom goes into chaos. Girls shriek. Books slap to the floor as kids crawl under desks, just like in our weekly atom-bomb drills.

O'Connor pulls back his fist and aims at Dwight's head. I run at Mr. O'Connor. Flying into him, my head catches his ribs with a crunch. The hallway seems to go black, but I can hear O'Connor's grunt of pain and feel the thud of our bodies landing on the linoleum-covered floor.

"Put it away, Dwight," I shout. "Get out of here with that thing."

As my vision returns, I see Dwight sit hard on his rear end, staring at Mr. O'Connor, the ugly gun still in his hand.

Mr. O'Connor grabs at my shoulders, and at the same time kicks shut the door on his classroom.

"No more!" Mr. O'Connor yells. "No more!" He tries to crawl over me to get at Dwight. Most of my air whooshes out with the weight of the man, but I hold onto O'Connor's belt, forcing him to drag my body with him. My Dracula cape strings stretch across my throat, strangling me.

"He's a kid," I gasp. "It's Halloween."

O'Connor swipes at Dwight's nearest boot. Dwight, terror in his wide eyes, scrambles backwards down the hall. Behind Dwight, Mrs. Hill and half her class have come out of her room. Beyond her, Mr. Marvin's class stands in the hall watching the whole scene.

Marvin laughs. The students stand, bug-eyed.

The string on my cape busts and I can breathe again.

"Stop," I yell. "Don't hurt Dwight. Mr. Marvin sent him."

Mr. O'Connor's body goes slack. A silence falls over the three of us.

"Oh, God have mercy," Mr. O'Connor whispers. "God have mercy."

Mrs. Hill orders her class back into their room. She directs one of the kids to call the office. "Tell Principal Patton we need him. It's an emergency."

She calls to Marvin. "Get your students in order and back into the classroom, immediately."

Marvin, startled, begins to obey her, then turns and says, "Do you need help?"

"Not from you," Mrs. Hill says, pointing her stubby finger at him. "Get into your classroom and control yourself."

He does exactly what she says.

Beyond Mr. Marvin, Rick stands near the steps to the playground, his knife still out. His mouth is open as if he can't believe what he sees. He looks at me, at the back of Mr. Marvin and then off toward the outside – toward our neighborhood. He seems to be thinking, adding things up. Next, without a word, he flips that knife into his pocket, strides down those steps and out the back door of the school building. It's like he's decided to do something.

And suddenly, I'm afraid of what Rick will do.

Mr. O'Connor pulls himself to a sitting position. "Son," he whispers to Dwight. "Put that thing in its holster and take off the jacket and hat." Dwight does as he is told.

"I'm sorry, Mr. O'Connor," I whisper.

"Thank you, Gib," Mr. O'Connor says, his hand resting on my shoulder. My throat hurts all across the front with a burning pain.

"Gib Evans here needs some medical attention," Mr. O'Connor says to Mrs. Hill.

I feel Mrs. Hill kneel beside me, her soft, fat hand on my forehead, her eyes on my throat.

Beyond her, I see Elizabeth Gray at the window of Mr. O'Connor's classroom door. Her glance assesses my throat, a frown on her face, her light- colored eyebrows pinch with worry. A moment later, she turns back toward the science class. Through the door glass, I hear her say, "Mr. O'Connor has everything under control. You can all get back into your desk seats, but stay quiet until Mr. Patton comes to take care of Dwight and Gilbert."

"I think," Mrs. Hill says, "that you three have had enough Halloween and ought to go to the hospital. Elias Marvin can very well take care of my class as well as his until we can get a substitute."

"My class is still on the floor," Mr. O'Connor groans as he tries to rise.

"No," she says. "Elizabeth Gray has them sitting quietly in their seats."

Mrs. Hill rises. In pained silence, we watch her open Mr. O'Connor's classroom door. "I want you students to get out whatever reading book you may have and stay in your seats until I come back from my classroom. I'll be a few minutes."

She closes the door on Mr. O'Connor's class and asks me. "You heard Mister Marvin send Dwight to knock on the door?"

I nod.

Dwight says, "I told him Mister O'Connor didn't know me."

She glances at Mr. O'Connor and says, "Vicious and stupid. A bad combination." Then she glances at Dwight. "I don't mean you, Dwight."

Mr. O'Connor stands up, reaching a hand down to help Dwight get up. Dwight hesitates, but after a moment, he puts his left hand out and lets Mr. O'Connor pull him to stand. Dwight's other arm, the one Mr. O'Connor twisted, hangs limply at his side.

"Your name is Dwight?" O'Connor asks.

"Yes, sir. I'm real sorry, sir."

"So am I, Dwight." O'Connor, though holding tight to his injured ribs, puts one hand on Dwight's good shoulder. "Excuse me. I need to say something to my science class." Mr. O'Connor opens the door and speaks quietly. "Ladies and gentlemen, I'm proud of you for hitting the dirt when I yelled at you. Good reaction time like that could save your life someday."

At that moment, Mr. Patton rushes up. "What's going on here?"

Mr. O'Connor is still talking to his class. "I want you to do whatever Mrs. Hill says until I return. We're going to make sure Dwight and Gib are taken care of."

In the hall, Mrs. Hill answers Mr. Patton. "Everything out here is taken care of," she says to Mr. Patton. "Mister O'Connor and these two boys have been hurt while trying to protect his class."

"What? Protect them from what?"

Mrs. Hill doesn't answer. Instead, she says, "I think we need an ambulance for Gib Evan's throat wound and Dwight's arm."

"Patients who can walk? No ambulances. We're not telling the entire school and the neighborhood that we've lost control over here at Eisenhower School."

"Mr. Patton," Mrs. Hill begins.

I break in. "We can go in Mister O'Connor's car."

Patton turns on me, surprise in his open face. "This your doing, Gib Evans?"

I'm too startled to answer, but Mr. O'Connor speaks. "While you drive us to the hospital, I expect we can fill you in on the details."

"I want a report now."

Mr. O'Connor's eyes narrow. "Let's start with the fact that Gilbert here saved me from doing something real stupid. As a result, he may have a concussion and we need to get to St. Joseph's Hospital."

"So it's you," Patton says, squaring off with Mr. O'Connor and staring straight at his tie clasp. "You'll have the parents and the superintendent even more down on me if you've hurt this kid."

I'm thinking, *Even more than what?*

Mrs. Hill steps between the two men. "Where is your car, Mr. Patton? You need to bring it to the side door now."

Mr. Patton stares at her as if she is the Wicked Witch of the West, but he pulls out his keys.

"Meanwhile," Mrs. Hill says, "I'll call a substitute for my class so I can help Mister O'Connor's class settle down."

Surprising to me, but not, evidently, to Mrs. Hill, Principal Patton nods and says. "I'm parked out here, right up Fourteenth Avenue."

As he ambles toward the door, however, his agreeableness evaporates. Over his shoulder he says to Mr. O'Connor, "I want a written report, O'Connor, and I'll need it by the time we leave the hospital."

Mr. Patton used to be a reasonable principal, but not since the board meetings and the oath letters.

CHAPTER THIRTY-SIX

Sometime later, in the waiting room at St. Joseph's Hospital, Mr. Patton says to Mr. O'Connor, "Here are three bus tickets for your return trip. I have to get back to Eisenhower School and take Mister Marvin's statement about what happened."

Mr. O'Connor lets Mr. Patton's hand hang in the air, tickets dangling.

"Mr. Marvin?" Mr. O'Connor asks. "Why not Missus Hill? Or Gilbert, here, who saw the whole thing? Or Dwight, who was sent to my door?"

Mr. Patton glances at me and Dwight, then speaks low, as if we can't hear him whisper.

"Mister Marvin is the adult."

"Are you certain?" O'Connor pauses. "And Missus Hill?"

Mr. Patton glances toward the door. "Oh. Of course. But she arrived after the fact."

Mr. Patton lays the bus tickets on a nearby chair and says, "I'll see you back at the school, boys." Then he walks toward the door that leads to the parking lot.

For a moment, Mr. O'Connor watches Mr. Patton's retreat, then he reaches into his jacket pocket and says, "Dwight, here are two dimes. I believe you should call your mother and father. Tell them what happened and where you are."

Dwight stares at the dimes, as if he's imagining how his mother will feel when she hears. Then he nods and leaves us to find the pay phone.

Mr. O'Connor's attention is on Dwight's back.

I say, "Mister Patton should have called Dwight's mother."

"Oh, he will do that. Right after he talks to Mister Marvin."

I sit there, stunned, thinking what Mr. Patton might say. And then I remember Rick's face right before he left the school.

"You know," I say, "Rick Johnson saw what happened to us in the hall, and I think it made him mad."

Mr. O'Connor looks puzzled. "Angry about what I did?"

"No. I think he left to have it out with his dad about what Mr. Marvin does, what the Senator and Marvin do together. He's pretty much done with his dad and his ways."

Mr. O'Connor's eyes open wide. He kind of whispers to himself, "Oh, that poor boy." Then he turns to me. "I need to talk to your mother or dad, right away."

I fish in my pocket for a dime to call Mom.

Mr. O'Connor stands, and walks to the Emergency Room check-in desk.

The woman behind the desk looks up. She winces slightly as she catches sight of his scarred face. "You really must just wait, sir," she says. "Doctor is very busy. He will get to your case as soon as possible."

"May we call this young man's mother and tell her where her son is?"

"Oh." She glances at me. "You aren't his father?"

Mr. O'Connor points at the papers we filled out when we arrived. "I am his teacher. May he call his mother?"

I show her the emptiness of my pants pockets. "No dimes."

She looks at Mr. O'Connor. "No dimes," he says. His hairless left eyebrow rises, waiting. It's the only eyebrow he has, so it's pretty obvious when he uses it. I can see the lady doesn't want to have to look at him much longer. She pulls her big black phone around so I can dial it.

I call Margaret Fox House for Women. When I get mom, I hand the phone to Mr. O'Connor. He tells her where we are and that we'll be taken care of. Then he turns his back on the secretary and talks a little more.

"Christine, call the judge. That boy is in danger again, right now."

I don't know what this is about with the judge, but within a minute, my mom is catching a ride to the hospital from one of the other volunteers.

*   *

Mom, Dwight, Mr. O'Connor and I are going to ride home from the hospital with Mom's volunteer friend. Dwight's mom, Mrs. Smith, is at work across town and has no car. She says his dad is on a business trip, so we're taking Dwight home first. Mom has called Mrs. Smith several times to let her know how Dwight is. His dislocated shoulder is fixed, but I can tell it hurts.

Mrs. Smith told Mom that Mr. Marvin called, telling her an entirely different story than Dwight did about how Dwight got injured.

As we leave the hospital, I see Mom's friend do a double-take on her three busted up passengers. Dwight's arm hangs in a sling. Mr. O'Connor's ribs are taped because when I tackled him, he fell pretty hard. The doctor covered Mr. O'Connor's hand in bandages because his little finger busted when he landed on the hall floor under me – one of the few fingers on that hand.

I have no concussion. I'm pretty hard-headed. A gauze bandage circles my throat where my Dracula cape tried to strangle me.

We climb into the back seat. Mom sits up front, but she rolls down the window and talks to Mr. O'Connor. "The mom said the boys weren't at home, but the social worker got a scare."

"Did she go inside?"

"She got run off the property."

Mr. O'Connor's mouth goes tight. He nods. I think they're talking about Rick, but I'm sure they don't want me to ask.

Mr. O'Connor grins at us boys as he climbs in back.

"You guys look a mess."

"And you're such a beaut," I shoot back, and then I'm embarrassed for talking to a teacher like he's one of the guys.

Dwight smiles, but his smile sits sadly in his face.

"Not feeling good, eh Dwight?" Mr. O'Connor's face grows serious again.

"I'm thinking about why Mr. Marvin did that."

"I'll tell you why," I start in, but Mr. O'Connor holds up his hand.

"Dwight," he says, "why he did it doesn't matter as much as what we all learned from it."

I frown, but Dwight nods his head and then drops his gaze to the floor. "Yes, sir. I should have done what my gut said. I should have walked away from him and not knocked on your door."

"And I," Mr. O'Connor says, "should have known a long time ago that inside, I am still fighting the war."

Dwight glances up at him and says, "You can't ever forget war, sir. My dad still ducks every time an airplane flies overhead. He scrunches down when we drive under a bridge, or when some car backfires."

Mr. O'Connor nods. "I know the feeling. I can fool myself for a while, but I'm not the calm person I hope to be."

I think none of us is what we hope. I believed I was this great communist hunter, and then I discovered I'm just some kid who understands nothing, whose writing got used – used against all the people I care about.

I don't think Mr. Marvin is really afraid of subversives any more than Senator McCarthy is. I saw how much Mr. Marvin enjoyed controlling all those people who came in a frenzy to the board meeting. And they enjoyed jumping on cars and threatening others. And after that meeting, did a real anti-communist throw the rock at our window? I believe somebody just loves to scare us. And they are doing a good job.

"Mr. O'Connor," I say, "Let's go back to school. Let's let everybody know we're okay. Let's let Mister Marvin know he can't do things to us anymore."

Mr. O'Connor looks at me, long and sad, then he studies his hands. "Gib," he starts, then has to take a long breath. "Gib, I have to resign."

"No!"

And I hear Mom whisper, "Oh, Brendan."

"Why quit?" Dwight asks. "Marvin hopes you'll quit."

Mom's friend glances into her rearview mirror, her eyes pinched with concern. Mr. O'Connor looks at his hands again for a long time. While he sits there, the brakes on the car squeak. We stop at a red light. Then silence closes in on the five of us.

Mr. O'Connor stares at his hands, closing and opening his right fist.

Finally, he says, "I'm a big guy, and I've hurt people badly because I thought they were after my crew or me. Back when we were hunted day and night, after we bailed out, I near killed a man who came into the woods where we hid. He came to offer us a hiding place."

He stops, still watching his knuckles whiten. "My crew had to haul me off him. And even after I beat him, he still helped us, limping back to his barn and signaling when it was safe to follow him inside. We hid there for two weeks before the Nazi's shot up his house and took his whole family with us to a prison camp. He still limped the morning they hanged him."

Mr. O'Connor looks up at us, then at me alone. "I can't take a chance anymore. I thought I was well, but I could have hurt you badly."

"But Dwight's right," I say. "That's what Marvin wants. He can't get Mr. Patton to fire you fast enough."

"Oh, sooner or later, Mr. Patton will have to fire me, all right," he says, "But today has shown me that I must quit now, before I hurt someone else."

Mom speaks up. "Wait, Brendan. Don't quit now. Give yourself the opportunity to argue against the oath in court."

Dwight says, "Don't just give up. That's what my dad did. Gave up and now he hides out in our house all the time."

Mr. O'Connor looks at Dwight. "No business trip?"

Dwight realizes his family has been caught in a lie. Then, slowly, he nods his head. "No business trip. My mom has a waitress job. And she couldn't leave to come or she'd be fired."

Mr. O'Connor puts a gentle hand on Dwight's hurt arm. "One thing I can do, Dwight, is talk to your Dad. Get him some help." And then he turns toward me, "But I can't be teaching kids anymore."

In the front seat, my mother drops her head to her hands. "No, Brendan," she whispers. "You're too good. And you've worked too hard."

"It will be all right, Christine." His voice breaks on her name, and in that moment, I know Mr. O'Connor has discussed this possibility with Mom and Dad many times before.

CHAPTER THIRTY-SEVEN

On the Monday after the Halloween party, the school district superintendent ignores the school board vote and allows the principals to 'answer their conscience' about the need to fire teachers who didn't sign the loyalty oath. The names and addresses of those teachers are all in the *Portland Journal*.

When I read that list, my skins grows cold.

After that article, ugly things begin to happen – one teacher's home caught fire when the burning cross fell from his lawn into his front porch. His family escaped out the back door. The fire department took forty minutes to get to the scene.

Before the firings, Mrs. Hill had planned ahead. She had lined up a job selling children's clothing at the Meier and Frank Department Store, but when the list came out, the store manager fired her. Said he couldn't have a communist working with little children.

"Gimme a break," Justine complained. "She going to sell them communist clothes? Or communist shoes?"

* *

Two days after the superintendent's announcement, the mayor has another. We hear the news on the radio – the one Mike moved into our garage office. As the news reader's voice oozes from a death report sympathy to his fun-times tones, every one of us in the office stares at the radio.

"In this year of grave danger from the Russian threat," the announcer says, "we will celebrate our Veterans with a Rally for Democracy. On Armistice Day, November 11, the city will hold a rally beginning at 11:00 a.m. to celebrate our veterans, our visitors from the House Committee, and our Democratic way of life. The rally will be in the natural amphitheater known as the Bowl, in Northeast Portland."

"Nice!" James says, "A party for the Spanish Inquisition."

"They might as well have a bonfire of the heretics," Elizabeth says. She holds our newspaper, a stomach-sick pallor on her face.

Mike is drawing fast. Over his shoulder, I see the rounded slope of the outdoor theater we call the Bowl. He's started drawing a stage. By the time he puts victims at a stake on the platform, I turn away.

I like the Bowl. It's where our All-City Student Orchestra puts on an annual concert. All Dad's choirs and bands from Portland State College have put on concerts there. The odd thing about this outdoor theater is how close it is to the Union Pacific tracks.

A band conductor has to know when the freight trains will rumble through. Dad always has his students plan a pantomime or a silent farce for the five minutes it takes to get rid of that train noise. The farces have been pretty funny, so people come partly to see what Portland State College will do during the train.

The Bowl is a great place for free events. HUAC and the mayor will want everyone to attend this celebration. The crowd will be huge.

I mention the announcement at dinner. "They said, 'Rally speakers include Portland's own Senator Roland Johnson and Mr. Elias Marvin, Chair of Educators for Democracy.'"

Mom says, "Gilbert, could you pass the jam?"

"Didn't you see this, Mom?"

Mom looks at me and says, "We are eating dinner, Gib. And we are going to let Mayor Peterson have his party without us."

But I'm thinking about an article I have pinned to my wall near my desk. I keep these old articles to remind myself of what I used to take in as the whole truth.

> *"The House committee on un-American activities renewed its recommendation that spies and saboteurs be subjected to the death penalty in peacetime, as they are in wartime."*
>
> *The Oregonian, Sunday, December 28, 1952*

This rally that Mayor Peterson plans, it's on the annual celebration of wartime.

*   *

After that, the *Portland Journal* carries a whole page advertisement for the rally every morning.

Pretty soon after the firings, Mr. O'Connor's landlady told him she needed his room in her boarding house for a relative who might move back to town. He's now renting a room in Mrs. Silverberg's house.

Mr. Halverson hired Mr. O'Connor on his construction crew, but Mike told me some of the guys were not happy about having "a proven Marxist-communist" working next to them.

Mr. Halverson thought their complaints would die down after they saw how hard Mr. O'Connor worked, but things got kind of ugly whenever Mr. Halverson or his manager, Mr. Burleigh, weren't at the construction site.

To solve that problem for Mr. Halverson, Mr. O'Connor found a job with men who work maintenance on the Portland streets. Even there, a group of men complained.

Mr. O'Connor told Dad what the crew boss said to his crew. "When you can spread asphalt as fast as O'Connor, I might listen to your whining."

For the last two days, though, something more is going on with Mr. O'Connor. He has called the house, talked to Dad and they seem to be whispering some of the time. The one thing I have heard is Rick Johnson's name. I'm not sure what's going on, but it makes me wonder about where Rick is right now. None of the kids have seen him since Halloween.

* *

Elizabeth Gray came to our next garage news meeting with an editorial about how unfair the firings were. Her editorial talked about how the *Portland Journal* and the school district went against the constitutional right to have a trial. "Those who feel free to burn crosses in lawns, and the firemen who decide to arrive late to put out the fire are just as unpatriotic as those who have decided a fair trial and a Grand Jury are not necessary. Portland has become part of the United States of Pretend Democracy."

After I read her editorial out loud, Mike says, "Mr. Sanderson, will never print this. It's too controversial."

James takes the editorial and starts fitting it into the page. "We won't know until we test him."

We took the paper to Mr. Sanderson the next afternoon. He read the editorial first and then scanned the rest. "Fine work. Better than that cowardly daily we could all use for wiping..." he looked at us and stopped. "Nice work," he said. "This will spice up the first issue nicely. You'll have a lot more subscribers than you can imagine."

* *

On Friday, we delivered the first issue of the *Eisenhower Community News* and an advertisement flier about how to subscribe. We actually covered about seven hundred houses, most of the school neighborhood. Some of the guys from the soccer team helped us, including a couple of fellows from Alameda's soccer team. Raymond

Byers, Alameda's goalie whispered to me, "It's not fair your mom was fired. She made school sane."

Saturday, the day after we delivered our first issue, I'm outside early in the morning. I feel better about things, because last night, several neighborhood businesses called to congratulate us on a great newspaper. We had done stories about businesses in the area and that really turned the paper into a big success. Those businessmen and some others want to be sure they get advertisement in the next issue. One dress store owner told me he had more people in his store that day than the whole previous week.

No one mentioned Elizabeth's editorial. Maybe they only read the first few pages. The editorial was part of a two page spread toward the back. Most of the editorials were letters to the editor written by adults we know in the neighborhood.

Today, the weather is very warm for November seventh – heat brought by a southern breeze we call a Chinook Wind. I glance across the driveway toward the newly planted garden in Mrs. Silverberg's yard. It's looking pretty good.

Mr. O'Connor sits on Mrs. Silverberg's front porch, so I go for a visit. A tray of food lies on the wicker table near him. Mrs. Silverberg has brought his breakfast outside, so he can enjoy the crisp air. I hear her inside, humming and washing dishes.

"Morning, Gib," Mr. O'Connor says, and he reaches over to the coffee table, gesturing that he'll pour me some coffee.

"No thanks," I say, plopping into one of the wicker chairs. "But I would eat one of those biscuits, if there are enough."

He smiles. "Thought you might." As he hands me one and a knife, he adds, "Have you seen your friend, Rick Johnson?"

"No, sir. And I'm kind of worried."

"How so?"

"The day of the Halloween party and he hasn't been back."

"Well, will you let me know if you see him? And let me know how his little brother is getting on?"

"Sure." I don't want to mention again that Rick seemed angry about what happened to Mr. O'Connor. Mr. O already feels guilty about that day. I ask, "You know Kenny has a broken jaw, don't you?"

"I do. Interesting newspaper you ladies and gentlemen produced this week."

I'm grateful that he changes the subject. "Thanks."

"That Elizabeth Gray doesn't mince words."

"She sure doesn't."

"She's a keeper," he says. I glance at him, afraid he knows what I think about Elizabeth. He winks and says, "I mean, keep her on the staff."

"Yeah, sure. She's a partner."

"Looks like you've got the beginning of a big success."

"I sure hope the newspaper is a success," I say. "We can't do it for free for very long."

"What would success look like to you, Gib?"

"Well, I guess that people would read it. They'd want to subscribe."

"What would the paper itself look like as you continue?"

"I got into doing it because I don't like how Mr. Marvin and the *Journal* used my essay. That was a way of lying."

"So, you want revenge?"

"No, I want to make a difference. The *Journal* says whatever is popular. I want to say what's real."

"Real, as you see it?"

I think about what he's saying and come up against a hard thing. "What I see isn't always real, either. I'll try to hunt out what is real."

"Even when it disagrees with you?"

I stop, and a picture flashes into my mind. I say, "Mr. Patton has a poster in his office. I'm trying to remember what it said."

He nods. "Freedom requires your search for truth."

"Yeah. That was it." I slice my knife through butter for the other half of the biscuit.

Mr. O'Connor says, "I've been thinking about the day we met. I did catch another fish that afternoon, but Sullivan's Creek was pretty dry."

"With last week's rain, the creek'll be up," I say, buttering the half biscuit.

"Shall we see if any fish are biting?" He pushes the raspberry jam jar toward me.

I'm really glad he wants to do something fun. "Sure," I knife into the jar. "I'll get a couple of new fishing poles, and some lines and hooks."

"Finish your biscuit. Then I'll help you cut switches from the Big Leaf Maple in your backyard. Isn't that where you usually get your fishing poles?"

"Yes, sir."

He gestures at my biscuit. I've put jam on my knife and it's about to fall off, so I shove the biscuit under and catch a big glob. I know, from the handwritten label on the little jar, that Mrs. Silverberg makes this jam herself.

An hour later, the two of us are hunkered over a wide spot in Sullivan's Creek. Two fish lie on the wax paper inside my wicker fishing basket. The leather strap holds the lid down, but the tail of one long trout is caught under the edge of the lid. Our lines are in the stream again, a worm on my hook, and a bird feather on Mr. O'Connor's "for an experiment," as he says.

Up under the Twelfth Avenue Bridge, I've seen The Emperor Maximillian puttering around his camp. No train is scheduled to come along for a while. And, until next Wednesday, November 11, no one is making speeches or setting up for a concert over at the Bowl on the other side of the bridge, so, it's very peaceful.

I can smell wet and mold in the nearby dirt. Blackberry brambles arch, leafless. A few dried up berries still hang on. Somewhere up on the south bank of the gulch, between the golf course and the blackberries, a bird sings one long buzzy whistle.

"A Hermit Thrush," Mr. O'Connor says.

"How do you know?"

"One of the fellows, a German fellow, in the POW camp, knew birds by their call. That's what kept him alive, I think, teaching the rest of us to recognize the life that hovered just beyond the barbed wire."

Mr. O'Connor stops, like he's remembering those days, those men. Then he says, "In Germany, while my crew and I were still free and hiding out, I used to fly-fish in small streams like this. It's a silent way of catching food. Only the birds know you're there."

"And the fish you catch," I add.

He chuckles. "The hardest part about hiding is cooking. Fire can be seen, if you're not careful. One of my men was badly injured, so we had to cook his fish, make it go down easier." Mr. O'Connor smiles, and he adds, "And his collard greens."

I recall James Wray's collard greens. "How'd you cook it?"

"Start a fire at dusk when it's hard to distinguish smoke from the gray of nightfall. Keep the fire low. Create enough coals to bake. And then bank those coals to cook several hours without another flame."

"Did any of your crew make it through the war?"

He stares at the creek surface, as if it holds the answer to my question. "I wish I knew. We were separated, moved around. For all I know, one or two of them are still in POW camps inside the Soviet Union."

"So, doesn't the U.S. Army know about these missing guys?"

"No matter how many letters we veterans write, begging them to look into it, we get replies like, "Thank you for your concern. The United States Armed Services are doing all they can to verify rumors about prisoners ..."and on and on like that. No answers."

I stare at the creek and wonder how it feels to know your own government is lying, and your friends might be dying in Siberia because the government won't push for their release.

Soon after that, we take our fish, wave to Max and climb the hill to go home. As we walk up Fifteenth Avenue, I hear the freight approaching, out at the Forty-Seventh Avenue Crossing.

CHAPTER THIRTY-EIGHT

It's Monday, November 9th. Rick Johnson has not returned to school for ten days. I wait outside Justine's class to see Rick's little brother because I've learned from Justine that Kenny's jaw still is taped up. He has a hard time opening his mouth.

When he comes out of class into the hallway, I ask him, "Where's Rick?" He points at his jaw and acts like there's no way to tell me. I hand him a pencil and paper, but he pushes them away, glares at Justine, and then me.

"Come on, Kenny," I say. "Take care of Rick. You guys can't stay there and just get beaten up again."

Kenny says. "What about Mom?" He grabs at his jaw. That little talk hurt something awful. Then he blurts, "I shouldn't make him mad."

"You mean your own dad?" I say.

Kenny stares at me a second, then he walks off and when I call to him, he refuses to turn around.

Standing next to me, Justine yanks on my shirt sleeve and says, "Leave him alone, Gib. He won't tell Mrs. Price anything, so he sure isn't going to tell you."

"Is Mrs. Price asking about Rick?"

"No, Dummy. She asks about how his jaw got broken. He won't talk or write. Fat lot of good asking does."

That afternoon, I sit in study hall, watching the rain outside the classroom window. The door opens, and Elizabeth comes into study hall this morning instead of to Journalism class. She hands a note to the study hall teacher and then sits at a desk, just looking at her lap. So, I go over there like I'm searching for a particular book in the shelves next to her.

"What's up?" I whisper, facing the bookshelf.

"Mr. Marvin doesn't want me in his classroom," she hisses.

I glance at her. "Why?"

"I'm a bad influence on the other girls."

I get down on my haunches as if the book I want is on the lowest shelf. I'm thinking fast about what this all means. "How can the best writer in the class be a bad influence?"

"I associate with the wrong type of boy."

My chest feels slammed. I grab at the bookshelf. That damned guy is giving her a reputation. I stand, about to leave and have it out with him when she looks up and shakes her head. I stop.

"I guess he's the only person in town who read the editorial," she says.

"He mentioned the editorial?"

"No. He just said I should know better than to meddle in men's work."

"I'm going ..."

"Not if you care about me," she says. "You fight, you make it worse."

"Then what?"

"Ignore him. For me."

I look at her pleading face and know she's right. I pull a book out of the nearest shelf and return to my desk, where I can't do anything but imagine Mr. Marvin's smug face. I'm beginning to know how helpless it feels to have people in charge who lie to you, like the government lies about POWs in Russia. In Elizabeth's case, the person in charge lies to ruin her reputation and if I do anything, the lie will go everywhere.

I wish I could rub Marvin's face in the mud puddle under the rhododendrons in the school's front garden. I get up to sharpen my pencil and watch that puddle grow deeper and muddier in the rain.

I look across the room and see again the empty seat where Rick usually sits. Ten days since he left with lightning in his eyes. I think he went home to confront his dad about using Mr. Marvin to get Mr. O'Connor fired. Another lie by two grown men to get rid of someone who is a threat.

I'm afraid of what Rick's courage may have cost him.

Elizabeth Gray suddenly stands behind me in line for the pencil sharpener. She whispers, "I've written the story of Mr. O'Connor's time in the prisoner-of-war camp."

I glance over my shoulder at the study hall teacher. She is working with Davie Dashlee on his math problems. In that glance, I also notice that Elizabeth has her hair in a ponytail today. She wears a blue sweater that looks really soft. I stare at the window and turn the pencil sharpener.

Elizabeth says, "Let's publish our second edition of *Eisenhower Neighborhood News* and spread O'Connor's real story all over the neighborhood. You can take a portrait of him with that old box camera of your dad's."

"I doubt we can still get advertising," I say. "Dad's name is in the newspaper today as a college teacher who refuses to sign the loyalty oath."

"Is Portland State College going to fire him?"

Still twisting the sharpener handle. I whisper, "Depends how much pressure the college president gets from the board of the college."

"They can't fire their best music teacher," she says.

Elizabeth is a great friend, but I understand people better than I used to.

"You saw what happened at Corbett College," I say. "The board caved in to HUAC, the House Committee. The teachers who didn't cave in and take the oath got fired. The ones with courage are ruined."

Elizabeth says, "It's not over, Gib. We can make a difference."

"Yeah? How?"

"I've arranged to interview the ex-mayor, Dorothy McCullough Lee, You've got Mr. Harl's interview," she says. "Think about that."

I see she is not about to let my negative feelings stop her. "Okay, then we're ready for the second edition," I say.

The study hall teacher speaks loudly. "Gilbert Evans, that pencil must be down to the eraser by now. You and Elizabeth save your date until after school."

Everybody in the room laughs at us. When I turn to bumble my way to my desk, I see that Elizabeth's face has grown as red-hot as I feel.

CHAPTER THIRTY-NINE

After school, I walk Elizabeth home. She'll talk to her mom and dad about Mr. Marvin's study hall move. I want to find Rick. So, I leave her at her house and wander down to the gulch, trying to get my mind around Kenny Johnson.

Kenny's afraid. After seeing how much pain he's in, I'm afraid for him, and for Rick. If his dad broke Kenny's jaw, then what did he do to Rick that day of the Halloween party?

I push my way into the brambles, this time using my notebook as a shield. Then, I hike down to the bottom of the ravine. I just stand there thinking and listening to the buzz of wings and the piercing whistle of the thrush.

I don't understand what brought me down here. In ordinary times, Rick is afraid of this place. He wouldn't be anywhere near here.

I glance up at the village of boxes under the bridge. Maybe Max can help me. That guy is all over this part of town in the night. People don't give him trouble at night. I climb up through the braided, almost obscure paths that Max uses to get to the creek.

When I get close, a tall man stands up from nowhere. His clothes are little better than Max's, but he's twice Max's weight. I stop climbing.

"What do you want?" His big voice says *this is no question*.

"I want to talk to Max."

"And if Max don't want to talk to you?"

"Then I'll leave."

"So, leave."

"I think that message should come from Max."

"Yeah? I got a fist says Max don't talk to nobody."

I'm looking up at this big man. He's got a right hand as big as a boulder and it's clenched tight. I step closer. "I don't believe Max asked you to speak for him."

The man's arm rears back. I move in closer, so I can get inside his power reach – maybe. At that moment, Max comes out of the crate behind the man.

"It's okay, Carlton. This kid is okay."

Carlton's fist comes down slowly.

Damn. I'm feeling like busting something.

Max smiles at Carlton, then turns to me. "Nice newspaper, Gib. The whole neighborhood is talking about it. But, you didn't interview me about life in Portland. That why you're here?" He's grinning, so I'm pretty sure he's kidding. I like the idea.

"I surely could do that, if you'll let me. But today, I need some help."

"About?"

I'm aware of Carlton looming, so I get my problem out fast. "My friend, Rick Johnson, is missing. Johnsons live on Seventeenth Avenue, just north of the gulch."

"So, you think I stole him?"

"No. I'm hoping you saw something, or heard something that can help me."

"If he's run away, maybe he don't want to be found."

"Maybe, but, I'm pretty sure his little brother's broken jaw is the result of his dad's temper. Little brother won't talk – or write – about what happened. I'm scared that Rick said something to his dad and got worse than Kenny."

"Johnson. That the Senator Johnson, the lousy dancer that I met at the school board meeting?"

"Yes."

Max thinks for a few minutes and then he says, "Carlton, you saw that at the old warehouse?"

I know that building. It's next to the tracks down near Twenty-Eighth Avenue.

Carlton nods. "Little stub of a guy."

"Rick is short and strong," I say.

"Okay, follow us over there," Max says.

A mile of tramping east along trails I can barely see, and we arrive at the south end of the Twenty-Eighth Avenue Bridge. An abandoned building sits north of the tracks and east of the bridge.

For the first time since we started, Carlton talks. "Little Stubby is afraid of me. I'll stay here."

"Good idea," Max says. "But point where you saw him go in."

"That door under the faded letter P. He skittered in there. I didn't foller. Figured he'd just go deeper."

"I'll go down," I say. "He might come out for me."

Long minutes of climbing bring me to the creek, which rushes deep. By the time I get across and up to the building, my shoes are soaked and muddy. The door under the P is narrow. I can see in the dirt that it has swung open recently. There are tennis shoe marks in the dirt, and blood.

I step into complete darkness. Plywood covers every window. The light switch next to the door does nothing. Of course, General Electric doesn't send current to abandoned warehouses.

"Rick?"

Echoes, and then silence.

"Rick, its Gib, Gib Evans. I'm worried about you. I've seen Kenny and I'm afraid of what happened to you."

Nothing moves. I feel the great emptiness waiting.

"Rick, I don't want you to go back there, but I don't want Kenny in more danger either."

I hear a short intake of breath.

"That guy who saw you come in here, that's Carlton. He's big, but he's a friend of Max, my friend in the gulch, so, don't be afraid of him."

There is a slight rustling of cloth above me. "How'd you know to ask him?" That voice is tired, but it is Rick.

I think about his question, surprised. "I don't know. I guess something told me you were in trouble, and something told me to come to the gulch to figure out what happened."

"That something, is that Quaker stuff?"

"Hell . . . I don't know what told me to come."

"I can't do much," he whispers."

My back goes cold. "Where are the stairs?"

"Right of the door, I think."

I swing the door out farther and let in enough light to see the bottom stair. Then I wave at Max and Carlton and I point up, so they know what I'm doing. I don't want to yell and scare Rick about them being near.

"Careful," Rick says. "The fourth step up is missing."

I leave the door as wide open as I can get it. Then I start up the steps, counting. He's right. On that fourth step, the riser and the tread, the place where a guy puts his foot, those are completely gone.

"Any other steps broken?" I ask as I reach for the fifth step.

"Some wobbly. Might break. I didn't count after I slipped on four."

I put my hands in front of me, climb over the missing step and work slowly on. The farther up I go, the darker it is. By the eighth step I can't see anything in front of me. I glance behind me to check on the door. The sun is getting low. The light stretches inside, but the angle is going to move fast, longer and longer. I've got to get to Rick as soon as possible.

"Are you close to the top of the steps?"

"'bout fifteen feet left of the stair top." His voice is weaker.

My hand reaches for the eighth step and I find the left end of the tread. When I lean on it, the other end flies up. As I dodge the slab of wood, I have to grab for the wall to keep myself from falling backward. The board hits the side of my head and then falls back onto the stringer, the frame for the stairs.

I remember helping Dad repair steps to our front porch in Germany. I know the nails holes are old, and so big they can't hold the flat tread in the grain of the stringer.

I work the tread of that step so the nails are over a slightly different part of the stringer wood. Then I pound on the board with my notebook. The nails sink in. I keep climbing.

By the twelfth step, I realize this place has a really high second floor, probably to make it easier to move heavy equipment around on the main floor. Thirteen, fourteen, fifteen. The sixteenth step needs to be hammered in just like the eighth. It doesn't go down as easily. There's a knot close to the top of the stringer. My notebook gives before I can get the nails in solidly. The cardboard of the notebook cover cracks. I have to stand, push against the sidewalls and stomp on the board with my shoe.

Back on my knees, I climb four more steps. Twenty, I tell myself. Sixteen and eight are iffy. Four is gone.

I turn left. "Rick, talk to me so I can find you."

"I see your shadow," he says.

"Boy, you can see more than I can."

"Been here three days," he whispers.

"Water?"

"Gone this morning," he says.

My throat dries. I cough to clear my fear for him. "Can you crawl?"

"I'm pulling myself toward you, but I can't move fast."

"Stay there. I'm coming to you, then we'll see what to do."

By the time I reach Rick, I can barely see him. There is a little light coming in through a wide space in the floor boards. His right eye is completely closed and bloody. Blood from some other cut soaks his pant leg. When he tries to stand, he screams and holds his stomach.

I try to remember what I should have learned in health class. "Are you bleeding inside, too?"

"How would I know, Butt-head?"

I want to cry and laugh at the same time. Same old Rick.

Rick grabs me. "Shh!"

Downstairs, I hear banging and see flashlight beams. Max's voice calls up. "Carlton is hunting a board for that missing step."

Beside me, Rick moans. I hold his arm. "It's okay," I whisper. "They're okay."

"Found one," Carlton yells.

"You have a hammer?" I call.

"A fist," Max says.

"Tell him steps eight and sixteen are loose on the right side."

Half an hour later, Carlton, Max and I carry Rick down the stairs in a piece of old canvas that keeps ripping around the frayed edges. Carlton takes over and carries him up the path to the empty lot on the north side of the gulch. He lays Rick down, and covers him with his own coat. Then Carlton hightails it back into the gulch.

"Afraid of people," Max says. "I'll stay here."

I run to Margaret Fox House and get Mom. She calls for help while I run back. Mom meets us with a police officer named Sergeant Robert Ryan.

Mom tells Max and Rick, "Sergeant Ryan comes to Margaret Fox House sometimes to protect women from mean husbands. I trust him."

"I've called for an ambulance," the sergeant says.

Sergeant Ryan takes Rick's vitals. Rick asks for water. Ryan says, "No water at the moment. You're probably bleeding inside. Don't want to work your systems 'til a doctor knows the damage."

While we listen to the approaching wail of the ambulance, Sergeant Ryan asks how this happened. Rick says, "Dad caught me packing. Kenny, too. Dad tied us. Mom was screaming for him to stop, but he whopped her. He beat on Kenny to force me to talk. I told Dad, 'I know you sicced Mr. Marvin on Mr. O'Connor like a dog on a cat. You're going to ruin him, just like Stockman.'"

Rick stops talking and holds his stomach. His skin is wet and gray. Sergeant Ryan says, "That's enough. We'll talk later."

But Rick grabs my hand, so I lean close. He whispers, "Dad left us on the floor of the bathroom to hunt for Mr. O'Connor."

Rick's voice goes. The ambulance arrives. Just before they put him in the back, Rick whispers, "I warned Mr. O. He asked, 'Where are you?' I said, 'I'm leaving town on the bus.'"

I say, "That didn't fool him. He's been looking for you, anyway."

Rick's smile isn't strong, but it's a smile.

Then they push the bed into the ambulance.

Sergeant Ryan and Mom go with Rick to the hospital. Mr. Halverson and Dad get a judge named Augustus Shalom involved. Somebody who works for the judge talks to Rick at the hospital. In half a day, Rick is taken out of the hospital to somewhere that I am not supposed to know about.

Dad says, "He's in protective custody and Kenny is next."

CHAPTER FORTY

On Tuesday night, the day has been hot for November. So, I open my bedroom window a crack. I'm having trouble concentrating, thinking about how bad Rick looked, and how Mr. Johnson is after Mr. O'Connor. He's telling lots of people that Mr. O turned his son into a communist.

When somebody gets that way, jazzing themselves up on anger and lies, nobody is safe.

On my desk, I study the layout Mike and I just did for the second edition of *Eisenhower Neighborhood News*. Our printer guy showed us how to fit in photos. We've got a great one of Mr. O'Connor that I took with Dad's camera. I hope other people will see Mr. O'Connor the way we see him. I hope this second edition keeps him safer.

But how safe can you be when so many believe the lies?

After a while, I give up concentrating on layout. I'm on my bed listening to Mom and Dad. They're down at the dining table, figuring ways to cut costs. Dad's music students are now our only income. This afternoon, two of his students didn't come. Their dads called. They won't take lessons anymore.

That starts me thinking about ways I can earn money to help at least buy groceries. This afternoon, Elizabeth has been up and down Broadway Street selling ads for our next issue. She is not related to hard-headed Quakers or to school teachers who make it a point of honor not to sign oaths. Plus, Elizabeth has this quiet way about her that makes it hard for people to say 'No'. She can really sell advertising.

People liked that first edition. They found the names of friends in there, and learned more about the little stores in the area. I guess that's what they've been wanting from the big newspaper.

Maybe doing the newspaper can bring in some money, but that money has to be split with our news partners. We've now got one hundred subscribers. That number barely pays for the printing. We've promised subscribers to put the news out every two weeks. I figure maybe we could also do a newspaper for the next neighborhood over – Alameda. Mom knows a lot of the Alameda families because she was their favorite fifth-grade teacher. Maybe their goalie, Raymond Byers, can help us.

Maybe not all of them think we are revolutionaries.

I hope there are other neighborhoods that will want a newspaper, too. The city news pays attention to national events and stories about their big advertisers. It's hard for regular people to get space in the *Portland Journal*.

But not everyone likes our neighborhood newspaper. Yesterday, Mom answered the phone twice and asked if she could take a message for the editor of the *Eisenhower Neighborhood News*. One guy told her, "Your boss, this Gilbert Evans character, he must be a commie and you should resign. Lots of places looking for a good secretary."

When the second call like that came in, Mom said, "Sir, could you tell me what communism is? I don't think I have seen it."

"Lady, if you don't know, I can't help you. Just tell the editor we don't want his kind in Portland."

On the other hand, Elizabeth says, "Three families so far have bought subscriptions because of my editorial, and one bought a subscription for her neighbor because she wants us to stay in business. The lady in the blue house up at the corner of Siskiyou Street says she's glad we're standing up for the U.S. Constitution."

So, who knows where that will all fall out? Maybe, when pushed, some of those people will stand up for our newspaper. Maybe. But I've seen grownups like our principal turn into somebody different. They crumble when somebody threatens to investigate them. I wonder what I'll do when that happens.

* *

Along about ten o'clock at night, I'm in bed, but hear a lot of noise out my window, the sound of an engine revving as if a truck were stuck, wheels squirreling, kicking up mud. The crack of wood and a humongous bang brings me right out of bed. I pull up my shade and look out, expecting that someone is driving into our front porch.

What I see is an old green truck running out of the side yard between our house and Mrs. Silverberg's. From the tracks, it looks like the truck is making its second trip across Mrs. Silverberg's front garden. He bumps his way down between the street light pole and her street trees. Then he's back onto the street.

I've already yanked on my pants and shoes by the time he hits the street and heads south. I grab my jacket, the Brownie Box camera and my under-cover-reading flashlight.

I'm out my bedroom door as Mom and Dad run onto the front porch. I don't want them to stop me, so I take the stairs three at a time, slide into the kitchen and race out the back door.

I hear the truck round the corner at the south end of our street, so I run through the mud of Mrs. Silverberg's ruined back yard, climb the old stile into Mrs. Moriarity's, and head down Seventeenth Avenue toward Brazee Street as fast as I can go. From the south corner, the truck headlights suddenly turn toward me. I dart behind the nearest tree in Mr. Stockman's parking strip. That green truck is still coming toward me. I hold as quiet as I can, next to the big Maple tree. The truck screeches to a halt right in front of Mr. Stockman's house.

And Mr. Stockman is in the truck. This truck must be in his garage all the time. I've never seen it before.

I know he'll see me when he walks past to get to his front stairs, so I try to stop breathing and become as tree-dark as I can. Mr. Stockman pushes open his old truck door. It groans and then shudders as he slams it shut. He doesn't pass me at all, instead, he goes around his truck's rear end and walks down the street toward Davie Dashlee's, crossing the corner of Seventeenth and Brazee.

He's wearing a long rain slicker and the same big hat. I saw that on him just before he broke my nose, but I didn't realize what it meant. He's the man who stared at our house in the rain. Is he also the person who threw the rock?

I hang out around the roots of Mr. Stockman's maple until he gets clear across Brazee Street. As soon as he is a ways down the next block, I step to the front of his truck and crouch down where I can take a photo of his muddy license plate. The flash on my camera whirs and crackles. I hear him stop walking.

He grunts, "Huh?"

I'm hunched over, below his hood, waiting. Finally, his shoes start slapping the pavement again. I don't know where he's going, but I decide I better find out.

I stand up and watch him walk down Davie's block. After a moment's hesitation, he crosses Seventeenth Street and climbs the stairs to the porch of Senator Johnson's house. I sling my camera over my shoulder and run across Brazee Street as silent as my tennis shoes can be. I dart from tree to tree in the shadows until I'm under Davie's Horse Chestnut.

I'm looking straight across the street at Johnson's porch. Mr. Stockman stands on the porch dripping mud. A moment after I arrive, the porch light goes on and Senator Johnson answers the door.

I unplug my flash attachment so it won't go off and alert them. I snap my Brownie Box and rewind as fast as it will work. I hope the porch light is enough.

I hope I've got three photos of Johnson's face talking to Mr. Stockman. There's a chance those are good enough to identify them.

As they face each other, I hear Johnson say, "I told you to stay away from my house after that window business."

"I done what you said both times, and now I want my money."

"Not tonight. Come to my office in the morning. We'll work...."

"Tonight, Senator. You promised. And the mortgage is already overdue."

"Tomorrow or never." Johnson says. His door slams.

The porch light goes out a moment later, so I wait.

Mr. Stockman knocks and rings the bell, yelling, "That's my house. My property." He rings again, "You said you'd take care of the back payments."

He rings and yells, again. Again. Again. Again.

All that noise gives me a chance to go down the street one house and cross to the driveway Johnson shares with his neighbor. I walk up the drive just far enough to be near a dark bush. Smells like a cedar. I blend in.

Inside the house, I can hear Senator Johnson's big shoes clomp down some stairs. He opens the front door and whispers. "My son is calling the police about an intruder. You better not be found outside my door."

"Your son's livin' on the streets, Johnson. And safer for it."

"Why you son of a ..."

"I seen the crack you give him. It's a wonder he can see outa that eye."

"You don't get out of my sight, you're going to look worse than him."

I hear Mr. Stockman back up. Senator Johnson's screen door squeaks open, like he's coming out on the porch after Mr. Stockman.

"You wouldn't . . ." Mr. Stockman whines.

"I see you near my office or my house . . ."

"You promised me."

"I promised nothing, Dirt Bag. I'm going to have you arrested."

"I'll tell about all you done . . ."

"Why would I ask you to do anything to that sweet old lady?

"But . . ."

"Nobody will believe you, Stockman. So, start packing and clear out of town because your house and your mortgage are a lost cause."

"You can't do this to me."

"You're trespassing. See this rifle?"

I see the shadow of the rifle and crouch lower. I hear Stockman back off the porch and Johnson walk out to the porch edge as if to make sure he's gone.

Stockman's boots retreat up Seventeenth toward his truck and house. Johnson goes back inside and slams his door. From upstairs, I hear his wife call, "Roland is that Ricky? Did Ricky come home?"

I stand next to the cedar for a long time, until I hear Mr. Stockman's front door, up the block at his house.

Inside, Senator Johnson yells at Kenny. "Where's your brother, you bastard?"

I hear him smack Kenny. My stomach rears into my throat. Kenny's jaw is still broken. The sound of Johnson hitting him comes clear out here.

"Don't know," Kenny whimpers.

"I can't believe either of you little shits. That O'Connor fellow took him somewhere, didn't he?"

How can he think that? Judge Shalom told the Johnsons about Rick being in the custody of the court.

Johnson hits Kenny again and I fold over as if he's hit me. Mrs. Johnson pleads. "Roland."

His dad's fist hits something hard like a wall. "You're a fat, coward, slob, the kind who would let the commies like O'Connor walk right into our country."

"I don't know – Rick is."

"Mildred, Get me that rope. I'm gonna teach this kid to keep secrets from me."

"Roland, he's just a child . . ."

"Get me that rope or else."

*   *

I'm halfway around the corner, running and breathing hard, when a voice says, "Gilbert, stop."

It's Mr. Stockman. In the light of the street lamp, he looms like the dark statue of a man. His eyes are big and black under his rain hat.

I back away.

He leans toward me. Sweat beads on his face, like he's been drinking or taking some kind of medicine. He says, "I gotta tell someone and you got that newspaper. You can tell it in there, right?"

"Tell what, Mr. Stockman?"

"That fellow Johnson, he'll kill me. I know it."

I back up and glance toward Johnson's house. Their house lights are out, but we're standing under the corner lamp. I turn and start to run, but Stockman grabs my coat.

"Wait, please hear me."

"Not in the light," I say. "He'll see us."

"In my yard, then. It's dark in my yard."

"Let go." I unzip my jacket, planning to leave it in his hands, but he grabs my arm and yanks me close to his driveway where it's black as tar. We're too alone here.

"Listen kid," he says, "you gotta tell everybody. Johnson started this. I wouldn't a done it, but he'll condemn my house, says it's a fire hazard for the neighborhood."

I look up the driveway where his house seems huge. "It's no older than our house."

"That's it, ain't it? He's lying, but he's got the power."

"How could he condemn your property?" I let my arm drop. He doesn't seem to remember he had a grip on it.

"He's already had inspectors in. That bathroom ain't permitted in the basement. The electricity is old and not up to code. I can't afford that."

"So, he wants you to do things for him?" I turn sideways, ready to run, but I want to know what he'll say, too.

"Where will Jeff and Randy come home to if I don't have that house?"

"He's asked you to do things, like what?"

A bead of his sweat drips, catching the light as it falls. He says, "You gotta believe me. I only did it because he threatened me."

"What did you do?"

"Johnson said I had to scare you and your folks, run off that foreigner next door to you, and that communist teacher."

"Can I quote you about that in the newspaper?"

Mr. Stockman backs up. He wasn't thinking it through until I asked that question. "Not quote me. Just tell that Johnson does those kinds of things."

"I've got to have specifics, and a witness to say things like that about him."

"But you are a witness. I saw you at the side of the house. You followed me there and you heard all of it, didn't you?"

"Yes. Yes, I did hear, but he denied it all, when you accused him. He never admitted to anything you said."

He backs up farther. "Damn you, kid." He turns away from me and starts up his driveway. "You heard it. You know it's true. What kind of newspaper man are you?

"I don't accuse without evidence. Bring me evidence."

"How'm I gonna get evidence?"

"I don't know. Maybe something he put in writing."

He turns back to me. "I got writing. His handwriting. I'll bring it to you tomorrow morning."

"So, I'll hold the newspaper and see if you really have something."

Mr. Stockman turns his back on me and climbs his driveway. My own back is cold.

I watch until he's in his house. Johnson's light is still out, but who knows if he's looking outside?

I stay out of the street light as much as I can as I run on around our block. Dad comes out of Mrs. Silverberg's side yard, running toward me. He hugs me real hard. "Your mother and I – about the whole neighborhood have been searching for you."

"I took pictures of Mr. Stockman's truck. Johnson hired him to do it, and now he's beating on Kenny."

He holds me away from him, looking at my face. "You ran down there? Kenny? Why's Johnson beating on Kenny?"

"Thinks Kenny knows where Rick is."

"Damn!" Dad never talks that way. Dad says, "Gib, you get home. Your mother is frantic."

"I didn't think you'd even know I was gone."

"Justine ran into your room for safety."

"My room? Why would she?"

"Because you are Justine's hero. She came downstairs hysterical because she thought the burglar kidnapped you."

We run to the porch where Justine won't let go of my legs, and Mom keeps rubbing my shoulder and whispering, "Safe. You're safe."

Just then, Mike's dad meets us wearing his plaid pajamas and a thick cotton robe. He's a big man. His slippers are a foot long and the belt on his robe looks like it might circle a hundred-year-old maple trunk.

"Johnson's beating Ken, to find Rick," Dad says to him.

Mr. Halverson closes his eyes. "I'll warn Judge Shalom," he said.

"Doesn't Mr. Johnson know Rick's in court custody?" I ask.

"He's been told, but won't admit it. He's never shown at a hearing to get him back and he's never allowed Mrs. Johnson to bring Kenny to court."

"And the court can't just go get Kenny?" I ask. "He's beating him with a rope."

"I'll call the judge," Mr. Halverson says, and then he eyes my Brownie Box. "Taking photos of a muddy truck?"

"Yes, sir. But Senator Johnson refused to pay Stockman."

"Ah," Mr. Halverson glances at Dad as if to pass him some message. Dad nods at him.

Off in the distance, I hear a police siren. Dad says, "We called the police to document the damage at Missus Silverberg's."

"Why did Johnson pick on her?" I ask.

Dad glances at Mr. Halverson. Mr. Halverson says, "Gib's out taking photos in the night. He's old enough to know."

Dad nods and says, "It's because Mr. O'Connor rents a room from her. Mr. Marvin told Johnson it was Mr. O'Connor who turned Rick against him. Marvin claims that's what Reds do."

"I gotta find a way to get Kenny out of there." I say.

The police siren grows louder down on Broadway.

Dad says, "Gib, we're working to keep Rick safe. You have to let the court take care of Kenny. Johnson will explode when he finds he's lost control of the situation."

Halverson turns to me. "And Gib. I'd keep your photo shoot under wraps until the photos are developed."

"Why?" I ask.

"The police may take the camera," Mr. Halverson says. "Some of them are in the Red Squad, with Roy Norene at Immigration, or they work with communist hunters like Johnson. We can't tell if one of the Red Squad will come tonight."

Dad says, "We need to give them copies tomorrow, and keep originals for Mrs. Silverberg's lawyer and for Rick's judge."

"Can't Judge Shalom take Kenny away from him?" I ask.

Dad says, "For Kenny's sake, you need to write down everything you heard tonight."

Now, I'm scared for all of us. A man as powerful and angry as Mister Johnson is not going to stop with destroying an old woman's garden and beating on his own sons.

At that moment, the police siren screams from nearby Brazee Street. Then it sweeps around the corner and starts up our street. When they arrive, Sergeant Ryan is not with them. My camera is in the garage in a box.

CHAPTER FORTY-ONE

This morning, Mr. Stockman doesn't answer his door. Maybe he never stayed in his house after he talked to me last night. Today, Tuesday morning, his house is dark, and his rusty truck is gone. I'm worried about him – not about what he might do, but about what has happened to him since last night.

Dad and Mr. Halverson drive around looking for that truck. By seven this morning, every guy working at Halverson-Built Homes is on the lookout for it.

I take Justine to school today, but I leave right away to come back to our garage. Mom's at Margaret Fox House and Dad's out searching, so when the phone rings in the kitchen, I run in to answer it.

"That newspaper your kid put out? That's a piece of trash, and you ought to control that kid better 'n that."

This person thinks he's talking to Mom. For a second I can't think. I make myself talk. "Sir, were you upset by the story about Roger's Five and Dime?"

"You know what I'm talking about. That E.L. Gray person had best learn to shut up and let adults take care of business."

I say, "You think you're an adult?" I wish I hadn't said that. I'm afraid for Elizabeth, and Mom.

"Lady, you should be afraid somebody's going to bust one of you."

He's said this before. I can tell. "Mister, I am the editor. Mrs. Evans has nothing to do with the newspaper."

He hangs up. It's like lightning has run through my body. I can't stop shaking. Mom has gotten other phone calls like this and hasn't told me.

I dial the operator. "Can you tell me who just now called this number?"

"Why would you need to know, ma'am?"

I go along with that, saying, "The caller threatened several people in my family and I need to report it to the police."

"Only the police can make that kind of request, ma'am. You need to call the police."

I hang up. I don't know who's on the Red Squad, who owes the mayor and the chief of police and who wants to be honest law men. I call the police and ask for Sergeant Robert Ryan.

"What is the nature of your call?"

"I wish to speak to Sergeant Ryan."

"You must leave a message. The duty officer will take care of it."

I hang up.

Out in the garage, I'm so nervous I have a hard time using the scissors and paste, but I lay out the second edition, and try to think how to get Sergeant Ryan without calling the dispatcher.

When I'm done, we've got sixteen pages of business stories, advertisements, stories about house renovations, park improvements, intersections that need stop signs and that kind of neighbor news. We've stories about church socials and a story about the new Pastor Fedje who recently came to Rose City Park Methodist Church.

James did that interview and Pastor Fedje was great about a negro interviewing him. He said he was glad to meet James, and that he'd accepted the position in Portland because he hoped to find that this city was a place where people hadn't bought into fear of change. I wonder what the pastor thinks about the *Portland Journal's* ads for the HUAC Rally tomorrow.

In this edition, Elizabeth has interviewed Mrs. Dorothy McCullough Lee about her campaign against corruption in the police and other city bureaus when she recently was mayor of Portland. I'm also printing my interview with Councilman Robert Harl.

Mr. Harl was great. He talked about why people who have advantages want to remain on top and in charge forever. Most importantly, he listed the tools those people use to get everyone who has no advantages to support those who have them. Top of the list is to make people afraid of each other. Second is make people afraid of change.

This *Eisenhower News* second edition is going to cause a ruckus. At least, I hope it will. Like Commissioner Harl, we want to be a threat to people who misuse power.

Mom comes home with Justine. A fourth graders' school day ends earlier than mine. She sets Justine up with toys and drawing paper in the kitchen, then she comes out to the garage.

"Gib, thee cannot avoid school for the rest of the year."

"I've got more important things to do than go to a school where the new teachers are all under the thumb of that idiot, Marvin."

"Elias Marvin is far from an idiot. He played this perfectly for what he wants."

"So, you're saying I could learn something from him?"

"I think you've already learned about as much from him as there is to learn, but you have to graduate and then go to high school."

"I won't graduate even if I go every day. Marvin has set me up to be three credits short by the end of the year."

She sighs. "We're working on getting that changed, but you have to be there."

I don't believe she was in any position to change things Mr. Marvin did, but I say, "Okay."

Mom smiles, then her smile disappears. "Gib, Sergeant Ryan called me today. He thought I'd called him this morning."

"Someone called and thought I was you. He threatened you, and me, and E.L. Gray because of the newspaper editorial. I tried to call Sergeant Ryan because only the police can ask the phone company to trace that call."

Mom takes in a deep breath. "I'm sorry that I haven't been more honest. I've gotten calls like that, too. Dad and I have Sergeant Ryan working on tracing those. So far, they are all from phone booths near here, or from other phone booths in towns down the valley."

"From Salem, where Mr. Johnson might be?"

She glances at me. "From every town down the valley except Salem."

"Ah."

"Will you please go to school, so I know where you are each day?"

I nod at her. "Maybe, I'll go tomorrow and see if any of the new teachers have any wisdom."

She tries to smile, too, but her eyes are tired. She gestures at our newspaper. "Persevere, but be careful of others. We don't know who the caller might be."

"Yeah, sure. Okay."

When James, Mike and Elizabeth get out of school, they come by and approve the layout. Then I tell them about the phone call and the threat to E.L. Gray.

James says, "Boy, using your initials was a good idea, Elizabeth."

"I just did that because people don't take women writers seriously. But I'm glad he doesn't know who I am . . . exactly."

I say, "I'm afraid Mr. Marvin knows who you are. And I'm afraid the caller knows Mr. Marvin."

Mike says, "George Sanderson, our printer, told Dad that a couple of businesses withdrew print orders because he did our first newspaper. They were mad about your editorial, E.L. Gray."

I shake my head. I should have expected this.

"So, he won't do this edition?" Elizabeth asks. "E.L. has this great interview in there!"

Mike looks around at the three of us. His face is all solemn. "Sanderson says bring the second one as soon as we can. He can hardly wait to show those two people what he thinks of them."

"Hoorah!" James yells.

In a moment, we're all up and dancing around, hooking arms and swinging each other like square dancers. James and Mike slap each other on the back. Suddenly, I put my arms around Elizabeth. I'm just thinking about dancing her in a circle, but she pulls me tight for a moment – a moment that lasts and lasts, and is over too soon. She steps back to take my hand and pull me around as if we'd been dancing.

For a minute, I can't think about anything but how good it feels that she hugged me. But then it hits me. Somebody, maybe more than one person, hates her. I have to watch, keep her safe.

Then I notice Mike and James are quiet and watching us. James breaks into a grin.

Mike pokes James in the shoulder. "'Bout time, eh?" he says.

"What?" Elizabeth and I say at the same time.

"Aw," James says, "Nothing. Let's get this newspaper out the door."

Mike takes it off the layout table and out the garage to Mr. Sanderson, the printer. We'll deliver it to our seven hundred-fifty houses tomorrow, if they'll still have us. Raymond Byers has rounded up even more Alameda guys to help us. We'll all meet here at the garage after school.

After Mike leaves, Elizabeth is all business. She and James start planning what we need for the third edition. But I'm just nodding and pretending to write down the ideas. What I'm really thinking is that her waist is a comfortable place for my arm. I'm not sure what happened to us while we danced. What I do know is I've got to make sure nobody hurts her.

CHAPTER FORTY-TWO

I take Justine to school the next morning and then head to the Bowl to report on the Rally. It only takes me eight minutes to get to there. I look sweaty, but I'm ready with pen and paper.

A huge sign hangs over the Bowl. It says *Rally for Democracy*.

For Democracy! What a crock!

Hundreds of people already push into the park-like amphitheater. Others hang out of windows in the Bonneville Power Building nearby, or stand on the roof near the air-raid sirens. In the lower part of the amphitheater, the city has put up a grandstand. Some well-dressed people already sit in that area, but policemen turn away most others. I bet they're expensive tickets.

I peer between the shoulders of grown men at the edges of the crowd. From here, I'll never hear anything. If anyone here knows I'm editor of the *Eisenhower Neighborhood News*, I'll be hustled off the premises.

I inch closer and closer to the front. The head of the rally stands on the stage at the bottom of the Bowl. He introduces the visiting dignitaries starting with the *Portland Journal* editor who waves at the clapping crowd. Next the announcer introduces "The honorable Peter Campbell Brown, Chair of the Subversive Activities Control Board." Mr. Brown pulls out a speech and steps to the podium.

I take notes on the Subversive Activities fellow, Brown. Then on Elias Marvin, who is introduced as the founder of Educators for Democracy. Everything he says is a parody of McCarthy's radio speeches. I move farther toward the front.

"Don't tread on me," a man whispers behind me.

I turn. There stands Mr. O'Connor, smiling.

"Aren't you working?" I ask.

"I came to tell you there is an alternative to this."

"Newsworthy?"

"Very."

I follow him up the curve of the Bowl to the road at the rim of the gulch. Then we walk a couple of blocks to Holladay Park which is closer to the Twelfth Avenue Bridge. In this park, every union banner I've ever seen hangs over many tables.

"It's an anti-HUAC rally," I say.

"No," Mr. O'Connor says, "It's a pro-U.S. Constitution rally."

People pour into the block from all sides. Many of them wear their work clothes, though some women are in Sunday dresses. The west end of the park has a temporary platform with red, white and blue skirts draped below the stage. Behind the speakers' podium hangs the U.S. flag.

Over the main southern and northern entries to the block, posters announce, "*Celebrate the Bill of Rights.*" Another sign says "*This event sanctioned with park permit number 2910.*"

"Why the sanctioned sign?" I ask.

"So the police have no excuse for what they might do."

"The unions are signing up new members?"

"And they explain rights to their members."

Mike and James come up to me. James carries my camera.

"Hope you don't mind," he says. "Mike knew where you put the camera and he wanted coverage of this event for the next issue."

"Great. But if the police come, you'll be a . . ."

"I know. I'll be a target in their sites."

"So how do we keep you safe?"

James says, "I've got my spot picked out, if you'll give me a boost." He looks up at the nearest tree. "I got this idea from your essay."

The tree is an oak. I glance at the first branch for climbing. Then, I get on my hands and knees, "Stay up there 'till the last policeman is out of here."

James hangs the camera over his neck and steps onto my back. In minutes he's hidden in the branches and calls, "Great view. Bought three extra rolls of film at Ventnor's Market."

"Stay hidden, no matter what," I say. "I want that film safe."

"So great that you care." He parts the branches and pretends to glare at me, but he knows what might happen better than I do.

"Did Elizabeth come with you guys?"

He says, "We skipped school with her. At the garage, Mike got Elizabeth to go advert selling before we came here. She is not here."

"Good."

Mr. O'Connor turns his attention to my notebook. "In a hostile crowd, you should keep that notebook close to your leg. Learn to take notes on the quiet."

I let the notebook rest against the corduroy on my pant leg. "Hard to see."

"Just keep writing. You'll know what it means when you get back to the office and clean up the notes."

From over at the Bowl, I can hear the voice of Mayor Peterson. He's welcoming the crowd, congratulating them for attending such an auspicious occasion.

But a microphone crackles near us. My history teacher, Mrs. Hill steps up to the stage. She is introduced as the chair of the Committee to Protect the Foreign Born. I start taking notes. She tells how the committee is paying legal fees for one of the organizers who is scheduled to be deported. "Mr. William Mackie decided to fight the system through the courts," she announces. "He's exercising his rights as long as he can, and as long as he has our support. If we win this one case, we have won for all. So, donate to protect our workers."

The next speaker, Reggie McDonald, says, "Our friend, Arturo Mendoza, wanted safety and a better life for workers. When he tried to organize, he was taken away as a communist. No trial. No justice. Mendoza deserves more than the cowering fear we have given him. He deserves our bravery in the face of the police and immigration threats."

Mr. O'Connor whispers to me, "Are you getting this?"

"Yes, sir. I think they can hear this crowd clear over at the Bowl."

"They should. See how this protest is growing by the minute?"

"Yes, but how many will stand up to pressure?"

"We'll see."

Another speaker moves to the podium. "We welcome to the stage one of our teachers, Mr. Brendan O'Connor. Fired because he would not sign the oath. His main accuser is Senator Roland Johnson, who always claims he worked for freedom during the war, when the truth is, the man raked in government contracts for transporting war material across the country. While our teacher was shot down, starved for his country and worked to escape his captors, his accuser became a rich man from a safe office right here in Portland."

Mr. O'Connor frowns. He walks forward and doesn't wait for the man to finish. I think he wants no more hate talk.

"Thank you, Mr. Olafsen," he says, and then he turns to the clapping crowd. They all quiet down.

"I refuse." He says, and waits during a puzzled silence. Then he gazes at his friends and says, "We refuse. We refuse to buy fear."

The crowd understands. They cheer and clap. Mr. O'Connor holds up his hands and continues.

"As a pilot, and then as a prisoner of war, I learned a fundamental truth. Fear is a train with no brakes. Once set in motion, the train takes those who drive, and all who jumped on for the ride to certain doom.

> *"Some of you have lived in Marxist countries with secrecy and total control over minds, but it was not the ideas of communism that caused secrecy and control. The cause was tyranny. Tyrannical despots caused human suffering in East Germany. Despots caused the deaths of thousands in the Ukraine, and deportation to Siberia from Estonia, Latvia, and other Stalin-controlled countries.*

> *"Joseph Stalin is not a Marxist. Joseph Stalin is a despot who claims to believe in communism.*

> *"And here, in the United States of America, Senator McCarthy is a despot who claims to believe in democracy.*

> *"A tyrant is a tyrant no matter what values he claims to hold.*

> *"Our government has become a tyranny under McCarthy and his fellows at the House Un-American Activities Committee. Joe McCarthy's rantings and his committee hearings are the most Un-American Activity in our country. Joseph McCarthy wants to peddle fear and keep us afraid of each other so he has control. He tells us we should be so afraid of each other we must ignore the Constitution of the United States. "*

The crowd around me hisses.

From the Bowl, I hear a fearsome roar. Mr. O'Connor acts like he never heard it.

He says, "Our Constitution is our law. McCarthy and his kind claim our law is inconvenient and dangerous in times of crisis. They want us to ignore law when danger threatens. If danger does not exist, they manufacture it. Crisis and fear gives them control.

"But our First Amendment gives you and me freedom – freedom of religion, freedom of speech and of assembly. Our First Amendment says that 'Congress shall make no law respecting the right of the people to petition the government for a redress of grievances."

"What greater grievance than that people like Arturo Mendoza, William Mackie and Margaret Hill, can be accused, lose their jobs, tried in secret, and never told who accused them or why? What greater grievance than that those citizens can be found guilty without redress to a court of law, a jury of their peers, and without defense? What greater grievance than to be shunned, deported or locked up with no hope of reprieve?"

He lowers his voice, slowing down his rhythm, but looking each of us in the eye. "Our accusers are despots, not supporters of democracy. They are lovers of power. We must have the strength to stop them. The price of our freedom is the courage not to buy what Power is selling. And once again, Power is selling fear.

"The measure of a good citizen is the courage to speak the truth, to speak loudly against the tyrant. The good citizen

refuses to bend. The tyrant sells an illusion of safety. And his price is too high."

For the first time, I hear out-loud the truth that I've been learning ever since I wrote my first essay.

Mr. O'Connor leans toward the crowd. Everyone around me stands still, their eyes wide with understanding. His voice rings soft and clear. "When we are asked to pay this price by signing an oath, we will always write, I refuse. I refuse. I . . . refuse."

The men and women around me are now clapping and yelling, "Refuse. Refuse."

Suddenly, Rick Johnson runs into the park from the direction of the bowl. He dodges past other speakers, and the union tables. He dashes up the stage steps and yells, "Mr. O'Connor, my dad is bringing part of that crowd here from the Bowl. He's got the craziest of the crazies. Please, Mr. O, get out."

Mr. O'Connor turns to the crowd, holding up his hands for attention. "They are coming from the Bowl. Please make certain those you love are with you and leave now." Then he turns toward me and urges, "Gib, take Mike, James and Rick with you, and do it immediately."

All around us, women and men are arguing, "Go!" or "No." and many are shouting, "We take a stand today."

Mr. O'Connor stands between me and the Bowl, and pushes me, "Go. Take the boys with you."

I pull at his arm. "Please, come. Don't get arrested. We want you to teach."

He turns his back to me, and puts his arms out as if to protect me from others. The union members rush toward us, trying to stand together against the onslaught of what looks like over a hundred people from the Bowl.

But it is too late. The mob is on us from the south, and from the north, the city police with dogs and guns. Among the mob, I recognize many who carried signs outside the school board meeting. As Mr. Johnson's crowd roars its approval, the union organizers are batoned and handcuffed by the police. Their papers scattered.

Off toward the Bowl, I can hear Mr. Marvin's voice on the loudspeaker, talking again to all who chose not to accompany Mr. Johnson. He says, "Reasoned disagreement with..." and then I can't hear anymore.

I grab Rick, pulling him off the stage, and shoving him under the skirted platform. "Stay hidden," I shout. "Your dad will kill you for this."

Mr. O'Connor stands in front of Rick's disappearing feet and next to me, but men are already on Mr. O.

Three big men pick me up. One of them is the man who jumped on cars outside the school board meeting. Others lift Mr. O'Connor. He twists in their grasp.

"Gib," he yells, "go limp."

I try. My body becomes very heavy, unwieldy. It takes more people to hold me. I see the face of a classmate's mother. Her eyes have gone dark and her face is an ugly red as she grabs my pant leg to pull at me.

Another man pulls her away, yelling, "Martha, don't be an animal."

A woman tries to pull on the two men who hold my shoulders. "He's a kid," she cries. But they push her away and keep moving.

I can't see faces anymore, but I hear part of the mob yelling, "Stop. Let the police...."

Others are yelling, "Commie unions." and "Red lovers."

Through all their arms and legs, I can see Mr. O'Connor being dragged on the ground. They haul us out of the park and toward the gulch. Part of the mob from the Bowl surrounds us, screeching, grabbing at my arms and legs.

I hear a woman screaming. "You worms."

Behind us, the police and union workers are a whirl of chaos. I can't see Mike. Please James, stay hidden in the oak. But I do hear the calm drone of Mr. Marvin speaking to the larger crowd still at the Bowl.

Mr. Johnson has taken over the microphone on our stage. He yells, "These traitors deserve no mercy."

Suddenly, a baseball bat hits my shoulder. I'm dragged to the edge of the gulch.

Far away, I hear Mr. Johnson still shouting. "Men, make certain the leaders will not rise again."

The men swing my body between them. Excruciating pain shoots through my arm and back.

"No!" a woman howls at the men. "You can't do this!"

"Never again," Johnson yells into the mike. "We shall not fear these, ever again."

Near me, other men swing and release Mr. O'Connor. He floats against the cold, blue sky.

But they swing me twice more. Through the pain, I try to concentrate on seeing, not feeling. Air-raid sirens on a roof. Dark trees, grass, the upside-down faces of my tormenters. My shoulder and arm crack.

I hear some in the crowd cheer. Others are yelling. "Stop!" "Leave him."

On stage, Mr. Johnson still harangues. "Let none escape."

My mind goes dark. They let go of me and I fly out over the gulch. In moments, blackberry canes stab my back. My head folds toward my chest, crushing air out of me. A cane scrapes the back of my head and then I'm through to the ground where the thorns are old and thick. I can't move.

I lie there, hurting all over. I hear screams of pain somewhere off closer to the Bowl.

Through my own pain, I hold onto hope for James and Rick. How many have the crowd torn apart this way? Where is Mrs. Hill?

Moments later, I hear a groan, and then Mr. O'Connor says, "Gib, they're coming again. We've got to move."

CHAPTER FORTY-THREE

I fight my way through the brambles. My right arm won't do anything, and every motion shoots lightening from my shoulder down my back. Finally, I can stand. Mr. O'Connor limps down to me.

Above, several young men push through the brambles to get at us. They have already grabbed Reggie McDonald, Mr. Mendoza's friend. I know some of those people. I've seen them at our school plays, our football and soccer games.

Mrs. Hill is at the edge of the gulch, reaching out to me as if to help. A woman spits on her.

"Stop," I shout. "Don't hurt her."

But that woman won't hear. The ones who came up here with Mr. Johnson are followers. Their twisted anger and their coiled force are like the pack of starving dogs in Germany that once attacked Mr. Grofmann's sheep.

From the Bowl, I hear Mr. Marvin's calming tones at their microphone. He's pretending he doesn't know what Johnson means to do. And Marvin's audience ignores the howls of the pack they sent to the Bowl.

They are clapping for every sentence Marvin says. Clapping with gloves on.

"Your arm?" Mr. O'Connor asks, touching it.

I wince. "Not sure."

"Dislocated," O'Connor says, "But, we have to run on top of the brambles and get away from them."

He holds my good arm and helps me scramble to stand on the bent vines which cut my hands and arms and grab at my pant legs. I move forward because I have no choice. If we stand still, we'll be attacked. But excruciating pain makes my stomach heave. We run-walk across and stumble through the tough blackberries. In minutes, we get to the far side of the Twelfth Avenue Bridge. We are well away from the men who tried to follow us into the blackberries, and blocks away from the crowd at the Bowl. In the depths of the gulch is the railroad line and directly across the tracks from us is Max's box village. We start to climb next to the bridge footings, trying to get to the streets.

A squeal below makes me turn around. A hand truck heads east on the single track. In it are three big men. Two of them pump the hand truck. The third man spots us, and points.

I push Mr. O'Connor up next to the bridge. "Climb faster."

But three more men are on the north rim of the gulch above us.

"Aw, shit." I say.

"Damn," he whispers.

Above us, one of the three men hits his open palm with a metal pipe.

"Come on up, commies," the biggest man says.

I've never seen these men before.

Off in the distance, I hear the train whistle near the Forty-Seventh Avenue Bridge, coming into town. The hand car sits on the one set of tracks. Oblivious of the approaching train, the men pile out of it and follow our trail up the hillside.

Mr. O'Connor says. "Well, Br'er Rabbit, dive back into the brambles and run."

I start to do what he says, but sense that he isn't following me. I turn around. He's facing downhill, waiting for the men who climb. I try to return to him, but my torn shirt catches on thorns. The men from below and above converge toward him.

The big man above says, "Shouldn't have taught your commie ways to kids."

I rip off my shirt and run to Mr. O'Connor. I face uphill, protecting his back from the three above us. My back is shredded.

"Go, Gib. Get help."

"No help can come. I stay with you," I say.

"You're a yellow-bellied commie teacher," one guy says.

"Marvin pointed you out to them," I whisper.

"You don't know that," he says. "Accuse with proof, news guy."

I know he's right, but Marvin's is the easiest face to hate right now. And hate, I've seen, creates energy.

Off to the east, the clamor of the train grows louder. Its headlight shows through the brambles as it roars toward the west. I glance over my shoulder. The three hand-car men are only twenty feet below us. The hand car still sits on the tracks.

The three guys above me will arrive first. They look huge.

The train whistle blows. The engineer must have seen the hand car.

Mr. O'Connor whispers, "Max. Stay hidden."

I glance around. Maximillian climbs down from the golf course above his camp. He's a long way from the track – a long way, but he's running.

Mr. O'Connor says, "Come on, train. Come on."

For a moment, I think he hopes the train engineer will save us, but then I know he wants the train to keep Max away from this fight.

I try to be Dad. I call to the men above. "Good morning, gentlemen."

"You're the newspaper kid," one man says.

"Yes, sir," I hear my voice waver, but I push on the way Dad would do. "I don't believe we've met."

The guy points his lead pipe at Mr. O'Connor. "That guy's speech, disgusting."

The man below yells, "Bobby, shuddup. Just get that kid."

I can tell the men below have climbed a lot closer to Mr. O'Connor.

Mr. O'Connor backs up against me. "Get ready to slide-tackle your front man," he whispers. "I'll take the front man down here."

Slide-tackle is a move we learned in soccer – illegal, but useful when you've lost control of the ball. And by now, I'm sure these guys are beyond Dad's way. There's no reason in them.

I keep my attention on the front man's eyes. He's got no thought I might do anything. Big, burly, and coming from above – the advantage is all his.

Mr. O'Connor has always told us players, "The big ones crack when they fall." I try to remember that because otherwise I'm shitting scared. I move uphill. When I bring this Bobby guy down I don't want his pipe to hit Mr. O'Connor.

Bobby is nearly on me. I crouch. He laughs again and raises his pipe, but I go for his legs, my right foot between his feet. My left hooks behind his knee and shoves downhill.

"Bastard!" he yells. His pipe hurls off into the brambles as he falls. He crashes into the black berries to my right. His weight traps me, like a boulder hitting my leg. I land on my bad arm and scream.

Others are running, so I wrench my body around to fight them. As I scramble, Mr. O'Connor leaps on top of his front man. The man brings his pipe down. Both the man and Mr. O fall onto the trail.

Mr. O'Connor goes down limp. All motion stops in that moment.

Bobby tries to grab at my arm. I yank away, hollering at him. "Get away from me, Jackass!"

I want to get to Mr. O., but I see only brambles near where he fell. I yell a lot of stuff as I pull out from under Bobby. My aching arm is useless. Yelling hate helps push me to action.

Near Mr. O'Connor, one of the men raises a crow bar. It thuds into something soft. My stomach lurches into my throat.

"Enough," another man says.

I jerk my foot out from under Bobby. He struggles against the blackberry vines, reaching for me, but his shirt is trapped by blackberry stickers. I'm sure the other two will hit me, but as I crawl toward Mr. O., I glance uphill. Bobby's two buddies run up the path toward the top of the gulch, leaving the fight.

Below me, Max starts to wade across the creek, but the train roars past, leaving Max only yards from the track.

The train whistle blares. There are witnesses. We won't die alone.

I scramble to my feet. My battered leg stabs as I limp downhill. Below me, two men stand over Mr. O'Connor. The first man who hit Mr. O'Connor is under him, cringeing. As I charge at them, the man pulls himself out, first one arm, then another. Mr. O'Connor doesn't fight to keep him down.

I leap between the standing men, and over Mr. O'Connor. Screaming, "No. No. No.", I land on the man who hit Mr. O'Connor, and then somebody pops me on the back of the head. And all that long moment, the train whistle blows a warning. A metallic grinding fills my ears. I close my eyes, waiting to die.

Bobby yells from above, "Get on with it. Kill the kid."

"But the train," one man says.

The grinding sound is the train hitting the hand car. Over that noise, Bobby yells, closer now, like he's climbing down the slope.

"You yellow bellied . . ."

I can't hear anything else he says. The hand car, or the train, or maybe both, will derail in a moment. Then these men will be aware of me again.

Suddenly there is a crushing blow to my chest. A boot, maybe. I've closed my eyes against the next thing they'll do. The face of Justine hovers in my mind. *Oh, baby sister, I want, Elizabeth.*

The train whistle wails. The hand car screeches. Something heavy turns over and over on the track.

Please don't let Max be in the way.

"Stop!"

That voice . . . it's Rick.

"Damn you, kid." The shadow standing over me yells, "Get outta here."

"Don't hit him." Rick's voice is hoarse with desperation.

"Shit, more witnesses," says a man near me. "We gotta disappear."

The ground next to my head thuds, loud and deep, a smack from a piece of dull metal. Dust jumps up into my face and my nose. I don't breathe.

"He's dead now," a voice says. "We gotta go."

Booted feet step over my body. One kicks me hard, low in the back, and then they are running down the hill.

I have to bite my lip. I can't let them know I feel. I let pain slide out of me and into Brendan O'Connor because he can feel nothing.

Above, I hear Senator Johnson's voice. "You bastard . . . Where've you been?"

"Let go of my shirt, Dad. Those men are killing . . ."

I open my eyes. Up at the rim of the gulch, the senator whacks Rick in the face. Rick crumples, but his dad lifts him over his shoulder. Rick's arms swing limply behind his dad's back as the senator hustles away.

God. Please save Rick.

Some of the men who beat us have already run uphill to get away. The rest are probably following that train, maybe hopping a ride as it slows to cross the Steel Bridge, or stops to deal with the handcar debris.

I look at Mr. O'Connor. I knew he died with that first blow – the limp way he fell.

I don't want to be a part of this world any longer. Next to me, his body is warmed by the sunshine. I feel the sun, but for me, it's fiery hell.

Silence.

I open my eyes again and look at him, dead and looking at me. I think about his German friend who knew the birds, about his crewmen, maybe still alive and wondering where he is. I hurt, but I can't feel much beyond my fear for Rick, and the pain in my throat from knowing Mr. O'Connor is gone.

Someone climbs from below us.

"God, I done good for you." Maximillian's voice is low and ragged. "I done good. Now you gotta do good."

He falls on his knees next to O'Connor, staring at him. His labored breathing stops, and I see the moment he recognizes death. Max drops his head against Mr. O'Connor's shoulder and roars. "No. You made me late. Your damned train."

"Max," I whisper.

"Uh!" His head comes up, a startled look in his eyes. "Uh, kid."

I try to nod, but I can't move my head. "Rick Johnson." I say.

"You got all that blood," he says. "Back o' your head. Bloody."

His eyes open bigger. "God," he says. "Don't be foolin' with me," he says. "You . . ."

He moves closer. "Gilbert." He touches my face. "You. You're alive?"

I can only blink.

"I'm gettin' help," he says. "George Fox House."

He touches my face once more, and then scrambles to his feet. "Help," he says, and then he runs up the hill. I have no chance to warn him. Those others, they still might be up there.

He's gone. I'm left to watch the warmth fade from Brendan O'Connor's face. The sun still shines. A fly buzzes. I try to move my hand, to cover his eyes from flies, but pain keeps my hand pinned at my side. Then, I grunt past the pain. I put my arm over his shoulder, and I strangle a sob. I stare at him, watching the change that death brings.

And then I hear feet, and James's voice. "Where are they?"

And Mike. "Climb down next to the bridge." I hear Mike's heavy footsteps running toward me, and James' lighter shoes.

Dad's voice, far above me. "Max, I see them." He crashes down the path as he yells, "We've found them."

"Lord, God-a-mighty," Max yells, "Ambulance driver over here."

Mike drops next to me, feeling my throat. James grabs Mr. O'Connor's wrist, looking vainly for a pulse.

In moments, Dad falls on his knees. "Gilbert." He looks old. Scared.

"Senator hit Rick," I say.

Dad leans close. "Hit him?"

"Took him home. Save Rick."

"I got photos of Johnson doing it," James says.

"He followed Rick out of the park," Mike says.

Dad stands suddenly. "Sarge!" he yells to Mike's dad, "Get Officer Ryan over to Johnsons. Roland Johnson's taken Rick. That boy was here, too."

CHAPTER FORTY-FOUR

In the hospital, tough little Justine pushed my wheelchair down to Rick's room. Rick was hooked up to tubes and monitors, had one leg in a contraption that held it up over his bed, and his head wrapped in bandages. He raised a hand to me and tried to smile around his swollen jaw, then he fell asleep. Kenny lay asleep or unconscious in the next bed, curled on one side, facing his brother, fear and pain etched into his gaunt face.

On the day of the HUAC Rally, Rick had run from under the speakers' stand and out of the park to try to save Mr. O'Connor from the crowd. His father saw Rick and followed him. When the police vans left the park, Mike helped James climb down from the oak. They followed Rick and Senator Johnson to the gulch. As they approached the edge of the gulch, James took photos of all that happened near the Twelfth Avenue Bridge. They found Mrs. Hill injured at the edge of the gulch. The ambulance drivers saved her life, and the life of Reggie MacDonald, Mr. Mendoza's friend.

Elizabeth took James's film to our printer, Mr. Sanderson. Nobody looked for incriminating film at Mr. Sanderson's shop – at least they weren't looking at Mr. Sanderson until the soccer teams and Elizabeth delivered the second edition of *Eisenhower Neighborhood News*. After that, Mr. Sanderson was a hero or a villain depending on your politics.

The morning after the murder, Dad had to move everything in our garage to Judge Shalom's for safe keeping – all our notes and my film of Stockman talking to Johnson. In the hands of the police, everything might have disappeared.

* *

I know I was at Brendan O'Connor's funeral because I remember speaking about what he meant to us kids.

"Brendan O'Connor planned for every student to become great. He taught science, and he taught curiosity. He rewarded the interesting questions as well as answers. Because of Brendan O'Connor, we expect to keep asking questions and seeking answers while we try to create an honest, caring world. Mr. O'Connor's death showed us that a good man is dangerous. For some people, honesty, questions and courage are the enemy."

Mr. Reese came to the funeral. He hugged me afterward, and I felt his ribs, all bones and sadness. I haven't seen him since. That day is the one thing I clearly remember in those many weeks.

Rick and Kenny finally recovered from the beating their dad gave them. But their mom never has been right since. She tried to stop him, and got the worst of it. Courage, one time in her life. She saved her sons.

Soon after the murder of Mr. O'Connor. Mr. Stockman was found hung from the ceiling of his own metal-clad bomb shelter. We've never known if he hung himself or was murdered. In that room, no one could have heard any cries for help.

After the trial, Mr. Johnson's company, Cargo-Car, went into a trust. It's still run by its workers. They formed a union. The Cargo-Car union leader set aside money quarterly to pay Mrs. Johnson's medical bills, and eventually to send Rick and Kenny to college.

My mom was right. Mr. Marvin is smart enough to get what he wants. A month after the Rally, Elias Marvin was appointed to Mr. Johnson's unfinished term in the Oregon State House.

*   *

It took a year of lawyer- maneuvering before Mr. Johnson went on trial. He was charged with inciting the members of the mob to murder.

In a separate court room, during the same month, the guys who attacked Mr. O'Connor and me went on trial. Their defense lawyer blamed Mr. O'Connor's murder on Mr. Johnson's leadership. In his trial, Mr. Johnson's defense turned on whether he told those people to capture suspected communist leaders or kill them.

The defense lawyers in both cases tried to say that fifteen-year-olds would not be reliable witnesses. But the prosecutor in each trial was allowed to call us despite that argument.

In the courtroom where Johnson was the accused, the prosecutor had many witnesses to Johnson's harangues. Two television stations had film of him yelling at the crowd. The anger he projected resulted in injuries to many, and the injured also testified.

On the day we were to be called, his defense lawyer kept talking about Mike and me as 'those loitering children', but he tried to dismiss James Wray's photographs as "the alleged photos of Senator Johnson taken by the Negro man."

When I was called to the stand, the prosecutor asked me "Why were you three young men in the area?"

"We run a neighborhood newspaper called the *Eisenhower Neighborhood News*. I first went there to report on the Rally at the Bowl."

"And then where did you go?"

"I later moved up to the *Celebration of the Bill of Rights* in Holladay Park."

"Who was with you there?"

"Mike Halverson and James Wray were already at Holladay Park taking photos and notes."

"What has happened with your newspaper since that day?"

"We now have enough staff to put out an Alameda Neighborhood News and a Fernwood Neighborhood News."

The defense asked a lot of questions that tried to show we couldn't be counted on as witnesses because we skipped school and ran around town on the loose.

Every time he asked questions, I tried very hard to be calm, and do what the prosecutor taught me. "Only answer the exact question he asks. Don't elaborate." That was the hardest part, because the defense twisted everything we did on that day to look bad.

When the defense attorney finished, the prosecutor stood up and asked.

"Do you attend high school?"

"Yes, sir. All of us do."

"Objection," the defense lawyer said.

The judge said, "Objection sustained." He turned to me and explained. "Speak only about what you do and know first-hand."

"Yes, sir.

The prosecutor asked. "What is your grade point average?"

"For the year it is three point eight five."

"Objection," the defense lawyer said. "Irrelevant."

The judge answered, "I believe you first brought up the idea that these students were delinquents. Objection over-ruled."

The prosecutor asked the next question. "And, Mr. James Wray is a part of your news staff?"

"Yes."

"How do you know James Wray?"

"We are friends at school and in the neighborhood."

I think the prosecutor was setting it up so that the jury would stop thinking of James as "That Negro man" which is how the defense talked about him. He is a kid, just like the rest of us.

After me, the prosecutor asked James questions about that day. The defense tried to make out that James was a friend of a deported family, but when the prosecutor objected, the judge agreed and put a stop to that defense tactic.

When it was all over, James's memories, his photographs, and Mike's and my notes from that day had an impact. Later that week, Mr. Johnson was found guilty of encouraging a mob to murder. He was sentenced to jail for a long time.

*   *

In the other courtroom, the state had the six men who attacked Mr. O'Connor and me. I could identify four of them on sight. James's photos identified the two who had run up to the streets after I brought down Bobby.

On the stand, I identified Bobby, who tried to hit me with his pipe and who yelled at the others to kill me. His name is Robert Adam.

His defense lawyer asked me, "Why did you have no injuries from your encounter with him?"

"I did have injuries from that."

He looked at me, puzzled, but didn't ask.

Later, the prosecutor asked me. "What injuries did you have after your encounter with Mr. Robert Adams?"

"He landed on my leg. It broke."

"Which of these men hit your teacher?"

"Mr. Oster, the man on the left at that table. He was the first man who hit him in the head."

"First?"

"There was a second hit at him after he went down, but I'm not sure who hit him that time."

"Objection."

The judge said, "Over-ruled."

The county coroner already had told the jury that Mr. O'Connor had been hit twice in the back of the head with a blunt instrument.

"And," The prosecutor asked. "Who hit you in the head?"

"I didn't see the person who hit me, but it could not have been Mr. Oster. I was on top of him when it happened. But," I turned to the judge, "your honor, one of these men also saved my life."

Our prosecutor jerked toward me, but the judge said, "Please clarify."

"After the first one hit me, Bobby kept yelling at them to hit me again, to make sure I was dead. One of those three men pretended to hit me. Instead, he hit the ground beside my head and told the others that I was dead."

"Which man was that?"

"I don't know who that man was, but I owe my life to his choice at that moment."

All six were found guilty of the murder, and attempted murder. I've never known which one saved my life.

*   *

After the trial, Kenny and Rick lived with Halversons and with us right up to high school graduation. For the few months that she lived, Dad or Sarge took Rick and Kenny to the nursing home every week. They tried to tell their mom she did the right thing, and they loved her, but she didn't any longer know who they were.

Rick went to university with Elizabeth, Mike and James.

Max Million became a manager at George Fox House. He died in my bed at our home, where he lived while I was in college. I had gotten out of town on an athletic scholarship – went as far away as I could.

In 1961, when Kenny turned eighteen, he left high school, joined the Army and went to fight in Viet Nam. He wanted to save the world from communists.

Kenny is buried in Willamette National Cemetery, in the same row as Brendan O'Connor.

AFTERWORD

It has been half a century since Mr. O'Connor died. I look back to that time with horror, and with sad fondness for the man.

Back in 1953, I wrote that essay. My youthful thoughts were misused. My damned essay helped others do unspeakable things. Brendan O'Connor understood why I wrote it. He understood better than any how the hovering threat of the bomb made our country ripe for takeover by people like Roland Johnson, Elias Marvin and Senator Joseph McCarthy.

From Mr. O'Connor, I learned to face power. Thanks to him, I became a writer who struggled to find the truth. I've never forgotten his last teaching to me: "Accuse with proof, news guy."

During the days of McCarthy's tyranny, the strain of our parents' isolation made all of us, Mike, James, Rick and Elizabeth rely on each other. We grew independent, yet inter-dependent, and adept at business decisions. Our company, Evans International Media, now runs one newspaper, radio and television station in each of the ten largest West Coast cities, and several in other parts of the nation. Our media includes the international reach of many online journalists. But we bought only one newspaper, and one television and radio station in each city. Great media needs great competition.

It is far too easy to convince ourselves that we own the only truth.

QUESTIONS FOR CLASSROOM
AND BOOK GROUP DISCUSSION.

Do you know the tradition of the 'scapegoat'? Here are definitions from a dictionary:

> **Merriam-Webster:** a goat upon whose head are symbolically placed the sins of the people after which he is sent into the wilderness in the biblical ceremony for Yom Kippur.
>
> *a*: one that bears the blame for others
>
> *b*: one that is the object of irrational hostility

You can find out more about this word through dictionaries and encyclopedia research and many folk stories.

1. How does the scapegoat tradition relate to the experiences Gilbert Evans has in this story of events during 1953? In what way does Gilbert's fear of communists fit the definition of using a scapegoat? How do people around Gib use scapegoats?

2. Do you know anyone who has become the scapegoat for things others do? How about those who may be the objects of irrational hostility or of hysteria in our present time?

3. Gib is embarrassed by his parents' religion and beliefs. What do they seem to believe? Why does that bother Gib? At what point does Gib begin to understand some of what his parents have been teaching? What brings about this change in him?

4. How does the setting of the story affect your understanding of Gib and of the community?

5. Gib meets at least two people whom, at first, he thinks are ugly – Mr. O'Connor and Mrs. Silverberg. What does he learn from them about appearances? How does the difference between appearance and reality affect many of the characters in Gib's stories?

6. What is the place of Gib's little sister, Justine, in his understanding of how the world and people work? What is his role in her life? Do you have younger brothers or sisters? What is your place in each other's lives?

7. Gib has many friends: Mike Halverson, James Wray, Elizabeth Gray, Billy Mendoza, Davie Dashlee, Rick and Kenny Johnson. What do these friends learn from each other?

8. Mr. Brendan O'Connor refuses to sign the loyalty oath because he believes signing will teach Gib and his other students the wrong lesson. What does he hope to teach them? What do you think he and the other teachers in the story should have done?

9. What do the other adults in the story teach Gib and his friends? Do the adults learn from the students?

10. How does the memory of the fired teacher, Mr. Reese, affect Gib?

11. How does the board meeting change Gib, and how does it change the town in which he lives?

12. James Wray says "At bottom, it's always about the money." How is that true or not true for James? For Billy Mendoza? For Rick and Kenny Johnson? For Mr. Marvin? For Max Million? For Gib's parents?

13. In his introduction, the older Gilbert says: "Two things I've learned from my years as a journalist: One: Fear is the easiest commodity to sell; and Two: Someone is always selling. In that essay, I was selling fear." What do you think of his statements?

14. Have you recently read the Bill of Rights of the Constitution of the United States, or other parts of the Constitution? How does the loyalty oath fit or not fit the U.S. Constitution?

15. Did you know that the oath taken by the president of the United States on first entering office is specified in Article II, Section 1, of the Constitution?

> *I do solemnly swear (or affirm) that I will faithfully execute the office of President of the United States, and will to the best of my ability, preserve, protect, and defend the Constitution of the United States.*

16. Read the addenda below about the loyalty oath. How is the presidential oath different from the loyalty oath that the teachers were asked to sign?

The rally and riot at the end of *The Price of Freedom* is based on similar events that did occur, but this scene is fiction. It draws especially on an anti-communist riot that occurred on September 5, 1949 in Peekskill, New York, where an anti-communist, rock-throwing mob attacked those leaving a concert given by Paul Robeson. Why do you think the author chose to include this scene? What does it tell you about those who are taught fear and hatred? (see archives, The Oregonian.)

STYLE AND CRAFT

a. The author tells the story from the point of view of Gilbert Evans as an eighth grader. Most of what the reader knows about others is what Gib recognizes about them. Does the reader get a chance to make an independent judgment of these people? How?

b. The author chose to introduce the game of soccer to students in this story twenty years before it actually became widely played in the United States (or thirty years before in some parts of the country). How does this new game (new to the characters) allow the author to bring up certain understandings about people and games, and life?

c. The Union Pacific tracks, Sullivan's Creek, Twelfth Avenue Bridge over-pass, The Bowl, the school, streets, neighborhood and playgrounds are all a part of the atmosphere of the story. These are real places in a real town, though the name of the school has been changed. Why would the author choose to set this story in these places? Do you think this seems to be an ordinary town? How do these surroundings affect Gib's understanding of what is happening in the United States during this era (1953)?

d. Dialogue is an important aspect of the story. Gib's family and other families have certain speech habits that they learned early in life. How do these habits reveal their world view? How are these speech habits of the 1950s different from those you know today? How do your speech habits change for different locations in your life: school, work, home, with your friends?

e. The author begins and ends in the point of view of Gilbert as an adult looking back on those times. How does this affect your understanding of the events in the story?

The sequel to *Scapegoat: The Price of Freedom* revisits Gilbert Evans, his friends and some very new people in a dangerous adventure. When you read *Scapegoat: The Hounded*, notice the very different style choices the author made for *The Hounded*.

HISTORICAL ADDENDA TO SCAPEGOAT:
THE PRICE OF FREEDOM

RESEARCH:

For help with research, the author thanks the Multnomah County Library, the Records Management and Archives of the Portland Public Schools and, also, the Legislative Library of the State of Oregon. At the Portland Public Schools' archives, Melinda C. Murray helped access PPS school board minutes, and patiently brought the next, and the next, and the next hefty tome. Her persistence and her suggestions were invaluable in helping discover that the loyalty oath was not a construct of the school district, but of the State of Oregon.

In researching the state oath, I thank Multnomah County Research Librarian Baron Schuyler for his thorough digging. It was he who discovered much of what is in print concerning the Oregon Constitution and loyalty oaths, including the notice of an earlier oath from 1921 (during the first Red Scare). Baron Schuyler also helped the author discover the Legislative Library as a resource. We have great historical resources in our state and wonderful people who support the researcher and author well beyond the call of a mere job.

HISTORIC TIMES:

Scapegoat: The Price of Freedom is a work of fiction set in the year 1953, a time now referred to as The McCarthy Era because of the power of Senator Joseph R. McCarthy and his investigative committee which kept the fear of communism before the American public. Throughout our history in America, insecurities have often been projected on a demonized group of "others". Catholics, Quakers, racial minorities and immigrants have each become a suspected threat within our community.

Following World War I, those who took over Russia preached exporting their methods and political beliefs. In the United States, the Communist Party U.S.A. reached its peak at 200,000 members during the Great Depression. Because of this growth, some U.S. leaders advertised that communists were a deep threat to 'the American way of life'. During the Depression, Eastern European and Russian immigrants, especially those who believed in the ideas of Karl Marx and Communism, or even believed in the rights of workers, were persecuted and vilified. This continued up until the beginning of World War II.

However, this scapegoating of communists calmed substantially during World War II. While the war raged, the U.S. and Great Britain needed Russia as an ally in the fight against Germany. At that time, our government downplayed any concerns about communist subversives within the country. After the war, when the Communist Party U.S.A. was on the wane and losing members, our previous ally, Russia, maneuvered for more control over territories of Europe, creating what was termed a Cold War.

In the United States, politicians and their media allies used the instability of the Cold War to fire up our fears again. Although membership in the Communist Party had dwindled, Congress passed the McCarran Act, which helped create a constant fear, not just of possible spies in our midst, but also of the investigators of subversion who, under the McCarran Act, had the power to accuse and destroy without proof.

Senator Joseph McCarthy of Wisconsin took advantage of the opportunity under the McCarran Act to make a name for himself as a fearless unmasker of communists. He held "investigative" hearings that accused, intimidated and ruined the lives of many citizens. McCarthy was not alone in using fear to gain power, but he was the most prominent among the many who did.

THE BILL OF RIGHTS AND THE CONSTITUTION OF THE UNITED STATES (SECTIONS DISCUSSED BY GIB AND FRIENDS IN *SCAPEGOAT: THE PRICE OF FREEDOM*)

AMENDMENT I

Congress shall make no law respecting an establishment of religion, or prohibiting the free exercise thereof; or abridging the freedom of speech, or of the press; or the right of the people peaceably to assemble, and to petition the government for a redress of grievances.

AMENDMENT VI

In all criminal prosecutions, the accused shall enjoy the right to a speedy and public trial, by an impartial jury of the state and district wherein the crime shall have been committed, which district shall have been previously ascertained by law, and to be informed of the nature and cause of the accusation; to be confronted with the witnesses against him; to have compulsory process for obtaining witnesses in his favor and to have the assistance of counsel for his defense.

ACTS OF CONGRESS DISCUSSED BY GIB, FRIENDS AND FAMILY
THE MCCARRAN INTERNAL SECURITY ACT

The Internal Security Act passed on September 23, 1950. The claim by its creator, Senator Pat McCarran, Nevada, was that the act would fight against allowing the U.S. to turn into a totalitarian dictatorship. President Truman had vetoed the act on the day before, but it passed over his veto by 89%. The act required communist organizations to register with the U.S. Attorney General. The definition of communist was very broad and open to interpretation.

The Act established the Subversive Activities Control Board to investigate people suspected of promoting the establishment of a totalitarian dictatorship, fascist or communist.

Members of these registered groups could not become citizens. Some were barred from entering or leaving the U.S.

Any citizen found in violation could lose his or her citizenship for five years.

Investigating subversive activities was the U.S. Senate Subcommittee on Internal Security, a senate equivalent of the already established House Committee on Un-American Activities (often referred to as HUAC). The Senate Subcommittee on Internal Security was chaired by McCarran and then Senator Jenner, Indiana, not by Senator McCarthy. However, Senator McCarthy turned one of his own subcommittees into the most noticeable investigator of communism.

Title II of the act established concentration camps and authorized the President to apprehend and detain each person for whom there is "reasonable ground to believe they . . . probably will engage in or probably will conspire with others to engage in, acts of espionage or of sabotage."

The authority of the McCarran Act was only to be invoked during war or during an "Internal Security Emergency". The definition of an emergency was wide open.

The act was the underlying reason for the type of hunt for communists that occurred all over the United States during the early fifties. Today, most of the act has been struck down by the Supreme Court as un-constitutional under the first amendment's protection of the right of association.

When President Harry Truman vetoed the McCarran Act, he said, "No considerations of expediency can justify the enactment of such a bill as this, a bill which would so greatly weaken our liberties and give aid and comfort to those who would destroy us." President Truman elaborated on the ways the Act would "destroy all that we seek to preserve, if we sacrifice the liberties of our citizens in a misguided attempt to achieve national security . . ." Truman's entire speech can be read at http://trumanlibrary.org/publicpapers/viewpapers.php?pid=883.

THE SMITH ACT

Generally referred to by the name of its main author, Representative Howard W. Smith of Virginia, this federal legislation was enacted June 29, 1940. It set criminal penalties for advocating the overthrow of the U.S. government and required all non-citizen adult residents to register with the government.

Approximately two hundred fifteen people were indicted under the legislation, including alleged communists, alleged Trotskyites, and alleged fascists. Prosecutions under the Smith Act continued until a series of United States Supreme Court decisions in 1957 reversed a number of convictions under the Act as unconstitutional. The statute has been amended several times.

QUAKER BELIEFS IN GILBERT'S FAMILY

Although in the past I, the author, was a member of the Religious Society of Friends and attended a silent meeting, I now am, for the sake of family members who like to sing, a member of a Presbyterian Church, which shares many beliefs with Friends. I do not speak for all Friends in my depiction of Gilbert's family. I speak only for the close friends I have had among the Society of Friends, of their beliefs as I understand them and of their experiences and habits of speech during the 1950s.

Very few West Coast U.S. Friends still use old speech in everyday conversation, though they may use it among Friends at gatherings.

Friends have a strong belief in Truth, Peace, Equality, Community and Simplicity. Many still speak of their belief that there is "That of God in every man". In my Silent Meeting experience, Gilbert would not be alone in his frustration that he "got no messages from the Big Guy". Meditation is a rewarding but difficult practice.

Friends believe that our acts should be our word, and that a requirement to swear an oath indicates that without the oath, a person may act without scruples. Quakers may affirm that they act in accord with their beliefs. The allowance for affirmation instead of swearing was not recognized in 1953.

Central to Gilbert's story in *The Price of Freedom* is the Peace testimony of his Friendly family. For Friends, the Peace testimony is much deeper than the simple idea that war is wrong. Friends have a commitment to work toward solutions to all problems without violence and threats. They, like many others, have witnessed how, when a problem is solved through the use of force, those against whom violence is used are left angry. The seeds of future violence are sown. Nonviolent solutions are more likely to last. The process for seeking non-violent solutions is more likely to bring harmony.

Friends also work to end the causes of violence: poverty, injustice, lack of access to basic education and other needs. Thus, Friends may refuse to work within the framework of force, may resist the draft and have been conscientious objectors in times of war. However, that doesn't mean Friends dodge the hard work of bringing help to the victims of war. And Friends believe they must work as hard for peaceful solutions to causes of injustice during times of peace as they do in times of war.

THE LOYALTY OATH IN OREGON

For many years, the Oregon State Constitution contained a loyalty oath. Public employees were required to swear to their loyalty to the Federal Constitution and the Oregon State Constitution. (ORS240.340) An early mention of this oath is from the Oregon Revised Statues in 1945. We do not know how consistently the oath was used. In fact, it appears that some did not think it was used enough. In 1951, the state legislature considered a bill to require teachers to sign a loyalty oath. An *Oregonian* article about this proposed legislation is entitled "Bill to Spot Red Teachers." This bill eventually failed, but in some places, public pressure caused the oath to be used for teachers anyway.

During the time of *Scapegoat: The Price of Freedom*, the oath included what is called a negativity clause. Those taking the oath were asked to swear that they had no beliefs 'inimical to the government'. The word 'inimical' has a wide range of meanings, from *opposed* and *unsympathetic* all the way to *hostile* and *malicious*, so it would be difficult for an oath taker to know if he or she had any beliefs that others might think were 'inimical'. An oath taker might also be correct to worry if his belief that he was being over-taxed or that children should be prohibited from owning bicycles could be construed as beliefs inimical to the government.

Further, the negativity clause, based on Oregon Laws 3871 allowed those hiring public employees 'any inquiry as to whether the applicant, ... has any beliefs inimicable to the government, who advocates **or is a member of an organization** which advocates the overthrow or resistance by force of our form of government.'

This mention of organizations was another possible pitfall for oath takers. At that time, such organizations as the film industries Conference of Studio Unions (CSU) were portrayed as Communist. During an eight-month CSU-led industry-wide strike in 1945, a rival union, the International Alliance of Theatrical Stage Employees

(IATSE), and the Motion Picture Alliance for the Preservation of American Values (MPA), a right-wing anti-communist industry group, launched a campaign to brand the CSU as 'communistic'. At the House Committee on Un-American Activities hearings (HUAC), a battle between Disney's cartoonists, (members of CSU) and the Walt Disney Company for higher wages was portrayed as a battle between forces for and against Communism.

This union was not alone in having to 'prove' it was not communistic. An organization, union or affiliation group could be assumed to support communism or other 'inimical' ideas because a rival organization or industry said they were 'leftist leaning'. The accuser did not have to prove the organization was against the United States government or democracy. The guilt of an organization could merely be assumed by someone in power.

Thus, the negativity clause forced both the person swearing and the organizations in question into the position of having to prove innocence rather than being presumed innocent under the law. This gave those requiring the oath an enormous power.

In February of 1959, Oregon's Congresswoman Edith Green offered an amendment to the National Defense Education act to repeal the negativity clause of the Federal loyalty oath. In April of 1959, the Oregon State legislature amended the state loyalty oath to remove the negativity clause, but the rest of the law remained in the state constitution for many years.

Public school teachers are public employees and therefore many were asked to swear by the oath during all the years of its use. I have talked to teachers who remember the oath being used when they took jobs in the Portland Public Schools during the late 1960s and 1970s. Some teachers remember that into the 1970s the oath still contained the negativity clause concerning membership in possible subversive organizations, the very type of clause that was *officially* struck out in 1959. In 1962, the United States Supreme

Court overturned the use of a similar clause in the state of Florida's loyalty oath for teachers (*Cramp v. Board of Public Instruction*). In 1979, the State of Oregon repealed the entire law concerning the administering of a loyalty oath.

HISTORIC FIGURES WHOSE ACTIONS AND STORIES INFLUENCED GIB AND FRIENDS IN *SCAPEGOAT: THE PRICE OF FREEDOM*

Senator William Benton, Connecticut, appointed to the United States Senate in 1949, and elected in 1950 as a Democrat, defeating Prescott Sheldon Bush, father of U.S. President George Herbert Walker Bush. In 1951, Benton introduced a resolution to expel Joseph McCarthy from the Senate. This resolution was a big part of Benton's defeat for re-election in 1953. (Chapter Five)

Peter Campbell Brown, Chair of the Subversive Activities Control Board 1952-56. (Chapter Forty-two)

Albert Einstein, Theoretical physicist, wrote a letter to President Roosevelt with a physicist colleague (Leo Szilard) urging the U.S. to study atomic power before Germany had mastered it. This study was to become the Manhattan Project to develop the atomic bomb. As the project developed, many of Einstein's colleagues were asked to work on the first atomic bomb, but Einstein was not one of them. According to several researchers who examined FBI files over the years, the reason was the U.S. government didn't trust Einstein's lifelong interest in peace and socialist organizations. FBI director J. Edgar Hoover recommended that Einstein be kept out of America by the Alien Exclusion Act, but he was overruled by the U.S. State

Department. After World War II, seeing the possibilities of atomic and hydrogen weaponry, Einstein regretted his letter to President Roosevelt as "the one big mistake in my life." (Chapter Seventeen)

Klaus Fuchs, physicist, worked on the development of the atomic bomb during the Manhattan Project. In 1950, he admitted that he was a spy and had passed secret information about bomb development to the Russians both from the Manhattan Project and earlier when he worked on a similar project in England. (Chapter Five)

Elizabeth Gurley Flynn, sent to jail in 1952 under the Smith Act, because of her membership in the Communist Party U.S. A. Flynn was a labor organizer and active in women's rights within labor. In 1920, she was a founding member of the American Civil Liberties Union, but was ousted from the ACLU because of her membership and leadership in the CPUSA. (Chapter Twenty-eight)

Portland City Councilman Robert Harl tried unsuccessfully to shut down the Portland Chief of Police and his Red Squad as an uncontrolled witch-hunting organization.(Chapter Twenty-eight and after)

Claudia Jones, born in Trinidad, immigrated to New York when she was nine years old. Her family was so poor they could not afford to attend her high school graduation. She joined the CPUSA because they were among the few organizations that supported the Scottsboro Boys, when a devastating injustice was perpetrated on several young black men. After the war, Jones became secretary for the Women's Commission of the Communist Party USA (CPUSA). She was convicted under the Smith Act in 1952, served in prison until 1955, and then deported to the United Kingdom in that year. (Chapter Twenty-eight)

Owen Lattimore, Educator and China specialist, The Tydings committee hearings (see Tydings, below) revolved around McCarthy's charge that the fall of the Kuomintang regime in China had been caused by the actions of alleged Soviet spies in the State Department, and McCarthy's allegation that Lattimore was a "top Russian agent." The Tydings Committee published a report denouncing McCarthy and these claims as a hoax. Nevertheless, Lattimore's life was scarred. (Chapter Twenty-Six)

Mayor Dorothy McCullough Lee After a scandal in the mayor's office involving the previous mayor, police officers and bribery, Lee was petitioned to run for office and served beginning in 1949. She was the second woman to serve as mayor of a major U.S. city. Her anti-gambling stance probably cost her a second election. (Chapter Thirty-Eight and after)

William Mackie (William Albert Niukkanen Mackie, Jr) Born 1908 in Finland while his U.S. citizen parents were there on a visit to family. Accused of being a communist 1952, fought deportation, but was deported to Finland in 1960. He was allowed to return, mainly through the efforts of his relatives, along with U.S. Sen. Mark O. Hatfield, R-Ore., and Hatfield's friend Mark Austad, at that time U.S. ambassador to Finland. Mackie became a U.S. citizen in 1978. William Mackie died in 1994. (Chapter one and after)

Hamish Scott MacKay Accused with three others of being a communist in 1949, was declared eligible to be deported in 1951, appeal was denied in 1955, Deported to Canada. (Chapter one and after)

The Marshall Plan Gilbert's family worked in Germany as part of their religious organization's contribution to the rebuilding of Europe after World War II. Under the insistent leadership of Secretary of State,

General George Marshall, the United States government recognized that the financial and social disintegration of Europe could only be halted with substantial financial and technical assistance from the United States. Many volunteers also worked with ordinary citizens to rebuild. Volunteers included members from churches including the Religious Society of Friends.

During the administration previous to Marshall becoming secretary of state, the U.S. government insisted that all citizens of Germany should have to prove they were not Nazis before they could have a job, and all industries were not to be rebuilt. The Marshall plan reversed this, understanding that a Germany that could not feed its people would be ripe for another demagogue like Hitler.

For many decades, a rebuilt Germany has sustained democratic and humanitarian values and helped to bring unity and peace to Europe.

Senator Joseph McCarthy: Chairman of the U.S. Senate Committee on Government Operations and its Permanent Subcommittee on Investigations during 1952 and 1953. Had accused others of being communists since well before becoming committee chair. (Chapter One and after)

Senator Wayne Morse, Oregon. McCarthy accused Senator Morse of being soft on Communism. Senator Morse tried unsuccessfully to stop the deportation of Mr. Mackie and Mr. MacKay and worked for their return during the 1960s. (Chapter Five and after).

Roy Norene, Director, U.S. Immigration for Portland District during the early 1950s. (Chapter Twenty-nine)

Robert Oppenheimer, theoretical physicist and technical director of the Manhattan Project to develop the atom bomb. He was Chairman of the General Advisory Committee to the Atomic

Energy Commission (AEC), serving from 1947 to 1952. It was in this role that he voiced strong opposition to the development of the hydrogen bomb. In 1953, at the height of U.S. anticommunist feeling, Oppenheimer was accused of having communist sympathies, and his security clearance was taken away. In 1963, President Lyndon B. Johnson tried to address this injustice by honoring Oppenheimer with the Atomic Energy Commission's Enrico Fermi Award. From 1947 to 1966, Oppenheimer also served as Director of Princeton's Institute for Advanced Study. (Chapter Seventeen)

The Red Squad, a sub-group of Portland police used accusations of communism as an excuse to harass and destroy community members who represented a threat to their friends, business associates, and allies. (Chapter Six and after)

Senator Millard Tydings, Maryland. In 1950, he headed a committee to investigate Joseph McCarthy's early claims of Communist infiltration of the federal government and military. Tyding's committee published a report denouncing McCarthy and his claims as a hoax. Tydings ran for re-election in 1950. McCarthy's staff distributed a composite picture of Tydings with Earl Browder, the former leader of the American Communist Party. The photo merged a 1938 photo of Tydings listening to the radio and a 1940 photo of Browder delivering a speech. The photo and story implied a friendship between Browder and Tydings that did not exist. Tydings lost the election. (Chapter Five)

ACKNOWLEDGEMENTS:

The quote that opens this story is from my mother, Wilhalmena Stamps Williams, who consistently showed her family how to pay the price of freedom. She recognized when the powerful sold fear for power's gain, and always spoke out against the resulting injustice.

My brother, Jim Williams, told me of an incident that occurred during his seventh grade year, a demonstration of the anti-communist hysteria of the 1950s. I knew that Jim's vignette should become part of a bigger story dealing with a young adult's understanding of the fear that drives people to irrational accusations. Jim became a consummate teacher and leader, vigilant in the protection of the vulnerable. The fact that he remembered this incident all his life reveals how story and memory can give life direction and purpose.

Early in life, I learned, from my brother, Al Williams, that there are times to mediate, and times to defend and protect. I watched his valiant attempts to define for himself what right action to take when others attempted to intimidate, harass or control the rightful freedoms of his family or friends. His thoughtful and courageous example has always been part of my definition of hero, though he would not recognize that about himself.

As late as 1955 or 1956, well after McCarthy was censured by the United States Senate, there were still some who found it expedient or profitable to give names of possible communists to various Red Squads and other witch-hunting committees in our town and across the nation. During one of those years, our father, Clifford Williams, came home one evening with a bootlegged record, given to him secretly by an educator friend. After closing all the windows and blinds in the house, he and our mother sat us all down near the record player.

They told us we could not talk about this recording outside of the house, never tell our friends, never quote it or mention it to any other person, even our other relatives. They let us know it represented a wrong that they, the adults, would take care of, but that they wanted us to know about it so we would know why they were working against its effects.

Then, they played *The Investigator* written by McCarthy victim, Reuben Ship, and read by the actor John Drainie. *The Investigator* was a serious and frightening, but also extremely funny, satire. It never mentions McCarthy by name. Drainie's Investigator-voice was recognizably McCarthy. I still have this recording, inherited when our parents died.

That hour with our parents also showed me the courageous trust they had in each of us. We were young enough that they could have kept the recording and their discussions hidden, and kept their work against McCarthyism in the schools and in our church separate from us. However, they wanted us to know that the hysteria controlling our country represented a deeply disturbing abrogation of human dignity and human rights.

McCarthy's exploitation of anti-communism exemplifies the type of fear-mongering that happens when one faction grabs power by selling hysteria. Our schools naively taught us that such thought-control movements happened only in dictatorships, or in Nazi or Communist countries on the other side of the world.

In the years that followed McCarthyism, other 'crises' have allowed our government to suspend freedom of speech and other rights. 'Crisis', defined by people who desire power, is an easy fog used to cover our exercises in inhumanity. We all need to recognize their true and disgusting character. We must fight them with clarity and courage.

Rae Richen
Portland, Oregon
2016 and 2024

ABOUT THE AUTHOR

 Rae Richen's short stories and articles have appeared in anthologies, newspapers and in handbooks for writers and teachers. She has taught middle school, high school students and adults and has always been impressed with the wide-ranging curiosity and the persistent search for answers among her students.

Her novels include the adventure novel, *Uncharted Territory*, and the historical *Scapegoat* series, *The Price of Freedom* and *The Hounded*. She has also written *To Serve Those Most in Need*, a non-fiction history of social services in the Pacific Northwest.

Her novels include questions for book groups dealing with story content and also with style and storytelling choices. They are appropriate for interested readers and also for students studying fiction writing.

The author is available for classroom presentations and discussions. She enjoys leading workshops for any age group on the writing of fiction and non-fiction. Contact her at:

Lloyd Court Press
3034 N.E. 32nd Avenue
Portland, Oregon
Or at www.raerichen.com

OTHER TALES OF ACTION AND ADVENTURE BY RAE RICHEN

For a good read of all first chapters, and the history and back story of these novels, sign in as the author's friendly reader at https://www. raerichen.com/guest-area .

Uncharted Territory – a father-son adventure in the mountains and in learning to accept and love despite the fragility of life. Learn more: https://www.raerichen.com/books

Scapegoat: The Price of Freedom – a teen and his friends struggle with a culture of easy accusation during the McCarthy Anti-Communist era. Learn more: https://www.raerichen.com/books

Scapegoat: The Hounded – after September 11, 2001, a grandfather and grandson work to create safety and freedom for friends falsely accused of treason.

Learn more: https://www.raerichen.com/books

In Concert – A novel of suspense and romance when a famous musician is stalked by a vicious man who wants to own her and her son. Visit https://www.raerichen.com/in-concert and read the first chapter for free.

Frozen Trust – a novel of espionage and romance within the United States during World War II. Visit https://www.raerichen.com/frozen-trust and read the first chapter for free.

Sentinels of Solitude – a novel of suspense and love during a murderous land grab in the lush Willamette Valley of Oregon. Visit www.raerichen.com/blog for the stories behind the story.

A Fool's Gold – a novel of treachery and romance in the Rocky Mountains of Colorado during the mining fever of the 1880s. Visitwww.raerichen.com/books for more information

Those Who Curse You – A Murder Mystery of Unlikely Bonds and Unrelenting Peril – Can inner-city architect, Sarah Rohann and her client, Abraham Hallowell save their families from the murderous drug gang that threatens all of their lives?

Without Trace: A Glyn Jones and Grandma Willie Mystery
When Trace Gowan, drummer in Glyn Jones' hip-hop band, goes missing, Glyn and his friends involve Grandma Willie and her connections to prison and police in the search. They find there is a lot more than a kidnapping going on and all of them are in danger. www.raerichen.com/books

Coming Soon: *Calling The Shots, An Anthology of Short Stories:* A confection especially for readers who asked "What happened to Elizabeth in The *Price of Freedom*? To Dick Street of *In Concert* and in *Those Who Curse You*?"

Learn what caused Gryf and his brother Sam to be the targets of a madman even before they came to the United States – the back story of *A Fool's Gold*.

And see what happened to Lewis James's missing brother, Dicken – a follow-up on Lewis's search for Dicken during *In Concert*.

In this and other anthologies soon to be published, Rae Richen has given us short stories to reveal where these characters lives intersected with the stories in the novels and where they went after we last saw them.

At the same time, in other tales, Rae Richen also has brought us whole new worlds and characters that we will want to follow and cheer for as they attempt to untangle their complicated lives.